CODE GREEN

ANDREW WARREN

Boldwood

First published in 2022. This edition published in Great Britain in 2025 by Boldwood Books Ltd.

Cover Design by Head Design Ltd.

Cover Images: iStock and Figurestock

Every effort has been made to obtain the necessary permissions with reference to copyright material, both illustrative and quoted. We apologise for any omissions in this respect and will be pleased to make the appropriate acknowledgements in any future edition.

A CIP catalogue record for this book is available from the British Library.

Paperback ISBN 978-1-83703-877-0

Large Print ISBN 978-1-83703-876-3

Hardback ISBN 978-1-83703-875-6

Ebook ISBN 978-1-83703-878-7

Kindle ISBN 978-1-83703-879-4

Audio CD ISBN 978-1-83703-870-1

MP3 CD ISBN 978-1-83703-871-8

Digital audio download ISBN 978-1-83703-872-5

This book is printed on certified sustainable paper. Boldwood Books is dedicated to putting sustainability at the heart of our business. For more information please visit https://www.boldwoodbooks.com/about-us/sustainability/

Boldwood Books Ltd, 23 Bowerdean Street, London, SW6 3TN

www.boldwoodbooks.com

1

BEIJING, CHINA

Years ago...

The upscale apartment's decor is cold and modern. Caine hides behind a curtain and peers out a towering floor-to-ceiling window. The street below is empty save for an occasional taxi-cab. From this high up, the tiny blue and green sedans look like beetles scurrying through the dark, empty lanes of the spiraling Chinese freeway system.

Caine adjusts his walkie's headset mic. 'Street looks clear. Jack, you got anything? Over.'

Jack Tyler's voice crackles softly in his ear. 'Besides a sudden unexplained craving for Peking duck? Negative. But tell Boone to speed it up in there, over.'

Caine smiles. He peers out at the building opposite the apartment high-rise. Like this one, it is a towering slab of steel and concrete. Dozens more line the hillside. Neon red Chinese characters adorn their roofs, but the thick, humid air gives the lights a hazy green glow in his night-vision goggles.

Most of the windows in the other buildings are dark. He

knows his partner, Jack, is stationed in one of those empty rooms, covering the entrance and lobby of the building Caine is in. Lying on a table, set back from the window, his eye pressed against the night-vision scope of a Chinese-made JS 7.62R sniper rifle.

Caine looks over his shoulder. He hears the third member of their team searching a small office connected to the living room of the spacious luxury apartment. Caine turns his wrist, examining the luminous numbers on his Casio G-Shock watch. 'We're still on schedule,' he replies. 'You getting nervous in your old age? Over.'

'Negative,' Jack answers. 'But I got a funny feeling about this one. Hairs on the back of my neck, you know? Over.'

Caine grins. 'I know the feeling. Maybe it's just too much Peking duck. Out.'

Behind him, a tall, muscular man enters the room. His steel-gray hair is cut military short, and his skin is tan and leathery. A pale scar runs down his right cheek, the thin white line of tissue standing out even in the dim light. Like Caine, he wears black street clothes.

'Anything?' Caine asks in a quiet voice.

The older man, Boone Riley, shakes his head. 'Negative. If this place is bugged, the bastards who put 'em there are better than I am. Made a full sweep, didn't come up with shit. You?'

Caine shrugs. 'Nothing in the bedroom or kitchen. Maybe this guy's clean?'

Boone shakes his head and gives Caine a crooked grin. 'Well, aren't you just the eternal optimist? Trust me, kid. He's dirty. Everyone is if you look hard enough. Grissom's been on this guy's ass for months. He doesn't make mistakes like that.'

Caine follows Boone into a small den on the opposite side

of the apartment and checks his watch. 'It's almost time to bug out, Riley. We should get—'

'Jack's got an eye on the building, right?'

Caine nods. 'Yeah, but—'

'So what's your rush? We clone the drive, then we leave.'

Caine glances over his shoulder at the apartment door. 'Fine. But make it quick. We should be leaving now.'

Boone makes his way to a large, dark wood desk. A laptop sits on the surface next to a folder of papers. He flips open the laptop. The screen lights up, displaying a secure log-on prompt. Boone slips a tiny USB drive from his pocket and inserts it into the side of the computer. The screen fills with static then flashes with random characters as the decryption key runs in the background.

Boone slides the folder across the desk to Caine. 'Here,' he snaps. 'Make yourself useful.'

Caine pulls a thick cell phone from his jacket pocket. The device resembles a commercially available model, but its camera has been modified to take high-resolution infrared pictures. He opens the folder and begins snapping photographs of the documents inside, briefs from the office of the US ambassador to China.

'Looks like normal stuff,' Caine mutters. 'The ambassador's schedule, notes on the trade talks, and—'

'Kid, we got a situation here,' Jack whispers in his ear. All traces of levity have vanished from his voice, he speaks in a calm, level monotone. 'Limousine just dropped off three subjects. They're walking into the lobby now. Over.'

'Copy that, over,' Caine answers. He shuts the folder and replaces it on the desk. 'Boone, they're here. Time to go.'

Riley glances at a progress bar on the laptop's screen. 'Stand by.'

Caine narrows his eyes. 'I said they're here, Boone. We have to—'

'I heard what you said. Sit tight.' The progress meter continues crawling across the screen.

Caine paces back and forth as Jack's voice crackles in his ear again. 'Are you guys clear?'

A brief hiss of static interrupts them as Caine toggles the talk button. 'Negative,' he whispers. 'We're still in the apartment.'

'Well, unless you're planning on leaving them cookies and milk, you better get a move on. I've got one guy in the elevator now. Judging by the cut of his jacket, I'd say he's armed. Looks military to me, probably a bodyguard.'

'Boone,' Caine snaps in a low voice. 'They're here. We have to go. Now!'

Boone draws a Sig Sauer P226 pistol from inside his jacket. 'Get in the kitchen. Take position behind the counter. The bodyguard will be first through the door. Neutralize him.'

Caine narrows his eyes and leans over the desk. 'Neutralize... Boone, what the hell are you talking about? We need to get this intel to the tech division. They have to examine it for—'

'This isn't intel. It's a nail in a coffin. This asshole's been selling out our agents. And he goes down for it tonight.'

Caine grabs Boone by the collar and hauls him to his feet. 'That's not the mission! What the hell has gotten into you?'

Boone breaks Caine's hold and shoves the younger man back. He aims his pistol at Caine's head. 'That *is* the mission. You and Jack are just too stupid to realize it. My orders came from Grissom himself. Why do you think he assigned me to this unit? He didn't trust you jokers to get the job done, that's why. Now get your ass in the kitchen and take down the bodyguard when he does his sweep.'

Caine mutters a curse under his breath then sprints toward the kitchen island. He ducks behind the counter as a beep sounds from the apartment door. A crack of light fills the entrance, and Caine closes his eyes. He flips up his night-vision goggles before the active amplification system turns the tiny sliver of light into a blinding glow. He hears footsteps move past his position. One set of steps... one man.

Suddenly, a burst of static fills his ears. 'Tom, do you copy? I—'

Caine turns off the walkie, focusing his attention on the shadowy figure pacing through the apartment. The man stops in the center of the room. Caine hears his feet shuffle as he turns left then right. The other man walks over to the wall, heading for the light switch.

Caine vaults over the counter and races across the floor. Before the man can turn on the lights, Caine is upon him. The bodyguard reaches into his jacket for a weapon, but he's a second too slow. Caine smashes the butt of his pistol into the base of the man's skull. A loud crack echoes through the apartment, and the bodyguard collapses to the floor. He lies motionless.

Caine kneels and checks for a pulse. 'He's alive.'

Boone steps into the room. 'Nice work. Drag him into the bedroom, quick.'

Caine glances at him. 'What about the family? Our orders were to gather intel, and—'

'I have new orders. Move!'

Caine drags the unconscious man across the floor and into the bedroom. As he stuffs the unconscious body in a closet, he realizes his walkie is still turned off. He twists the knob on the unit clipped to his waist. A burst of static fills his ears.

'*Zzzzst*—do you copy? Repeat, family is in the elevator, over!'

Caine presses the talk button. 'Jack? I had to go radio silent for a minute. What do you mean, the—'

'They didn't follow procedure! They're not waiting for the guard to signal all clear... They got in the elevator a few minutes ago!'

Caine rushes back into the living room. 'Boone, we have to leave now!'

Before Boone can answer, the apartment door swings open. Boone presses himself against the wall next to the door as a Caucasian man enters the room. He wears a dark overcoat over a tailored navy-blue suit. A Chinese woman and a young girl follow, both wearing expensive-looking designer dresses.

'John?' the man calls out. 'Cici had to use the bathroom, so we figured—'

The door slams shut behind them. The woman gasps, and the man spins around. 'What the—'

'You figured wrong,' Boone says. He steps out into the sliver of light from the windows. He aims his pistol at the man in the suit.

Caine stands frozen in place. His emerald-green eyes dart back and forth between the family and Boone. Static blares in his ear, followed by Jack's frantic voice. 'Tom? What the hell is going on in there? This isn't the plan!'

'We... we have money, in a safe,' the surprised man stammers. 'I can—'

'On your knees!' Boone shouts. The woman screams, and Boone points the gun at her. 'You too, lady. All of you!'

The three of them kneel on the floor, and the little girl begins to cry. Caine watches the woman wrap the wailing child in her arms. The girl is young, no more than six or seven years old. Boone looks like a giant, looming over her as she cries in her mother's embrace.

Caine holds his pistol at his side in a white-knuckled grip. 'We should leave,' he growls.

The woman cranes her head, staring at him with dark, pleading eyes. 'Yes, please leave. We won't say anything! I swear, I—'

'Shut your damn mouth!' Boone shouts. The child screams again, and her sobbing grows louder.

'Tom, Boone...' Jack's voice crackles in their ears. 'This is not the plan!'

'New plan,' Boone snaps. 'Tyler, repo to the lobby. Make sure the street's clear, then make your way to the rendezvous point. Tom and I will meet you shortly.'

'Boone,' Tyler hisses. 'Come on, man. The kid—'

'That's an order, Tyler!'

The radio goes silent.

He used our names, Caine thinks. Bad sign...

Boone presses the Sig's barrel into the kneeling man's forehead. A puddle of liquid spreads across the floor... The man has pissed himself in fear.

Boone crouches next to him. 'This is what happens to traitors, Phil,' he whispers in the terrified man's ear.

'Please... just let my family go...'

Boone stands up. 'Sorry. I don't make deals with traitors.'

He pulls the trigger. Caine winces as the weapon's muzzle flash lights up the room. Even with the silencer, the gunshot is deafening at close range. The Chinese woman shrieks and crawls to the man's body. In the sliver of light, Caine sees black tears trickle down her face as her mascara begins to run.

Boone steps into the kitchen. Reaching behind the stove, he grunts as he yanks a hose free from the wall. The hiss of escaping gas fills the room.

'Now, lady, I don't know if you're MSS or just a freelancer.

For all I know, you turned poor Phil over here. Maybe this whole thing was a honey-trap operation.' Boone steps back into the room. He aims the gun at the sobbing woman. 'Or maybe you're just in the wrong place at the wrong time.'

She turns to Caine, pleading with her eyes. The child hides her face in her mother's arms.

Boone raises his pistol. 'Truth is, I don't much care.'

'Don't,' Caine says quietly. 'This isn't why we're here.'

Boone does not take his eyes off the trembling woman. 'Wrong, Caine. This is exactly why we're here.' His lips curl into a cruel grin. 'End of the road, lady. But just in case you are MSS, I have a message for you. Walter Grissom says hello.'

Blam!

Another gunshot roars inside the apartment. The woman screams and closes her eyes, holding the girl tighter.

Boone looks down in shock. A dark stain spreads across his chest, nearly invisible against the black fabric of his clothes. A drop of liquid spatters on the floor. It shimmers bright crimson in the moonlight, like the neon letters outside.

Boone clutches his chest and turns to face Caine. 'You... You motherfu—'

Caine's face is pale. His pupils are two pinpricks of black, nearly lost in the emerald-green seas of his irises. But his grip does not waver as he fires the pistol again. Another explosive blast echoes through the room.

Boone staggers back. His arm falls to his side, and his gun clatters to the floor.

He collapses in a heap, his breath a wet, ragged rasp.

'Caine?' Tyler's voice crackles in his ear. 'You still there?'

Caine does not answer. The woman looks up at him, her eyes dark pools of shock and surprise. More inky black tears stain her cheeks.

'I... I'm sorry,' Caine mutters.

He turns and rushes from the apartment, barely remembering to hide his pistol in his waistband as he jogs down the corridor.

The journey to the lobby is a blank. He does not remember his panicked breathing as he waits for the elevator or the long, silent descent in the tiny mirrored car. All he can think of is the Chinese woman's terrified face. And the child peering up at him from her arms.

And Boone Riley... His sudden surprised look of pain. The rage and betrayal in his voice...

Somehow, Caine makes it outside. The thick, humid night air embraces him, dulling his senses. The memory of the woman's face fades into the haze. The apartment complex is dark, and no pedestrians walk the street. Tyler deactivated the parking lot surveillance cameras earlier. There are no witnesses.

He tenses as he hears the squeal of brakes and the roar of a powerful engine. An unmarked van screeches around the corner. It pulls into the parking lot and skids to a halt. The side door rumbles open. Tyler crouches in the rear of the van, gesturing to him.

'Move your ass, Caine!' his partner hisses. 'Police band's blowing up about you and Riley. The wife just called, told them—'

Kaboom!

An explosion lights up the parking lot with a bright orange flash. Caine spins around, squinting in the harsh light as a blast of hot air ripples through his hair and clothes. A pillar of fire erupts from the window of an apartment near the top of the building.

The apartment he was just in.

Jack stares in awe at the destruction as burning debris pelts the parking lot. 'Fucking Christ... Tom, what the hell did you do up there?'

Caine climbs into the van. 'Go!' he shouts. 'Now!'

The driver, a local contact, steps on the gas. The van lurches out of the parking lot, leaving the burning building behind.

Caine leans against the vehicle's cold metal wall and stares blankly into space.

Tyler takes a deep breath. 'We're about twenty minutes from the extraction site. If we can make it to the boat, we should get away clean.'

'Boone,' Caine mutters. 'He must have set incendiary charges. This was never about finding evidence. This was revenge.'

'Tom... I didn't hear everything that happened. But I heard enough, man. I mean, Christ, there was a kid up there. You tried to stop him... You tried...' Tyler's voice trails off.

Caine closes his eyes. The van rumbles and squeaks as it carries them deeper into the shadows of Beijing.

* * *

Virginia, USA. Present Day.

Caine shot up in bed. His throat felt dry and parched, and he was panting for breath. The muscles in his arms and legs were stretched taut, and his heart pounded in his chest. Wiping the cold sweat from his forehead, he fumbled around the night-stand and reached for his phone. He tapped the screen and checked the time. It was 5.00 a.m.

Sighing, he slid his legs from under the covers and sat on the edge of the bed. He rubbed the sleep from his eyes as his heart slowed its frantic beat, and his breathing returned to normal.

Another nightmare, he thought.

His nightmares were almost always memories... Brief snippets of brutality, horrors he had witnessed. And the pain he had inflicted on others...

Boone Riley... Why the hell did I dream about him? he wondered. That night...

That cold, dark night in China, the woman's pleading eyes, staring at him from the shadows... The explosion, the building engulfed by flames. More horrors he had pushed into the dark recesses of his mind. More echoes of the past, cursed to haunt his dreams.

He stood up and paced over to his dresser. Outside, the sun began its ascent over the rolling green hills and oak tree groves. The chill in the air carried with it the promise of fall. The leaves on the trees surrounding the safe house had begun to turn orange, red, and yellow.

Grabbing the TV remote, he pressed a button, and the small, flat screen glowed to life. A newscaster's voice filled the room.

'We're live from the Pan Asian Alliance Trade Conference, where the Chinese president stunned spectators by walking out on United States President Garrick in the middle of the first day of negotiations.'

The footage on the screen showed a small group of Chinese diplomats and officials flanking the tall, portly figure of their president, an older, stern-looking man with a stiff, steady gait. A blaze of camera flashes caught the surprised expression on President Kyle Garrick's face. The dark-eyed, steely-haired man huddled with his advisors as the throng of reporters closed in around the now-empty negotiating table.

'If these talks fail to move forward,' the newscaster continued, 'the results could have crippling effects on the United
States economy as jobs numbers plummet due to the ongoing
trade war between these two superpowers.'

'Mr. President, Mr. President,' one of the reporters shouted.
'Do you have any insight as to why the Chinese have put a
stop to—'

'You'll have to ask them,' President Garrick snapped as he
stood up and ran a hand down the front of his suit. 'We've come
here in good faith, to discuss a new vision for American–
Chinese trade policy. And I remain committed to the idea that
our cooperation will be mutually beneficial to both America
and the Chinese people.'

Another reporter held a microphone over the crowd,
desperately trying to catch one last sound bite as the president
walked toward the exit. 'Does the Chinese reaction signal the
talks are over, Mr. President?'

Garrick turned and flashed the camera an election-winning
smile. 'I'm not going anywhere, I assure you. I can only hope
that the Chinese delegation feels the same—'

Caine pressed a button on the remote, and the sound cut
out as the screen went dark. Caine tossed the remote back on
the nightstand.

Same old story, he thought. Same old lies.

He fished out a pair of sweatpants and a hoodie from the
drawer. After throwing on his clothes, he sat on the edge of the
bed and slipped on a pair of running sneakers. As he tightened
the laces, he glanced up at the ceiling. Even in the dim morning
light, he could see the tiny black dome mounted above his bed.
No lights or any other indication showed the camera inside was
operational. But he knew it was recording his every move.

He was always being watched.

He left his room and exited the house. Built on the shore of Lake Jackson, the structure dated back to the fifties and had the dubious honor of housing several Russian defectors during the Cold War.

Caine's breath misted the cool morning air as he began his run. After making his own journey in from the cold, he had spent several uncomfortable days in a CIA interrogation cell in Guantánamo Bay. Once Director Paulis was satisfied that he was not, in fact, a traitor, Caine was transferred to the palatial safe house in Virginia. The modern contemporary building was comfortable, and its grounds boasted a pool, a spa, and decent gym facilities.

But as he glanced up at the hillside, he saw shadowy figures standing against the horizon. They were as still as statues, but Caine knew they were armed with automatic rifles, and they watched his every move.

As beautiful as the grounds were, the house was still a cage. And he was still an ex-spy. Despite Rebecca's assurances, he knew it would be a long time before anyone trusted him again. Least of all the director of the CIA.

The feeling was mutual.

Hunching his shoulders, he began to shadowbox as the trail sloped up the hill. His breathing sped up as he increased his pace, jogging into the black shadows that loomed beneath the bloodred leaves.

2

TEXAS, USA

Morning sun peeked through the rippling horizon of pink and gray clouds as a team of armed men raced across the cracked, faded pavement. The empty field surrounding the parking lot was flat and barren save for a few clumps of dead weeds. Despite the cool early-morning temperature, heat from the previous day had baked into the dark asphalt and now radiated around the group.

The men wore uniforms covered with MultiCam, a mottled pattern of brown, green, and gray suitable for use in a variety of environments. Most of the team carried short-barrel Colt M4 rifles, but a few hefted suppressed HK 416s with red dot sights. Black balaclava masks hid their faces, and Kevlar vests protected their chests and vital organs. Black lettering on their vests identified them as FBI.

The team moved at a lightning-fast pace despite the heavy gear and equipment they carried. Twenty men sprinted across the cracked pavement, but a group of ten peeled off to surround the parking lot perimeter. The remaining group split into two teams of five and flanked the side door of a sprawling warehouse complex standing at the end of the lot. Behind the building, empty grasslands stretched as far as the eye could see, meeting up with a pitch-black line of trees in the distance.

Two of the men pressed their backs against the warehouse walls and faced the empty lot, checking the ground behind the team. The rest took up positions along the door, covering an operator as he slid a black cylinder from his tactical vest.

The operator shattered the window of the door with his elbow and tossed the grenade into the dark room beyond. He held up three fingers and silently counted down.

Three... Two... One...

A bright flash erupted in the dark room, and the hiss of tear gas filled the air.

The men pulled breathing masks over their mouths, and the point man kicked the door open. The team swarmed into the room.

'FBI, nobody move!' the squad leader shouted.

Flashlights mounted on the men's helmets crisscrossed through the thick haze. The warehouse floor was dusty concrete, and tall support columns reached up to a high ceiling. As the smoke cleared, the men moved into a standard breaching pattern, kicking down office doors and making sure no attackers were hidden inside.

Finally, the leader toggled the radio mic in his helmet.

'Area is secure, ma'am. Looks like nobody's home.'

A woman's voice crackled through his earpiece. 'Hold your positions and stand by. I'm sending in a special observer.' She spoke with a slight accent, but it was difficult to place.

The squad leader pursed his lips. 'Observer? Agent Zavala, I don't think—'

'That's Special Agent Zavala, Commander. He's an expert

witness regarding this group's activities. Don't interfere. Don't get in his way. Just let him do his job.'

'But ma'am, the procedure for—'

'I'm in charge of this operation, and I'm changing the procedure. If you'd like to file a protest in your report, that's your prerogative. Zavala out.'

The warehouse's metal doors rolled up, and a lone figure walked into the room. He wore the same camouflage and body armor as the others, and a green balaclava mask covered his face. His skin was dark, and he spoke in a deep, commanding voice.

'Okay, I need you all to fan out and search the premises. We're looking for any sign of chemical accelerants or pyrotechnic devices. If you find anything, and I mean anything – iron shavings, ethyl alcohol, hell, even an empty gas can – don't touch it. Alert me on the radio and pull back. Understood?'

The squad leader nodded. 'You heard the man. Move out!'

The FBI team stalked through the shadowy interior of the warehouse, moving in coordinated pairs.

As they fanned out, the squad leader approached the special observer and held out his hand. 'Don't believe I got your name, Mister...'

The observer shook his hand but ignored the question. 'Agent Ricardo, right? I know this isn't exactly standard procedure, but I'll be out of your hair shortly. In the meantime, you're with me.'

He shifted his rifle and advanced down a narrow corridor. Ricardo followed, sweeping his rifle left and right, covering doors and darkened rooms as they stalked past a row of abandoned offices.

'Whoever was using this place, looks like they moved out before we got here,' Ricardo muttered quietly.

'That's what I'm afraid of,' the other man replied in a low voice.

* * *

The woman staring at the bank of monitors squinted, wrinkling the skin at the base of her nose. One of her eyes was a brilliant sapphire blue, the other dark brown. A pair of slim metal-framed glasses perched above her nose, reflecting the glare from the glowing screens on the side of the van. Each screen displayed a wireless video feed from one of the men in the Hostage Rescue Team inside the warehouse.

Despite the team's name, Zavala did not expect to encounter any hostages within the building. HRT was considered the FBI's elite special forces team and was often deployed on counter-intel operations like this one to keep their skills sharp.

'Same deal as last time, AJ,' a man in a white dress shirt said with a sigh. He leaned back in his chair and rubbed his eyes. 'Empty warehouse. Nothing but dirt and dust, just another wild goose chase.'

Special Agent Alejandra Zavala peered at the top row of tiny monitors. Her different-colored eyes darted over the various video feeds as she tucked a strand of light-brown hair behind her ear. She watched each man's camera feed as the squad fanned out and searched the empty warehouse.

'More watching, less complaining,' Zavala said. '*Más ven cuatro ojos que dos.*'

Her partner, Special Agent Pete Tarpin, sipped cold coffee from a Styrofoam cup and rolled his eyes. 'What the hell does that mean?'

Zavala shot him an annoyed glance. 'We've been working together for six months, and I haven't taught you any Spanish?'

The younger man smiled and tossed the empty cup at a plastic bag hanging from the corner of the monitor bench. The cup missed the bag and tumbled to the floor. Zavala rolled her eyes. 'No wonder it smells like sour milk in here.'

Pete grinned and bent over to pick up the trash. 'Guess my hook shot is out of practice. Too much time sitting in the back of dark, cramped vans with—'

'Hold on,' Zavala said. She focused on the bottom-right monitor. 'What do we have here?'

Pete leaned forward, following her gaze. Each monitor had a strip of tape bearing a name above it: Ricardo, Maz, Terrill, Bailey, and Murkowsky. But the last monitor was blank, with no name attached.

'That's your mystery man,' he said.

'Special observer,' she corrected.

'Well, whoever he is, looks like he found something.'

The two of them continued observing as the camera feed darted down a cramped, narrow passage. Zavala tapped the microphone in her ear. 'Zavala to Bluejay. Do you read?'

A burst of static filled the van. 'Found... door. Squad Leader... Stand... *zzzzt!*' The garbled transmission cut off suddenly, and the video feed began to flicker.

'Something's interfering with the signal,' Zavala said.

Pete furrowed his brow, noting the hint of concern in her voice. 'You sound worried. Wait, do you know this guy?'

'Yeah, I know him,' she muttered, keeping her eyes on the scenes.

'You did clear this with our section chief, right?'

'*No me hagas preguntas y no te diré mentiras...*'

'What?'

Zavala shook her head. 'Ask me no questions, and I'll tell you no lies. You're hopeless, Pete.'

The young agent stroked his stubbled chin. 'AJ, just being on-site for an HRT op is already pushing things. I don't know how you pulled this off, but if things go south and—'

He paused, watching the screen as the video signal continued to degrade. 'You're right... Something's interfering with the signal.' He looked up at the top row of monitors and frowned. 'Same with Agent Ricardo. He's squad leader on this one, right?'

Zavala triggered her microphone again. 'All agents, I need a twenty on Squad Leader Ricardo,' she said, asking for any nearby agents to report the man's position. 'Please acknowledge.'

'Copy that. I do not have eyes on Ricardo.' The voice was from Maz, a recent addition to the HRT team. One by one, the other operators reported in, all negative.

'Wherever Ricardo and your observer went, looks like they're on their own,' Pete said, eying the screens.

'I don't like this,' Zavala replied in a low voice.

'Hey, we're missing a response.'

She looked up. 'You're right.' She activated the microphone again. 'Murkowsky, please respond.'

A soft, buzzing static was the only reply.

She narrowed her eyes. 'Agent Murkowsky, do you copy? Does anyone have eyes on Murkowsky?'

Another chorus of negatives crackled through the speakers.

Zavala stood and grabbed a Kevlar vest hanging on the back of her chair. 'Something's wrong. I'm going in.'

'What?' Pete looked up at her in surprise. 'We're not cleared for—'

'Just stay here. Keep me updated if you hear anything.' She

slipped on the Kevlar vest, tightened the straps, and pulled down the back flap, revealing her FBI markings. Then she grabbed her sidearm from the desk and clipped the leather holster to her belt.

Pete nodded. 'You got it.'

Zavala slid open the van's side door. A burst of early-morning sunlight filled the dank interior. She squinted then jumped to the pavement.

'Hey, AJ...' Pete called after her.

She turned to face him.

'Be careful.'

She nodded. '*Gracias*,' she said with a smile. Then she slammed the door closed.

* * *

'Special Agent Zavala, this area is not secure! You aren't supposed to—'

'Enough, Agent Maz. I know the rules. Has anyone put eyes on Murkowsky or Ricardo?'

'Negative,' the lanky man replied, shaking his head. 'We're still checking all the nooks and crannies in here, making sure those bastards didn't leave us any surprises.'

'Found anything so far?' she asked, peering through the swirling air.

'Nope. Empty as a whisky bottle at closing time. There's a second level you can only get to by freight elevator. We're moving up there now to—'

Suddenly, three loud pops echoed through the warehouse.

'What the hell was that?' Pete's voice crackled over Zavala's walkie.

'Shots fired, shots fired!' a voice cried out.

Zavala drew her pistol. 'Maz, you're with me!'

The man followed as she sprinted across the warehouse, moving toward the direction of the shots. 'All units, converge on my position,' Maz shouted into his microphone. 'Be advised, shots fired, hostiles in building!'

They turned a corner and walked down a dim, narrow corridor, keeping close to the wall.

Zavala paused halfway down the passage, feeling a light breeze stir her hair. 'Wait,' she whispered. She examined the wall to her right. A thin black line ran between the drywall panels. A mild wind blew through the crack in the smooth, featureless wall.

Before she could examine the fissure, a pair of men rounded the corner from the opposite side. Zavala raised her pistol but lowered it when she saw the FBI markings on their fatigues.

She pointed at the dark slit in the wall. One of the men advanced and felt around the edge of the crevice. He glanced at the other agents. They aimed their weapons at the wall as he depressed a hidden switch.

With a click, the panel slid aside, revealing a dim corridor, barely wide enough for a grown man to walk through. Without waiting for a signal, Zavala darted down the passageway.

'Pete, are you getting this?' she whispered.

'Yeah,' her partner's voice crackled in her ear. 'Still no signal on Murkowsky or... zzzzt.' His voice faded into static.

Something in the walls, she thought. She turned around and pointed at the entrance behind them. One of the men nodded and hung back, ensuring that Pete could still reach someone on the team.

Then she continued down the narrow passage, her pistol drawn. The remaining men filed behind her and spread out as they entered an empty office. The fragments of a wooden desk lay in the corner, and a pile of charred files and papers sat in the center of the floor. The corridor stretched on, turning to the right.

Zavala drew a pen from her jacket and prodded the pile of ash. She separated a few scraps that retained traces of a computer printout. 'Pete, I've got some evidence to pick up once we secure the area. Do you copy?'

Again, all she could hear in her earpiece was soft, buzzing static.

Another round of gunfire echoed from farther down the corridor. Before Zavala could respond, the other men charged ahead. She heard a different gun return fire. The corridor turned left and opened into a vast loading dock. A metal door hung halfway open, and she could see a figure slumped on the ground. A dark pool of blood spread underneath him on the concrete floor.

The two HRT agents pressed forward, spraying fire into the loading dock.

'Shoot to wound,' Zavala shouted. 'I want to take them alive. We need answers!'

Gunshots ricocheted off the concrete, and one of her men collapsed.

Zavala skidded to a stop and dropped to the ground. A hail of bullets streaked beneath the metal door. She rolled across the floor, firing wildly into the room. A shadowy figure sprinted toward the sunlight outside. She stopped behind the body of her man. Then she reached over and felt for a pulse.

He was gone.

She lowered her head as more bullets streaked above her. A few slugs thudded into the dead body, and she fought back a sick, nauseated feeling in the pit of her stomach.

The gunfire ceased. She muttered a silent curse then leaned

over the corpse and braced her shooting arm on his lifeless chest. She fired three shots and saw the figure stumble. He fell down behind a rack of computer servers. She narrowed her eyes, staring at the blinking equipment. Several identical racks behind it stretched toward the far side of the loading dock. The computers mounted in the metal frames looked modern and expensive. She had seen nothing else like them in the warehouse.

Another man lay on the floor of the loading dock. He crawled toward her, leaving a trail of blood across the floor. He was almost at the opening. He looked up at her...

It was the special observer... CIA Officer Clayton DuBose.

'Too late,' he hissed. 'Get your men back!'

'Clayton!' She stood up, sending a hail of bullets toward the other man's last position.

'Clayton, hold on. I'll get you out of—'

'No!' He pulled himself forward and reached for something on the wall.

Zavala ran toward him, but before she could get to the opening, the man behind the barrels staggered to his feet.

She threw herself against the wall as he opened fire. His bullets clanged against the corrugated metal door, sending sparks flying through the air.

He lowered his weapon. 'I had no choice!' he shouted, limping toward the loading dock's exit. 'I... I'm sorry!'

She recognized his voice... It was Murkowsky. And Clayton was still in there with him.

Zavala leapt from her cover and sprinted for the door. But before she could reach it, DuBose punched his bloody fist against a button on the wall. The metal door slammed shut, striking the ground with a loud clang.

She pounded on the door. 'Clayton, get your ass out—'

Kaboom!

An explosion thundered on the other side of the door. The metal slats buckled and exploded outward. Zavala felt herself fly through the air. She slammed to the ground, instinctively covering her face with her arms as crumbling Sheetrock and debris rained down from above.

Her vision grew dark. A distant ringing filled her ears, and she felt herself slipping into the warm, liquid embrace of unconsciousness.

3

VIRGINIA, USA

24 Hours Later

Caine sat alone in the stark white room. Another camera dome hung from the ceiling, and once again, he knew he was being watched. He had just completed yet another series of questions with yet another staff psychiatrist. A warm, friendly woman who gently probed him about his past.

As usual, he had no answers for her. He had spent years running from his past.

Now, as before, he sat waiting. Waiting to see what blood-stained memory they would pry up next. What dark corner of his psyche they would ask him to describe using pictures and inkblots on cards. Not for the first time, Caine asked himself what on earth he was doing here. The CIA had hung him out to dry long ago. He didn't owe them anything.

You know why you're here, a voice in his head answered. *Rebecca...*

Suddenly, the door opened, and a tall, heavyset African American man entered the room. He wore thick-framed black glasses, and his short hair was gray around his temples. A neatly trimmed mustache and goatee framed his lips. He walked with a slight, almost unnoticeable limp, as if one of his legs was stiff.

The man carried a folder of papers in his hand. He sat down at the table opposite Caine and began flipping through the files in silence.

Caine laughed, a short, cynical bark. 'Michael Paulis. The God on the Seventh Floor himself, come to visit little old me. I'm flattered.'

Paulis ignored him and continued studying the file.

Caine stared at him for a moment then shook his head. 'Yeah, good morning to you, too, sir.'

'Don't call me sir,' Paulis answered, keeping his eyes on the file.

'Excuse me?'

Paulis peered up at him over the rims of his glasses. 'I haven't approved your return to duty, Caine. Don't call me sir.'

'What should I call you? Mike?'

'Director will be fine.' Paulis closed the folder and removed his glasses. He puffed on them with his breath then wiped the lenses clean on the sleeve of his jacket. 'You know, I haven't done the math, but I have to assume it's costing the US taxpayer a small fortune to keep you here. Food, healthcare, daily psychological evaluations. Not to mention a team of analysts to dig through your debriefing reports, sift fact from fiction.'

'You think I'm lying to you?' Caine snarled. 'About what Bernatto and Grissom did to my life? To Rebecca, and—'

Paulis held up his hand. 'No, that's not what I meant. I'm satisfied that you're telling the truth about all that. The incident in Sudan, Josh Galloway's murder... Those are just the tip of the iceberg. I'll tell you what I told Rebecca. Walter Grissom and this rogue network of his may be the most dangerous enemy this country has ever faced. And working on your own, you uncovered intel that's been critical in getting a handle on the situation. If not for you, we'd all still be in the dark about Grissom, Blackwing. All of it.'

He took a sip of coffee. 'Frankly, I've never seen anything like it. A privatized intelligence network. HUMINT, SIGINT, Spec Ops... Grissom can pull off anything from boots on the ground to sophisticated cyberwarfare. And despite your efforts, the Senate Intelligence Committee still doesn't seem to grasp the threat that's been sitting under their nose.'

Caine stared back at him. 'So if you believe me, why the third degree? Why the armed men on the hill and the cameras and all these damn tests? What more do you want?'

Paulis leaned back in his chair. 'Isn't it obvious?'

Caine laughed again. 'Enlighten me.'

The older man pointed at him. 'See, I think that's part of the problem right there. You've been working on your own for so long now, you can't see it. Hell, even your last few years in active duty in SAD/SOG, you were under Bernatto's thumb. A secret division within the CIA, carrying out unsanctioned operations. Missions you hid from Rebecca and anyone else in the official command structure.'

'I paid the price for that, didn't I?'

Paulis set his coffee cup on the table and steepled his fingers under his chin. 'Maybe. But at the end of the day, what I need to know is, can I trust you? And more importantly, can you trust me? Or anyone, for that matter.'

'Trust? Afraid that's in short supply these days, Director.'

'Indeed it is. More than you know. I understand Rebecca briefed you on the raid Grissom arranged in DC.'

Caine nodded. 'To set up something like that... the men, the planning, the firepower... Takes a lot of money. And the right people in your pocket.'

'Based on your reports and what little we've been able to uncover, Grissom's influence reaches into the highest levels of this country's intelligence apparatus. He's been able to compromise high-ranking NSA officials, the former director of National Intelligence, countless private military contractors and local officials. Hell, even operatives within China's MSS.'

Caine clenched the side of the table with a white-knuckled grip. 'So why are we sitting here and talking?'

Paulis stared at him for a moment, then sighed. 'If I send you after Bernatto, Grissom, or anyone else... Well, like we used to say in JSOC, it's "weapons free" out there. I have neither the time nor the inclination to babysit you. I can't micromanage your every move. If I can't trust you to make the right decisions, if you're permanently damaged and broken by the things Bernatto did, the betrayal you suffered... If you can't trust, you're useless to me.'

Caine stood and placed his hands on the table. 'You've had me caged up here for months. That's months of Bernatto and Grissom doing who knows what out in the real world. So don't talk to me about trust. I trust Rebecca. I trust DuBose. As for you, if you want my trust, maybe you should try earning it for a change. I don't give it blindly anymore.'

Paulis looked up at him. 'Sit your ass down, or you can go back to your room.'

Caine glared back at him but said nothing. He remained standing.

Paulis shifted in his chair and cleared his throat. 'DuBose is part of the reason we're here,' he continued. 'All the doctors and psychological tests in the world don't mean shit to me, Caine. I need to look a man in the eye before I make a decision like that.'

'And?' Caine growled.

The director stared back at him.

'According to the staff here, you're suffering from classic PTSD symptoms. Paranoia, nightmares, mood swings. You lash out at anyone and everyone who tries to get close because you don't want to remember what happened to the people you used to give a damn about. How am I doing? Sound familiar?'

Caine returned the man's stare. 'Why do I feel like there's a "but" coming?'

Paulis gestured to the chair. 'For the love of God, Caine, will you please sit down!'

Caine slid into the chair. 'Well?'

Paulis slid the folder out of the way and rested his hands on the table. 'Clayton DuBose is down. He's alive, but he's not returning to active duty anytime soon. And given Grissom's track record of infiltrating US intelligence agencies, that narrows down the list of people I can trust to exactly three. My D/NCS, an FBI special agent who's barely able to contact me... and you.'

Caine narrowed his eyes. 'What happened to DuBose?' he asked, unable to hide the note of surprise in his voice.

Paulis pushed the bridge of his glasses up with one finger. 'While you've been cooling your heels in debriefings, Walter Grissom has been systematically wiping out loose ends. Anyone who could hurt him or his organization or that could be vulnerable to CIA pressure is turning up dead or missing without a trace. We sent DuBose as an undercover observer on one of Special Agent Zavala's operations. The raid in Texas. They took down a warehouse belonging to a Blackwing front company called Agromex.'

Paulis slid another folder across the table. Caine flipped it open, grabbed a picture, and held it up. He whistled when he saw the satellite photo of the obliterated warehouse.

'What the hell did this?'

'Some kind of high-grade explosive, military for sure. We believe the building housed a massive data server for Blackwing. The FBI cybercrimes unit is sifting through the rubble, but there obviously isn't much left. They haven't released their findings yet, but whatever was on those servers, someone clearly didn't want it to be found.'

'Which begs the question,' Caine muttered. 'How did you know it was there?'

Paulis grunted. 'An asset in Singapore tipped us off... He used the codename "Larkspur." For obvious reasons, we've been keeping his identity classified.'

Caine continued flipping through the photos of the obliterated warehouse. 'Larkspur, huh? Apparently, his intel was good. So who is he really?'

Paulis tapped the table with his fingers and sighed. 'His real name is Andrew Seng, a financier Grissom used to launder money. After you blew up their operation in South Sudan, I guess Seng saw the writing on the wall. He wants to cut a deal, protection in exchange for what he knows. He contacted my office and revealed the location of that warehouse to establish his bona fides. Then he turned himself over to the Internal Security Department in Singapore.'

'Which means he's probably next on Grissom's hit list.'

Paulis leaned forward and stared at Caine. 'That's right. So I don't have time to read a stack of reports about your nightmares or a list of your physiological anxiety symptoms. I can't make sure you're eating properly.'

'I'll save you the trouble,' Caine replied. 'The food here is shit.'

Paulis adjusted his glasses. 'You suffered. You were betrayed. I get that. But right now, my only link to Blackwing is holed up in another country with a target painted on his back. So I need you to look me in the eye and tell me... Are you code green or code red? Go or no-go? That's the only answer that matters to me right now.'

Caine closed the folder and looked up at Paulis. 'Honestly? I have no idea.'

Paulis stared at him in silence for another few minutes. Then he stood up, gathered his folders, and marched toward the exit. 'You leave Dulles Airport in three hours. Car's waiting outside. Pack light clothes. Gets hot in Singapore this time of year.'

He closed the door behind him. Caine remained in the chair and looked up at the ceiling.

Code green... Go or no-go...

'Guess we'll see,' he muttered.

4

REPUBLIC OF SINGAPORE, CENTRAL BUSINESS DISTRICT

It feels strange to be back...

As the thought crossed his mind, Caine lowered his head and peered over the rims of his metal-framed aviator sunglasses. A petite woman sat ahead of him in the front passenger seat of the white Volvo SUV.

Her hair was short, dark, and razor cut. She pressed a cell phone to her ear and spoke in Malay, uttering a series of fast, clipped words and phrases that Caine could not understand. Her voice was low-pitched for such a small woman, with just a hint of a throaty rasp. Caine had noticed she was a chain smoker. In the brief time he had spent with her, she had already gone through half a pack of Viceroy cigarettes.

'*Lima minit. Saya faham. Siap sedia,*' she said into the phone. She glanced back at Caine and gave him a brief smile. '*Orang Amerika ada bersama saya. Jumpa lagi,*' she added, replying to the person on the other end. Then she hung up and slid the phone into the pocket of her dark blazer.

She turned her head to face Caine. 'I directed a STAR team

to lock down the hotel's service entrances in the rear,' she said, switching to English for his benefit.

Caine nodded. 'STAR... that's special tactics and rescue, right? Your version of SWAT?'

'Yes. I also stationed two of my Internal Security Department colleagues in the corridor outside the asset's room. No one has entered or left since their last sweep.'

Caine forced himself to return her smile. 'Thank you, Miss Yeoh. I appreciate you checking. In my experience, you can't be too careful with these people.'

She nodded. 'Please, call me Sasha. And you need not worry... Singapore is not like Africa or China or even America. Violence is very rare here. We are a country of law and decency.'

Caine cocked his head. The woman sounded too naïve and earnest to be serious, but nothing in her expression indicated she was joking. Her dark, almond-shaped eyes observed him with quiet curiosity. He was, after all, a stranger in her country. An operative of a foreign intelligence service sent to interrogate and possibly take custody of a potential asset.

Sasha Yeoh raised an eyebrow as she read Caine's bemused expression. 'You think I am kidding? But Singapore has not had a terrorist incident in over fifty years. As a country, we are a mix of Chinese, Malaysian, Indian... Cultures and religions from all over the world mingle here, and yet violent crime is almost unheard of.'

Caine glanced at the man sitting next to him. Tony Lim, a junior ISD agent, wore a masculine version of Sasha's dark, stylish suit. His eyes, hidden behind tortoiseshell sunglasses, betrayed no trace of emotion. He faced straight ahead and seemed to ignore their conversation.

'That's true,' Caine replied, looking back out the window.

'Then again, I wouldn't want to get caught spitting gum on the sidewalk.'

The woman laughed. 'Please, Mr. Caine. Don't believe everything you read. We don't cane people for littering. But we do cite them and charge expensive fines. Some think we are too strict here. But perhaps that is the price we pay for safety and security.'

'Well, can't say I blame you,' he grunted.

Caine watched the scenery speed by the window. He had to admit she had a point. Against all odds, Singapore had prospered and developed into an unrivaled economic destination, brimming with wealth and luxury. Outside the window, thick groves of green palms and vibrant floral gardens streaked by in a blur of color. Golden sunshine reflected off the rippling water of Marina Bay to his right. The sky above was as bright and blue as a carpet of sapphire gems.

Technically, Singapore was designated a sovereign city-state. The entire country was smaller than the state of Rhode Island, yet the tiny island nation boasted one of the highest GDPs per capita in the world and had been granted a triple-A rating by all major credit agencies. Singapore even ranked at highly on the United Nations Human Development Index.

But despite Sasha's optimism, Caine knew the region's safety and prosperity came at a cost. The government enforced order through strict and, some would argue, overzealous regulation. Historically, the powers that be restricted freedom of speech and other rights to maintain control over the populace. The ruling party used broad powers to limit civil liberties and political opposition. And the country's Internal Security Act allowed authorities to detain potential suspects indefinitely, without charges or trial, and had been used in the past to silence rival political parties.

As to whether it was a fair trade... Caine watched the water zip past in silence. It was not for him to say.

As a CIA paramilitary officer, he had worked with and against citizens from just about every developed country in the world. He had learned that if you went back far enough, every nation had blood on its hands.

His own hands were also stained.

'We are almost at the hotel,' Sasha said, pulling him from the cloud of his dark thoughts. 'Look, there.' She pointed out the front windshield.

Ahead of them, the Marina Bay Sands hotel swept up against the azure sky. Caine had seen the hotel before, on previous trips to the country. But the sight never failed to dazzle him. The three towering slabs of glass sparkled in the afternoon sun. Each glittering edifice rose fifty stories into the air, gently curving from the base to the top. Together, they contained over two thousand luxurious hotel rooms, a casino, and multiple clubs, spas, and restaurants.

Above the towers sat the world-famous SkyPark. This massive, curved observation deck was nearly a quarter mile long. The SkyPark presented guests with an unparalleled view of Singapore and access to an exclusive bar, lounge, and the breathtaking infinity pool.

As far as luxury hotels went, the Marina Bay Sands was considered a feat of luxury and engineering. Few places in the world could match its splendor.

'We've held security drills at the hotel before,' Sasha said as the driver sped around the sparkling bay waters. 'The management is used to ISD using the service elevators to access the upper floors. Shouldn't attract too much attention.'

Caine nodded. He shifted in his seat and drummed his fingers on the armrest. He was uneasy, on edge.

It felt strange to be back.

Again, the thought echoed through his mind. And he knew his return to Singapore was not what filled him with nervous energy.

No, he thought. *It's not this place. It's being back in the field. Working with someone.*

Trusting someone.

Sasha lit another cigarette and rolled down the window a few inches. Caine smelled the acrid smoke wafting through the interior of the car. Then the sultry tropical air blasting in from the window filled the cabin with the scent of flowers. 'This will all be over soon,' she said. 'We are just *lim kopi*.'

Caine nodded. '*Lim kopi*,' he repeated. The phrase was local slang and literally translated to 'having coffee.' But locals used it to refer to government authorities applying subtle pressure during chats with criminals and informants in shadowy backrooms. Chats from which some individuals never returned...

Their vehicle pulled behind the three sparkling towers and came to a stop. The driver remained seated as Tony exited the SUV and held the door open. Caine followed, stepping out into the thick, damp air. Sweat beaded on his forehead, and the tinted lenses of his sunglasses fogged. The intense humidity hit him like a brick wall. Caine wore a thin white linen shirt with the sleeves rolled up and olive-green lightweight pants. But the heat from the late afternoon sun was still oppressive.

Four white Volvo sedans with orange police markings fanned out around the rear loading dock of the hotel. Two men wearing camouflage uniforms held assault rifles across their chests and stood guard at the doors leading into the central tower. Other officers marched about the concrete expanse, speaking with anxious hotel managers in low, clipped grunts.

Sasha stubbed out her cigarette in the vehicle's ashtray and shot a nervous glance at the other men. Caine grinned. Singapore had some of the toughest anti-smoking laws on the planet. Clearly, Sasha didn't want word of her habit spreading up the command structure.

She stepped out of the vehicle and stood beside Caine as one of the uniformed men jogged over to them. He shouted some words in Malay to her, but Sasha ignored him and grabbed a walkie clipped to her belt.

'*Unit satu, apakah keadaan anda?*' she said into the radio.

No reply came. Only the static and hiss of an empty channel.

The officer in the uniform lowered his rifle and gestured at Caine. '*Kami diarahkan untuk memeriksanya. Tiada senjata yang dibenarkan!*' he shouted in a gruff voice.

'They want to search you before you enter the hotel,' she whispered in English. 'As a foreign operative, you're not allowed to carry a firearm in the country.'

She turned to the officer. 'It's fine,' she said, raising an open hand to placate the man. '*Saya memeriksanya di lapangan terbang*... I searched him at the airport.'

The man gave Caine an uneasy look then continued jabbering at Sasha. She ignored him and spoke into the walkie again. 'Unit 1, *sila jawab*,' she said into the walkie, a frown marring her delicate features.

'*Saya mesti memeriksanya dia, tiada pengecualian,*' the uniformed man shouted again. Several more officers ambled over. Caine narrowed his eyes... Something didn't feel right. But the last thing he wanted was to create a territorial dispute between local law enforcement and the CIA.

'Fine, fine,' he muttered, raising his arms. 'Knock yourself out.'

The officer grunted and began a thorough pat down, checking all of Caine's waistband and his pockets and ankles.

Sasha continued speaking into the microphone, but static was the only response. She tucked a strand of ebony hair behind her ear and gave Caine a nervous look.

He turned toward her as the officer continued searching him. 'What's wrong?' he asked quietly.

Sasha shook her head. 'Probably just interference from the hotel. But the men I stationed outside the asset's room are not responding.'

Caine felt a familiar tingle on the back of his neck. He cursed himself for being so slow to respond to his instincts. From the moment they reached the hotel, he sensed something wasn't right. But he had failed to listen. Now they were wasting precious time.

He slid off his sunglasses and squinted in the harsh light. 'Something's wrong. We have to get up there. Now!'

The woman looked up at him. His green eyes shimmered in the light, peering down at her like two glittering emerald shards.

Sasha grabbed the officer's arm and pulled him back. '*Cukup*... That's enough!' She held up her ISD badge. 'I take full responsibility. We must get up there. Now!'

She shoved her way through the armed men. Caine followed, gritting his teeth as he shouldered past the officer who had searched him. Tony walked with them, murmuring in Malay to quiet down the other men.

Sasha marched through the doors and into the loading dock. Another pair of STAR officers guarded a row of service elevators in the warm, antiseptic concrete-and-metal room.

'We're going up,' Sasha snapped. '*Biar kami lalu.*'

The men shot each other nervous glances then moved

apart. Sasha pushed the elevator call button. The doors slid open with a chime. Caine, Sasha, and Tony stepped inside.

'Still no response from your men?' Caine asked as the doors shut.

She shook her head. 'No. It could be Wi-Fi, cellular phones, something like that. But—'

'It's not interference,' Caine growled, cutting her off. He looked up at the glowing numbers as the elevator car glided up the tower.

'How can you possibly know that?'

Caine's hand dropped to his waistband. The gesture was pure instinct, and he frowned as he remembered he was unarmed. 'Trust me... I just do.'

The woman looked him in the eye and gave a nervous laugh. 'Do you always think the worst, Mr. Caine?'

He nodded. 'Pretty much.'

She glanced up as the numbers continued to rise. 'Sounds like a terrible way to live.'

'Maybe,' Caine replied. 'But the alternative is an excellent way to die.'

They stood in silence as the elevator continued moving up the tower.

The elevator doors slid open, revealing a sterile white service corridor. Sasha and Tony drew their pistols and crept along the walls, moving in tandem. Caine ignored their command to wait in the elevator and moved behind them, staying close to Tony.

The white corridor led to a gray metal door. Sasha signaled to her partner as she took up a position next to the exit. Tony nodded and moved to cover the doorway. Caine took a step back, making sure he was out of the firing line of any assailant who might be on the other side.

The woman turned the knob then cracked open the door. She peered through the narrow opening.

'*Sudah jelas...* It's clear,' she whispered.

They advanced into the luxurious hotel corridor.

The long hallway was dim and warm. A rich orange carpet, inlaid with a golden leaf design, ran beneath their feet. The wallpaper matched its sunny, gem-like hue. Amber light streamed in from a floor-to-ceiling window at the end of the hall, adding to the warm ambience.

Sasha looked back at Caine. 'My men,' she whispered. 'They are gone.'

Caine said nothing. He pointed at his eyes at the door ahead of them.

Room 1471. The asset's room.

She nodded and continued forward until she and Tony flanked the door. Caine squinted. He could hear a rhythmic sound coming from the other side of the door. The noise sounded like a distant tapping.

Caine pressed himself against the wall. Sasha slipped her key card into the lock. She reached down and turned the knob.

The door swung open.

Tony moved forward, sweeping into the room with his gun extended in a two-handed grip. Sasha followed. Caine heard her gasp. He peered around the corner of the door and looked inside.

The room was a luxurious suite. White furniture sat upon a beige throw rug. A rolling bar cart stood askew in the center of the room, and bottles lay tipped over on its metal surface. Broken glass fragments lay in a puddle of spilled liquid on the polished wood floor. The harsh tang of alcohol filled the air.

The curtains were drawn, allowing a thin sliver of sun to pierce the black shadows. But even in the dim light, Caine could see their asset clearly...

The Asian man hung above the floor, suspended by a thin cord noose. The corpse's face was pale, his lips blue.

Tap... tap... tap...

Caine heard the noise again, louder now. He turned and nodded toward the bedroom.

The sound echoed again in the distance.

Tap... tap... tap...

Sasha met his gaze and nodded back. She advanced,

creeping along the wall toward a wood panel door. She threw the door open and swung into the entrance, weapon at the ready.

The room was as dark and shadowy as the first. Empty suitcases lay on the carpet, and a pile of clothes and toiletries spilled across the rumpled bed.

A stiff wind rustled the heavy curtains, and Caine heard the muted sound of traffic from below. Sasha and Tony advanced toward the open window. The junior agent grabbed the curtain and yanked it open.

Blinding sunlight flooded the room, and Caine shielded his eyes. The wind gusted again, stronger than before. They were on the twenty-seventh floor, and the breeze filled the room with the scent of tropical flowers and the bay waters outside. It whipped the loose clothes and tissues off the bed.

One of the towering windows hung wide open, allowing the wind to blast into the room. The tapping sound came again, this time accompanied by a metal twang.

Caine squinted his eyes. An empty window-washer's cart thumped against the side of the building, buffeted by the powerful wind. Tony reached through the open window and grabbed the railing of the long, narrow cart with his free hand. As the curtains shifted in the wind, a starburst of light on his left side caught Caine's eye.

A massive pane of glass lay at an angle against the far wall of the room. He felt the familiar tingle at the back of his neck once more.

The window isn't open, he realized. *Someone removed the glass!*

As Sasha approached the open space left by the missing panel, Caine saw something move in the plate of glass. It was a reflection from outside the hotel... Workers in a second cart, ascending the side of the tower.

'Sasha, look out!' Caine shouted.

Charging forward, he grabbed her arm and yanked her back from the window.

Before she could even scream, the staccato beat of automatic weapon fire slashed through the air. Tony's body jerked and writhed, and one of the other windows exploded into glittering shards.

Caine rolled with Sasha across the bed and onto the floor, dragging her with him. As another volley of bullets screamed overhead, he gritted his teeth and pressed her to the carpet. The gunfire shredded the pillow and linens above them, sending tiny white feathers drifting to the floor like falling snow.

'Men outside,' Caine grunted. 'Three of them, on another cart. They're moving up the building.'

Sasha barked a series of commands into her walkie.

'I've ordered men to lock down the elevators on every floor.' She looked deep into his eyes. 'You... you saved my life,' she murmured.

Caine realized his arms were still wrapped around the petite woman. He let go and peered over the shredded mattress. The other cart's reflection moved across the pane of glass, rising higher up the tower. He leapt to his feet and ran over to Tony. A scarlet puddle stained the carpet around Tony's lifeless body.

'Stopping the elevators won't help if they're taking the cart all the way up.' Caine reached down and felt the agent's neck. There was no pulse. He pried the pistol from the dead man's grip then slipped a spare magazine from his shoulder rig.

The gun was a CZ P-07, a Czech-made pistol chambered in 9mm Luger. Out of habit, he ejected the magazine and checked the load. Then he slammed the mag back into the pistol and released the slide. He leaned out the window and glanced up the towering structure. The wind whipped through his hair as he watched the cart, now just a tiny sliver, climbing higher and higher up the shimmering hotel.

'They're not stopping at any floors,' he muttered, turning to Sasha. 'I don't think that's their plan. The floor just below the SkyPark... what's there?'

Sasha stared at Tony's corpse. Another gust of wind blew the curtains aside, and sunlight slashed across her face.

Caine grabbed her arm. 'Sasha?'

She pulled back her hair and turned to face him. 'Sorry. Above the towers are spas, restaurants, a nightclub... and service areas for hotel employees. After that is the SkyPark.'

Caine nodded. 'Post men outside this room. We'll have to search it later, in case the attackers left anything behind. Then send whoever's left up to the SkyPark.'

'Here,' she said, her voice still shaking. 'You'll need this.' She handed him her key card. 'It opens most of the doors in the hotel. But why would they be going up there? What could they hope to—'

'I have no idea,' Caine said, cutting her off as he moved toward the door. 'But what goes up must come down.'

6

Caine took the service elevator up as far as it would go, to the fifty-seventh floor, where the doors opened with an electronic chime. He stepped out, sweeping left and right with the pistol, and followed the corridor until it turned to the left. Peering around the corner, he saw a service door several meters down another identical corridor.

He stalked forward, gun at the ready. As he approached the door, he spotted some scuff marks on the white floor and a small crimson stain near the metal door's card key reader. He touched the sticky patch with his finger.

It was blood.

He slid the key Sasha had given him into the lock. The door beeped then clicked open. He pulled it aside and darted through.

He was in a dim supply room that smelled of scented oils and candles. Metal shelves reached the ceiling, filled with towering piles of fluffy white towels. A second door, unmarked, stood on the opposite wall.

He cracked the other door open and looked through. It led

to a dim, narrow corridor. Caine crept through it, moving silently across the bamboo floor. Soothing music played overhead, and a series of doors flanked the serene corridor. They were all ajar, and as he stalked forward, he looked through one of the doorways.

In the low, flickering candlelight, he saw massage tables draped with colorful linens. Translucent curtains hung over curved floor-to-ceiling windows, dimming the sunlight. Through the sheer fabric, he could just make out the city skyline in the distance.

He moved on, glancing into the next room. It was identical to the last save for one detail. A body lay on the floor. The corpse was an Asian woman dressed in a white masseuse uniform. A crimson stain spread across her chest, and her glazed, lifeless eyes stared up at the ceiling.

Caine pressed on. The corridor opened into a lobby. Two more employees lay dead on the floor, and a man in a white tunic sprawled over the spa's front desk. A glass wall separated the lobby from the hotel corridor outside.

He saw movement in the distance... blurry figures sprinting beyond the translucent wall. Caine dove behind the desk as the roar of gunfire filled the air. The glass barrier exploded into a falling cascade of glittering shards. He heard the thud of bullets slamming into the desk, and wood splinters dusted his hair.

A moment later, the gunfire ceased.

Caine sprang up, holding the pistol in a two-handed grip. In the distance, he saw the figures racing down the corridor, four men in blue workers' coveralls carrying submachine guns. Caine suspected the weapons were HK MP5s, but it was difficult to tell through the broken glass.

An older woman shrieked and fell to her knees as the

gunmen rushed past her. They ignored her, continuing toward a bend in the passageway.

Caine returned fire, sending a double tap through the broken glass. One of the men stumbled. A teammate helped him up, and they hurried around the corner.

Muttering a silent curse, Caine vaulted over the desk and scrambled through the shattered glass panel. He helped the older woman to her feet. 'Which way to the SkyPark?' he shouted in a commanding voice.

The woman was in tears. She spoke in a language he did not understand, gesturing in the direction the men had gone.

Caine pointed at the shattered window that led to the spa. 'Get back there, find a room, and stay down!' he said, not knowing if the woman could understand him.

He darted down the corridor, pressing himself against the corner wall. Taking a deep breath, he swung around and peered over the barrel of his pistol.

The corridor was empty. An elevator stood at the end, and another service door hung ajar. He charged ahead, ignoring the elevator and kicking the door open. Before he could enter the stairwell beyond, gunfire ricocheted off the wall and floor. Caine ducked back, wincing as the men continued firing from above.

He waited until the shooting died down, and then he popped back into the stairwell. He fired a quick double tap, but he was shooting blind. He couldn't see anything, but he heard the men's footsteps clanging up the metal stairs. Another barrage of gunfire rained down the stairwell.

Caine ducked back into the corridor and pressed the elevator call button. As the doors slid open, he leaned back into the stairwell and fired again. More bullets streaked down in response as the shooters continued up the stairs.

He stepped into the elevator and pressed a button marked SP. He was certain there was only one place the armed men could be heading.

The SkyPark, he thought.

His chest heaved as he panted for breath. His nerves crackled with energy. Chinese pop music played over the speakers in the elevator, but he barely heard it over the roar of adrenaline pumping through his veins.

Then the chime rang, and the doors slid open. Caine raced out, joining a crowd of tourists as they exited from one of the main elevators. The stream of people headed toward the massive SkyPark's entrance. Hotel staff and security guards manned a series of turnstiles, blocking the guests from entering the complex.

Caine narrowed his eyes. In the distance he spotted the four men hustling through the crowd on the other side of the turnstiles. They all carried canvas bags slung over their shoulders.

Their guns must be inside, Caine thought. *That's how they got through security.*

He shouldered his way through the crowd. Spotting security up ahead, he shoved his gun into his waistband. Assorted Asian and European families ambled alongside him, wearing loose shirts, bathing suits, and lightweight robes. Caine grabbed the arm of a heavyset man in front of him and pulled him out of the way.

'*Vad fan?*' the man grunted in a thick Swedish accent. Caine ignored him and shoved on, threading through the tourists until he stood face-to-face with one of the security guards.

The man's hand dropped to his belt as he eyed Caine with a suspicious glare. 'Sir, the SkyPark is closed. All hotel guests are directed to—'

'Listen to me,' Caine said. 'I'm working with Sasha Yeoh,

from ISD. Four men in workers' uniforms just came through here. They're armed and dangerous. You have to evacuate—'

He stopped in mid-sentence as he spotted another security guard jogging across the pool area, moving to intercept the men.

Caine realized that news of the carnage downstairs had already reached security. That was why they had closed the deck. But they had not yet evacuated the guests already in the park.

'No!' Caine snapped. 'Call your man back. If he stops them now, they could—'

Before the security guard could answer, the gunmen yanked their weapons from the bags and opened fire. Screams erupted throughout the complex as bullets riddled the guard's body. The men fired again, sending a crowd of tourists scurrying toward the entrance. Then the attackers sprinted across the curved deck, heading for a cluster of red umbrellas near the infinity pool.

Caine pushed the security guard aside and vaulted over the turnstile. He drew his gun and sprinted after the men, turning to run along the length of the SkyPark. He leapt up onto a low stone wall as a throng of terrified hotel guests in dripping swimwear rushed past him.

As the crowd fled the area, Caine ran along the top of the wall. Once the other people were clear, he jumped down and continued chasing the men down a meandering stone path. Rows of palm trees flanked him on either side. It was as if a city park had levitated hundreds of feet in the air.

Gunfire screamed past him. He heard wood snap as the bullets tore into the surrounding trees. Cursing, Caine ducked into the garden and crawled through the grass. He took cover behind a palm tree as more bullets flew overhead.

He peered around the tree trunk. The gunmen were running past the infinity pool in the center of the park.

Caine lowered his pistol and raced after them, pumping his arms to increase his speed. His heart pounded in his chest, and he panted for breath as he sprinted toward the rear man. Gritting his teeth, Caine burst from the trees and raced onto the flagstones surrounding the pool.

He barreled into his target at full speed, tackling the man like a football player. The two of them fell into the pool with a loud splash. Caine wrapped his arms around the man's torso as they sank into the sloshing water. They slammed into the concrete bottom with a dull thud then floated toward the surface. Caine lost his grip on the gun, and the weapon sank to the bottom of the pool.

The man kicked and struggled, breaking free of Caine's grasp. Caine felt a burning pain slice across his shoulder. Opening his eyes, he saw a pink cloud obscure the surrounding water. The man had cut him with a knife. Bubbles exploded from his mouth as he hissed in pain.

Caine broke the surface and wiped his eyes to clear the droplets of water from his vision. He felt his feet touch bottom. The man lashed out again... A razor-sharp blade glinted in his right hand. Caine backpedaled through the water, and the attack missed his torso by inches.

'Who are you?' Caine snarled, circling around his opponent. 'Who hired you?'

Looking over the killer's shoulder, he saw the other men pause and watch him.

'What are you waiting for?' one of them shouted. 'Move your ass!'

No local accent, Caine thought. *Sounds American...*

They turned and continued racing toward the end of the SkyPark deck.

The man in the pool focused on Caine, splashing toward him with rage simmering in his eyes. Behind them, the modern Singapore skyline glittered in the distance.

The edge of the infinity pool was an invisible line between water and sky. Ripples sloshed over the side, falling off into nothingness as the men splashed and moved about. It was as if they were fighting atop a waterfall, perched high above the shimmering city.

The man slashed with the knife again. Caine kept his hands in close, guarding his face with his forearms. The strike went wide, and Caine dropped his arm, grabbing the man's wrist. He twisted the arm, struggling to lock his attacker in a hold. But before he could complete the maneuver, the man's foot lashed out in a sweeping kick, knocking Caine's legs out from under him.

As he fell beneath the water, Caine felt chlorine sting his eyes. He reached up, grabbing his attacker's knife arm with his free hand. He had to gain control of the weapon before the man stabbed him again. He kicked out, slamming his foot as hard as he could into his enemy's shin.

Caine heard the man's muted cry, and another splash echoed beside him as his attacker plunged below the surface. The two men spun around in the water, sending a trail of bubbles exploding through the azure depths. Caine struggled to plant his feet on the bottom of the pool. But before he could regain his balance, his opponent shoved him through the water. Caine drove his elbow down, slamming it into his attacker's back as he felt himself propelled backward.

Caine felt fire in his lungs. His chest burned, his body crying out for oxygen. But he couldn't surface without relinquishing his hold on his adversary's knife arm. One quick jab would be all it would take... a thrust into a vital organ, and he would bleed out in the luxurious pool's crystal waters.

Bubbles spewed from his mouth as his back slammed into something hard. They had collided with the far wall of the pool. Caine threw his head forward, striking his opponent with a headbutt. But the water slowed his movements, rendering the attack weak and ineffective. Through the swirling water, he saw his opponent clench his teeth, his dark eyes like two obsidian stones in the bubbly haze. The man thrust forward with the knife. Caine managed to block the attack, pushing his opponent's arm aside. He heard the scrape of metal against concrete as the knife struck the side of the pool.

His attacker snorted another burst of bubbles, and they both broke the surface of the water, still grappling for control of the weapon. Caine gasped, sucking in a deep lungful of air. He caught a brief glimpse of the pool deck over his enemy's shoulder. The red umbrellas twisted in the wind, and water sloshed over the edge of the pool as their battle whipped it into a frenzy.

His attacker placed a hand on his head, shoving him back underwater. Chlorine stung his eyes as they both spun around in the depths. Again, Caine's back scraped against the concrete wall of the pool.

He closed his eyes briefly, letting the darkness calm his frenzied thoughts. He kept his grip on the man's wrist and oriented himself. He remembered the Singapore skyline, yawning beyond the horizon of the infinity pool's cascading waters.

The pool deck is in front of me, he thought. *That means behind me is...*

The man thrust the knife again. Caine shoved the blow aside again then released the man's wrist. The weapon scraped against the wall of the pool, just under Caine's arm.

Before his opponent could recover his balance, Caine grabbed his collar with one hand and the belt of his jumpsuit with the other. Off balance from his attack and slowed by the water, his opponent could offer no resistance. Caine pushed off the floor of the pool with both feet.

He broke the surface, grunting with exertion as he heaved the man up and over his shoulder.

The Asian man screamed as he saw the skyline looming before him. Caine tossed him over the side of the pool, and he tumbled out of sight.

Panting for breath, Caine turned and looked over the edge. Contrary to his belief, the side of the infinity pool was not a sheer drop over the edge of the building. Instead, a narrow trench ran alongside, allowing the water to spill back into reclamation vents.

His attacker sprawled across a walkway below. He had struck the ground headfirst, and a dark pool of blood stained the concrete beneath his crushed skull.

Caine took a deep breath then leapt out of the pool and hopped over the edge. He flexed his knees as he landed, allowing them to absorb the shock of the fifteen-foot drop. Sprinting forward, he grabbed the corpse's shoulder bag and tore it off. Then he kept running, following the trench to the end, where a set of concrete stairs led back up to the SkyPark.

He raced up, taking the stairs two at a time, then ripped open the assassin's duffel bag, exposing the barrel of an MP5 submachine gun. The weapon rested atop a plastic case of tools and cables and a slim metal rectangle... a computer hard drive. Caine pulled out the gun then slung the bag around his neck.

Leaping over a low gate at the end of the stairs, Caine saw the two remaining men standing at the end of the platform.

The SkyPark resembled the deck of a ship with a subtle

curve running along its length. The men stood at the park's 'bow.' Shimmering buildings and blue sky lay beyond the metal guardrail. A flagpole rose from the deck, topped with a crimson wind sock. The fabric flapped due north, pointing straight away from the platform.

As Caine sprinted closer, he saw the men strip down and remove their coveralls. They wore sleek black jumpsuits underneath. Loose flaps of fabric stretched between their arms and legs.

'Freeze!' Caine shouted, aiming the weapon as he ran. 'Don't move! It's over!'

One of them turned to face him. Black balaclavas covered their faces, and goggles hid their eyes.

'See you around, Tom,' the man shouted back. Caine could barely hear him over the wind. But he heard enough.

That voice, he thought. *It can't be...*

Caine narrowed his eyes and fired. His bullets sparked off the guardrail, but it was too late. The two men jumped off the platform, falling away from the structure into the wind.

Caine reached the railing and looked down at the two figures, already tiny black dots, streaking away from the building at incredible speed. They spread their arms and legs wide, and the flaps of fabric running along their suits stretched taut. The men whipped through the surrounding buildings like tiny fighter jets, banking and turning as they adjusted their course.

Wingsuits, he thought.

He pressed the gun's stock to his shoulder and pivoted, tracking the lead flyer in the weapon's sights.

Then, with a hiss of frustration, he lowered the gun. They were just barely within the MP5's effective range. But they were moving too fast. They had to be traveling over 100 miles per hour. Trying to hit a flying target at that speed would be nearly impossible. And given the heavily populated city, there was no telling where his errant shots might land.

They had escaped. He had failed.

Caine heard footsteps clattering behind him. He spun around as a squad of STAR officers raced across the deck. They fanned out around him, weapons at the ready.

'Drop the gun,' one of them shouted. 'Now!'

Caine slowly crouched, lowering the MP5 to the ground. He stood up again, raising his hands.

'*Hentikan!*' a woman's voice shouted. Sasha pushed her way through the men, blocking their line of sight. '*Lelaki ini bersama saya...* Stand down, he's with me!'

The men lowered their weapons. One of them secured Caine's MP5 as the others spread out along the SkyPark deck, searching for anyone who might need medical assistance.

The squad leader approached Caine. 'Sorry, sir. After all the shooting, we thought—'

Caine nodded and raised a hand, dismissing the officer's apology. 'I get it. Were there any more of them?'

The officer shook his head. 'No one came down to the twenty-second floor. The hotel shut down all the lobby elevators. We're searching them now, but I don't expect to find much.' He gave Sasha a nod then marched off to join his men.

The woman's hair whipped around her face as the wind picked up again. 'We found my men in a supply closet,' she said to Caine. 'And several IRT members assigned to the hotel's shopping mall have gone missing.'

'IRT?'

'In-Situ Response Team. Security forces deployed to prominent public locations, like the hotel. They carry MP5s, so we suspect the assassins killed them and stole their weapons.

Smuggling that kind of hardware into Singapore would be extremely difficult.'

Caine nodded and walked next to her as they stepped away from the guardrail.

'Makes sense. And the asset?'

'Preliminary findings indicate he was dead before they strung him up. We don't know how, but we did find a tiny puncture behind the right ear.'

'Poison,' Caine said. 'Maybe KCl... potassium chloride? It breaks down into common organic elements in the body. Hard to trace.'

She nodded. 'One more thing. We found the asset's computer, but the hard drive was removed.'

'That's what they were after,' Caine said. He slipped the bag off his shoulder and held it out to the woman. 'One of the men was carrying this. There's a hard drive inside. My guess is it came from Seng's computer.' Sasha reached for the bag, but Caine held on to it. 'It's important that you share this with my people.'

'Of course,' she said, giving him a surprised look. 'You have my word.'

He released the bag then shot a glance at the STAR officers sweeping across the SkyPark deck. 'Sasha, I've crossed these people before. They have a certain MO. They find a weak element in the power structure and apply pressure, corrupt from within. If we had been a few minutes later, they would have gotten away clean.'

Sasha followed his glance. He was staring at the officer who had searched him on the ground. 'You think they delayed us on purpose?' she murmured.

Caine thought for a moment then turned to face her. 'I don't know. But it's possible. Either way, you don't set up an operation like this without help from the inside. If I were you... I'd be careful who you trust.'

They continued walking toward the elevators that led down to the hotel. They stopped and waited for the car to arrive. Sasha looked up at him as the wind rustled through the nearby trees. 'Tom... I... I think I need a drink. Several, in fact. I know a place. It's close by.'

Caine looked her in the eye. He squinted but said nothing.

'It's near my apartment,' she added. 'Would you... care to join me?'

He realized he had misread her before. It wasn't curiosity he had seen in her eyes. It was attraction. He shook his head. 'I'm sorry, but I'm afraid I have to debrief with my people.'

She nodded. '*Sudah tentu*... Of course. Another time, perhaps?'

The elevator chime sounded. 'You never know,' he replied with a gentle smile.

Sasha remained where she was. She gave him one last smile as the metal doors slid shut.

As the elevator traveled down the length of the tower, he held up his hand. It was shaking. He clenched it into a fist and took a deep breath. His body ached, and the cut in his shoulder throbbed.

He leaned against the wall and closed his eyes. The tiny metal car carried him farther and farther down.

7

REPUBLIC OF SINGAPORE, KALLANG AIRPORT

The old Kallang Airport was a crumbling edifice of white concrete walls and shattered glass windows. Its faded, cracked tarmac sat near the city's Geylang District, infamous for its brothels and 'gentlemen's clubs.' As the blazing sun lowered over the stark, empty buildings, far in the distance, Geylang's colorful neon lights flickered in the dim streets, like fireflies darting through the night sky.

Thick groves of trees obscured the view of the old art deco buildings from the street, and a metal slat fence blocked off the rear. Inactive for decades and closed off to tourists, the airport was now an abandoned curiosity, a long-forgotten reminder of the country's colonial past.

Inside the crumbling central tower, two men's footsteps echoed through the ruin as they jogged up a metal spiral staircase. Every footfall shook the old stairs, sending chips of rust and paint showering down from above.

The lead man pulled a black balaclava off his face and stuffed it into a Velcro pocket on the side of his parachute pack. After gliding across the city, they had triggered their chutes at the last minute, swooping in low and fast over the old airport's main runway. Within minutes, they had stowed their chutes and sprinted into the abandoned structure.

Bands of purple and orange lit up the sky as the sun began its final descent. Darkness slithered across the streets and alleys. The crowds of workers and pedestrians thinned out, giving way to the denizens of the neon-tinged shadows. Those who sought the pleasures of the night ventured out into Geylang.

As the men ascended the tower, a distant sound cut through the wind... a rhythmic thumping, growing louder and louder. The lead man turned to his partner. His skin was sun-bronzed and leathery, weathered by age and the elements. His eyes were dark, almost black, like a shark's. His steel-gray hair was buzzed military short. Despite his age, his jaw was as chiseled and angular as an armored tank.

'You said your man would take care of things,' he grunted. 'Give us a window before ISD arrived at the hotel.'

The other man yanked off his own hood, revealing Asian features and a scruffy mop of dark hair. 'Someone went over his head at ISD,' he muttered as they exited the stairwell. They kept moving, entering a circular, dust-filled landing. 'You didn't tell me American operatives would be on the scene. My guy got spooked!'

The leader shoved open a rusting old door. Countless layers of industrial white paint covered the metal slab, and a screech echoed through the building as the old hinges moved for the first time in years. 'It could have been worse. Still, I don't like it. Sloppy work.'

They emerged onto the roof of the old airport. The thumping noise grew louder, and a black shadow descended from the clouds. A sleek helicopter came into view, moving down toward the building.

The Asian man knelt and rummaged through a pouch at his belt. 'Quit complaining, Riley,' he snapped. 'We got what we came for.' He removed a silver hard drive from the bag and handed it to Riley. 'Whatever compromising intel Seng had on your organization, it's on this drive. I cloned it before we left.'

Boone Riley took the drive and held it in his gloved hand, examining it in the dim light. The helicopter continued its descent, hovering just over their heads. His black clothes rippled in the heavy prop wash. 'What about the original?' Riley shouted over the noise of the rotors.

The Asian man shrugged. 'That was with my partner. He didn't make it. Either way, you hired me to retrieve the intel. I did my job. The rest is your problem.'

Riley nodded and stowed the drive in his pack. 'You're right,' he shouted back. 'I'll take care of it.' He stood up and raised his arm, a silenced 9mm pistol in his fist. 'Nice working with you.' His lips curled into a manic grin.

The Asian man raised his hands and stepped back. 'Wait, Riley, you can't—'

The gun barked twice, the sound barely audible over the roar of the helicopter. Crimson holes opened in the other man's forehead and chest. He coughed, and a thin line of blood trickled from his lips. Then he collapsed to the ground.

The helicopter set down on the roof behind Riley. The structure groaned and he felt the metal plates beneath his feet buckle. But the crumbling building still supported the aircraft's weight. The helicopter was long and coated in solid black paint. The hull had a matte, almost rubbery texture.

A door slid open in the rear of the helicopter. Riley ducked down as he jogged beneath the spinning rotors. A crewman wearing an unmarked jumpsuit and helmet leaned out and offered a hand. Riley took it and hopped into the rear cabin. As they took off, he chuckled and turned to the crewman. 'First class all the way, huh? Grissom must have paid a fortune for this.'

The man nodded. 'Yes, sir,' he shouted back. 'MH-X Stealth Black Hawks don't come cheap. But the engine is shielded for noise, and it has a second main rotor. Slows down the spinning blades, makes less of a racket.'

'Could have fooled me,' Riley shouted back. The thumping of the rotors filled the rear of the cabin, which made hearing difficult.

'Trust me, the engine noise carries less than a block. And we're invisible to radar, more or less.' The man handed him a chunky satellite phone. 'He wants you to report in ASAP.'

Riley grabbed the phone and sat down on a bench at the rear of the cabin. He fished the hard drive out of his pack and connected it to a Toughbook laptop with its own secure satellite connection. Then he entered a number on the phone's keypad, dialing from memory.

He heard a lengthy series of beeps then a burst of static. A gruff, rasping voice answered the call. 'Riley, you're bang on time, son. Efficient as usual.'

'Thank you, Mr. Grissom. I'm transmitting the contents of Seng's laptop now. Hopefully your techs can use it to pinpoint the leak.'

'I think we both know who the leak is, Riley. Finding him... Now that's another story. Hopefully Seng wasn't as careful as our old friend. Any problems?'

Riley leaned back and peered out the tinted rear window. The helicopter soared high above Singapore's neon lights and misty streets. He knew they would be out over the ocean within minutes. By the time local authorities pieced together the few eyewitness accounts of the helicopter's sudden appearance, the aircraft would have safely landed on a freighter in international waters.

The escape was clean. Relatively clean, at least.

'Some local help lost their nerve. There were a few bodies. But nothing that can blow back on you, sir.'

Grissom made a clicking sound with his tongue on the other end of the line. 'Well, situation like this, I suppose it can't be helped. It's a cliché, but you know what they say about omelets.'

'One more thing, sir. Caine was there.'

The voice was silent for a moment. 'He was, huh? Looks like you were right. That boy's a dog who's got himself a taste of a bone. He just can't seem to let go.'

'Like I told you, sir, he won't stop.' Riley paused for a moment, thinking. He watched the dark water unfold beneath them as the chopper flew out to sea. 'It's all he has left, sir.'

'Doesn't change a thing. You just settle in for the flight. I'll call you as soon as my men pick over this bastard's hard drive.'

'Understood,' Riley said. He hung up, leaned his head against the wall, and closed his eyes. It was time to rest. He knew he would be busy again soon.

See you around, Tom... He grinned as he remembered the look of surprise on Caine's face.

Yeah, he thought. *I'll see you soon. Sooner than you think.*

The familiar beat of the helicopter's rotors lulled him to sleep.

8

Caine peered out the window of his room at the Quincy Hotel. Outside, the humid air had finally cooled. The light breeze carried a hint of brine as it blew across the bay. The sky was a canvas of pastel hues, fading to black as the last remains of daylight sank beneath the horizon.

After operating on his own for so long, he felt a vague sense of unease, bordering on panic, at the thought of allowing the agency to know where he was staying. Out of habit, he called several other hotels in the city, booking reservations under various aliases in case anyone tried to determine his whereabouts. But out of all the hotels available, he chose to stay at the Quincy.

At just 108 rooms, the boutique establishment was tiny compared to the palatial luxury of the Marina Bay Sands. The building was a single wedge of glass and steel, rising above the tree-lined streets of the Orchard shopping district. From the ground, its facade presented a glowing checkerboard of purple and orange, like a neon Mondrian painting. A glass-enclosed cantilevered pool deck on the upper floors jutted out over the busy street.

Caine's room was on the fourteenth floor. It was comfortable, quiet, and modern, decorated in wood and leather tones. Muted electronic music played on the sound system, helping to soothe Caine's jangled nerves. He lifted a glass tumbler to his lips and swallowed the last drops of scotch.

Reaching into an ice bucket on the bar, he fished out a fresh cube and dropped it in the glass. He poured another measure of Ballantine's Scotch Whisky into the glass. He took another sip, barely tasting the smooth amber liquid.

See you around, Tom...

The words echoed in his mind, like a tune he just couldn't get out of his head. The rushing wind, the screams of the panicked crowd, the roar of gunfire... So much had been happening. Had he possibly misheard the man?

No!

He played the scene from memory once again. *You know what he said. He called you by name. He knew you.*

And you know him...

A loud buzz sounded in the room, dragging Caine from his melancholy reflection. It was his phone, vibrating on the nightstand. He paced over to the bed and eyed the screen. The complex string of digits signified an agency call.

Great, he thought. *Another debrief...*

'Yes,' he said, answering the call.

'Hey, you,' a woman replied. 'I just got in. Read more of that Murakami book you recommended.'

Despite his somber mood, Caine grinned from ear to ear. 'I thought you'd like it. It's a bit of a mystery.'

'And a bit of a meditation,' she replied.

'Yeah. Just like life.' Their odd speech pattern masked a

series of code phrases, meant to establish that neither was speaking under duress. Caine had worked out the routine with her long ago. 'Rebecca!' he continued, unable to keep the pleasure out of his voice any longer. 'I wasn't expecting you to—'

'Oh, I'm full of surprises,' she replied, cutting him off. He could almost hear her smile through the phone. 'Check your door.'

Caine stepped over to the door and removed the strip of electrical tape covering the security hole. He peered through the tiny circle of light. His grin widened as he unlocked the door.

A woman stood framed in the doorway. She was tall and athletic looking, with fiery copper-red hair. She wore a navy-blue woman's suit. Caine couldn't identify the brand, but he knew she had a penchant for Helmut Lang. She peered up at him, a mischievous smile tugging at the corners of her lips.

'Rebecca!' Caine said in a loud whisper. 'What are you... It's not safe for you to—'

She nodded over her shoulder. Caine peered down the hall behind her. A large, beefy-looking man in a charcoal suit stood near the elevator.

'I have men positioned throughout the hotel,' Rebecca said in a low voice. 'Trust me, my security team has it covered. Now, are you going to invite me in? Or do you expect me to stand in your door all night?'

Stand...

Caine realized how long it had been since he had seen her out of her wheelchair. The chair Bernatto and others had put her in after a brutal gunfight in Thailand left her... He blinked, banishing the painful memories. 'Sorry, it's just—Please, come in.'

He stood aside, and Rebecca stepped into the room. As he

softly closed the door behind her, he noticed she walked with a slight limp. She held a wooden cane in her left hand, and it made a tapping sound as she moved across the wood floor.

'Nice!' She glanced around at the room. 'I can see why you like it here.'

'It's just a place to sleep,' Caine said, watching as she sat down on the bed. 'Nothing special.'

She glanced around, taking in the details. The rich wood floors, the slate-gray headboard, the clean, modern lines... 'No, it's relaxing. Comfortable but not ostentatious. Reminds me of you.'

Caine walked over to the bar and refilled his drink. 'Your surgery was a success, I take it?' he said, using a corkscrew to pop open a bottle of red wine then pouring some into a glass.

'So far, so good. I'm not running any marathons yet, but... baby steps. It got me out of that damned chair, so no complaints here.'

Caine offered her the glass of wine. She took a long sip, peering at him over the rim of the glass. 'I heard you could be pretty dangerous in that chair,' he said, sipping his own drink.

She smiled, but something in her eyes looked pained. Caine gritted his teeth as he remembered Josh Galloway, the former head of her security detail and the man who had trained her to fight in her wheelchair. She had grown close to him during Caine's self-imposed exile. Galloway was another victim of Caine's former boss, Allan Bernatto, Rebecca's predecessor as the director of the CIA's National Clandestine Service.

'Rebecca, I'm sorry,' he muttered. 'I didn't mean to—'

She shook her head. 'Forget it. The past is the past.'

Caine grabbed a chair and pulled it close to the bed. He sat down, hunched over, and looked up at her. 'So... Did you really come to debrief me?'

'What did you expect?' she said, taking another sip of wine.

He chuckled. 'Just like old times.'

She raised an eyebrow. 'Old times? I seem to recall our old operations being more successful. Singapore's ISD is breathing down my neck for intel after what happened at the hotel.'

Caine shrugged and swirled the ice in his drink. 'Can't say I blame them. Dead tourists, a gunfight in one of their most famous hotels. Any luck IDing the attackers' corpses?'

Rebecca ran her hands through her crimson hair then tied it back in a ponytail. 'Yes and no. We identified the two that you neutralized. Both were Indonesian. Former military, spotty service records. Freelancers now, known associates with several terror groups on the ISD's watch list.'

Caine sipped his scotch. 'Makes sense. So let me guess – ISD is chalking this up as an extremist terror attack?'

Rebecca nodded. 'Got it in one. After the bloodshed at the hotel, they're under massive pressure to make this all go away. And it's not like I can offer them a better explanation. Not without revealing the truth about Bernatto, Grissom, and a bunch of other things the CIA does not want to discuss.'

'Any lead on the surviving men? Like where they might be now?'

She bit her lip and sighed. 'Negative. Singapore air traffic control didn't log any unauthorized flights out of the country. ISD officers are stationed at all the airports and train stations. Surveillance cameras are active throughout the city, but so far, there's been no sign of them.'

'Those cameras rely on facial recognition software,' Caine said. 'Grissom and Blackwing have access to the most advanced tech companies in the world. They could have slipped a virus into the network before his men landed here. Some kind of algorithm to erase their records if their faces got flagged in the city.'

Rebecca crossed her legs. She tried to hide her pain, but he saw her wince. Caine narrowed his eyes.

'Right,' she said. 'So that angle's a dead end. But it's not a total loss. Our techs got a look at the hard drive you dropped off at the station house. Whoever killed Seng removed it from his laptop, but it looks like they made a clone first.'

'Interesting.'

She took another sip of her wine. 'They've barely had time to sift through it all, but they did come up with one tidbit. Seng's tip about the Blackwing mainframe in Texas. We found an encrypted email with those same coordinates. Someone fed him the intel. And whoever it was, they called themselves "Larkspur".'

Caine rubbed his shoulder and grunted again. His muscles still throbbed from the battle in the pool. 'So Seng was just a cutout. The real Larkspur is still out there. Do we know where?'

'Whoever sent Seng that email was using a Tor network to hide their tracks. But the NSA recently found a flaw that could be exploited in the Tor software. The latest builds are immune, but Larkspur is using older version. We haven't been able to pinpoint an exact location yet, but our techs are confident the email originated in Vietnam. Somewhere near Hanoi.'

Caine took a sip of whisky then focused his emerald gaze on Rebecca. 'Then I take it that's my next stop?'

She brushed a strand of copper hair behind her ear as she met his stare. 'You leave in the morning. There's nothing more to be gained here. Andrew Seng died in his hotel room, Blackwing got whatever intel he was looking to trade, and we're back at square one. We have a highly skilled former CIA official operating his own deep-state intelligence network and no idea where or when he'll strike next.'

Caine stared at the whisky in his glass. Rebecca arched a single eyebrow. 'You're hiding something,' she said.

Caine chuckled. 'You know me too well.'

'Or maybe not well enough,' she replied. 'We made a promise to each other. No more secrets.'

He shook his head. 'It's not a secret. I just... I'm not sure I...'

She followed him with her eyes as he stood up and paced over to the window. All traces of the colorful sunset outside had fled, leaving the sky dark.

'One of Seng's killers said something to me before he jumped off the building.'

Rebecca leaned forward, and her eyes opened wide with surprise. 'Well, that's one detail you left out of your report to the ISD.'

Caine nodded. A gentle breeze filled the room, rustling the curtain. The air smelled of tropical flowers and sea salt. 'Yeah. I wanted to tell you first. He spoke to me in English. I can't be 100 percent certain, but I think he was American.'

He swirled his drink, letting the ice rattle in the glass.

'Go on,' Rebecca said, peering at him with an intense stare.

'He seemed to know me, and I think I know him.'

'OK. So who was it?'

Caine turned to face her. He threw back the rest of the scotch and set the glass down on the table. 'Boone Riley.'

Rebecca narrowed her eyes. 'That name sounds familiar.'

He nodded. 'He is... was... an operator. Worked with Jack in Delta Force for a while. When Jack came over to SAD/SOG, Riley followed a couple months later. Bernatto recruited him for our team.'

'Operation Blackwing,' Rebecca murmured.

'Yeah,' Caine replied. He looked her in the eye. His emerald stare blazed in the dim light like a pair of verdant suns. 'Like I said, I can't be 100 percent sure. I didn't see his face, and as far as I know, Riley is dead. But I could have sworn it was his voice.'

She bit her lip, thinking. 'I'll pull his file, see if we can make any connections. After I get back to D.C.'

'You're going back?' He tried to hide the disappointment in his voice.

She nodded. 'I leave tomorrow as well. Director Paulis has been called to testify at a Senate Intelligence Committee hearing. Fallout from... well, from everything that's happened lately. He wants me running point on this from home, in case—'

'In case the suits decide Paulis is their new fall guy.' Caine shook his head. 'Every one of them knew Grissom and Bernatto were dirty. They let them skate to keep their own hands clean. When do you leave?'

Rebecca took another sip of wine, then looked up at him. 'In the morning.'

Caine sat down next to her on the bed. 'Rebecca, it's incredible to see you walking again. But I can't help but feel that... what happened was my fault somehow, I—'

She rested a hand on his shoulder and peered into his eyes. 'Tom, do you remember what I told you the first time you saw me in the chair? Back in Thailand?'

He nodded once more. 'You said we both made our share of mistakes.'

'And to leave them in the past,' she added. 'Maybe it's time I listened to my own advice.'

She leaned in and kissed him. Caine felt his heart race. Instinct took over, and he wrapped his arms around her, crushing her to him. For a moment, it was like nothing had changed at all. All the lies, secrets, and death that had surrounded them like a fog for so many years... they vanished, blown away by the tropical night winds.

Then their lips parted, and he pulled away. 'Rebecca, are you sure? I don't want—'

She put a finger over his lips. 'Why do you think I came?' she said in a low voice. 'You think the D/NCS personally flies out to debrief all her officers in the field?'

Caine chuckled. 'I certainly hope not. But what about your surgery? I don't want to—'

She wrapped her arms around his neck and pulled him down on top of her. Caine tore open her jacket as his lips traced feverish kisses down her neck. 'Don't worry,' she breathed into his ear. 'You won't break me.'

She groaned and locked her legs around him. Her fingers darted through his hair, pulling his lips to hers. He felt his doubts melt away, swallowed by the burning hunger of her kiss.

He grinned. 'I'll try to be gentle,' he whispered as he unbuttoned her blouse.

She pulled away and stared into his eyes. 'Don't you dare.'

The warm breeze stirred again, blowing the curtains aside and sending the candles flickering as the two of them writhed on the bed. For once, Caine was eager to give in to the past.

9

WASHINGTON DC, USA

SCIF (Sensitive Compartmented Information Facility)

'Order, order! The gentleman from Arizona has exceeded his time!' The chairman's gavel cracked against the podium three times as the angry shouts and cries faded to an inaudible murmur. Director Paulis leaned back in his chair and took a sip of water. A hush fell over the dim chamber.

He set the glass down then leaned forward, toward the gooseneck microphone that hung from his desk. 'I'm sorry, I don't believe I heard a question in there?'

Again, the excited murmuring rose. The twelve men and women seated at the curved bench before him frowned. Paulis had been in these hearings before, although never in the hot seat, as he was now. He knew each elected official on the Senate Intelligence Committee was running their own series of mental calculations... an internal debate upon whether the excitement in the room ran for or counter to their respective agendas.

The Sensitive Compartmented Information Facility, SCIF for short, was located in the basement of the Capitol and used by both the House and Senate Intelligence Committees when reviewing classified information. The chamber's walls were designed to block both audible conversations and electronic signals. All computers operating in the room were required to follow the NSA's TEMPEST emissions security guidelines, to prevent unauthorized parties from gaining access to classified intel through unintentional radio or electrical signals, sounds, or vibrations. And on top of all that, a skeleton of metal beams in the doors and ceiling made forcible entry into the chamber nearly impossible.

Ostensibly, they were all gathered in the vault-like room to get to the truth. But in the wake of Blackwing and the revelations of Walter Grissom's manipulations, his deep penetration into the country's intelligence apparatus... As far as Director Paulis was concerned, the truth wasn't as cut and dried as it used to be.

Correction, Paulis thought, watching an aide lean over and whisper into the Arizona senator's ear. *It never was...*

The senator from Arizona cleared his throat. 'I yield back,' he muttered into his microphone.

His aide probably warned him that his financial records tied him to at least six Blackwing-owned companies, Paulis thought.

That alone was hardly evidence of collusion with the private intelligence network. But if the man had done favors for Grissom's personal army of mercenary soldiers and killers, the last thing he would want was anyone looking too closely into his financial records.

The chairman banged his gavel again. 'The gentleman yields. Next, we shall hear from the honorable gentleman from Virginia.'

Jeff Kemper, Paulis thought. The Virginia senator was an enigma. Recently elected, he had a reputation for ruffling feathers and seemed willing to go against members of either party when it suited his interests. What those interests were, few could say. To Paulis's eye, it looked like the tall, portly man wearing an ostentatious bowtie was a huckster, just another fat cat touting a populist message while looking to line his pockets as fast as he could while in office.

Doesn't exactly make him stand out in this group, Paulis admitted grudgingly. He took another sip of water. His CIA-appointed legal counsel, Darren McCaffrey, sat next to him in stoic silence.

Senator Kemper consulted his notes then cleared his throat. Once again, a hush fell over the room. 'Director Paulis. Good to see you again, sir.'

Paulis offered a thin smile. 'I'm sure we would all prefer to meet under different circumstances.' Polite laughter ran through the crowd.

Kemper cleared his throat. 'On that, at least, we agree. Are you aware, Director Paulis, of the FBI's investigation into a warehouse owned by the entity your report refers to as...' The Senator paused and made a show of shuffling papers.

Flair for the theatrical, Paulis mused.

'I believe the entity you're referring to is Blackwing Capital,' Paulis said into the microphone.

Darren glared at him over the rims of his glasses. Previously, they had agreed to answer only direct questions asked by the senator. But Paulis was already losing patience with this show of political theater.

The microphone amplified the rustling of the senator's papers. 'Yes, that's right. And let us not forget the brave FBI personnel who lost their lives in this operation. An operation, I am told, that the CIA inserted an unauthorized operative into, with tragic consequences.'

'Clayton DuBose was assigned to the task force as a special observer. As someone with firsthand knowledge of Blackwing's methods and tactics, we felt he could provide an invaluable perspective on—'

'We?' Kemper said, interrupting Paulis mid-sentence. 'And who exactly is this "we" you're referring to, Director?'

'Myself, the Director of the National Clandestine Intelligence service, and the FBI special agent in charge of the investigation.'

Kemper shot a thin grin at Paulis. 'You mean Special Agent Alejandra Zavala, correct?'

Paulis nodded.

'And were you aware,' Senator Kemper continued, 'that the director of the FBI's Houston office has filed a complaint, indicating that Special Agent Zavala never cleared this special observer of yours with the proper authorities?'

Paulis gave the man a blank expression. 'I was not aware of any such complaint. That being said, I have no reason to doubt my esteemed colleagues at the Bureau. And this matter falls under their jurisdiction, of course.'

'You're referring to the domestic nature of this counterintel operation. Is that correct, sir?' the senator asked, twirling a pen in his fingers. Despite the shadowy conditions of the room, a spotlight beamed down on Kemper, giving his thinning hair a golden glow.

'Yes,' Paulis said, shifting in his chair. 'As I'm sure you're aware, the CIA's charter does not allow us to operate on domestic soil or pursue domestic targets unless—'

'I assure you, Director, every member of this committee understands the Central Intelligence Agency's charter of operations. But speaking candidly...' Kemper paused and twirled his pen again. He leaned back in his seat and pursed his lips. 'Well, let's just say those rules don't seem to apply across the board, do they?'

Paulis's nostrils flared, and his dark eyes flashed with obsidian fire. He leaned forward to speak, but Kemper raised a hand.

'Now, before you answer, Director, please let me make something clear. This committee recognizes and appreciates your decades of service to our country. But there are those under your command who may have—'

'Let me stop you right there.' Paulis locked eyes with the senator. 'When I took this position, the Central Intelligence Agency had been rocked by years of scandal. The National Clandestine Service was in disarray, its officers betrayed by the very men who swore to do right by them and their ideals. I vowed to uphold the integrity and honor of the agency. If you have reason to doubt the sincerity or actions of any officer under my command, let me assure you: their conduct is my responsibility.'

The senator cleared his throat. 'Well, of course, Director. But you can't deny that some officers working beneath you may have exceeded their—'

'Let me clarify further,' Paulis said, cutting the man off. 'The buck stops with me.'

Kemper glared at him from the raised desk of the committee. 'Very well.' He shuffled his papers again, peering over the rims of his glasses at the documents before him. 'Then by your testimony here today, you are giving explicit approval to an illegal operation conducted by Rebecca Freeling, whom you appointed as the Director of the National Clandestine Service? An operation, I might add, that she conducted on private property, within the great state of Virginia?'

Paulis was silent. He stared up at the senator with a blank, unreadable expression on his face.

Once again, the speaker banged the gavel. 'The witness is directed to answer the question,' he said.

Paulis nodded. 'Apologies. I was just trying to remember which operation the senator was referring to. Did you mean the attempt by a compromised NSA employee to kidnap a Chinese national, assassinate an employee of my agency, and interfere with a presidential order?'

'Reclaiming my time—' the senator began, but a chorus of whispers and murmurs ran through the chamber like a wave cresting toward the shore.

Paulis raised his voice as he spoke over the muttering crowd. 'Correct me if I'm wrong, Senator, but it seems like Director Freeling's actions were in response to one of several illegal operations we could discuss in this committee.'

The speaker pounded his gavel. 'Order! The gentleman from Virginia may respond.'

'Director Paulis,' Kemper continued, raising his voice. 'I'm well aware of this conspiracy theory you and your office have promoted. But I have yet to see any concrete proof of these outlandish claims. And from where I'm sitting, your propensity for breaking the law to pursue this radical agenda looks an awful lot like a personal vendetta!'

Paulis narrowed his eyes. 'Senator, I can assure you, I have no personal stake in this matter whatsoever. Members of this very committee confirmed me to replace my predecessor, who resigned after Allan Bernatto went rogue and nearly—'

'Yes, yes, we're all aware of the unfortunate incident in Tokyo,' Kemper snapped, interrupting the Director. 'But since that time, you and those under your command have demonstrated a single-minded determination to somehow link a private citizen and his assets to this so-called "conspiracy." An individual, I might add, who has offered his services in support of our ongoing mission to confront and eliminate violent extremist groups abroad. An issue which seems of little concern to you.'

'You can't be talking about Walter Grissom? Senator, Grissom is responsible for the murder of a federal witness and the destabilization of—'

'Again, Director, I've read your reports. But all we have for now is your word and that of D/NCS Freeling. And both of you have broken standard protocol and the law! Beyond that, what proof do you have? Some vague rumors from a classified asset? A man no one here has questioned or even seen?'

'I questioned him,' Paulis snarled. 'That will have to be enough.'

'Well, forgive me, Director, but it's not. Walter Grissom has offered the US government favorable terms to deploy his private military contractors in key strategic hotspots throughout the Middle East. That alone could free up over twenty thousand National Guard troops deployed to those regions. We have an obligation to our brave men and women in uniform, and we must do whatever we can to bring them home safely, wouldn't you agree? Therefore, I intend to submit Mr. Grissom's proposal to this very committee. And, subject to our vote, of course, to recommend it to the president!'

Director Paulis stood up and rested his hands on the table. 'Senator, I have the utmost respect for our soldiers. And as someone who has served with them, fought with them, I trust them a hell of a lot more than Grissom's army of professional mercenaries.'

The director paused. His stern gaze traveled across the shadowy faces before him. 'When I look at you all today, I see more than a few familiar faces. Many of you have served on this committee for years. Several of you, in fact, served during Walter Grissom's tenure at the CIA. And when confronted with evidence of Grissom's unsanctioned, extrajudicial killings, you chose to allow him to resign rather than prosecute him for his crimes. For reasons of political expediency.'

'Director Paulis,' Kemper snapped, wearing a look of dismayed confusion. 'I must insist we return to—'

'You were present at Grissom's hearing as well, Senator Kemper,' Paulis continued, interrupting the sputtering politician. 'Now, your lack of action has allowed this man to become even more dangerous. Walter Grissom is an existential threat to our nation's security. If you can't see that, then I believe there are only two plausible explanations. Either you lack the intelligence required to hold your office, or you lack the integrity. Either way, this conversation is over.'

Paulis turned and strode down the corridor. Behind him, the crowd erupted into shouts. Kemper stood and shook his fist.

'You can't walk away from this, Paulis! We'll subpoena you and Director Freeling! Who is your source? I demand to know who your source is for these outrageous accusations.'

Paulis ignored the man as he stepped out of the darkened room. As the door thudded shut behind him, his security team closed in around him. They had been waiting outside in the darkened corridor that separated the SCIF from the horde of press outside.

Paulis slipped his cell phone from his pocket. Now that he was outside the secure chamber's armored walls, he could once again make and receive calls.

'Sir,' a tall, stocky man named Curtis said in a low voice. 'We have your car and usual driver waiting outside.'

'And about a hundred reporters standing in our way. That's a lot of "no comments." Best let me catch my breath, Mr. Curtis.'

The man nodded. 'Of course, sir.'

As Paulis's slim, angular phone reconnected to the network, a text message appeared on the screen, followed by a quiet buzz. He frowned as he examined the name of the sender. Then he picked up the phone and dialed their number.

'Hello,' a woman answered. 'I wasn't sure if you could take my call.'

'I can now,' the director replied, glancing back at the thick wood doors. 'But I'm not sure I should. For your sake.'

'I have to talk to you. White Pine... *Entiendes*?'

He consulted the gold watch strapped to his wrist. 'I'll see you in one hour.'

'See you then.' The woman hung up.

Paulis turned to Curtis. 'Call my office. Tell them to cancel all my meetings and send any calls to the deputy director. And reroute Director Freeling's connecting flight. I believe she's overdue for an inspection of our station house in Prague.'

'Yes, sir,' Curtis replied. Ahead of them, the crowd of reporters pressed in, held back only by a thin line taped on the floor. 'Seems like you're trying to keep her at arm's length from all this. Is there something I should know, sir?'

'Not if you're interested in keeping your job,' Paulis muttered. 'These days, ignorance is bliss.'

His bodyguard's reply drowned in the sea of shouted questions as dozens of reporters pressed forward in the dim, shadowy hall.

10

HANOI, SOCIALIST REPUBLIC OF VIETNAM

After a four-hour direct flight, Caine exited the jetway into Noi Bai Airport. Although Noi Bai was the largest airport in Vietnam, it couldn't compare to the decadent lounges, stunning gardens, and indoor waterfall of the opulent Changi Airport in Singapore.

As he walked through the open-air terminal, the heat and humidity hit him like a ton of bricks. Sweat trickled down his forehead, and he took a moment to catch his breath in the thick air. He slipped his agency-issued smartphone from his pocket and checked the weather app. The temperature and humidity were in the mid-nineties. Within seconds, he felt his linen shirt sticking to his skin.

Ignoring the heat, Caine grabbed his single bag from the carousel and made his way outside. Despite the high chance of rain, the sky was a brilliant blue. The blistering sun hung overhead, and rows of palms waved gently in the distance. A line of white and green taxicabs idled outside the terminal. Caine moved away from the crowd and tapped a number from memory into his cell phone.

A long beep followed by a series of clicks indicated the signal was passing through the agency's encrypted network. A few seconds later, Rebecca answered.

'Hello?'

Her voice sounded heavy and tired. Caine glanced at the chunky metal dive watch strapped to his wrist. He estimated she would still be in the air, on her way back to D.C.

'It's me. Wanted to let you know I arrived safe and sound. Just getting my bearings before the big meeting.'

'Nice of you to let me know. How was your flight?'

'Not bad. Gave me a chance to catch up on that Basho book you recommended.'

'What did you think?'

Working with her again, using their old coded phrases and signals, brought a smile to Caine's face.

Careful... Remember what happened the last time you worked with her. She paid the price.

'I enjoyed it,' he said, his voice cold and flat. 'Still think I prefer Murakami, though. Perhaps because I read him first.'

Rebecca seemed to key off Caine's change in tone, and her voice took on a businesslike demeanor once they'd passed the duress test. 'I've arranged a meet and greet with our local representative,' she said. 'And I've sent you the latest info from your meeting in Singapore. It should be quite useful.'

'Skip the local rep. I'm not sure their heart is in the right place,' Caine said. 'I'll make arrangements with my people.'

'People you trust?' she asked.

'No,' he replied. 'The exact opposite. Safer that way. I have to go.'

'I... Okay. Good luck.'

'Thanks. You too. I'll contact you soon.'

He hung up and stared at the phone. He could barely

remember what it felt like to work with agency support, to report to a handler, someone he trusted. But after his meeting with Paulis, he knew this assignment didn't need that. If Paulis was right, Grissom had other moles within the CIA and other intelligence agencies.

He trusted Rebecca with his life, but the local safe house, the CIA's contacts in the Vietnamese government... they could all be compromised. He had come in from the cold, but he had to keep operating as before. On his own, trusting no one.

Alone.

He powered down the phone and slung his bag over his shoulder. Then he stood in line, waiting for a taxi. After a few minutes, a tiny hybrid sedan pulled up to the curb. The driver emerged from the vehicle and opened the rear door. The man was over six feet tall, comically large for the tiny car.

'Bag heavy?' he asked, speaking in broken English. 'I take for you?'

Caine shook his head and climbed into the rear seat. 'No thanks. I'll keep it with me.'

The driver got back into the car. The vehicle's hybrid motor was surprisingly quiet as they pulled away from the airport. They drove in silence past a long patch of dry grass and flatland. Caine rolled down the rear window. Once again, a wave of heat blasted his face. He dropped his cell phone out of the car then rolled the window back up. The driver peered back at him in the rearview mirror, looking confused.

'Roaming charges,' Caine said with a grin.

'You need phone? Local SIM card, I know good place.'

'That's OK. Just take me to the old quarter.'

The driver nodded. 'No problem. Thirty minutes, no traffic. First time in Vietnam?'

'No,' Caine replied. He glanced out the rear window to

make sure no one was following them. The long, heat-blasted road behind them was empty.

He turned back to face the driver. 'I used to come here often, for business.'

The driver regarded him for a moment. The dark-haired man had a long, narrow face and five-o'clock shadow. He rubbed his stubbly cheek with one hand as they sped past an emaciated cow that stood alone in a parched field.

'Ah, what kind of business you in?' the driver asked.

Caine settled back in his seat. 'The unfinished kind, apparently.'

The driver seemed confused by his response and turned back to the road. They continued on in silence, speeding toward the city.

* * *

Forty minutes later, Caine wandered through the narrow, congested streets of the Old District. Also known as 36 street Hanoi, the area had once been a nexus of trade unions. Each guild controlled a single street, known for a specific *hàng*... a set of commercial skills or wares. The streets still had their original names, such as Hang Dong – meaning Copper Wares Street – even though the city and its businesses had evolved decades ago.

As Caine made his way down Hang Tre Street, an area once known for its bamboo wares, he marveled at the eclectic buildings crammed along the narrow road. Shop owners hawked their wares from colorful Vietnamese shop houses. The two-story buildings were decorated with sloped tile roofs and hanging paper lanterns. Some sold street food, such as *bánh mì* sandwiches or fried rice-flour crepes. Others beckoned tourists to sample fine silks or purchase local crafts and works of art.

Nestled alongside the shop houses, crumbling French colonial buildings flanked the street. Their wrought-iron balconies looked out over the crowd of pedestrians. Many of the older buildings were coffee houses, and patrons sat above the hustle and bustle of the street, sipping the strong local brew mixed with coconut cream and condensed milk.

A web of power lines crisscrossed overhead. The skies above were gray. Ominous clouds rolled across the horizon, and the air had cooled slightly. Rain seemed imminent despite the earlier sun.

Caine glanced left and right then walked out into the tiny street. Colorful motor scooters zipped around him, weaving through the traffic in a random pattern. The tiny vehicles were everywhere. Their little engines buzzed and growled as they darted around one another in an elaborate mechanized dance. The drivers wore long-sleeved shirts, sweaters, or jackets. The locals prized a pale complexion, and despite the heat, riders bundled up to shield their skin from the sun's rays.

Caine glanced left and right as he ventured into the buzzing traffic. If there was any pattern to the chaos, he couldn't see it. Finally, he made it across the street and stepped into the open lower level of a shop house.

The cramped boutique sold a variety of cheap electronics and used devices, including cell phones. The shopkeeper, a young woman with long raven-black hair, wore jeans and a pink T-shirt with kittens and hearts on the front. She looked to be in her early twenties and wore little or no makeup.

She greeted Caine with a warm smile as he stepped through the beaded curtain that separated the store from the chaos outside. '*Xin chào*,' she said in a quiet voice. The phrase was a traditional greeting, and she bowed her head as she spoke.

'Good afternoon,' Caine said. 'Prepaid cell phone?' He held up his thumb and pinky finger, mimicking talking into a phone.

The girl laughed. 'I know what "cell phone" means,' she said, shaking her head.

Caine smiled back. 'Well, your English is better than my Vietnamese.'

'We have a few models,' the girl replied, rummaging through a glass cabinet behind the counter. 'You can choose.'

She placed three Ziploc bags on the counter, each containing a battered but functional-looking smartphone. Caine elected an older Samsung model. 'I'll take this one,' he replied, sliding some crumpled Vietnamese dong notes across the counter.

As the shopkeeper inserted a fresh SIM card into the phone, Caine glanced at the horde of scooters buzzing down the street. 'Does the traffic ever slow down here?'

She shook her head. 'It's always bad on weekends. They close the streets around the lake for the festival.' She handed him the phone, cupping it in both hands. Caine returned the gesture and examined the phone's screen.

'The lake,' he said. 'You mean Hoan Kiem?'

'Yes,' she replied, a note of surprise in her voice. 'You know it?'

'I'm looking forward to seeing it.' Caine held up the phone and smiled. 'Thank you... *Cảm ơn.*'

Again, she bowed. '*Không có chi*,' she said.

He pushed aside the jingling beads and left the store.

As he walked down the busy sidewalk, the grating of coffee grinders from a nearby cafe drowned out the buzz of the motor scooters. He turned down an alley, walking past a row of slanted bamboo poles and wood carvings arranged behind a shop. The street noise grew distant, and he was alone save for a few pedestrians.

He texted Rebecca his number, along with a coded message indicating that she could reach him on the burner phone for the next twenty-four hours. Then he dialed a number from memory.

The phone rang five times. He was about to hang up when a gruff voice answered. '*A lô?*'

'I need to speak with Le Duan.'

'Who is this?'

Caine grinned. 'Tell him Mark Waters wants to discuss some business.'

'What kind of business?'

'The kind that makes him money,' Caine replied. 'I need to go shopping. And I'm looking for some information on a competitor.'

'Information?'

'I'll text you the details.'

'Hold on,' the man replied. Caine heard some muted voices in the background, chattering in rapid-fire Vietnamese. Then the other man returned to the phone. 'Ha Long Bay. Bo Han Island. Be there before sundown.'

'What do I do when I get there?'

'You wait. We find you.'

He hung up, and Caine slid the phone back into his pocket.

He felt droplets of water splash in his hair. The sky had grown darker. Tiny raindrops pattered against the cobblestones. The few merchants in the narrow alley scrambled to gather up their wares and stashed them under canvas awnings.

The storm was finally rolling in.

11

GENEVA, SWITZERLAND

Deep in the countryside, the chirping birds and buzzing insects went silent as a distant thumping filled the air. The sound grew louder, faster. A black dot descended from the sky, and the swaying trees seemed to part and lean away from the strange intruder. A helicopter burst through the clouds and lowered to the ground. The aircraft touched down on a patch of grass next to a long, winding road that led off into the distant trees.

The side door slid open, and a man in a business suit and tan trench coat hopped out. He stumbled as his polished dress shoe sank into the damp, soft ground. His thin brown hair whipped across his face in the violent wind generated by the rotors. He squinted as he saw the gate at the end of the road swing open.

The noise of the helicopter died down as the pilot slowed the rotors. The man in the trench coat stepped away from the aircraft and made his way toward the opening gate. A tiny white dot motored down the driveway – an electric golf cart, being driven by a large man in a black cashmere sweater.

The cart sped through the gate and stopped. The man in the

trench coat hurried over to it as the driver stepped out of his seat.

'Mr. Bernhardt,' the towering man shouted over the sound of the helicopter. 'Welcome to Ticino. I'm Karl.'

The man called Bernhardt eyed the towering brute before him. Karl was at least six foot three and built like a linebacker. His chiseled jaw, brilliant blue eyes, and thick blond hair gave him the appearance of a male model. Only the steel clamp at the end of his right arm marred his physical perfection. The artificial limb looked blunt and heavy, more like a bludgeon than a medical prosthesis.

Bernhardt reached out and shook Karl's left hand. The man's strong grip left Bernhardt with no doubt that Karl could crush every bone in his hand if he so desired.

'Mr. Grissom is expecting you. He hopes you'll join him for lunch.'

Karl climbed back into the seat of the tiny vehicle, and Bernhardt sat in the back. 'If you don't mind, I'd like to get this over with,' he replied as the cart turned and hummed back down the driveway. 'I have important business in Zurich tonight, and I...'

Bernhardt's voice trailed off as a massive structure loomed over the horizon. The building looked like something out of a fairy tale... A medieval castle, complete with stone walls, towers, and minarets, nestled in the rolling green hills.

'My God,' he said. 'I knew this place was huge. But I never—'

'Yes, impressive, isn't it?' Karl said with a smile. 'It's a recreation, of course. The original castle was destroyed in World War II. Mr. Grissom had it rebuilt, along with his home, when he acquired the land.'

'His home? You mean... there's more?'

Karl laughed. 'Oh yes! The castle is just his hobby. The house is around the bend.'

He continued driving, and a massive, mid-century house came into view, standing behind the ancient fortress. The estate was a sprawling labyrinth of slate and glass, a Zen-like enclave of peace and quiet, secluded by the beautiful countryside.

The cart continued motoring along, darting behind the sleek home. The sounds of workers and heavy machinery rose in the distance. 'Sorry about the mess,' Karl shouted. 'We're building a second pool. Bit of chaos back here, I'm afraid.'

Finally, they stopped next to a gravel path. The two men dismounted the cart and walked beside a towering hedge wall. The path led to an Olympic-size swimming pool, hidden behind the wall of greenery. One half of the pool's veranda was complete, a long stretch of smooth white concrete gleaming in the sun. Umbrellas and teak furniture dotted the surface.

On the opposite side of the deck, a backhoe tore into the green hillside, gouging out a perimeter around the pool. Workers poured fresh concrete into the foundation. Other men smoothed the surface of the thick liquid with trowels and shovels.

Karl led Bernhardt to a circular table on the finished side of the pool. A short, stocky man sat in a white chair beneath a blue umbrella. He had a craggy, wrinkled face. His skin was pale, and a pair of bushy white brows framed his blue eyes. Unlike Karl, the man's irises were a pale, soft blue, the color of fresh ice.

A breeze rustled his gray hair as he sipped beer from a tall glass. He flashed a smile at the two men as they approached. 'René! Good to see you, son. I appreciate you making the trip. Have a seat.'

'Thank you, Mr. Grissom. I assure you, it was no trouble at—'

Grissom waved a hand and chuckled. 'René, please, call me Walt. I refuse to drink beer with a man who calls me by my last name. That's for business talk. This is personal. Now, what can I get you?'

Smiling, Bernhardt shook his head. 'Thank you, Mr... Walt. That's kind of you, but I'm rather—'

Grissom took another sip and licked his lips. 'You know, I've tried French wine, Spanish wine, Australian wine. Hell, even California wine. And guess what?'

Bernhardt shifted in his seat. 'Sir, I don't know what—'

'It all tastes like wine. I couldn't tell a Sauvignon from a Chablis if my life depended on it. Now, beer, on the other hand... Well, take this here.'

He held the glass up to the light. Tiny bubbles fizzed in the thick, amber beverage. 'Rosengarten Maisgold. It's made from corn. Nothing else I've tried tastes quite like it. You gotta have one of these.'

He looked over his shoulder. 'Karl, be a pal, would you? Bring us another round from the kitchen. And some sandwiches. Tell the chef to slice off some of that leftover roast beef. And throw on some horseradish.'

'Copy that, sir.' Karl spun around and marched toward the sprawling estate house.

'He's a wonderful boy, Karl. Used to be a soldier. Swiss Special Operations Command, kind of like your Special Forces. Then he went freelance, hired gun on the circuit. Lost the arm in Afghanistan.' Grissom made a clucking sound with his tongue. 'That's war for you. If it was pretty, they'd call it something else.'

He took another sip of beer then set the glass down on the

table. 'I take it you heard what happened to your partner, Mr. Seng?'

Bernhardt cleared his throat. 'Mr. Grissom... Walt... I assure you, I had no idea my associate was in communication with American intelligence organizations. We built our firm on a foundation of trust and discretion. I would never—'

'Oh, all right, I don't need you to tickle my belly. And hell, if there's one thing you Swiss excel at, it's failing to take sides. I only need to know one thing. Then I can get back to my lunch in peace, and you can get back to whatever the hell it is that occupies a Swiss banker's time.'

Bernhardt sighed in relief. His eyes darted up as he watched Karl returning from the house, balancing a silver tray on one hand. A white napkin was draped over the tray, covering the food beneath. 'I can offer whatever assurances you require, Mr. Grissom,' he began. 'You have nothing to—'

'See, there you go again, calling me Mr. Grissom. Now, just a few minutes ago, did I or did I not ask you to call me Walt?'

'Yes, sir, Walt. Sorry, I—'

Grissom shook his head and took another sip of beer. 'If I can't trust you to follow a simple instruction like that, how the hell can I trust you when you tell me my former colleagues didn't reach out to you as well?'

'I beg your pardon?'

Grissom did not answer. The man looked calm, relaxed even. His eyes had a soft, drooping quality. But something about his gaze was unsettling. It took Bernhardt a moment to realize what it was.

Grissom didn't blink. He and Bernhardt locked eyes for several moments as Karl paced closer to the table. The entire time, Grissom did not blink once.

'Walt,' Bernhardt said. 'You must realize, governments reach out to my firm all the time. It's not unusual, but in all my years, I've never broken confidentiality with a client. Especially not one such as—'

Karl stepped up to the table. He set the tray down between the two men.

'Sir,' he said, interrupting Bernhardt's nervous backpedaling. 'As you requested.'

'Good, good,' Grissom said. He pulled aside the napkin, revealing a silenced pistol on the silver tray. He picked up the gun, racked the slide, and pointed it at Bernhardt. The weapon was an FN-509 pistol, a tactical model, with raised metal wings protecting the front and rear sights. The metal flanges gave the barrel an enlarged appearance, and Bernhardt sucked in his breath as the empty black dot of the silencer hovered before his eyes.

'René, I want to give you the benefit of the doubt here. I really do. So let me make myself clear. Did you speak with anyone from the CIA? Or any other American intelligence agency?'

Bernhardt leapt to his feet and backed away from the table. 'This is crazy! I can't believe you—'

'I wouldn't do that, René. I may not be much of a shot these days. But I assure you, Karl here has lost none of his accuracy. And he's left-handed, in case you were wondering.'

Bernhardt glanced at the towering blond man. The valet clutched an identical pistol in his left hand.

'Mr. Grissom, please! I swear I—'

Grissom rolled his eyes. 'Oh, for the love of Christ. You just don't listen, do you, René?'

He pulled the trigger. Muzzle flash exploded across the table, and the weapon made a sound like a loud cough. Bernhardt screamed and fell to the concrete. He clutched his leg and writhed in pain. A fountain of blood gushed from a wound in his thigh.

Grissom winced. 'That's a bleeder, son. Gonna need to get that looked at. Karl?'

The hulking brute stomped over to Bernhardt. The injured man flailed his arm, struggling to push Karl away. But the massive valet ignored his feeble swipes. Karl hoisted the banker up into the air. The terrified man kicked and swung his feet beneath him, and he cried out in pain once more.

'Please, Mr. Gris—Walt, please, I swear, I didn't tell them anything!'

'I think we'd better stick with "Mr. Grissom" now. It's time to talk business.'

Grissom stood up as Karl carried the dangling banker across the pool's veranda. He held the man out over the freshly poured concrete foundation. Bernhardt grunted a strangled plea for help, but no workers were in sight. The construction equipment sat idling.

'René, I've worked with cutthroats and con men all my life. In America, we call them politicians. I've been lied to by the best, and I still came out on top. So believe me when I tell you, when I look you in the eye, I'll know if you're full of shit. So why don't we save ourselves some time here?'

He turned to Karl. 'Put him in.'

Karl heaved the wounded banker into the pool of wet concrete. Bernhardt disappeared beneath the surface for a moment. Then a burst of bubbles exploded from the smooth white liquid. His face emerged from the cement. He spit the thick sludge from his mouth and gasped for breath.

'Please! Mr. Grissom, I swear, I told them nothing! Nothing! I told them Seng had a drug problem, that he was unreliable. I told them I had severed our partnership. That was all I said, I swear.'

Grissom looked down at the floundering man. 'Hard to swim in concrete, isn't it? It's like quicksand. The harder you struggle, the faster it pulls you down.' He shook his head. 'I wouldn't know, but I have to assume it's not a pleasant way to die. Trapped, suffocating as the rock hardens around you. Wouldn't wish it on my worst enemies.'

'Please, sir, just tell me what you want to know! I swear I would never betray you!'

Grissom grunted as he squatted down. He grabbed Bernhardt's slick, cement-crusted hair and yanked the man's head up. Then he peered into the banker's cement-crusted eyes. 'Think carefully, René. Did you tell them anything... anything that might lead back to me?'

'They... they asked about Blackwing Capital. But I told them I could... urgh!' Bernhardt spat out another mouthful of wet cement. 'I told them I couldn't discuss our clients or their business. I gave them nothing, I swear!'

Grissom was silent for a moment. He let go of the man's hair. 'Good boy. I believe you.'

'Oh, thank God. Thank you, sir, thank you!'

'You're welcome, René.'

Grissom raised the pistol and fired again. Bernhardt gasped as a red dot exploded in the center of his forehead. A swirl of crimson spiraled through the wet cement. His body sank deep into the gray sludge.

Grissom handed the gun to Karl, who gripped it in his metal claw. 'When the boys get back from lunch, tell them I spilled some wine. Have 'em pour another layer over this mess. Oh, and do me a favor?'

Karl gave him a questioning look.

'Bring down those sandwiches now.'

'Will do, sir.'

As he paced back to the house, Grissom picked up the satellite phone and tapped a number on the keypad.

'Go ahead, sir,' Boone Riley answered.

'Seng's loose end is tied off,' Grissom replied. 'But we've got a bigger problem. My men were able to extract an IP address from the hard drive you sent me. I need you in Hanoi, Vietnam.'

'I can be there in three hours.'

'Good, good. And keep an eye out, Riley. I have a feeling you won't be there alone. You might bump into an old friend.'

'I certainly hope so, sir.'

Grissom hung up the phone. He took a deep breath and stared out at the waving trees and hazy mountain in the distance. It was beautiful here in the countryside.

But it wasn't home. Home was where you could die at peace.

He glanced down at the crimson swirl of blood in the smooth liquid concrete. He took another sip of beer then dialed a new number on his phone.

12

SOCIALIST REPUBLIC OF VIETNAM

After checking in at his hotel in the old district, Caine booked a seaplane tour from the front desk. The flight was expensive, but it was the only way he could make it to Ha Long Bay before nightfall. By car, the drive would take four hours or more.

After a relaxing forty-five-minute flight along the coast, the tiny aircraft landed in the shimmering green waters of the bay and motored up to a launch ramp. A few minutes later, he boarded a boat that ferried tourists out to the stunning rock formations.

As they neared the famous rocks, Caine gripped the railing and looked out over the bay. The sun hung low in the sky, and the ocean waves filled the air with a cool mist. A tour guide spoke over a PA system as they cruised between the towering slabs of volcanic rock. The guide spoke in Vietnamese first then translated their words into English. Caine ignored their patter and allowed himself a few minutes to soak in the natural beauty of the scenery.

The dark, craggy spires broke the surface of the calm green water and stretched hundreds of feet into the sky. Green tropical plants clung to the rocks like a carpet of jade velvet draped over the jagged cliffs. At the base of the rocks, gentle waves lapped against sandy beaches, where the seawater had carved away at the earth to form inlets and harbors.

It was one of the most beautiful places Caine had ever seen.

The boat motored into one of the many harbors and moored at a long, rickety pier. Caine filed out with the other passengers. He watched as the tourists followed a guide up a steep trail that wound up the side of the island. Caine hung back and bought a coconut from a tiny shack near the dock. He listened to the waves lapping against the pier and sipped the coconut's cool juice through a paper straw.

A few minutes later, a battered old fishing boat motored up to the dock. Chipped, peeling green paint covered the boat's hull. A faded red canopy flapped above the deck in the breeze.

The driver stayed in the boat and kept the engine idling. He was a lanky young Vietnamese man with messy hair and tan skin. Dark sunglasses covered his eyes. Engine oil and grease spattered the front of his sleeveless white T-shirt.

He scanned the beach and gestured to Caine.

Caine sucked the last bits of pulp and juice from the green coconut then dropped the fruit in a metal trash can. He walked over to the boat.

'Le Duan?' he asked the driver.

Up close, the youth barely looked old enough to drive the boat. His arms were rail thin, and his long, narrow neck gave him a bird-like appearance. 'I take you,' he said in a high-pitched voice. 'Get on.'

Caine climbed into the boat and sat in the back. The youth kicked the dock, sending the tiny craft drifting away from the pier. The engine rumbled back to life, and they motored around the base of the rock formation.

Zipping under a rock arch, the tiny boat hugged the island's rugged coastline. Ten minutes later, they motored into a sprawling inlet nestled between the rocks. A low mist hung in the air. At first, Caine saw nothing... just the dark peaks in the distance, thrusting up from the pale fog.

Then tiny shacks came into view – bright-green and pink dwellings, bobbing up and down in the iridescent water. The homes sat upon a cluster of barges, lashed together to form a floating village hidden between the rocks.

'Cua Van,' the driver called to him, grinning. 'Biggest fishing village in Ha Long Bay.'

'It's beautiful,' Caine shouted back.

The man shrugged then spat in the water. He slowed the boat and drifted closer to the maze of buildings. Caine watched as they floated past the tiny shacks. A man in denim coveralls hung a score of fish on a drying rack. Next to him, a woman wearing a conical straw hat known as a *nón lá* hung dripping laundry from a line strung between two barges.

Caine felt the deck shudder as they brushed up against a dock. The driver leapt onto the platform and lashed the fishing boat to a mooring cleat. He pointed at the nearest floating shack.

'Le Duan inside. You go.'

Caine climbed out of the boat and walked to the bobbing shack. A pair of men lounging in hammocks flanked the rickety structure's entrance. They rolled to their feet as he approached.

'Hey, *đợi tí*... Wait a minute,' one man grunted.

Caine glared at them then sighed and lifted his arms. The men patted him down, checking for weapons. Satisfied, the guard grunted again and nodded to the other man. '*Anh ấy sạch sẽ*... he's clean.'

The second man opened the door to the shack and stepped

inside. Caine blinked as his eyes adjusted to the dim light. Another pair of men sat in wicker chairs, smoking hand-rolled cigarettes. They glanced at Caine as he stepped in but made no move to stop him.

A third man sat with his back to Caine, bent over a battered old rolltop desk. He appeared to be counting something. Caine could hear him muttering numbers in Vietnamese. He wore a faded green army jacket and gray acid-washed jeans. The pony-tail hanging down his back was long, stringy, and streaked with gray.

'Le Duan,' Caine said. 'Been a long time since—'

The man raised his hand in a silencing motion. 'Shhhhhh... Wait a minute!' he snapped in English.

Caine was silent as Le Duan continued his work. The man stopped counting and sighed in frustration. 'Bah... Twenty cards, no winners. Not my lucky day.'

He swiveled around in his chair and faced Caine. Le Duan's face had a gaunt, hollow look, and sunburn chapped his lips. He grinned, flashing a mouthful of crooked yellow teeth. He was missing an eye and wore no prosthetic. The empty pink socket gaped at Caine from above the man's hooked nose.

Le Duan held a small stack of colorful cardboard rectangles in one hand and a balisong knife in the other. 'Scratcher cards,' he said. 'My new addiction.' His laugh was a dry, raspy cackle.

'Could be worse,' Caine said, shooting a look at one of the smoking men.

Le Duan tossed the old cards on the desk and flipped the knife closed with a flashy gesture. 'Mark Waters... As you say, been a long time. You far from Japan, my friend. Last time I saw you, you were brokering a deal for the Yakuza. Selling them some đồ tầm thường... Chinese shit from that Saudi dealer.'

'Turel was Turkish, not Saudi,' Caine said. He offered no

further information. A long time had passed since he had operated under the cover of Mark Waters, posing as an international arms dealer. Although the details were still fresh in his mind, he knew the less he said, the better. Le Duan would seize on any inconsistencies in his story.

'Right, right.' Le Duan tilted his head and closed his good eye. The fleshy pink hole on the opposite side of his face leered at Caine. 'So, what brings you to Vietnam?'

Caine glanced at the other men from the corner of his eye. One of them stubbed out his cigarette and began fiddling with a cell phone, playing a game of some sort. The other blew a puff of smoke toward him. The air reeked of sweat and the sickly-sweet residue of *kretek*, an Indonesian blend of tobacco, cloves, and spices.

'Look, Le Duan, I'm sorry, but I don't have time for small talk. I'm here on business. Personal business. And I need some... protection.'

The man's good eye opened wide with surprise. 'Protection? In our glorious communist paradise? It is very safe here. You must be in some big trouble, eh?'

Caine stared back at him. 'If you can't help me, I can always call someone else.'

The Vietnamese man raised his hands and laughed. 'Chill out. Damn, Waters. I don't remember you being so touchy. OK, let's see what we got.'

He turned and shouted to one of the men lounging in the chairs. The one on the phone ignored him. The other stood up and grabbed a fishing gaff off the wall. A curved metal hook glinted at the end of the long wood pole. The man positioned himself between Le Duan and Caine. He kicked up a moldy, faded carpet, revealing a hatch in the barge's deck.

'Most of my inventory is off-site,' Le Duan said, leaning back in his chair. He lit a hand-rolled cigarette and took a long drag then winked at Caine with his good eye. 'But I'm sure we have something that can suit your needs.'

The man inserted the gaff's hook into an iron ring on the hatch. Rusty hinges creaked as he pulled the heavy slab of wood up, uncovering several trunks nestled in a hollow compartment below the deck.

'*Này, đừng lười biếng!* You gonna help?' the man grunted. The other thug set down his phone. The two of them dragged a footlocker out of the compartment, hauled it up, and set it on the deck with a heavy thud. One of them twisted the dial of an old combination lock that held it shut. The lock clicked open, and the men lifted the trunk's lid. Inside, a variety of pistols and long guns lay in neat foam cutouts.

'Most of these are CZ,' Le Duan said between puffs on his cigarette. 'But I have some IWI as well. Czech, Israeli... excellent guns. Better than Chinese.'

'Very nice,' Caine said, peering into the trunk. 'May I?'

Le Duan grinned. 'That's why you here, yes? To shop?'

Caine reached into the trunk and pulled out a CZ-P07 pistol. The weapon looked identical to the gun he had used in Singapore, and the grip felt snug in his hand. He peered down the barrel, testing the sights. 'No Beretta?' he asked.

Le Duan laughed. 'Beggars can't be choosers. You come busting into my shop after hours, asking to go shopping? Well, this is what I got.'

'I'll take it,' Caine said, handing the gun to the man who had opened the hatch. 'Ammunition?'

The thug set down the gaff and balanced it on a cylindrical buoy that lay on the floor. Then he gave Le Duan a questioning look. The one-eyed man grinned and tossed him a worn duffel bag. 'Oh, Waters, I got your text. I looked into your guy. What was his name again?'

Caine reached into the trunk and drew out a chunky, solid-looking black rifle. 'Boone Riley,' he replied as he tested the magazine release. Then he pressed the stock into his shoulder and peered down the barrel.

'Yeah, right,' the arms dealer continued. 'Sounds like a badass. Former CIA, Special Activities. Before that, US Army. He customer of yours or something?'

Caine shook his head. 'No. Let's just say he's bad for business.'

Le Duan shrugged. 'Whatever. Either way, he's no problem. File says he's dead. KIA, killed in action.'

Pivoting his body, Caine aimed the rifle at the man playing on his cell phone. 'The file's wrong. He's alive. Most likely a private contractor now. I need to know if he enters the country.'

The thug pointed the phone's camera in his direction and whispered in Vietnamese. Caine narrowed his eyes... A tiny Bluetooth earpiece rested in the man's ear. Caine felt the tingling sensation on the back of his neck once again. The familiar feeling of danger, an instinct honed by too many near-death escapes to count.

Something's wrong, the voice in the back of his head hissed.

Ignoring the man on the phone, he tossed the rifle to Le Duan, who caught it in midair and lovingly caressed the stock.

'Sure, sure. That's easy!' the one-eyed man said. He gazed lovingly at the rifle in his hands. 'Galil ACE rifle. Left-mounted charging handle. Lightweight polymer. Perfectly balanced. Accurate. You want ammo for that too?'

The man on the phone continued muttering behind them. Caine stared into Le Duan's one good eye. 'You know,' he said in a steely voice, 'I have to admit, I'm surprised you agreed to see me. Word on the street was, you were pissed that I stole the Yoshizawa contract out from under your nose.'

Le Duan tossed the gun to the other thug. The man dropped it into the canvas bag, slid some ammo boxes off the shelf, and placed them in the bag as well, keeping his eyes on Caine.

Caine stared into Le Duan's empty eye socket. The arms dealer gave him an exaggerated smile. 'Eh, who has time for that BS? I was tired of dealing with those Japs anyway. Bunch of stuck-up *lũ khốn nạn*. Think they're better than everyone else.'

Caine nodded. 'That's big of you. Still, I've been here for at least ten minutes. And so far, you haven't asked me about money once. That's not like you, Le Duan.'

The arms dealer kept smiling, but he made a gesture to the thug with the duffel. The man dropped the bag and drew a pistol from his waistband. It was another CZ, identical to the gun in the bag.

'Fuck you, Waters,' Le Duan hissed. 'Let me help you out. This guy you're looking for, Boone Riley? He's closer than you think.' He laughed again. 'He gave me a call, told me an interesting story about you... And after that shit you pulled in Japan, well, I was happy to listen. So tell me, did that prick Isato Yoshizawa go to the grave knowing you were working for the CIA?'

Caine's emerald eyes blazed in the shadows. He stared back at Le Duan but said nothing.

The Vietnamese man chuckled. His laughter grew to a high-pitched cackle, like a hyena's. 'Please... Please tell me that stuck-up piece of shit died knowing he got played by a *gaijin* bastard like you!'

Caine took a step back. The man with the gun reacted,

shifting forward. The pistol's barrel hovered in the air between them...

Right over the gaff's hook.

Caine stomped down on the end of the pole. The hook flew up, knocking the pistol aside. A bullet exploded from the barrel of the gun, but the wild shot struck the other thug. The wounded man gasped, and his phone clattered to the floor. Caine ducked and grabbed the pole. He jabbed forward and drove the metal hook into the gunman's groin.

His opponent grunted and stumbled backward. His eyes bulged with surprise as he fell through the hole in the deck and tumbled down into the hidden compartment. Caine kicked the trunk of guns. It slid forward, falling on top of the man and pinning him to the floor. He screamed as the heavy box slammed into his ribs.

Caine grabbed the duffel bag and swung it, knocking the hatch shut.

Le Duan jerked up from his chair. He had already drawn a pistol from his waistband, but before he could line up a shot, Caine swung the duffel bag again, striking him in the face. The one-eyed man grunted and fell to the deck. Caine stomped on his wrist, hard enough to break the bones in his hand. The arms dealer howled as Caine pried the pistol from his limp fingers.

'Who did you talk to?' Caine snapped. 'Who was asking about me?'

Le Duan's good eye peered up at him from the floor. The man chuckled. 'They were very interested in you, Waters. Or should I say Thomas Caine? Either way, you a dead man now...'

Caine heard the distant roar of boat engines outside. The sound grew louder... Speedboats were closing on the village.

Must be whoever was on the other end of that phone call, Caine thought.

The gun roared as Caine fired a shot into the deck. Le Duan winced as the bullet struck the wood inches from his face.

'Last chance. Who did you call? Who's after me?'

The sound of the boats roared closer.

Le Duan laughed. 'It doesn't matter. If they don't get you, I will. You think you can screw me over in my own country?'

The engine noise grew even louder. Whoever it was, they were closing in on his position.

Le Duan continued, 'There's nowhere you can go, Caine. Nowhere you can hide that I won't find you.'

'I believe you,' Caine replied. He pulled the trigger. A bright-red hole exploded in Le Duan's forehead, and a wet cough rattled in his throat.

The men outside began pounding on the front door. Caine slung the duffel bag over his shoulder. He glanced up and saw an open skylight covered by a moldy canvas tarp. He backed up a few steps, took a running leap, and jumped off the edge of the hatch. The man trapped in the compartment howled as the full weight of the footlocker crushed his chest.

Caine grabbed the edge of the skylight. He hoisted himself up and shimmied through the gap onto the roof.

Caine wobbled on the shack's roof. The barge beneath him rocked back and forth on the undulating green water. Before he could recover his balance, he heard the crash of breaking wood. The scream of gunfire filled the air, and the skylight shattered behind him.

The armed men had broken into the shack.

Caine turned and sprinted across the roof. He heard muted shouting behind him, both Vietnamese and English. But in the chaos, he could not understand what they were saying.

He reached the end of the flat roof and leapt over to the next barge. It was only a scant distance away, but the barge dipped in the water as soon as his weight slammed down on it. Caine lost his balance and crashed face-first into the roof. He rolled away from the gap as more bullets streaked overhead. Turning on his side, he raised his pistol and aimed at his pursuers, three men clambering up onto the roof of the shack behind him.

Two looked to be Vietnamese and wielded razor-sharp knives. The third man was Caucasian and wore black body armor over a gray T-shirt. Wraparound sunglasses hid his eyes, and he had shaved his head bald. He carried a Tavor 21 assault rifle in a two-handed grip.

Mercenary, Caine thought. *Grissom's private army...*

He aimed at the rifle-toting merc and squeezed off three shots. The bullets slammed into the man's body armor, sending him staggering backward. His boot teetered over the edge of the mangled, shattered skylight, then he fell through into the shack.

The other two men leapt over the gap. Caine rolled again, tumbled over the roof's edge, and plunged down into the gap between the two barges.

Wet rope bit into his skin. Something broke his fall... He had landed in a coarse net strung between the two buildings. The smell of fish assailed his nostrils. Hundreds of dead grouper surrounded him, hauled from the bay by the local fishermen.

As he thrashed around in the pile of fish, he heard more shouting and footsteps clambering across the barge. More men were coming.

He rolled out of the net and struck the barge, wincing as his back slammed into the damp wood planks. Then he picked himself up and sprinted between the buildings. On the other side, he saw several more thugs racing toward him. Caine fired a double tap in their direction, dropping the lead man. The others dove for cover in the gaps between the fishing shacks.

Caine turned and continued sprinting in the opposite direction but stopped when he heard more shouting up ahead. Another group of men, led by a blond mercenary in body armor, charged toward him from the opposite side of the village.

He spotted a gap between two bright-blue shacks and

darted into the narrow alley. Only a stack of crates blocked his way.

Leaping onto the nearest crate, he raced up the stack, climbing them like stairs. Then he jumped onto the roof of the nearest shack and continued running. He sprinted across the length of the tiny village, leaping from roof to roof.

Screams rose from the barges below as gunfire tore through the air. Caine ducked, struggling to stay as low as possible. Tiny puffs of dust kicked up from the roof as a few shots struck near his legs. He reached the roof's end and leapt over to the next shack. In the distance, he heard the muted buzzing of a boat's motor. He was nearing the end of the barges...

As Caine leapt across the next gap, he felt a sudden tug on his leg. He fell short, slamming into the wall of the opposite shack. Someone between the buildings had grabbed his leg and pulled him down. As he crashed into the barge beneath him, his pistol tumbled from his grasp.

Before he could even catch his breath, a powerful kick struck his abdomen, blasting the air from his lungs. He looked up and saw a blurry figure standing over him. A Vietnamese man, one of Le Duan's thugs, scowled back at him. The man kicked him again, and Caine gasped as the blow sent him rolling across the deck.

Caine landed in a pile of torn canvas, rotting wood, and moldy rope. He groped about, searching for anything he could use as a weapon. There was no time to open the bag of guns, but as he scrambled to his feet, his fist wrapped around something hard and metallic.

He hefted a heavy, four-pronged boat anchor in both hands. Then he jabbed the makeshift weapon at his attacker. The man leapt back, dodging the blow. His hand whirled in the air, and Caine saw a blade glinting in the sunlight. The man slashed with the knife, but Caine stepped back, increasing the distance between them.

Snarling and cursing in Vietnamese, the man stabbed again. Caine raised the anchor, and the knife clanged against the metal shaft. Then Caine lunged in close, pressing the prongs into his enemy's chest.

Caine twisted his body, blocking a knee strike as he shoved the man backward, toward the sloshing water. Before he could push the man over the edge, the thug dragged his blade across Caine's side, cutting a bloody gash through his shirt. Caine winced in pain and took a step back. The man hacked again with the blade, this time swinging high.

Caine ducked under the attack. As his opponent struggled to recover his balance, Caine grabbed the thug's knife arm and spun the man around, making him face the water.

Hooking the anchor into his opponent's belt, Caine kicked him over the edge. The flailing man struck the water with a loud splash. Panic filled his face as the heavy anchor dragged him under the water's surface. With a final sputter of terror, he slipped beneath the waves.

Caine panted for breath. He heard footsteps thudding across the barges to his left... There was no time to lose. He jumped up, grabbed the edge of the nearest roof, and pulled himself up. As he leapt over to the next shack, gunshots nipped at his heels. He heard a panicked scream. An elderly woman darted into her home and slammed the door.

The sound of the motor grew louder. A fishing boat puttered in from the bay, several meters ahead of him. Caine leapt onto another roof and raced toward it as fast as he could run. Tiny chips of wood exploded through the air as the bullets tore into the house beneath him. One of the armed mercenaries ran toward him and aimed his rifle.

Caine leapt again. As he touched down, his feet tore through rotting, waterlogged wood. He fell straight down into the shack. A burst of agony rippled through his back as he struck a solid wood table. Grunting in pain, he rolled off and fell to the ground. Plates and utensils flew around him, shattering on the floor.

A woman stared at him in shock as she stirred a pot of soup on a stove. Her two young children backed away from the table, screaming.

Caine heard shouting from outside her shack. He looked into the woman's brown eyes then pointed at the terrified children. 'Get down!' he shouted. He kicked over the table.

The woman grabbed the children and huddled behind the overturned furniture. Caine grasped the wok's handle and yanked the pot off the stove. Then he pressed himself against the wall next to the door. The wood splintered as the mercenary outside kicked the door open.

A burst of gunfire filled the air. Caine heard the bullets thud into the heavy wood table. Praying the thick planks would provide enough cover, he swung the wok. The man with the rifle howled as boiling oil sloshed across his face. He dropped the gun and backed up, cradling his scalded eyes with both hands. Caine charged forward and swung the empty pot down, bludgeoning him on the back of his head. The man grunted and went limp, falling motionless to the ground.

At the end of the barges, the boat roared closer, kicking up a spray of water as it pulled alongside the dock. Caine looked up and saw an elderly local fisherman in a conical hat and loose cotton clothes piloting the boat. His dark, sunken eyes stared at Caine and the armed men in shock. The fisherman spun the steering wheel, struggling to maneuver away from the barge.

As more men raced toward him, Caine grabbed the

discarded rifle at his feet and fired a burst into the air, forcing his attackers to take cover.

As they ducked behind other shacks and piles of crates, Caine turned and sprinted toward the end of the dock. Leaping over the water, he landed in the fishing boat's stern as it drifted past the village. He crashed into a stack of wood traps, sending a swarm of crabs, lobsters, and other crustaceans scurrying onto the deck.

'Hey!' the old man shouted. '*Ra khỏi thuyền*! Get off my boat!'

Caine grabbed the man and dragged him behind the side-wall. More gunfire erupted from the floating village, and bullets splintered the boat's wooden hull.

Caine crawled forward, keeping low as more gunfire whizzed overhead. Reaching up, he pushed the throttle lever forward. The boat roared away from the village, churning up the water into white, frothy foam. A few more bursts of automatic weapons fire lit up the mist behind them. Then they sped off into the fog, leaving the black rocks and colorful floating shacks in their wake.

The old man huddled in the back of the boat, regarding Caine with a nervous stare.

'I'm sorry,' Caine said, trying to sound reassuring. He pulled out his wallet and counted some bills. 'I'd like to buy your boat. Here.'

He handed the man half the cash from the wallet. The man counted the money, looked up at him, and shook his head. Caine handed him the rest of the cash.

The man counted again and nodded. 'Boat yours.'

'Thanks.' Caine took the wheel and set them on a course back for the mainland. 'Pleasure doing business with you.'

A cool breeze whipped through his hair as they sped across the waves toward the dim lights in the distance.

14

WASHINGTON DC, USA

The grounds of the National Bonsai and Penjing Museum were simple, quiet, and peaceful. Occupying over 400 acres of the United States National Arboretum, the museum served to promote the Japanese art of bonsai, as well as the related Chinese discipline known as *penjing*, to guests from all over the world. Although not as popular as some of the more well-known attractions in the D.C. metro area, the museum hosted more than 200,000 visitors annually, including many distinguished federal and foreign guests.

Michael Paulis meandered through the open-air complex alone. His bodyguards hung back, at his insistence. Few other guests walked the stone path with him, and after the display at the SCIF on Capitol Hill, he valued privacy more than security.

The stone walkway curved up, leading him past a grove of colorful flowers and dense greenery. Birds chirped in the distant trees, and a breeze whispered through the leaves. Paulis drew his dark trench coat a bit tighter.

The ground leveled out as he entered the Japanese pavilion. The wind ceased, and as he walked between a pair of bamboo fences, the only sound was his leather shoes tapping on the flagstone. A stillness filled the air, and a peaceful aura settled across the grounds. Even the chirping of the birds seemed muted and distant.

A row of miniature bonsai trees ran alongside a stone wall. Each specimen stood less than three feet tall, but the twists and curls of their trunks, the delicate patterns of their leaves and buds, seemed to contain a galaxy of minute detail. Most of the trees were green, but a few boasted purple, red, or orange blossoms.

A lone woman stood in the center of the row of trees, her back to Paulis. She glanced over her shoulder when she heard his footsteps approaching.

FBI Special Agent Zavala.

The woman gave him a thin smile. Although the day was overcast, her mismatched eyes squinted in the light. A mottled bruise marked her left cheek, and her right arm hung in a sling. She glanced at his cane.

'I might need one of those myself,' she said as he stood next to her. She groaned as she rolled her neck in a circle. '*¡Ay de mí!* Every morning, it feels like my neck hurts more than the day before.'

'I spoke with the hospital where you were treated,' Paulis said, staring down at the curved brown trunk of a tiny Japanese yew. 'They say the pain will fade with time.'

The woman glanced around the pavilion, confirming they were alone. 'And Clayton?' she asked, a note of concern in her voice.

'He's stable,' Paulis replied quietly. 'Looks like he'll pull through. As far as active duty goes... We'll have to see.'

Together, they slowly walked along the row of trees, stopping to examine the tag hanging from each ceramic pot.

'Ms. Zavala, I am truly grateful for your assistance with the Texas operation,' he said, giving her a warm smile. 'But I should warn you, based on what I heard in this morning's hearing, it's probably in your best interest to stay as far away from the CIA as possible right now.'

'Too late for that,' she replied with a bitter laugh. 'I was suspended this morning.'

Paulis stiffened. He looked around again, once more confirming they were alone in the quiet pavilion. 'Then it's probably even more important that we aren't seen together.'

She nodded. They walked further and then stopped to admire the pink blossoms of a miniature Satsuki azalea. 'I agree. But there's something you need to know, something I saw before the regional director called me into his office. And given what I know about Blackwing, I don't trust phones or computers. Or people, for that matter.'

'I understand certain members of the HRT team may have been compromised?'

She grimaced, took a long, slow breath, and nodded. 'Agent Murkowsky was trying to destroy the server in the warehouse when I found him. Clayton was trying to stop him. That's how he...' She paused, staring down at the beautifully sculpted tree. Her eyes seemed to glaze over. 'That's how he got hurt,' she finished.

'What did they have on him?' Paulis asked. 'Murkowsky, I mean?'

She shook her head. 'I don't know for sure. He had a wife, a history professor. She was traveling abroad, in Germany for a conference. We've tried to contact her, but as of now, she appears to be missing.'

'Grissom got to her. That's how he turned your man.'

She nodded. 'That's my best guess.' A shudder ran through her body. '*Es una tragedia.*'

'And your director? Is he compromised?'

'I don't know. I don't think so, but...' Zavala adjusted her glasses. 'This man, Grissom. It seems like he can get to anyone, make them do anything he wants. I thought after what happened here, with Ted Lapinski and the federal marshals, that would be as bad as it got. But it just keeps...'

Her voice trailed off. Paulis stood in silence, remembering seeing Rebecca Freeling in a hospital bed after Grissom unleashed Armageddon on the streets of Washington DC. Armored vehicles, a squad of heavily armed men with automatic weapons, and explosive military ordnance. All to kill a single witness...

'It seems hopeless,' she muttered finally.

They strolled on to the next tree. A thick, squat white pine with emerald-green leaves sat in a rectangular ceramic pot.

'You know,' he said, 'the word bonsai means "tray planting." It's a simple art, really. A patient art. They don't modify genes or make special breeds to get the trees so small. They just cultivate them from cuttings over many years. Bonsai masters shape them, trim them a certain way. Everything, from the size of the leaves to the shape of the trunk, is chosen and shaped with purpose. These trees can live for centuries. Most of these specimens are older than this country.'

She laughed. 'So you're telling me to be patient?'

'Take this tree here,' he continued, pointing at the white elm. 'It survived the bombing of Hiroshima. Almost 100,000 people died that day, but it lived. And now it stands here. A symbol of peace between two countries that were once at war.'

Zavala looked up at him. As the wind picked up again, she shivered. 'I didn't know you liked these little trees so much.'

'I respect them. They're survivors, like me. And like you.'

She smiled back at him, and they continued walking. 'I have to go, but there's something you need to know. I saw the report the director filed with the Senate committee. About the server equipment we found in the raid.'

'Yes, so did I,' Paulis replied. 'It said the hard drives were destroyed in the explosion.'

'They were, but the computer crimes task force at the Bureau was trying to reconstruct whatever data was left. They managed to retrieve a portion of a file, something called ACHERON.'

Paulis stopped and stared down at her. 'Well, that certainly wasn't in the report. What was in the file?'

Zavala bit her lip. 'I don't know. The equipment was badly damaged, and we only retrieved a tiny portion of code. But before the team could finish their work, three Secret Service agents stormed into the lab. They said they had orders to confiscate all the equipment salvaged from the raid. They took everything, even the technicians' personal computers.'

'Orders? Orders from who?'

'Alex Maddison,' she whispered.

Maddison, Paulis thought. *The new DNI. John Blayne's replacement.*

'Ms. Zavala, you should go,' Paulis said. 'You've done enough, and I don't want this to blow back on—'

'Wait, there's one more thing.' She pulled her cell phone from her purse and opened her photo gallery. 'A friend upstairs alerted me before they got to the lab. I knew whatever was going on, it had to be bad. So I took a picture of the screen with my phone and left before they could take it from me. About twenty minutes after that, my regional director called and suspended me.'

She held the phone out to him, and he peered over the rims of his glasses.

Row after row of glowing green characters filled the tiny screen. The shot was blurry; Zavala had obviously taken it quickly. But even at a distance, he could tell the writing was not in English.

It was Chinese.

'What the hell is going on?' Zavala whispered. 'What does this mean?'

Paulis handed the phone back to her. 'It means I need to have a sit-down with the new DNI. And you need to leave town.'

'¡Que se joda, peleamos! I'm not going to run,' she snapped, sliding the phone back in her purse. 'I want to get these bastards! I want to help—'

'You've helped enough. Go, be safe. The ball is in my court now.'

He turned and walked away, leaving the surprised woman and the peaceful row of trees behind him as he descended the stone walkway. Overhead, the swirling clouds in the sky grew darker, and the wind rustled through the leaves once more.

15

HANOI, SOCIALIST REPUBLIC OF VIETNAM

Despite the blasting AC, beads of sweat still dripped down Caine's face. He sat alone in his room at the Essence Hotel in Hanoi. The windows looked out over the bustling street. Outside, a throng of pedestrians filled the narrow road, and music blared from a tiny stage at the end of the street. Tourists and locals alike flocked to the stalls of the night market, where local vendors sold food, silks, toys, and anything else imaginable.

Caine peered through the curtains at the pedestrians and motor scooters weaving through the street. He sipped whisky on the rocks from a glass tumbler as he examined the crowd below.

His phone chirped. Without even looking at the screen, he knew who was on the line.

'Hello,' he said, setting down his glass.

'You had a busy day,' Rebecca replied. He couldn't miss the hint of annoyance in her voice.

'Not a very productive one, though, I'm afraid,' Caine said. 'The local supplier I was hoping to use was—'

'I heard,' Rebecca snapped, ignoring their prearranged code. 'Maybe if you took my advice and worked through our normal distribution channels like I asked, things would have gone smoother.'

Caine fell silent. The phone crackled and hissed in his ear. He pulled the curtains closed and turned away from the window.

'Is this line secure?' he asked finally.

'As secure as it will get, Tom. Now enough with the codes and secret signals. I'm hearing reports of the National Police investigating a shootout in Ha Long Bay... Was that you?'

'Yeah... Grissom knows I'm here, Rebecca. I'm blown.'

'What? How do you know—'

'I spoke with a contact... an arms dealer named Le Duan. I worked with him when I was undercover in Japan. He said someone had called him, asking about me. He knew my real name, and he—'

'So let me get this straight,' Rebecca snapped. 'You refused to work with my contact at the safe house because you didn't trust our network. So instead, you alerted an international criminal that you're in the country, and he sold you out to Grissom?'

'It's not like that, Rebecca...' Caine paused.

'Tom?'

'Look, I don't know how he knew... Maybe showing up after all these years tipped him off, made him do some digging. But he confirmed Boone Riley is alive. And the men who chased me – some of them were American. I'm sure of it. Guns for hire, mercenaries. Probably Delta Blue, like Grissom and Bernatto used before.'

Rebecca sighed. 'Delta Blue... Funny you should mention them. I've been working with Special Agent Zavala at the FBI.

She's kept Director Paulis and me in the loop, following up domestic leads. The paper trail on Delta Blue has changed. Blackwing Capital sold them to a European conglomerate. Now they call themselves Axion. They're up for a government contract, believe it or not.'

'What?' Caine snapped. 'That's insane. It doesn't matter what name they're using. Grissom is obviously still pulling their strings. Paulis must have briefed—'

'The Senate Intelligence Committee has Paulis tied up in hearings. They have an axe to grind, and they're painting all this as some kind of personal vendetta. You know, Grissom is just a private citizen. Investigation wasn't warranted.'

'The same BS they always trot out when they don't want their own dirt exposed,' Caine grumbled.

'Maybe. But Paulis isn't playing ball, so they want his head. And mine as well.'

'You okay?' A note of concern crept into his voice.

'So far. Paulis took the heat for my snafu in Virginia. He sent me to run things from the station house in Prague, to keep me at arm's length. But I don't know... This is all political, and whoever's running Axion now, you can bet they made some heavy donations to the senators on the committee. Director Paulis can only hold them off for so long.'

'Business as usual,' Caine muttered.

He heard her take a deep breath. When she spoke again, her voice was all business. 'So, what's your status? Do you require extraction?'

Caine thought for a moment. He took another sip of whisky and sat on the edge of the bed. 'No. Only a few people got a close look at me. And Le Duan won't be talking to anyone. Not anymore.'

Rebecca made a clicking noise with her tongue. 'I've worked

with you long enough not to ask what that means. The good news is our people pulled some more data from Seng's hard drive. We've narrowed the probable source of transmission to the lake district in Hanoi.'

'Good,' Caine said, peering through the shades at the street below. 'That's near my hotel.'

'We've also confirmed that the Tor network they used to contact Seng was compromised by an NSA exploit. It's a new piece of malware. Larkspur likely doesn't even realize it exists. The next time they try to make contact, we'll be alerted. Their computer will run a background process and send us their exact location.'

'So we wait until they make contact again, then I secure the asset?' Caine asked.

'Exactly. Based on the pattern of emails, they seemed to be in contact on a weekly basis. With any luck, they'll try again tomorrow. But given the mess you caused today, I'm not sure how long I'm willing to wait. If Larkspur doesn't make contact soon, I'm pulling the plug on this operation.'

Caine drained his glass. The liquor left a bitter taste in his mouth. 'Understood.'

'I'll have a contact leave you a secure phone at one of the dead drop sites we approved. Understood?'

'Yeah, I got it.'

'Good. Keep it with you. I'll contact you—'

'I'm sorry,' he said, spitting out the words as if they left a sour taste in his mouth.

'What?'

'I'm sorry,' he repeated, softening his tone. 'You're right. Le Duan was the wrong move. I should have expected that he—'

'Tom, I get it. You have no reason to trust our people. Hell, I don't know if you even should. You're good at working alone.

That's why Paulis wanted to put you on this. But Grissom, Bernatto, Larkspur... Someday, this will be over. And then you, me... Things will have to change. I need to know you understand that.'

'I do,' he replied. 'It's just—'

'Complicated?' she said, finishing his sentence.

He smiled. 'You know me too well.'

'At least one of us does,' she replied. 'I'll contact you with more info soon. And Tom... Be careful.'

'I will.'

With a click, the line went dead. Caine slid the phone into his pocket and sat in silence for a few minutes. Then he got up, poured more whisky into his glass, and pulled the duffel bag of guns out from under the bed.

He removed the CZ pistol and three magazines, stripped the gun down, and laid out the pieces on a towel. He wiped down the barrel and action, using a rag and some mineral oil he had purchased earlier. Then he reassembled the weapon.

As the music and crowd noise echoed in the noisy streets, Caine lay down on the bed. He pulled back the pistol's slide then released it with the decocking lever. He repeated the action over and over as the ceiling fan spun in an endless circle above.

16

PRAGUE, CZECH REPUBLIC

From the street, the building standing at the corner of Karmalitzka and Trziste looked like most of the other structures in the area: old, colorful, and quaint. Nestled in the heart of Mala Strana, one of the area's most historic neighborhoods, the blue brick building was within walking distance of the US Embassy, as well as the KGB Museum. A brass plaque mounted next to the entrance simply stated the building's street address. A second plaque, a black plastic rectangle mounted beneath the first, read '*Poradenství*' – the Czech word for 'consulting.'

Unlike the quaint exterior, the corridors inside were clean, white, and modern. The tapping of Rebecca's cane echoed off the gleaming tile floor as a short, gangly man led her past a series of frosted glass office doors. A shock of white hair framed his hawkish features. The plastic ID badge hanging from a lanyard around his neck identified him as Joseph Wimmer.

Rebecca knew him as the head of the CIA's Prague station house.

As they walked past the translucent panels, she caught a glimpse of the workers in the offices beyond the doors. They were all young, well-dressed professionals. The muted chirps of phones and conversations drifted through the hall.

Joseph coughed and cleared his throat. 'As I was saying, Director Freeling, we were quite surprised to hear of your arrival. It's somewhat irregular for a... err, high-profile client such as yourself to visit us in person.'

She nodded as they approached the silver metal doors of an elevator at the end of the hall.

'It's a surprise to me as well,' she replied. 'But here we are.'

Wimmer shrugged. 'Ah, well, it's not as though the Czech authorities don't know who we are or what we're doing here. So long as we supply them with intercepted Russian and German transmissions, they look the other way when necessary. All very polite and discreet.'

Rebecca smiled. 'Sounds like the stories my father used to tell me about the Cold War.'

Joseph stood straight and clasped his hands behind his back. 'I assure you, we're much more modern than that here.' He swiped his badge over the elevator's control panel, and the doors slid open. He gestured inside. 'I've had people working around the clock running the VPN exploit your people at Langley sent us. If this so-called Larkspur logs in, we'll be able to pinpoint their precise location within minutes.'

He followed her into the elevator, and the doors slid shut.

A few seconds later, the doors chimed open. Rebecca stepped out and blinked. They were in a dark, concrete basement. The fluorescent bulbs overhead flickered and hummed, giving off a dim glow. The dank, stagnant air smelled of vinegar and mold, and black stains marred the featureless walls. Stacks of rotting papers and waterlogged books covered most of the furniture in the chamber save for a pair of desks near the far wall.

Two technicians – one male, one female – sat beneath the sickly green lights. They were slim and pale, and they seemed focused on the computer monitors mounted above their desks. A stream of data and code filled the screens, and the girl typed quickly on her keyboard as her coworker leaned back in his chair and chewed on the cap of his pen.

Rebecca looked around the room. Her eyes began to water, and her nose twitched. When she sneezed, the technicians spun around in their chairs.

Wimmer cleared his throat. 'Anastazie, Lukas... Allow me to introduce Director Freeling. I presume you'll see to it she has everything she needs?'

Lukas smiled. 'Welcome to the pit.'

Rebecca turned to Joseph. 'But... upstairs was so...' Her voice trailed off as she glanced at her dismal surroundings.

The older man gave her a curt nod. 'Yes, I'm afraid we suffered some flooding down here a few years ago. Developed a slight mold problem. But I assure you, the area has been properly disinfected.'

'Yes, but—' Before she could continue, another sneeze exploded from her nose.

Anastazie stood up and handed her a mug from her desk. The blonde girl gave Rebecca a sympathetic smile. 'Here... This place gives me the sniffles as well. I find hot tea helps.'

Rebecca took a sip then coughed.

'With some schnapps,' Anastazie added, shooting a nervous look at Joseph.

Rebecca gazed at the screens. 'Do we have a satellite feed of the area?' she asked.

Lukas nodded. 'Of course. No sign of the Tor exploit we're targeting yet, but I can access traffic cams and satellite views of the lake district as we speak.'

Rebecca sneezed again. She took another sip of the warm tea and cleared her throat. Then she handed the cup to Wimmer. 'Could you have someone please bring up two more of these?'

Wimmer hesitated for a moment then gave her a slight bow. 'Certainly. I'll see to it.'

As he headed off into the shadowy recesses of the basement, Rebecca returned her attention to the screens.

'All right then,' she said as Anastazie took her seat. 'Let's get to work.'

17

HANOI, SOCIALIST REPUBLIC OF VIETNAM

Crack crack crack... Crack crack crack...

The sound of bamboo poles slapping against pavement rang out over and over, a steady percussive beat rising above the sounds of cooking food and the chatter of the crowd. Caine couldn't tell where the sound was coming from, but it had been a constant presence, always in the background as he meandered around the banks of Hoan Kiem Lake in the center of Hanoi.

Its name meant 'Lake of the Restored Sword,' or so the short, portly old man working in the tiny cafe told him. Caine listened to the shopkeeper's story as the man poured a cup of aromatic local coffee then blended it with ice and coconut cream. According to the legend, a Turtle God visited an emperor on the lake, demanding the return of a magical sword that belonged to the great Long Vuong, the Dragon King. After the emperor finished his revolt against Vietnam's Chinese rulers, he returned the sword and renamed the lake for the occasion. A small octagonal temple sat on the island in the center of the lake's placid waters. The building was the Thap Rua, or Turtle Tower, named in honor of the ancient legend.

As Caine walked among the fragrant gardens surrounding the lake, the sound of clacking grew louder. A crowd of pedestrians filled the street, blocking his view of the road ahead. It was the weekend, and the street that circled the lake was closed to all vehicles. Only foot traffic was allowed, and hundreds of locals strolled around the beautiful lake with their families, enjoying the day. The smell of grilled pork and spices wafted through the air, mixing with the sweet scent of flowers, the hundreds of tulips and orchids surrounding the banks of the lake, arranged in beautifully kept gardens.

Caine sipped more of the potent coffee concoction from a plastic cup as he maneuvered through the crowd. He emerged into a circular clearing of people.

Crack crack crack!

Crack crack crack!

The sound was louder here. In the clear circle of pavement, two rows of teenage girls in white shirts and blue skirts knelt across from each other on the street. They each grasped the opposite ends of bamboo poles, arranged in pairs. The long, narrow sticks measured about eight feet long, and the girls sang a song as they slapped them against the pavement, giving their tune a percussive rhythm.

Crack crack crack!

Crack crack crack!

The staccato beat continued like clockwork. Each time a pair of sticks hit the road, the girls moved them farther apart. Then they slid them together again. A group of younger boys and girls laughed and screamed as they tried to hop through the gaps between the sticks, playing *múa sạp*, a traditional Vietnamese folk dance that blended rhythm, agility, and teamwork.

The elder members of the crowd smiled as they watched the awkward children jump and sway on their tiny legs.

Caine grinned in spite of himself and glanced up at the buildings surrounding the lake. Dozens of cafes and coffee houses circled the placid green water. Some had outdoor seating, and their chairs all faced the walking street. Their patrons enjoyed the people-watching almost as much as the strong, delicious coffee.

Caine pulled a cell phone from his pocket and checked the display just to make sure it was working properly. It was, but it showed no missed calls.

Where the hell is she? Caine thought. *She should have made contact by now.*

He felt restless, ill at ease. After the events of yesterday, he could no longer have any doubt. Their enemy knew he was here, which meant they knew what he was after. His jaw clenched as he remembered Rebecca's phone call the night before. The anger and frustration in her voice.

It stings because you know she's right. For what seemed like the hundredth time, he wondered if reaching out to Le Duan had tipped off Grissom... *No. Grissom's men were already in the country, waiting for you. The old man had to know the asset was here...*

But no matter how hard he tried to convince himself, he couldn't shake the nagging suspicion that he had made things worse. That by being here, he was putting their mysterious asset, whoever it was, in even greater danger. But he wasn't operating alone now. He was working with Rebecca. She was calling the shots, and if he left now, Grissom would win.

He couldn't allow that to happen.

Turning down a side street, he stepped into an open-air cafe decorated with bright-yellow walls and natural-wood tables. He purchased a *bánh mì* sandwich for a few dong notes. The meal consisted of lemongrass-roasted chicken, served on a crusty fresh-baked baguette, a reminder of Vietnam's French colonial history. Crisp pickled vegetables and jalapeno peppers gave the sandwich a fresh, vinegary tang that helped counteract the oppressive heat and humidity in the air.

He continued walking, eating the sandwich straight from its plain brown wrapper. He washed it down with the remains of his coffee. As he tossed the empty wrapper in a trash bin, he felt the phone vibrate against his leg.

Rebecca was finally calling.

He tapped the Bluetooth bud in his ear, connecting the call. 'Caine here. Go for response code: Whirlpool.'

'Response code: Peninsula,' Rebecca answered.

Caine nodded and kept walking. The codes confirmed that the mission was a go, and neither side suspected a communications breach. He slowed his pace, scanning the faces of the local pedestrians as they strolled past him. 'Copy that,' he said in a low voice. 'I'm in position, near the lake.'

'Stand by. The asset tried to initiate contact with Seng. We should have a—' Her voice was lost in a loud burst of static.

Caine frowned. 'Come again?'

'Sorry, my allergies are killing me down here. I said we should be able to pinpoint their IP address and location shortly.'

Caine didn't answer. He glanced up as something buzzed across the sky. A tiny black drone hovered above the crowd, swooping over the locals' heads like a giant dragonfly. Caine averted his eyes and looked down as it flew over him.

'Copy that. Standing by,' he answered.

Rebecca noticed his hesitation. 'What's wrong?'

He moved away from the crowd, following a path that

wound through a series of rocks and pagoda statues. Low-hanging trees formed a dark leafy canopy overhead, bending their boughs to kiss the lake's emerald waters. After a short pause, he answered, 'Nothing.'

'I can tell by your voice something's not right. Do you want to abort?'

Caine eyed the foot traffic heading toward him through the rocks. Families, teenagers, couples enjoying the view of the lake...

'No,' he replied. 'I saw a drone. Consumer model, nothing special about it.'

'They're everywhere now,' Rebecca said, a note of caution in her voice. 'But Grissom's used drones before.'

'I know. But I don't have any reason to—'

He paused in mid-sentence. As he glanced over his shoulder, he spotted a man standing by the edge of the lake. He wore a black leather jacket and dark jeans. His attire was odd considering the heat. But many of the locals seemed comfortable in far heavier clothes than he would have expected.

Caine felt the familiar tingling sensation on the back of his neck... Something about the man was wrong. He didn't belong. It wasn't the clothes. It was something about his body language, the way he stood out from the crowd. Caine couldn't say how or why, but he was certain of one thing.

Someone was following him.

'Rebecca, I have to go.'

'What is it?'

'I think I've been made. Give me a few minutes, and I'll call you back.'

'Tom, I can't have a repeat of last night. If we need to pull the plug on this thing...'

'We already know Grissom's men are here. If you pull me

out, then this asset, whoever they are, is as good as dead. Just give me a few minutes. It might be nothing.'

'Tom, I—'

He tapped the earpiece, disconnecting the call. Then he continued walking, moving at a leisurely pace through an ornate gate framed by carved stone reliefs. The wall to his left displayed a white tiger prowling through grass. On his right, a golden dragon breathed a mosaic of fire over curling turquoise waves.

The path led to a bright-red bridge that curved over the lake and ended at a small, forested island. Caine paused in the middle of the wood arch, glancing down at the leathery turtles paddling in the brackish water. A low wind picked up, rustling the branches of the tree groves on the other side. The trees were in bloom, and an explosion of purple and orange blossoms drifted through the air before falling to the water's surface.

From the corner of his eye, he saw a man pushing his way through the pedestrians moving over the bridge. The man paused and turned away, pretending to look at the moss-covered temple sitting in the center of the lake.

It was the man in the black leather jacket.

Caine continued walking across the bridge. The wooden slats dipped down, and he stepped onto the tiny island on the opposite side. The path led through a gray stone arch decorated with stunning blue mosaic tiles. A short, heavyset woman sat at a wood desk beside the archway. A small blue plaque identified the spot as the Moon Contemplation Pavilion. Caine, noticing the dented metal cashbox on the desk, set a few notes down. The woman took them with a smile and gestured to the path.

'Ngoc Son temple on right,' she said in a lilting, high-pitched voice. 'Very beautiful, famous national treasure.'

Caine returned her smile and strolled down the path. He

did not look behind him to see if the man was still following. He could still feel the skin on the back of his neck crawling. He knew he was being watched.

The path led to a stone square surrounded by a collection of temples. Golden pagoda roofs rose above him, and the boughs of surrounding trees hung low, shrouding the tiny clump of land in their colorful embrace.

A metal urn sat in the center of the square, and fragrant incense wafted through the sultry air. Caine followed a group of locals as they strolled through a pair of red columns and entered one of the temples. The building smelled of damp wood and age. All around him, treasures from the surrounding area rested on display platforms or hung from shelves. Porcelain vases, metal statues, wood carvings, faded scrolls. Centuries of history were collected and displayed in the tiny, cramped building.

Unlike the other tourists, Caine spent little time observing the beautiful relics. Instead, he made his way to the rear of the building and darted behind an ornate carved wood screen. Glancing at the ceiling, he spotted a glowing red exit sign hanging in the corner. A black iron wedge propped the rear door half open, letting a breeze waft through the temple. He ducked through the opening and grabbed the wedge as he slipped outside. The door swung shut behind him and closed with a loud thud.

He hefted the lump of metal in his hand... The doorstop was shaped like a dragon, and its surface was pitted and dull. He couldn't risk a gunshot in such a heavily trafficked area – the sound would alert authorities instantly. But the metal wedge would serve as an adequate bludgeon.

Caine vaulted over a low stone wall behind the temple and entered a grove of trees near the water's edge. He pressed himself behind one of the thick trunks and listened. In the distance, he still heard the muted sounds of the festival on the lake's shore.

Crack crack crack!

Crack crack crack!

An unfamiliar sound joined the distant beating sticks. Footsteps snapped across the broken branches and tangled vines surrounding the grove. They moved closer. A shadowy figure rounded the low wall and advanced toward the water's edge. As the figure stalked past the tree, Caine gripped the metal wedge and raised it in both hands.

He stepped out from his hiding place and swung...

18

Even as Caine lunged forward, he felt something was wrong. His target, a tall, gaunt man in jeans and a black linen shirt, pivoted to his left as if sensing Caine's approach.

Caine swung the heavy doorstop, but instead of striking the base of the man's skull, it slammed into his shoulder with a dull, fleshy thud. The man stumbled forward, but he recovered and whirled around. Caine saw a glint of metal in his hand... a steel ring looped around his index finger, just below the thumb of his right hand.

Brass knuckles? Some kind of force multiplier?

The man lashed out with his fist. Caine leaned back, and the blow missed his chin by inches. He threw up the statue, clubbing the man's arm away. But his opponent seemed to anticipate the block once again. He dipped low, and Caine felt a punch slam into his left side. He gasped in pain and staggered backward, struggling to put some distance between him and his target.

His attacker's shirt billowed in the hot breeze as he swung

his arms in a series of intricate circles. Caine kept his eyes on the steel ring...

He's good, Caine thought, *but his technique... Looks more like a knife-fighting style than—*

Before he could finish his thought, the man locked eyes with Caine and struck again. Caine swung the statue up, trying to block the attacking arm once more. But again, his attacker ducked, dropping to one knee. Caine heard a metallic click... Glancing down, he saw the shimmer of a blade emerge from a handle attached to the ring.

The curved metal claw slashed across his midsection, tearing through his shirt and cutting a gash across his right torso. Caine winced in pain, but he did not retreat. The attack left his opponent open. Now was the time to strike.

Caine swung the doorstop overhead, clubbing the man's right shoulder again. He heard a loud crack as the heavy metal bludgeon slammed into flesh and bone. His attacker gasped and fell to the ground. Caine raised his foot and aimed at the fallen man's neck. But before he could stomp down, his attacker rolled away.

The man leapt to his feet and slashed with his blade, cutting a wide arc through the air. Caine shunted the strike aside, but his attacker wasn't finished. With a twist of his arm, his opponent spun the curved blade around and drew his arm back. Another bloody gash tore across Caine's skin.

Caine adopted a boxing pose, keeping his fists close to his face. His attacker shifted his weight back and forth on his feet, bobbing and weaving like a dancing cobra. Caine saw an opening... He jabbed, snapping a quick punch into the man's face.

Circling to his right, Caine jabbed again, but this time, his attacker was ready. Swinging up his left arm, he knocked the blow aside and trapped Caine's arm in a lock. The man's right arm snapped forward. Caine saw the blow coming, but it was too late. The metal ring slammed into his jaw, sending a blast of white-hot agony through his skull. As he pulled free and stumbled backward, he felt the cold touch of the metal blade sliding across his neck.

His fingers shot up to his throat. He expected to feel hot blood gushing across his hands. But to his surprise, he was uninjured.

Single-edged blade. Otherwise, I'd be dead by now...

He leapt backward as his attacker advanced, swinging the knife in a wide arc. The man grinned as he continued pressing forward. He spun the weapon around his finger in an elaborate flourish then winced in pain. Caine watched as his attacker transferred the weapon to his left hand. Judging by the way the man rolled his shoulder, Caine guessed his last strike with the statue had dislocated it.

Caine grinned back at the man as they circled each other. The distant beat of the sticks accompanied their movements, turning their fight into a graceful dance of death.

Crack crack crack!

Crack crack crack!

His opponent advanced, moving on the balls of his feet. Again, the curved metal fang lashed out, but Caine pivoted sideways, denying the man a clear target. The killer tried to reverse course, but his feet slid on the soft ground, carrying him forward a few inches before he could adjust.

Caine swung the heavy weight like a baseball bat. He heard a wet thud, followed by the snap of breaking bone, as the blow connected with his attacker's skull. The man stumbled then fell face-first into the mud. His body twitched and writhed as blood gushed from the back of his head.

Caine fell to his knees and swung again. His target lay still.

Panting, Caine dropped the bloody statue in the mud. He pried the knife from the man's limp fingers then staggered to his feet. On the opposite shore, the distant beat of the sticks continued.

Crack crack crack!

Crack crack crack!

Then...

Crack...

The sound of breaking twigs broke the rhythm. Caine spun around just in time to see the man in the leather jacket barreling toward him.

Caine stepped back as another curved blade glinted in the sunlight, cutting a silver trail through the air. The man in the jacket slashed again as he lunged forward.

Caine kept backing up, struggling to put some distance between them. He felt the back of his head slam into rough wood. He ducked low, dipping under the branches of the trees. They were nearing the edge of the lake...

The man in the leather jacket swung the knife in a wide arc. Caine blocked the attack and tried to hook the man's right arm. But as he trapped the limb, he realized too late that his attacker had slipped the blade into his other hand.

His opponent's left hand snapped forward. The metal ring of the karambit slammed into Caine's face, barely missing his eye. Caine's head snapped back. Before he could recover, his attacker flipped his knife around and dragged his blade across Caine's arm. Another gash opened in his right shoulder, and blood ran down the front of his shirt.

Caine spun around the tree, keeping it between him and his attacker. The man bounced left and right, unsure which way to press his attack. He stepped forward...

Come on... a little closer.

Suddenly, the man darted right. Caine slipped left, keeping the gnarled trunk between them. He reached out with his free hand, grabbed the man's shirt, and yanked forward as hard as he could. His enemy grunted as Caine slammed his face into the tree.

Using the momentary distraction, Caine pivoted behind the stunned man and grabbed the back of his jacket. He threw the man forward again, sending him careening into the tree even harder. He heard a loud snap as the cartilage in his opponent's nose broke.

The man stumbled backward, dazed from the sudden impact. Caine hooked an arm around the stunned thug's neck then drew back the knife. His opponent uttered a startled gasp, followed by a gurgle of pain. He fell to his knees as blood streamed from a gash in his neck. Caine glanced down... The bloodied iron statue lay in the mud near his feet.

Taking a deep breath, Caine picked the statue up and swung. It struck the top of the dying man's head, and he pitched forward into the mud.

Caine glanced through the trees, peering at the temple behind them. No one exited the rear door, and all foot traffic seemed concentrated on the other side of the building. But he knew that could change at a moment's notice.

He stripped off his bloody shirt and tore it into pieces of cloth. He used them to bandage his wounds as best he could, tying the strips off with his teeth. Then he removed one of the thugs' shirts and threw it on. As he dressed, he glanced at the lake's edge. A pair of tiny wooden boats, moored to a rickety pier, bobbed in the water.

He returned his attention to the pair of dead bodies lying in the mud. Patting them down, he found no identification or weapons other than the karambit knives. The man with the leather jacket carried a cell phone in his pocket and had a push-to-talk radiophone clipped to his belt. Caine grabbed these items then thumbed the locking lever on the knife he had acquired. The blade retracted, folding back like a cat's claw. He slid the weapon into his pocket then hurled the other knife into the lake.

He grabbed the two men by their feet, dragged the bodies to the island's edge, and sent them floating out into the water. He shoved the corpses under the two boats, tying their shoelaces to the mooring ropes to keep them from drifting away. He didn't know how long they would remain hidden, but it was better than leaving them out in the open.

Then he took another deep breath. He could feel his heart racing, and his right hand trembled. He clenched it into a fist several times, waiting for the rush of adrenaline to subside.

When he was no longer shaking, he slipped the dead man's cell phone from his pocket. It was not locked, and the screen showed what looked like a constant stream of data: letters, numbers, symbols...

IP addresses. The drone... It's intercepting nearby Wi-Fi signals. They're running the same exploit Rebecca is.

He slid the phone back into his pocket then jogged from behind the temple. He pushed his way through the crowd of people in the center pavilion then headed back across the bridge, moving as fast as he could without drawing attention to himself.

He pulled out his burner phone and redialed Rebecca's number. She answered on the second ring.

'Tom, where the hell did you go? Something's wrong. We just lost contact with—'

'We have a problem,' Caine said, cutting her off as he stepped off the red bridge onto the lake's shore.

'What do you mean? What's wrong?'

'Grissom's people are here. That drone I saw... I think they're using it to intercept Wi-Fi data.'

'But that data is encrypted. How could they—'

Caine peered at the skyline as he paced around the lake. 'You really think a coffee shop's Wi-Fi encryption is going to stop an operation like Blackwing? We have to assume they have the same capabilities we do.'

'Maybe you're right. But we lost the signal. We can't pinpoint the asset's location.'

Caine froze and narrowed his eyes. He spotted the tiny black drone hovering in the distance, above a row of red tents. Behind the food vendors, cafes and coffee shops lined the sidewalk.

'I know where they are. And so does anyone else looking for them. Might as well have a bullseye on their back.'

'Tom, this is our only shot. If Grissom gets his hands on them, we're cut off from any more intel.'

'Copy that. I'll contact you as soon as I can.'

He hung up and pushed his way through the crowded street. In the distance, the sticks continued to beat their steady rhythm.

19

Caine glanced left and right as he wove through the throng of bodies. Between the music, the people, and the incessant pounding of the bamboo poles, it was chaos. The streets were a riot of color... Crimson tents serving crepes and grilled meats, bushels of pink and orange fruit, Buddhist temples covered in flaking gold paint. He couldn't spot anyone in the crowd that stood out, but he knew they were there. Someone was receiving the same data stream as the phone in his pocket, IP addresses matched to the physical location of the hovering drone.

Caine glanced up. The tiny insectile-looking craft still hung in the air, drifting over a row of cafes beyond the sidewalk. He continued advancing, keeping his eyes on the tiny black dot hovering above. The buzzing aircraft settled over one of the coffee shops and remained stationary in the sky.

Suddenly, someone slammed into him. Caine reacted instinctively, knocking the body away from him. His free hand darted to the knife in his waistband.

'*Chào! Nhìn đường đi!*' an angry voice shouted. 'Watch where you going!'

Caine blinked. A short, withered old man picked himself up off the ground. A wicker basket lay overturned on the street, and an avalanche of pink-and-green dragon fruit tumbled across the pavement.

Caine bent down and picked up the nearest fruit, keeping his eyes on the hovering drone. 'Sorry... *Xin lỗi*.' He handed the colorful fruit to the old man then continued moving through the crowd. The elderly shopper muttered and cursed behind him, but Caine paid him no mind.

When he reached the sidewalk, he looked over his shoulder again, scanning the faces around him. He spotted a Caucasian man near the lake, heading in his direction. The man wore a loose-fitting linen shirt and gray canvas pants. He looked young and fit, early thirties, with a lean, muscular build. His hair was buzzed short, and wraparound sunglasses covered his eyes.

Caine watched as a crowd of pedestrians surged between them. Their bodies blocked his view as the man tried to cross the street.

Caine spun around and threw open the glass door to the cafe beneath the drone's position. Bells mounted above the entrance jingled as he stepped through. Inside, the air smelled of roasting coffee and freshly baked pastries. The tiny shop was clean and modern. American pop music played at a low volume over the speakers. Condensation covered the windows, and an air conditioner blasted the place with cool air.

A loud metallic grinding sound exploded from behind the counter. Caine tensed, then he realized it was the sound of an espresso machine preparing a coffee drink. A teenage Vietnamese girl wearing glasses and a dark apron stood behind the counter, spooning foam from a steel pitcher into a paper cup. She slid the steaming drink across the counter to a waiting customer.

Caine let the door jingle shut behind him. He reached down and surreptitiously locked the door with a twist of his fingers. Scanning the crowd, he saw they were all young, mostly locals. Nearly everyone's eyes were focused on their laptop screens. A few younger girls in the rear corner swiped at pictures on their cell phones.

'What can I get you?' the girl behind the counter asked.

Caine smiled. 'Nothing, thanks. I'm looking for a friend.'

She shrugged and turned away as a customer approached the counter for a refill.

Caine turned his eyes back to the crowd. A slim figure in a dark hooded sweatshirt abruptly left their chair and darted down a dim corridor in the cafe's rear. Caine narrowed his eyes. Whoever they were, they had left their laptop on the table unattended.

He chased after them, ignoring the annoyed glances of the other patrons as he bumped into their tables. He caught up with the figure in the corridor and grabbed their arm.

The figure spun around. He stared into the face of a youthful Vietnamese woman. She looked to be in her late twenties, and her dark, almond-shaped eyes squinted at him in annoyance.

'Hey!' she snapped. '*Đừng chạm vào tôi!*... Don't touch me!'

His green eyes locked on to hers. He could tell she was trying to project anger and confidence. But her eyes twitched, and her voice cracked as she spoke.

She was afraid.

'Listen,' he said in a low voice. 'The man you were trying to reach is dead.'

'What are you—' she began.

'I said listen!' he snapped. 'The people who killed him

traced your internet connection. I'm here to help, but we don't have much time.'

'You're fucking crazy!' She turned away, but he yanked on her arm again, spinning her around to face him. A concerned murmur rose from the other patrons.

Caine muttered a silent curse and pulled the girl farther into the corridor. 'His name was Mr. Seng, right? The man you were trying to reach in Singapore?'

She stared up at him but said nothing. A loud pounding echoed through the cafe. The bells jingled as someone shook the door.

'Hey, let us in!' a muted voice shouted from outside.

Caine glanced toward the entrance. The man with the buzz cut stood outside the glass, pounding on the door.

'Sorry, sorry!' The girl running the cafe ducked under the counter. 'Door locked... One second!'

Caine turned to the girl in the hoodie. 'Last chance. Are you with me or not?'

The girl bit her lip. 'I don't know who I was contacting,' she finally said. 'My grandfather sent me. He couldn't make it, so he told me to make contact from here.'

Caine nodded. He heard a click then a jingle as the door swung open. 'Right. Let's go. Stay behind me.'

He pulled the girl down the corridor, past a pair of restrooms. The corridor turned right then led to a rusted metal door. Caine drew his pistol from his waistband.

'Are you crazy?' the girl hissed. 'You can't bring a gun in here!'

'Tell that to the men on your tail,' he muttered back. He swung open the door and stepped out into an alleyway running alongside the cafe. Sweeping the gun left and right, he pulled the girl after him. He slammed the door and looked down the alley.

To their right, a battered truck faced them, and a stooped, elderly Vietnamese man unloaded silver canisters of propane gas from the back. A younger man wearing an apron carried them into a restaurant on the opposite side of the alley. Farther down, Caine caught a glimpse of the crowds around the lake and heard the rhythmic beat of the sticks again...

Crack crack crack!

Crack crack crack!

He turned to his left. The mad rush of Hanoi traffic rumbled past the alley's entrance. Bright scooters buzzed and wove between the endless cars and trucks, speeding past the narrow gap between buildings.

A dented metal dumpster, painted bright turquoise blue, stood against the wall, a few meters away.

'Quick, help me!' Caine shouted.

He raced to the dumpster and shoved it toward the door. The girl jogged over and pushed with him. 'Who the hell are you?' she asked.

'Call me Tom.'

With a harsh grinding sound, the dumpster slid in front of the exit. The metal door clanged as whoever was on the other side tried to open it.

'Come on,' Caine muttered. He pulled her toward the truck. The motor was still running, and a wispy cloud of exhaust fumes filled the narrow alley. Caine helped the girl up into the cab, and she slid over into the passenger seat.

'Hey, you can't just take this guy's—'

'Put on your seat belt and get down,' Caine snapped.

The delivery man hobbled over to them, shaking his fist and cursing in Vietnamese.

Caine ignored him and slammed the door closed. He shifted into gear and stepped on the gas. The truck roared to life and rumbled down the alley toward the traffic. A loose silver canister rolled out between the wood slats surrounding the rear bed. It struck the pavement like a gong and rolled backward.

'Sorry... *Lấy làm tiếc!*' the girl shouted out the window to the old man. He stood in the center of the alley, waving and shouting as they pulled away.

'I said get down,' Caine snapped. 'We're still in—'

The squeal of brakes echoed at the end of the alley. A black SUV pulled in, blocking their view of the traffic beyond. The dark vehicle's windows were tinted, and Caine couldn't see the driver. The vehicle stopped, its engine growling like an angry tiger as it blocked the alley's exit.

Caine slammed on the brakes, and the old truck groaned to a halt. The canisters behind them clanged like gongs as they slammed into one another and rolled through the pickup bed.

'Who's that?' the girl said, grabbing the armrest.

'I don't know,' Caine replied.

He shifted the truck into reverse but kept the clutch disengaged and his foot on the brake. A man in a navy-blue shirt leaned out the SUV's passenger window. Like the other, sunglasses covered his eyes, and his hair was military short.

He held an AK-47 rifle in a two-handed grip.

Caine released the clutch and slammed on the gas. The truck roared backward down the alley. The sudden acceleration caused the vehicle to lurch sideways. Sparks flew as the passenger door scraped against the alley's wall.

The girl screamed and threw herself down on the seat. The rifle spat a burst of orange muzzle fire. The chatter of automatic gunfire echoed through the alley. Caine ducked as the windshield exploded into a spiderweb of cracks. Bullets ricocheted off the truck's metal grille.

The vehicle continued scraping along the alley wall. Uttering a startled shout, the old man ducked back into the restaurant just as the vehicle lumbered past. With a shriek of rending metal, the truck tore the open door off its hinges. The old vehicle's shocks and suspension squealed as it bounced over the metal panel. A muffled explosion sounded under the truck... The loose propane canister crumpled beneath its wheels.

As the end of the alley sped closer, another volley of gunfire struck the windshield. The panel of glass exploded into glittering fragments, raining down on top of the screaming girl.

Caine drew his pistol and aimed through the shattered glass. The gun roared as he fired three shots into the SUV. The bullets tore divots in the vehicle's windshield, but they did not penetrate into the cabin.

Caine continued pulling the trigger until the slide snapped back. He ejected the empty mag, tossed the weapon to the girl and fished two spare magazines from his pocket.

'Reload!' he shouted.

She looked back at him, her eyes wide with terror. 'What? I don't know how to do that!'

'Figure it out. Quick!'

She grabbed the magazines, promptly dropping one to the floor. Her trembling hands struggled to shove the other into the butt of the gun. 'It won't go in!' she shouted.

'Other way!' Caine snapped. He glanced up at the rearview mirror. Pedestrians screamed and dashed through the streets behind them, struggling to clear a path for the reversing truck.

The girl flipped the magazine around, drove it into the grip of the gun, and handed the weapon back to Caine.

'Here... I think?'

A hail of bullets tore into the upholstery between them. Chunks of foam and fake leather exploded into the air. Caine grabbed the pistol from the girl's trembling hands and flicked the slide release. The gun snapped shut with a loud click.

The gun roared as he sent three shots into the front right tire of the SUV. The tire exploded and the vehicle jerked to the side, its nose crumpling against the wall of the alley. Steam erupted from the mangled hood as men leapt from a rear door and opened fire.

Caine slammed the shifter into neutral, spun the steering wheel, and skidded out of the alleyway. Bullets sparked off the rear of the flatbed. He leaned on the horn again, sending pedestrians scrambling out of his way.

Popping the clutch, he shifted into first, stomped on the gas, and maneuvered the lumbering vehicle through the panicked crowd.

20

'Watch where you're going! The street festival is packed!' the girl shouted.

Caine glanced up at the rearview mirror as he swung the truck around and roared down the street. He saw no sign of the black SUV. It was still trapped in the alley. The armed men vanished in the sea of bodies behind him.

A frenzy gripped the crowd. Screams and shouts echoed through the street. He knew the police would arrive in minutes.

He pressed the horn again, and the crowd slowly parted before him. The truck's engine groaned and squealed as it lurched forward a few meters at a time.

Reaching out the window, Caine pointed his pistol straight up and fired three quick shots. The crowd screamed louder and ran to either side, desperate to put as much distance as possible between themselves and his vehicle. Caine leaned back into the cab and shifted into a higher gear. The truck roared off the circular walking street.

As he turned left onto Dinh Teng Hoang Street, Caine

looked over at the girl. 'Who are you? Why were you trying to contact Seng?'

She sat up in her seat and glanced out the rear window of the little truck. As she turned, her hood fell from her head, revealing a short, sleek razor cut. It was a modern reverse bob, longer in the front than the back. A strand of hair on the left side of her face was dyed bleach blonde.

'My name is Trina Phan,' she said, her voice trembling. 'I already told you, my grandfather sent me. He told me I couldn't use my phone, only email.'

'Why there?' Caine asked. He swung the wheel to the right, swerving onto a street that split off from the crowded, narrow road.

The girl shrugged. 'How should I know? I just came down to help my grandfather. I had to cancel all my tours when he got sick.'

Caine shot her a questioning glance. 'Tours? What are you, some kind of guide?'

She nodded. 'I study geology at the National University, but I lead caving expeditions to make extra money on the side. I was supposed to take some photographers into Hang Son Doong cave next week. Then my grandfather called me. He said he was sick and needed my help. I—'

Before she could finish, Caine heard the squeal of brakes. A powerful engine roared behind them like a tiger running down its prey. He glanced in the rearview mirror. A pair of black SUVs swerved onto the street, closing in at top speed.

'Fill me in later. Get down!'

Trina ducked again as a hail of gunfire tore into the rear of the truck. She screamed as the window behind them exploded and sparkling shards rained down on her head.

Caine winced as a sliver of glass cut across his cheek. He

threw the wheel left, and the truck skidded onto a side street. Rows of parked motor scooters formed long barricades on either side of them. The crimson canopies of rickshaws wove in and out of traffic, their sweating drivers pedaling as fast as they could.

Neon lights blinked in the shop windows as Caine and Trina roared past. Caine threw the wheel to the left, and they skidded onto another street. Ahead of them, a circular fountain sent plumes of water spiraling through the air. More neon lights flashed on all sides. They sped into a roundabout, curving around the fountain. To his right, a five-story building packed with fast-food eateries and local cafes towered above the smaller street food stands. A cluster of scooters parked around the fountain, and a stream of traffic merged in the circle, exiting to the right of the town square.

'This is Dong Kinh Nghia Thuc Square,' the girl said, grabbing the dashboard in a white-knuckled grip. 'Go right, go right!'

Caine did as she asked, maneuvering the truck into the right-hand lane and merging with the other traffic. The truck's engine sputtered and roared as it picked up speed. Caine darted around another mass of scooters that spilled out into the street.

'We have to ditch this truck,' Caine snapped. 'Do you know anywhere we—'

Before he could finish his sentence, more gunfire erupted behind them. Caine winced as bullets studded into the thin metal wall behind them. Suddenly, an explosion rocked the truck bed, and the vehicle lurched across the road.

The girl screamed. She looked up at him, her dark eyes wide with surprise. '*Cái quái gì vậy?* What the hell was that?'

Caine glanced through the tiny, shattered window behind them. A splintered hole gaped through the wood slats that formed the truck's bed. He heard the loud clank of scraping metal. Several battered cylinders, each about a meter long, rolled back and forth in the bed.

'CO_2 canister,' he said. 'Restaurants use them to carbonate soda. A bullet must have punctured one.'

Trina gasped. 'You mean they could explode?'

Caine shook his head and spun the wheel left, skidding onto another side street. 'Not like a bomb, no. But I wouldn't want one to fly into the cab. Here, take the wheel.'

She squinted at him. 'What?'

Caine grabbed her hand and put it on the wheel. 'Drive... I'm going in the back to see if I can discourage your secret admirers.'

Caine grabbed a rag on the seat of the truck and swept away the jagged broken glass lining the window. Then he shimmied through the opening and fell onto the rattling truck bed.

The truck lurched and groaned as the girl slid behind the wheel. Then it surged forward, picking up speed once again.

Caine looked around. A frame of wood slats surrounded him, and the road noise was louder in the open truck bed. A sheet of canvas stretched above him, but he saw no roof. The air reeked of dust and exhaust fumes.

With an angry roar, the black SUV closed the gap between the vehicles. Caine saw a figure lean out the rear passenger window. Dropping to one knee, Caine raised his pistol in a double-handed grip. He squeezed the trigger, sending a double tap into the man before he could aim his rifle.

With a grim smile, Caine watched as his target jerked and fell out the window. The man landed in the street, where he was immediately struck by a buzzing motor scooter. The tiny vehicle flipped as it hit the body, throwing its rider to the pavement.

The truck made a sharp turn. A CO_2 canister slammed into Caine's leg, knocking him sideways. He fell against the side of the truck, and more bullets streaked into the open bed. Another gunman emerged from the pursuing SUV, this time behind the driver. The wood beams splintered around him, and he heard Trina scream as a stray shot ricocheted through the cab.

Recovering from the impact, Caine sent another double tap into the SUV's windshield. The slugs merely carved white divots in the tinted bulletproof glass.

Muttering a silent curse, Caine ducked as the gunman returned fire. He heard the staccato patter of bullets striking metal. Then the whoosh of pressurized gas drowned out all other sounds. Caine saw a flash of silver streaking toward him.

Something large and heavy slammed into his shoulder, knocking him backward. He barely managed to keep hold of his gun, as he felt the wind whip through his hair. The initial burst of pain faded, and he quickly realized what had happened.

A punctured canister had rocketed into him, smashing him through the side of the battered truck. One of his legs was wedged between two wood beams. He was dangling upside down, hanging alongside the speeding vehicle.

He struggled to grab hold of a beam so he could pull himself back in, but the splintering wood snapped off in his hand. He fell back, and his head barely missed the pavement streaking by below.

Caine heard the roar of an engine drown out the wind and other traffic. He turned to look behind him. The SUV drifted to the truck's left. Its gleaming front grille bore down on him, speeding closer and closer.

Raising his gun in a two-handed grip, Caine opened fire. He sent two shots into the grille, with no effect. He adjusted his aim and fired more slugs into the cracked windshield. The vehicle sped up, lurching close. The front end of the SUV filled his vision.

Lowering his aim, Caine sent another barrage into the driver's front tire. As the gun went empty, the rubber tire exploded. The vehicle lurched to the left, riding up and onto the sidewalk. Caine watched as the SUV crashed through the front window of a tiny art gallery. A confetti of sixties propaganda posters fluttered through the air as the vehicle careened into the building.

Caine heard a chorus of screams in front of the truck. Turning his head, he saw a crowd of pedestrians scatter as the vehicle plowed through a red tent. He raised his hands, protecting his face as the flapping canvas and metal poles battered his body. As they cleared the tent, he saw rows of blinking neon lights ahead, stretching over the street. They had entered another market. A stall in the middle of the street served fried dumplings to a crowd of locals and tourists.

Caine slammed his empty gun into the side of the truck. He saw Trina look over in the side mirror. Her jaw dropped.

'Turn!' he shouted. 'Turn right, now!'

The truck's tires squealed across the pavement as Trina spun the wheel. Caine flew back into the truck bed. He rolled across the floor, gasping for breath. His shoulder throbbed, and a bloody gash cut across his leg where the broken wood beams had torn through his pants.

Before he could assess his wounds, the chatter of gunfire tore through the air. Caine heard screams, and the surrounding crowd dispersed. Another black SUV screeched into the night market, roaring into position behind them.

Caine ducked as bullets whizzed past his ear. One of them thudded into a nearby canister. A rush of escaping gas blasted his face, and the metal cylinder flew out of the truck.

Caine glanced down at the empty pistol in his hand. The slide had racked back, and the trigger was dead. He tucked the useless weapon into his waistband and grabbed another canister. Then he peered through the shattered window that led into the cab.

'Get onto a side street,' he shouted. 'Try to shake them off!'

Trina looked back. 'What? I don't know where to—'

'Just give me a few minutes!'

The girl threw the wheel to the left, and the truck tore through a row of tents selling fresh seafood. A wall of glass tanks shattered, and murky green water sloshed across the hood of the truck. Trina shrieked as a swarm of crabs and lobsters flooded the cab. The angry crustaceans scurried across the seat as the vehicle skidded through the market.

Caine looked out the back of the truck. For the moment, they had lost their pursuer. But he knew that wouldn't last long. And the police would set up roadblocks soon. They would have to end this now if they hoped to escape the city.

He bent down and grabbed a canister, ignoring the pain lancing through his bruised shoulder. Grunting with exertion, he stacked the heavy tube on top of two more cylinders. He spun the canister around until the tiny release valve faced him and the bulbous end of the tank protruded from the rear of the flatbed.

Bright headlights pierced the shadows behind him. He raised his hand, shielding his eyes from the blinding light. The SUV had caught up with them. He saw another man lean out the rear window and aim his rifle.

Before the other man could fire, Caine grabbed a splintered wood beam running along the side of the truck and snapped it loose. Wielding the wooden beam like a club, he raised it up over his head. Then he swung it down with all his strength.

White-hot agony screamed through his shoulder as the wood connected with the end of the tank. With a loud metal clang, the blow tore off the release valve. Caine heard the whoosh of escaping gas as the canister shot out the back of the truck like a missile.

The flying metal cylinder struck the windshield of the pursuing vehicle, crumpling the bulletproof glass like a battering ram. The tinted glass panel dislodged and slammed into the driver's head. Caine grinned as he watched the man slump over the wheel. The SUV swerved sideways, tearing through a row of parked scooters. Then it flipped and rolled into a telephone pole. High-tension wires sparked and crackled as the crumpled vehicle fell to the ground.

Caine rubbed his aching shoulder. He sat down and looked into the cab. The girl's dark, frightened eyes darted up to the rearview mirror, meeting his gaze.

'Are you okay?' she asked.

'I'm fine, but we need to ditch this truck.'

'I know a place. It will take the police days to find it there.'

Caine nodded. 'Sounds good.'

'And after that?'

He narrowed his eyes, sizing her up as she turned the wheel and darted down another tiny side street. 'After that, we'd better go see your grandfather.'

'Is he in danger?' Her eyes were wide, and her voice quivered.

Caine winced as he shifted his weight and cradled his wounded shoulder. He leaned his head against the wall and closed his eyes. 'Yeah. I'd say he's definitely in danger.'

21

WASHINGTON DC, USA

Director Paulis peered through the crowd as he marched at a steady pace through the open-air fish market of the District Wharf. The air smelled of brine, smoke, and sweat, and a throng of bodies shoved around him on all sides. Most were making their way toward a long, brightly painted shack covered in neon signs.

Even in daylight, the bright lettering could be seen across the outdoor square. 'Seafood City! Jumbo crabs, cooked crabs!' Above the lettering, a cartoon sea captain gripped a ship's wheel and glowered at the crowd below. As the CIA director pushed his way past a group of teenagers plucking fried shrimp from a greasy paper cup, his bodyguards moved around him, shielding him from the crowd as best they could.

Each of his men was handpicked by the CIA's Security Bureau. Led by Mr. Curtis, they were all tall and muscular and moved with a quiet, athletic grace. They wore dark suits, and wraparound sunglasses covered their eyes. Their heads swiveled left and right as they scanned the nearby pedestrians for potential threats.

'Sir,' Curtis murmured into the director's ear. 'This area is impossible to secure with a team this size. I recommend we return to the car, and—'

Paulis raised his hand and continued pressing forward. 'I understand your concern, but sometimes the risk is worth the reward. Right now, I'm flying blind. And that's far more dangerous than a few tourists eating overpriced seafood.'

They continued walking across the square. The crowd thinned slightly as Paulis and his bodyguards turned onto a cobblestone street and headed southwest, toward the water. The air grew cooler, and salt stung Paulis's skin. Towering masts and white sails came into view, bobbing up and down in the distant gray water. 'Besides,' Paulis added, 'at my age, I'll take any excuse I can get for a stroll along the pier.'

They turned left, onto Wharf Street, heading away from the main pier. A few boats were docked to their right, and a pair of white gulls circled overhead. The late-afternoon sun sank lower on the horizon, and the atmosphere took on a still, electric tension, as if impatient to transition from day to night. Paulis glanced around and took a deep breath. Despite the tourists flocking to the wharf, the cool sea air and classic architecture made the spot one of his favorite retreats in the city.

As they walked away from the District Pier, they passed a gray stone-and-glass building that housed a popular oyster bar, a parking garage, and several smaller cafes. Paulis turned to his left, heading for the Recreation Pier. Unlike the other long, narrow docks, this one was curved, ending in a circular deck. A smaller dock curved off from the pier, where tourists could catch the Wharf Jitney, a water taxi that took passengers on sightseeing cruises around the area.

As he approached the Recreation Pier, Paulis spotted a pair of beefy men, dressed in similar clothes as his bodyguards, flanking the wood posts at the pier's entrance. Their eyes followed him as he walked closer, and he spotted the telltale bulges of pistols beneath their jackets. He was certain his men would notice those as well.

'Easy,' he murmured under his breath. 'We're all friends here.'

'I don't like it,' Curtis said, spitting out the words as if they left a sour taste in his mouth.

'I don't like it either,' Paulis replied. 'But you know how the song goes. We can't always get what we want...'

He approached the two men. They stepped into his path and smiled. The movement was slow and non-threatening, but the message was clear:

Stop. Go no further.

Paulis stopped. He sensed the tension in his men but raised his hands and spoke in a calm, level voice. 'Beautiful day, isn't it? Be a shame to spoil it.'

The two men smiled back at him. 'We're all friends here, sir. He's waiting for you at the torch.'

Paulis nodded. Before he could continue walking down the street, one of the guards put a hand on Curtis's shoulder. 'Just you,' he snapped to Paulis. 'The others can wait here.'

'Director—' Curtis snapped back, glaring at the man grabbing his shoulder.

'It's all right,' Paulis replied. 'Like the man said, we're all friends here. This won't take long.'

Curtis nodded, and Paulis continued down the pier on his own. His cane made a tapping sound on the gray wood slats as he left the other men behind. The calm water beneath the pier slapped against the wood with a slow, gentle rhythm. Ahead of him, a metal-and-stone sculpture sat in the center of the circular deck at the end of the pier. An orange flame flickered in the center of a twisted mass of gleaming steel. Known as the Torch, the metal rungs simulated the wood of a bonfire, and the gas-powered flame jetted up from the center of the sculpture. As the sun descended farther, the dancing flame glowed orange against the purple-and-gray sky.

A few cushioned benches surrounded the base of the sculpture. Most were empty, but a good-looking man in his early fifties sat alone with his back to the other piers. He wore a dark-blue trench coat over a gray suit and a crisp white shirt. His collar was unbuttoned, and he wore no tie. He looked up as Paulis approached, and the director noticed a cunning gleam in the man's eyes.

'Michael, good to see you!' The man held a greasy paper tray of fried clams in one hand and a toothpick in the other. He stabbed the pick into one of the doughy masses, holding the tray away from his clothes as a stream of juice squirted from the clam. Then he brought it to his mouth and chewed vigorously.

Paulis sat down next to him.

'Alex Maddison,' he said in a deep, slow voice. 'Been a few years since we last crossed paths. I suppose congratulations are in order.' He grimaced as he watched the new Director of National Intelligence swallow the clam then pick up a plastic cup of beer and take a sip.

As far as Paulis was concerned, Alex Maddison was appointed for purely political reasons, with little or no qualifications for the role. He was a former congressman who served on the House Intelligence Committee. Maddison's confirmation hearing was a bitter, partisan affair, split straight down party lines. Since replacing the missing and presumed dead John Blayne, the new DNI had mostly stayed out of the spotlight.

Maddison offered Paulis the tray of clams. 'You gotta try one of these,' he said, speaking between bites. 'Fuck Maine, Cape Cod, wherever. Nothing else comes close.'

Paulis glanced at the pool of grease surrounding the food in the tray. 'Just looking at that could give my cardiologist a heart attack.'

Alex chuckled and popped another clam in his mouth. 'You sure? The wharf is the oldest seafood market in the country. Been operating since 1805. They know what they're doing.'

Paulis shook his head, and Alex tossed the tray into a nearby trashcan. He leaned back and took another sip of beer. The two men gazed out over the sun-dappled water.

Paulis broke the silence first. 'I appreciate the meeting. So... You want to tell me what the hell is going on?'

Alex grinned. 'Kemper blindsided you at the hearing, didn't he?'

'You might say that.'

Maddison took another sip of beer. 'I want you to know I respect you, Director Paulis. You're a good man with a distinguished record of service to your country. That's why I wanted to talk to you alone, one on one. Consider it a professional courtesy.'

'I'll consider it whatever you like, as long as you can explain to me why the Senate Intelligence Committee is suddenly considering making deals with Walter Grissom.'

The DNI shook his head. 'Nothing sudden about it. Oldest story in the book, Michael. Corrupt politicians, dirty laundry, blackmail. It's business as usual, but now things are so bad, they don't even bother to hide it. It's out in the open for anyone to see.'

'Look, I know Grissom has dirt on some senators, but you can't expect me to—'

The DNI shook his head. 'You're thinking too small.'

Paulis gave him a quizzical look. 'Beg your pardon?'

Maddison lowered his voice. 'Grissom doesn't just have *some* dirt. He has *all* the dirt. Personal and professional. And not just on the senators.'

As the sun sank lower, the sky took on a deep blue cast. The dancing orange flame within the Torch lit the men's faces with a sinister crimson glow. 'Are you telling me the president is—'

Alex shook his head. 'No. I've managed to keep him out of this so far. That's the last thing we need. You remember right after the time you took over, that hacking scandal with the NSA?'

Paulis nodded. 'Of course. TANGENT and the mess in China. I filed several reports on that incident. The cyberattack was actually carried out by private individuals, using stolen NSA software to implicate a Chinese state-sponsored hacker. They weren't working with the MSS.'

Maddison glanced out over the water as one of the bright-blue Jitney boats buzzed by. 'Oh, I read your reports, Michael. Fascinating stuff. What was your asset's name again? The rogue SAD/SOG officer the FBI tried to take down in Louisiana?'

Paulis said nothing. Alex took another sip of beer. 'Well, we can discuss that later. Point is, whoever was behind it, the info was still hacked. And somehow, it ended up on the black market. Guess who acquired it?'

Paulis gritted his teeth. 'Walter Grissom.'

Alex looked him in the eye. 'It's not just about blackmail. All the dirt Grissom has on us? Illegal operations in China, unsanctioned killings, NOC personnel in the field... He's got the same thing on China's MSS.'

ACHERON, Paulis thought. He remembered the tiny fragment of data on Zavala's phone. Row after row of glowing green Chinese characters...

Paulis exhaled and leaned back on the bench. 'My God.'

Maddison cocked his head and smiled. 'Yep. Grissom's acquired enough dirt to reach critical mass. He's got leverage on the senators, plus enough embarrassing intel to tip the trade talks in our favor. Or in China's. Do you understand the kind of money we're talking about here?'

Paulis stared at the water in silence.

'The second I bring the president in on this,' Maddison continued, 'I can tell you exactly which way the hammer will fall. And you're not going to like it.'

'The Senate Intelligence Committee is recommending we give a known terrorist and international criminal immunity and safe passage into the country. At the taxpayers' expense, I might add. And you're keeping the president in the dark?'

'An old spymaster like you knows the value of plausible deniability,' Maddison replied. 'Grissom's got us all over a barrel. You know as well as I do, this is how things are done. America deals with enemies in two ways. Either we take them out, or we turn them into friends. Grissom is no worse than anyone else we've shared beds with lately.'

Paulis stood up and glared down at the DNI. 'The man turned Washington DC into a war zone. He deployed armed mercenaries less than a mile from the White House and assassinated a federal witness on US soil!'

Alex nodded. 'Right. At least, according to your report. But now the Senate Intel Committee has a whistleblower that calls your intel into question. Everything you just said has either been credibly refuted, or they've reframed your findings as some kind of personal vendetta against Grissom.'

Paulis shook his head. 'Whistleblower? You mean a compromised IG, someone Grissom already got to?'

The DNI stood and drained the last dregs of beer from his

cup. 'Most likely. But look at it from their point of view, Michael. If Grissom releases his intel to the press, a bunch of senators lose their careers, the trade deal with China crumbles, and America is publicly embarrassed. Everyone loses. Or we make peace with Grissom, and everybody wins.'

'Until the next time Grissom wants something. What happens then?'

The DNI shrugged. 'Guess that's a can they're willing to kick down the road.'

'He's responsible for the death of hundreds of people, Alex!' Paulis thundered.

Maddison glared back at him. 'The US makes deals with killers every day. They're just taking the path of least resistance.'

'Then they're cowards,' Paulis snapped.

Maddison shrugged. 'No, they're politicians, but that's splitting hairs. What do you expect?'

Paulis sighed. He looked Alex in the eye as the man tossed his empty plastic cup into the trash. 'Fine. So what if I put a little resistance in their path?'

Maddison grinned. 'Now you're thinking like one of them.'

'God help me.'

'What kind of resistance are we talking here?'

'Grissom's operation has a leak, and I have a man in the field. If he can retrieve the intel first, we take it out of play. I'll deliver it right into your hands. Then you can let the president decide what he wants to do with it.'

Maddison thought for a moment. 'Personally, that would be my preference. That way, the president's free of political entanglements with those vultures on the hill. Do you have a lead? We don't have much time.'

'How much time?' Paulis demanded in a low voice.

Maddison turned and began walking back toward the street.

'I can give you forty-eight hours,' he called over his shoulder. 'After that, the president will weigh in on the committee's recommendation before the Chinese leave these trade talks for good.'

'Alex...' Paulis shouted. The DNI spun around to face him, his dark coat fluttering in the sea breeze. 'Why are you telling me all this?' Paulis asked. 'You're hardly what I'd call a maverick. I figured you'd side with the senators on this.'

The man shrugged. 'Me? Oh, I'm just a survivor, Michael. When it comes to politics, there's only one side... mine.'

He turned and ambled away. 'Get me something I can bring to the president in forty-eight hours, Michael. Or I'll shut your operation down.'

As the sky darkened, the towering jet of flame burned brighter. Paulis felt the heat of the fire against his back. The warmth was comforting, a shield against the cool night wind whipping across the river.

That's how you get burned. First, everything's nice and toasty. Then, before you know it, your feet are in the fire...

22

SOCIALIST REPUBLIC OF VIETNAM

After leaving Hanoi, Trina guided Caine to a secluded dirt road, little more than a path carved through the dense leaves and vegetation. The winding trail led to a reed-choked stretch of water, a tributary of the nearby Red River. Caine pushed the battered truck off the trail into the deep water, watching the surface bubble and churn as the vehicle sank out of view. He doubted it would remain hidden for long. He just hoped it would stay submerged long enough to avoid notice for a few days, enough time to put some distance between themselves and the city.

Trina used Caine's burner phone and placed a call to a friend. An hour later, a surly-looking man in his twenties showed up, wearing a sleeveless T-shirt and baggy jeans. His hair was swept up in a short mohawk, and black tattoos covered his arms. Caine watched as the two argued in Vietnamese. Finally, the angry man tossed her the keys to his car, a white Honda City sedan. Mud and dirt flecked the paint of the four-door vehicle, and Caine knew the common sedan would attract little attention on the road.

'That your boyfriend?' Caine asked her as they sped away, leaving the scowling young man standing next to the river.

Trina reclined her seat and closed her eyes. 'His name is Vinh, and that's none of your business,' she muttered.

Caine glanced over at her. 'It's both our business if the police stop us. Are you sure this car isn't stolen?'

She shook her head. 'Vinh's not a car thief. He's a chemistry student. I know him from school. Besides, this is the best I can do. I wasn't planning to flee the city tonight, được?'

'Really? He doesn't look like a chemistry student.'

Trina turned her head and looked Caine up and down. 'Yeah? Well, you don't look like a cop.'

'I'm not a cop.'

She narrowed her eyes. 'Then what are you? What are you doing here, and how did you know those men were after me?'

Caine thought for a moment. 'It's complicated. Let's just say you were lucky I was there.'

Trina sat up straight. 'Look, let's get one thing straight. I appreciate you helping me out back there, but I don't know you, and I don't owe you, got it?'

Caine nodded. 'Got it.'

She took a deep breath. 'Good. Now, who were those assholes anyway? What do they want with my grandfather?'

Caine thought for a moment as they turned back onto the main road. He wondered how much he should tell her. The more she knew, the more danger she would be in. But despite his best efforts, the Blackwing thugs back in Hanoi had seen her face. She was a target now, regardless.

'Your grandfather contacted a banker in Singapore named Andrew Seng.'

She stared at him and blinked. 'Never heard of him. My

grandfather can barely afford groceries. What would he want with a banker?'

Caine gripped the wheel in his hands. 'Look, all I can tell you is, someone went to great lengths to make sure Seng couldn't talk. And they followed his trail back to you...'

'Which means they could be looking for my grandfather next?'

Caine nodded. 'Exactly.'

Trina exhaled, blowing her long strand of blonde hair out of her face. She tucked it behind her ear and slumped in her seat. 'This must have to do with Sam.'

Caine raised an eyebrow and shot her a suspicious glance. 'Sam?'

She closed her eyes. 'Old white guy, American. He and my grandfather go back to the war. The guy's shady, it's obvious to me. But my grandfather says he owes him. Some kind of old debt. Ancient history.'

'What's this Sam look like?' Caine asked.

The girl sighed. 'I don't know. Like I said, old. White.'

Caine grinned. 'Old and white, like me?'

She closed her eyes and rested her head on the seat. 'No, old. Like, really old. Fucking *xưa*, man.'

'Well, maybe this Sam will know more about what's going on.'

'Maybe,' she said, her voice low and heavy with exhaustion. 'My grandfather lives in Ha Tinh province. It's south on the 1A. Just get to...'

Her voice faded to a murmur then silence. Caine looked over at her. Her eyes were closed, and her mouth hung open. He could hear her soft breathing over the buzz of the car's engine and the steady rhythm of the tires thumping against the road.

Adrenaline rush. When the backlash hits, it hits hard.

He drove in silence, letting her sleep a bit. The skies above shifted from bleak gray to the purple velvet of night. The tiny car sped along, vanishing into the shady depths of the countryside.

* * *

Caine wiped sweat from his brow as he drove through the dark, humid night. A warm breeze drifted through the window, rustling his sweat-soaked hair. The night air smelled damp and salty. For a while, the southern road followed the serpentine curves of the Song Nghen River, a narrow, snake-like ribbon of muddy brown water. And a few miles to the east, Caine knew the dark waves of the South China Sea lapped against the sands of Cua Lo and Bai Bien beaches.

But now they were inland. The street was a narrow stretch of rough pavement, surrounded on either side by dense, shadowy jungle and vast plains of tall grass. Billowing gray clouds filled the sky above. He could barely see the hazy outline of the moon behind the wispy dark curtain, and the hazy air snuffed out the stars.

A soft, quiet sound broke the monotonous thud of the tires against the road. The white noise of static. Caine glanced down at the seat... A red light flickered on the walkie he had taken from the man on the island.

He grabbed it and used his teeth to rotate the dial on top to the next channel. The static was replaced with a soft crackling... a live channel.

He held the walkie in one hand, listening as he drove through the gloomy night.

'That you, Tom? You there?' a voice drawled.

Caine was silent. A low chuckle, disrupted by the bad connection, came from the tiny speaker. 'Yeah, you're listening. I can tell. I could always read you like a book.'

Caine debated replying to the transmission. It was possible, though unlikely, that his enemies had set up a network of antennas to triangulate the walkie's signal. But unless they knew his route in advance, he doubted they would have had time to position receivers in the miles of dense jungle surrounding him.

He depressed the talk button. 'Hello, Riley.'

'Told you I'd see you again, Tom. You weren't expecting it to be so soon, huh?'

'Too soon,' Caine said, his voice cold as ice. He looked down, making sure Trina was still asleep. She moaned and shifted her head.

'That hurts. After all this time, I was hoping we could put the past behind us.'

'I already have, Boone. It's dead and buried. Just like you.'

'We're both ghosts, my friend. Dead to the world. Or maybe it's more accurate to say the world is dead to us. It doesn't want us back, buddy. We don't belong out there.'

Caine stared ahead, peering into the shadows behind the car's headlights. 'Speak for yourself.'

'You had a change of heart, huh? Back on the inside? We'll see how long that lasts.'

The girl's head slid down in her seat, and she rolled away from him. Another soft groan escaped her lips.

'What do you mean?' Caine asked, lowering his voice.

'I mean you and me... we're wolves. You can try to live among the sheep all you want, but we'll never be one of them. And the sheep know it. Sooner or later, they'll get tired of having you around. They'll kick you out of your warm, comfy doghouse. Send you back out in the cold and the rain... Back with me.'

'Sounds like you need to ask Grissom for a pay raise.'

A slow, deep chuckle crackled over the radio. 'Glad to see you've developed a sense of humor over the years. Jack must have rubbed off on you. Too bad about poor old Jack. Guess he didn't get the memo after you left me to burn. He made the same mistake I did... He trusted you to pull his ass out of the fire.'

'We all made the same mistake, Riley... We worked for Grissom and Bernatto.'

'Look, Tom, much as I'm enjoying this trip down memory lane, I've got a job to do. And I'm gonna make this easy on you for old times' sake. Give us the girl. Drop her off at a hotel or a gas station, anywhere. Give me an address, and I'll pick her up. Just walk away, buddy. Fire and forget. I'll take care of the rest. You can go settle down with that redhead who took Bernatto's job. What was her name again? Beautiful girl...'

Caine triggered the walkie but said nothing. The words seem to catch in his throat at the mention of Rebecca. He released the switch.

'I saw her, you know,' Boone continued. 'Back in DC, when I took out that NSA rat. I had her in my crosshairs. So close I could reach out and touch her, know what I mean? I know you understand. How it feels when you have prey in your sights. No wind, no drift. I could count the freckles on her nose, and she didn't even know I was there. Just a tiny bit more pressure on the trigger and... Hell, it's the closest thing in this world to perfection. But I didn't take the shot. I let her live. I gave her to you, Tom. So how about you return the favor?'

Caine's jaw clenched. His knuckles were white as he gripped the walkie tighter.

'You're thinking about it, aren't you,' the voice continued. 'Come on, I know you want another piece of that—'

Caine pushed the talk button and interrupted him. 'I was thinking about the last time I saw you. Thinking I should have gone back to check.'

'Aww, you wish you helped me get out of that building before it went up in flames? I'm touched, brother. You're getting me all misty-eyed here.'

Caine triggered the walkie again. 'I wish I went back and made sure you burned to a crisp.'

Boone laughed. 'I bet you did. You hightailed it out of there so fast, you forgot to confirm your kill. Rookie mistake.'

'I saw the explosion. How did you survive?'

'Trash chute. Managed to climb maybe a quarter of the way down before I felt the flames on my back. Blacked out after that, but the chute must have slowed my fall. Broke my hip, my right arm. Hurt like hell, but that was nothing compared to what the Chinese MSS did when they found me in the garage. I'll tell you all about it next time I see you.'

Caine held the walkie close to his lips. 'The next time I see you will be the last time. Count on it.'

'Heh... We'll see, Tom. You never had a taste for the messy stuff. Just give me the girl, and no one else has to get hurt.'

'Go fuck yourself, Boone.'

Caine turned off the walkie and tossed it down on the seat. Trina sat up and rubbed her eyes. She yawned then looked over at him through half-closed eyes. 'Did you say something?'

Caine kept his eyes on the road and tightened his grip on the wheel. 'No.'

She brushed her bangs from her face and peered out the window. A sliver of orange fire rose on the horizon, casting a faint glow over the rice fields and distant mountains. 'What time is it?'

'Near dawn,' Caine said, guiding the car down the dark, winding road.

She nodded and closed her eyes again. 'Good. We're almost there. Almost home.'

Within moments, she fell asleep once more.

Almost home, Caine thought. The words had an ominous ring to them. He pressed the accelerator. The car roared ahead, speeding faster toward the distant glow of the horizon.

23

GENEVA, SWITZERLAND

Walter Grissom leaned back in his chair and took a puff of a thick hand-rolled cigar. Made by Gurkha Cigars, the tobacco was a blend of Dominican and Cameroon varieties. The dried leaf wrapper was a five-year-old Connecticut Broadleaf Maduro. Grissom glanced down at the cigar and nodded with satisfaction. Known as a Black Dragon, the smoke left a rich, earthy taste in his mouth, finishing with notes of sweet spice. A single Black Dragon cost over a thousand US dollars, and Grissom kept a humidor full of the cigars next to his desk.

He took another puff then sipped some Cognac Gautier from a crystal tumbler. The carved facets of the glass twinkled in the dim light, giving the reddish-brown liquid inside a warm amber glow.

Expensive extravagance. But then again, sometimes you get what you pay for.

His office occupied a loft overlooking the grand foyer downstairs. Decorated in stained wood and leather furniture, with a row of taxidermy animal heads lining the far wall, the room had a rustic, masculine feel. A few glass display cases stood between his desk and the door, containing dried bugs, tribal crafts, and other curiosities acquired from his expeditions around the world.

Grissom took another puff of his cigar then blew a trail of smoke up at the ceiling. His melancholy gaze traveled over the grisly trophies lining the room. The animals' glassy, lifeless eyes glared down at him in mute rage – a snarling tiger, a grinning hyena, and a magnificent horned black rhino. And in the center of the wall, a thick-maned African lion reigned supreme.

The king of the beasts, Grissom thought. The animal's gaping maw hung frozen in an eternal snarl, and its ivory teeth glistened in the dim light.

'Don't feel bad, sport,' Grissom muttered. He set his cigar on an ashtray and rose from his chair. After grabbing the cognac, he meandered through the rows of glass cases and stood before the lion's head. He raised his drink in a toast. 'Sooner or later, it happens to the best of us. But you had a good run.'

A knock sounded on the door.

'Enter,' Grissom shouted.

The door creaked open, and Karl entered. The tall, muscular man wore a thick gray roll-neck sweater and dark flannel trousers. He carried a satellite phone in his good hand. 'Mr. Grissom, I believe you were waiting for this call?'

The squat older man nodded and ran his fingers through his wispy white hair. 'Hell yeah, I was. Beginning to think the boy forgot whose payroll he's on.'

Karl gave a brief bow and held out the phone. Grissom took it and cupped his hand over the mouthpiece. 'You can go now, Karl. Appreciate it.'

The towering blond man gave another quick bow then left the room, shutting the door quietly behind him.

'Boone, good to hear from you, son,' Grissom grunted into the phone. 'Hope you have some good news for me.'

'Negative, sir,' Boone Riley's voice crackled back. 'Those Axion fuckups managed to shoot up half of Hanoi, but they missed the target.'

Grissom chuckled and took another sip of cognac. 'Well, don't be too hard on the boys. Caine's managed to piss off just about every paramilitary force in the world, and the son of a bitch is still breathing. Where are our men now?'

'I kept a few key personnel I could trust here. Sent the rest out of the country.'

Grissom nodded. 'Understood. And what about this asset? Seng's contact?'

'A woman was seen leaving Hanoi with Caine. We hacked into the area's traffic cam network, and they caught a shot of her. Running it through facial-recognition software now. But Mr. Grissom... After what happened at Long Bay and the lake, I think we're going to need local help on this one. Anything else will attract too much attention.'

Grissom took another sip of cognac. 'Agreed. I have a contact, someone who owes me a favor. I'll send you his information. Maybe it's about time you pay him a visit before...'

His voice trailed off. He blinked as the image of the snarling lion's head grew blurry and dark. He could hear Boone speaking, but the man's voice sounded faint and distorted, as if he was shouting from the end of a long tunnel.

'Sir? Are you there? Can you hear me?'

The words echoed through his mind as the shadows in his peripheral vision closed in. He felt faint, light-headed... He was stumbling, falling... The lion's snarling maw loomed before him. The beast's eyes glinted with predatory hunger.

Everything went dark. Grissom heard Boone shouting

through the phone, but the words sounded slow and distorted. Grissom was simply gone, adrift in a void, barely capable of conscious thought. Time seemed to slow down then stop utterly. He heard a growl then a roar. The sound rumbled in the pit of his stomach, flooding his body with adrenaline-fueled dread.

Then there was no sound at all. He was alone in utter blackness. Drifting... Falling...

A tiny pinpoint of light appeared. Thought and sensation came rushing back. He felt pain... His head hurt. His shirt was cold and wet. He tasted something salty in his mouth. He blinked, and his vision cleared.

He was looking up at the rafters in the vaulted ceiling overhead. Boone's voice crackled through the sat phone's speaker again. The phone lay on the floor, a few feet away from him.

Grissom groaned as he picked himself up. His shirt was damp and stank of cognac.

'God damn it,' he muttered to himself. 'One hundred dollars a glass, and I go and spill it on myself.'

He took a deep breath, steadying himself on a wood support column that rose from the floor. When the haze in his mind cleared and his breathing returned to normal, he bent over and grabbed the phone.

'Boone,' he wheezed, cutting off the other man's frantic shouting. 'Boone, it's all right. I'm here.'

There was a pause on the other end of the line. 'It happened again, sir. Didn't it?'

'What the hell do you think?' Grissom snapped.

'How long?' Boone asked. 'How much time do we have?'

'Enough,' the older man grunted. 'If we play our cards right. Now, as I was saying, I know a certain colonel in the special forces over there. We helped him move some cargo across the border that... Well, let's just say I doubt his superiors would approve. He owes us. Owes me, anyway.'

'Sounds perfect, sir. I'll reach out to your contact as soon as we have the info.'

'You do that. And Boone, if Caine gets in your way again...'

'Oh, I'll be seeing him again, sir. Count on it.'

Grissom nodded. 'Well, you know what to do.'

He hung up the phone, stumbled to his desk, and fell into his chair. Then he slid open a drawer and removed a small plastic pill bottle. He popped the cap, shook two pills into his hand, and tossed them into his mouth. He swallowed them dry. His glazed eyes once again examined his wall of trophies. The animal heads stared down at him, silent stares of beastly rage frozen on their faces.

He locked eyes with the lion. 'Like I said, King. You had a good run. But sooner or later, it comes for us all.'

He grabbed his cigar, pleased to see it was still lit. He narrowed his eyes as he took a puff. Then he exhaled, breathing a long stream of smoke toward the ceiling. 'But don't you worry. I plan to go out on my own terms.'

He continued puffing on the cigar until a thin gray haze hovered above the dead menagerie mounted to the wall.

24

HANOI, SOCIALIST REPUBLIC OF VIETNAM

Lt. Colonel Tranh Nguyen of the People's Army of Vietnam closed his eyes and grinned from ear to ear. The delicate fingers of the girl next to him in bed caressed his bare chest, her nails circling across his skin in slow motion. His shirt lay in a crumpled heap on the hotel room floor, next to his pants. Sweat glistened on his skin and plastered his thinning gray hair to his scalp. They had turned off the AC in the room, and the window was open. A ceiling fan spun overhead, circulating the languid air through the luxurious suite.

'Tốt quá, em yêu,' the girl whispered in his ear. 'So good, baby...'

Tranh sighed. 'I can't feel my toes. Where you learn to do that?'

The girl laughed and slid out of bed. Tranh turned his head, watching the silhouette of her slim, naked body cross in front of the window. Behind her, the neon lights of Hanoi twinkled in the haze.

'Hey, I pay for longer!' he said, propping himself on the bed by his elbows. The girl draped a silk robe over her shoulders and belted it at the waist. The shimmering red fabric hugged the tiny curves of her firm, pert body. Her inky-black hair cascaded down her back like a waterfall. Tranh found himself unable to tear his eyes away from her as she padded toward the door.

'Relax, baby. I order some food, room service.'

Tranh stood up and stretched. He glanced down, noting with some pride that his gut only partially obscured his toes. He grabbed his pants and stuck one leg in. 'I'm not hungry,' he said with a yawn. 'Not for food, anyway.'

'You need to keep your strength up, I think.'

Tranh grabbed a tiny blue pill sitting on the nightstand and tossed it in his mouth. He swallowed it down then took a sip of warm beer from a bottle of Tiger. 'Not with this, I don't. Get back here, *người yêu*.' He drank more beer and glanced at the bright lights outside the window. As a high-ranking officer in Vietnam's Special Operations Group, he had some latitude when it came to reporting back to the base. But he couldn't stay away forever. Eventually, his men could no longer cover for his absence. He wanted to make the most of the time he had.

He turned to the dark hallway that led to the door. The girl was nowhere in sight.

'Hey, is the food here or not? Come on, I'm ready to go, baby!'

A deep, guttural laugh echoed through the room. 'Oh, I bet you are...'

It was a man's voice.

Tranh jammed his other leg into the pants and spun around. He yanked open the nightstand drawer. Inside, a pistol lay next to a Catholic Bible. But before his fingers could close around the butt of the gun, he felt powerful arms grab him from behind. Two men in dark clothes exploded into the room.

An arm looped around his throat, and his attacker dragged him away from the gun.

As he struggled to break free, he felt the butt of a rifle crack against his chin. He fell back onto the bed, blinking as blood streamed from his mouth. Then he heard a familiar clicking sound... the charging handle of a rifle being pulled back.

A tall, muscular man stepped into the room. He wore baggy khaki cargo pants and a thin gray T-shirt that stretched over his broad shoulders. His hair was cut military short, and dark sunglasses covered his eyes. He cradled a Galil assault rifle in a loose two-handed grip.

Tranh stared up at him in shock as the man stepped over to the bed. He struggled to get up, but the two other men pinned his arms to the mattress.

'You dead!' he hissed. 'You know who I am? I kill your—'

Releasing the barrel of the rifle with one hand, the man held his fingers up to his lips.

'Shhhhhh...' he said. He pulled off his sunglasses and regarded Tranh with a pair of obsidian eyes. One of them twitched slightly. He turned to the men holding Tranh. 'Let him go.'

The men released their grip, and Tranh leapt to his feet. He charged toward the rifle-toting man and raised his fist. But before he could strike, his target ducked and snapped the rifle up, slamming the stock into his jaw again. Despite his size and age, he moved faster than Tranh's eyes could follow.

The big man lashed out with a low punch. Tranh grunted as he felt a blow thud into his kidneys. He bent over, coughing and gasping in pain.

'Good, you got that out of your system. Now sit down, shut up, and listen to the grown-ups talk.'

Another man grabbed a chair and set it on the floor in front of the bed. Then he slid a laptop from his backpack and set it on the chair. He opened the lid, and it powered up. An image faded in on the screen.

It was a man's face, blurred by an electronic masking filter. Tranh could make out soft, baby-blue eyes and white hair. But he couldn't pinpoint the man's exact age or appearance through the blurry haze.

'Lt. Colonel Tranh. You're a hard man to get a hold of. Guess those drug runners on the border must keep you busy.' The voice was slow and relaxed, with a trace of a Southern accent. 'Course, seeing as I helped you out with that Laos thing last year, I thought you might be more amenable to taking my call.'

Tranh's eyes went wide. 'It's... It's you!'

'Yeah, it's me. Apologies for the scrambler, but these days, you never know who's listening. Or rather, I should say, you always know who's listening. Everyone. Now, as for the surly gentleman holding the gun? That's Boone Riley. Consider him my official representative. Hope we didn't catch you at a bad time?'

Tranh's eyes opened wide as he stared at the screen. He stopped struggling and looked up at the man named Boone. 'The girl... you—'

'Hey, Tranh,' the blurry face on the screen snapped. 'Eyes front. Mr. Riley may be holding the gun, but make no mistake – it's my finger on the trigger.'

'What... What do you want?' the Vietnamese man stuttered.

The blurred face chuckled. 'That sounds like a much more constructive attitude. What do I want? Well, way I see it, the intel I've given to you over the years has made you a rich man, powerful in your own little neck of the woods. But everything has a price, Tranh. And now it's time for you to pay the piper. I need a favor.'

'Favor?' Tranh looked up at Boone, but the man's granite features betrayed no emotion. Tranh's eyes darted back to the screen. 'What kind of favor?'

'Manpower. There's a dangerous foreign agent loose in your country, Tranh. And I need you to help me catch him. See? This will be good for both of us.'

'But how...' Again, the man's terrified eyes darted to the rifle-toting Boone. 'I mean, what do you—'

'Christ, Tranh, do I have to spell it out for you? I need a hunting party. You're a high-ranking officer in TC2, your beautiful little country's military and domestic intelligence service. That gives you the direct authority to deploy a team from your so-called Special Reconnaissance Unit, isn't that right? Or did I get my hopes up for nothing?'

'Yes, but you must understand, I can't—'

'Oh, you can't? I see. Well, sorry for the inconvenience, friend. Course, if you can't help me, there's really no point in continuing this conversation, is there? Wouldn't want to waste your precious time and all. What's left of it, anyway.'

The men tightened their grip and threw the military officer back on the bed. Boone raised the rifle and flicked a tiny switch near the guard. A dot of red light drifted along the bed. The crimson laser traced a glowing path across Tranh's chest and neck. He could see motes of dust swirling through the brilliant beam as the dot settled on his forehead.

'You might want to rethink your answer, Colonel Tranh,' Boone hissed.

Tranh struggled to raise his head, but one of Boone's men clamped a gloved hand on his forehead and slammed it back down. With a loud thud, the back of his skull slammed into the headboard.

'Okay, okay! Whatever you want! I get you men, weapons, whatever you want!' the man sputtered, his voice rising in pitch.

'Oh? So you can help me? Well, ain't that a peach. Appreciate it, Tranh. I'll leave you with Boone here to settle the details. And don't worry... I'll be in touch.'

The screen went dark. Boone lowered the rifle and gestured to the men. They released their hold on Tranh. The man rolled off the bed and fell to his hands and knees. He shuddered then vomited on the floor.

Boone laughed. 'Jeez, Tranh, thought you were some kind of hard-ass. Here.' He tossed an iPad on the bed. 'There's a list of what we need. The file will erase itself in ten minutes, so memorize it and get cracking. I'll send you coordinates tomorrow at 6 a.m. Got it?'

Tranh staggered to his feet. His skin was pale, and his legs quivered. 'Okay, fine. Just go. Leave me alone.'

Boone slung his rifle over his shoulder. 'We're leaving. But if you tell anyone about our little meeting, I'm afraid I'll have to visit again. And next time, things won't be so friendly.'

Tranh nodded. 'I understand.'

Boone's eyes twinkled in the dim light. 'Have a lovely evening, Colonel.' His gaze darted down to the man's groin, and he cracked a smile. 'Sorry to make you waste your little blue pill.'

He turned and followed the other men out the door.

Tranh collapsed on the bed as they slammed the door behind them. He knew Grissom was not someone he wanted to cross. But this other man, Boone... Looking into those pitch-black eyes had been like staring death in the face. Another shiver ran through his body. He grabbed his cell phone off the nightstand and dialed a number.

It took his shaking fingers three tries to get it right.

25

It was early morning when the tiny winding road curved out from the dense jungle and hugged the shore of the Eastern Sea. Dark, slate-gray water stretched as far as the eyes could see, and the blazing orb of the sun peeked above the distant horizon. The sky overhead was a mural of purple and orange fire, painted across rolling gray clouds.

Trina shifted in her seat. She raised her head and rubbed the sleep from her eyes then peered out the window. They motored past a street sign mounted on a crooked metal pole.

'Ha Tinh Province,' she said, reading the characters on the sign. 'We're almost there. Take the next right.'

Caine nodded. He scanned the horizon. A few rotting wood piers stretched off into the water, but they were mostly empty. The few boats docked there listed in the water. Faded but colorful paint peeled off their barnacle-crusted hulls.

'This where you grew up?' he asked.

She nodded. 'My parents were from Saigon, but they died when I was very young. Car accident. My grandfather raised me himself, pretty much.'

She sighed, glancing at the water as they sped past the old boats. 'It used to be beautiful here. The fishermen painted the boats all these bright colors, and the water looked like blue glass. My grandfather made a good living as a fisherman, and he'd take me out with him on the water. Then they built that.'

She pointed out the window. Caine narrowed his eyes and peered through the haze. A white-and-red smokestack rose from a sprawling industrial complex. The buildings looked out of place nestled among the green hills and sand dunes of the coast.

'The Formosa Steel plant,' Caine said, eying the plume of white smoke billowing from the building. 'I remember seeing that on the news. Some kind of ecological disaster?'

She made a clicking sound with her teeth. 'Yeah... As soon as the plant went active, the fishermen started complaining. Each year, the haul got worse. Some locals protested, but the Chinese had invested hundreds of millions of dollars in the plant.'

'And I'm sure the local government took their cut,' Caine said as they turned off the road and left the ocean view behind.

Trina glanced at the billowing smokestack in the rearview mirror.

'Maybe. All I know is people who complained tended to disappear. Then, a few years ago, things got so bad the government couldn't hide it anymore. Millions of dead fish washed up on the beaches. It decimated the fishing industry here. Turned out an underwater pipe had ruptured. It dumped millions of gallons of industrial waste into the ocean. Cyanide, arsenic, iron hydroxide... The spill killed off the fish in four provinces. They even linked it to some swimmer and diving deaths. Not to mention the people who had been eating all that fish for the last year... Wasn't exactly great for tourism. The Vietnamese government ordered the Chinese to pay half a billion dollars in damages, but they let the plant stay open.'

Caine navigated the tiny car down a dirt road that cut between a pair of lush green fields. 'How much of that money made it back into the locals' pockets?' he asked.

The girl laughed bitterly. 'See for yourself.'

As they wound their way through the village, Caine understood what she meant. The buildings lining the dirt road were a far cry from the quaint, well-kept structures in the city. Most of the homes here were little more than shacks. Bundles of straw covered holes in the sloped wooden roofs, and their walls were held together with nails, twine, and whatever else the locals could scavenge.

An emaciated cow grazed on weeds in the front yard of one of the tiny houses. The animal's ribs jutted beneath its mangy fur, and a cluster of flies hovered near its tail.

Following Trina's directions, Caine maneuvered down a series of paths, most barely wide enough to accommodate the tiny vehicle. Finally, they stopped in front of one of the larger homes in the village.

The shack was in better shape than the others. Its roof seemed intact, and a fresh coat of green paint covered its walls. Red wood shutters blocked the windows in front, and a screen door led to a small front porch.

Caine parked and stepped out of the car. He closed the door as quietly as possible. His piercing green eyes swept the fields in the distance. Next to the house, a cluster of reeds and vines clung to the rotting hull of an old fishing boat. The wreckage was propped up on cinder blocks, and an enormous hole pierced the side of the collapsed watercraft.

'That your grandfather's boat?'

Trina stretched and yawned. 'Yeah. He used to take me out

on that old boat every day. Then a tropical storm knocked it into the pier. Tore a hole through the side. After the fishing money dried up, he couldn't afford to fix it.'

'What's your grandfather's name?'

'Nhan. Nhan Thien. Come on, I'll introduce you.'

He followed her toward the screened porch. As they neared the house, a whooping cough echoed from inside. Trina pursed her lips and furrowed her brow. 'He sounds worse,' she said in a quiet voice.

Caine didn't know if she was speaking to him or just thinking out loud. He said nothing in reply.

She knocked on the door. 'Grandfather? It's me, Trina.'

'It's open,' a voice croaked back.

Trina swung open the screen door and stepped inside. The interior of the house was dim. The musty air inside had a vaguely pungent smell, a mix of spices and menthol. To Caine, something about the still, dusty air reeked of age and death.

The floorboards creaked beneath their feet as they entered a cramped sitting room. A pair of rattan chairs flanked a battered coffee table, and an old futon lay folded against the wall.

A low shelf ran along the opposite wall, and old pictures in wooden frames stood on the narrow wood beam. Caine walked closer and picked one up. It was a black-and-white photo of a Vietnamese soldier in his twenties wearing a mud-stained military uniform.

Another picture on the shelf showed the same man but older, in his forties. He stood next to a beautiful young woman with brown, almond-shaped eyes and shoulder-length dark hair. She wore an *áo dài*, a traditional Vietnamese tunic, over loose pants. Colorful embroidery of birds and flowers adorned the front of her dress. The beaming woman cradled an infant in her arms.

'I'm in here,' the old man croaked again, his voice echoing from a dark, narrow corridor.

Caine set down the picture and followed Trina through the house. She opened a door at the end of the hall. Sunlight spilled into the cramped, dim corridor.

An old Vietnamese man sat in a chair, facing an open window. His face was a tapestry of wrinkled, leathery skin, and wisps of white hair covered his head. He held a cigarette in a trembling grip. He smiled, and Caine saw that despite his age and apparent illness, his teeth were still strong and white.

'Ah, Trina. Good to see you. *Rất vui được gặp con.*'

'Grandfather, what are you doing?' Trina stormed into the room and yanked the cigarette from the man's hand.

He shook his head and muttered a curse under his breath as she stubbed it out on the windowsill.

'It's just one little cigarette. What difference does it—'

'What difference does it make? You have to take better care of yourself, *ông nội*!' Caine watched as she helped the old man out of the chair and led him back to his bed. Nhan's dark, sunken eyes peered up at him as he lay down in bed. Trina followed his gaze.

'Grandfather, this is—'

'I know who he is,' her grandfather snapped, closing his eyes. 'His name is Caine.'

Caine stiffened. 'Who told you that?' he asked.

'Him,' the old man replied, nodding to the door.

Caine spun around. A shadowy figure stood in the corridor behind him. The man stepped into the light, and Caine stared into a pair of dark, beady eyes. Rectangular steel-framed glasses perched on the man's nose above a frowning, thin-lipped mouth.

Allan Bernatto.

'Hello, Tom. I figured Paulis would send you.'

Caine drew his pistol from his waistband. Trina screamed and grabbed his shoulder as he aimed the weapon. 'Tom, what the hell are—'

The roar of gunfire drowned out the rest of her words as Caine pulled the trigger three times.

26

Bernatto spun in the hallway as the first shot slammed into his shoulder. The weight of the girl on Caine's arm dragged his aim to the right, and the remaining shots thudded into the wall at the end of the corridor. The slugs gouged ragged holes in the drywall and threw plaster dust into the air.

Caine shook Trina off his arm and charged forward, sprinting down the hall toward the injured man. He snarled in fury as Bernatto staggered away from him.

The older man raised an arm. Caine glimpsed a metal canister in his fingers...

Pepper spray or mace.

Before Bernatto could depress the red button on top of the can, Caine's forearm pressed into his throat. Using his weight and momentum, Caine slammed the older man's back against the wall. He grabbed Bernatto's wrist with his left hand and twisted back, hard. With a loud hiss, a jet of mist exploded from the can. Caine squinted as the burning mist stung his eyes and nostrils. The thick white haze expanded quickly, filling the narrow hallway behind them.

Caine dragged Bernatto along the wall until they staggered into the sitting room. He swung his right arm down, slamming the butt of his pistol into the older man's wrist. Bernatto yelped in pain, and the metal canister fell from his fingers. It clattered to the floor, and Caine kicked it away.

Bernatto threw a punch with his free arm, but Caine easily dodged the feeble attack. He jerked Bernatto's arm up and behind him as he stomped the back of his knee.

The older man dropped to the floor, and his glasses skittered away. Caine kicked him in the side, sending him scurrying across the carpet. Bernatto rolled to a stop. His hands patted the floor, searching for the canister of mace.

Caine raised his pistol. 'Don't,' he growled.

Bernatto froze. 'Tom, wait! Before—'

'No more deals, Allan. Not after Josh.'

'If you kill me, Grissom wins. I'm the asset, dammit! I'm Larkspur!'

'Don't care. Goodbye, Allan.'

Before Caine could pull the trigger, an explosion boomed through the tiny room. He ducked as bits of plaster and wood rained down on his head. Caine spun around, aiming his pistol down the corridor.

A stooped figure limped out of the mist-shrouded hallway. It was Trina's grandfather, Nhan Thien. He held a smoking shotgun in a shaky two-handed grip. 'That's enough,' he wheezed. 'No fighting in my house.'

Caine glanced over the man's shoulder. Trina stumbled behind him, coughing and gagging as she stepped through the cloud of acrid mist.

'What the...' She rubbed her eyes, and tears streamed down her cheeks. She squinted at the old man lying on the floor. 'Sam, is that you? What the hell are you doing here?'

Caine returned Nhan's stare but kept his gun aimed at Bernatto. 'Sam? This is Sam?'

'Yes,' Trina said. 'Tom, please, this is—'

'His real name is Allan Bernatto,' Caine snapped. 'Whatever he's told you, it's a lie. He's put you both in danger just by being here.'

'I know who he is,' Nhan said. 'Put down gun. Then we talk.'

Bernatto grabbed his glasses and put them back on. A tiny crack ran across one of the lenses.

'Tom, listen to me. I came here because I had nowhere left to run. I want to turn myself over to Paulis and the CIA. I have critical information. If you kill me, that intel is lost forever.'

Caine tightened his grip on his pistol. The gun shook, and a muscle in his cheek quivered.

'I stopped Grissom before,' Caine growled. 'Why do I need you?'

Bernatto smirked. 'You think you stopped him? You're wrong. You hurt him, yes. Backed him into a corner. But we all know what happens when you corner a wounded animal.'

'What's this intel you have? Where is it?'

'I'm not a fool, Tom. It's not here.'

'Where is it?'

Bernatto looked up at Trina. Her eyes opened wide, and her lips parted in a silent gasp of surprise.

'I think I know where it is,' she said. She turned to Caine and wiped more tears from the corners of her eyes. 'Just... put the gun down. We can figure this out.'

Caine thought for a moment. Then he lowered the pistol.

'I told you I'd kill you the next time I saw you, Allan. And I meant it.'

'I know,' Bernatto said, peering over the rims of his glasses. 'But if you want to stop Grissom, you need me alive.'

'Maybe for now.' Caine shoved his pistol into his waistband. 'But the second that changes...'

Nhan lowered his shotgun and sighed. He turned to Trina. 'I start making food. Trina, you bandage his wound. Then give them time to talk.'

The girl gave Caine a confused look then followed her grandfather into the kitchen.

Bernatto grunted as he staggered to his feet. 'He's right. We do need to talk.'

Caine glared at the man, his emerald gaze blazing like jewels in the sun. 'Fine. Start talking. And you'd better pray I like what I hear.'

Bernatto winced as he cradled his injured arm. 'I don't believe in prayer,' he muttered.

Caine grabbed a chair and pulled it across the floor. He sat down and drew his CZ pistol. He set the gun on his leg, keeping it within easy reach.

'That makes two of us.'

27

Bernatto limped over to the shelf of pictures. He picked one up and cradled it in his hands, sighing. 'Nhan and his wife,' he said. 'Her name was Mai. It's been so long... I forgot how beautiful she was. Forgot a lot of things. Mostly by choice.'

'Who are these people?' Caine said in a low voice, keeping the gun trained on the old man. 'Why did you come here?'

Bernatto set the picture down and picked up another. In the photo, the same woman, Mai, brushed a young girl's hair. 'This is Mai and her daughter, Linh. Linh was Trina's mother. She's gone now. Hard to believe.' He replaced the picture on the shelf and went over to the futon 'Nhan saved my life during the fighting here.' Bernatto sat down facing Caine with his hands on his knees. 'Later, he became an asset of mine.'

'You were in the war?' Caine did some quick calculations in his head... Bernatto was old enough to have served, but he had a hard time picturing the cold, imperious man as a fresh-faced GI.

'I was. This place was my first lesson.'

'First lesson in what?'

Bernatto looked him in the eye. 'My first lesson in what happens when you let politicians wage war instead of soldiers.'

'That's rich, coming from you.'

Bernatto hung his head. 'You never understood, Tom. You never understood what Walter and I were trying to do. What we were trying to prevent.'

'Save it for your memoirs,' Caine snapped. He gestured toward the kitchen with his gun. 'Nhan, Trina... Who are they?'

Bernatto coughed and turned his gaze back to the pictures. 'Some of the bloodiest battles in the war were fought here, in Ha Tinh Province. I was a marine, fresh out of boot. My platoon was sent here to help reinforce southern troops as the North pushed through on the road to Saigon.'

'Didn't go well for you.'

Bernatto gave a bitter laugh. 'As usual, we had already lost. We just didn't know it yet. We would have needed ten times the men we had to hold the road. All we did was slow them down. Gave the politicians at home time to win more elections. And spread more lies.'

'Keep talking.'

'Nhan was a conscript in the Northern army. He had recently married, and his wife's family lived in the South. He... he saved my life in battle. Defected to our side. And in the aftermath, I did my best to repay him.'

'Aftermath? But the US withdrew after—'

'Officially we withdrew, yes. But the CIA continued operations in the area for several years. You've heard of the Phoenix Program?'

Caine nodded. 'Counterinsurgency op during the war.'

'We knew the Vietcong had infiltrated the joint southern military effort. The CIA was working in the region, neutralizing suspected VC operatives.'

'Yeah,' Caine said with a cynical laugh of his own. 'And killing thousands of innocent civilians in the process.'

'That's what happens in a war, Caine. People die. Guilty, innocent... We all bleed the same.'

'So you recruited Nhan into the program?'

Bernatto nodded. 'After the US pulled out, the CIA continued covertly supporting resistance efforts in the South. They renamed the operation Plan F-6 and recruited me to help coordinate local assets like Nhan. But it never amounted to much. The higher-ups had lost their appetite for crawling around in the muck here. They mothballed the op a couple years later, but I still did my best to look out for Nhan and his family.'

'Bullshit. You never look out for anyone but yourself.'

Once more, Bernatto's eyes darted to the pictures on the wall. Caine watched the old man's features soften. His face, his entire body seemed to sag under the weight of his memories.

'Think what you like. You asked who he was, so I told you. He's one of the few people left in this world that I trust. When you dismantled the operation in Sudan, I knew Grissom would see me as a loose end. My only chance was to trade what I knew for asylum.'

He turned and glared at Caine. 'But I had no desire to rot in a concrete cell in some godforsaken desert. If I was going to crawl back to the CIA, I would do it on my own terms. I needed a place to hide. To plan and gather intel.'

'So you came back here.'

Bernatto nodded again. 'Here was where it all started for me. Seemed as good a place as any. And Nhan let me stay, no questions asked.'

'All right. So what about this intel... What do you have?'

'What do I have?' Bernatto raised a single brow. 'I have everything. I have ACHERON.'

'What the hell is Acheron?' Caine snapped.

'In Greek mythology, Acheron was the River of Woe, one of five waterways that led into Hades.'

Caine glowered at the older man and clenched his fist. 'I'm not interested in fairy tales, Allan.'

'ACHERON is Grissom's scorched-earth policy. All the blackmail and intel he's gathered. Years of dirt on the past and present members of the Senate Intelligence Committee and the CIA's illegal black ops programs. The names of assets he controls within our nation's intelligence apparatus. Along with similar material on the CCP and MSS in China.'

'And what does he plan to do with it?'

Bernatto tilted his head and gave Caine a puzzled look. 'Isn't it obvious? The same thing I plan to do. Trade it to whichever side will grant him asylum.'

'Bullshit! Grissom is the biggest China hawk there is. You expect me to believe he'd willingly turn over US intel to the Chinese?'

Bernatto shrugged. 'You know better than anyone what happens when people are driven to extremes. Regardless, do you think the United States can afford to take that risk? Especially given our trade war with China?'

Caine narrowed his eyes. 'China walked away from the negotiating table a couple days ago... Grissom leaked some of his intel to them, didn't he?'

'Of course,' the older man answered. 'He's leveraged the Senate Intel Committee and the president into the same position. They both have something to gain by helping him. And everything to lose.'

'So Grissom gets immunity for his crimes, and Axion gets a

big, fat military contract. What about you, Allan? What do you get?'

'A bullet in the head, most likely,' Bernatto grunted. 'Unless you help me get ACHERON into the president's hands first. Take away Grissom's bargaining chip and expose his network all at once.'

Caine felt his face flush, burning rage simmering beneath his skin. *He's using you again*, the voice in the back of his head whispered. *Don't believe his lies. Kill him now and walk away.*

He clenched his fist and took a deep breath. 'Let's say I believe you. Where is ACHERON now?'

Bernatto shook his head. 'I sent the drive here to Nhan before I arrived. Told him to hide it, keep it safe.'

'And he gave it to Trina,' Caine said.

'Poor judgment on his part. But I didn't realize how ill he had become. I suppose she was the only one he could trust.'

'So where is it now?'

Caine tensed as Bernatto stood up. But the old man just shoved his hands in his pockets and glared down at Caine. 'I have no idea. We'll have to ask Trina.'

Caine peered at Bernatto over the barrel of the pistol, his eyes as cold as green ice. 'There is no "we," Allan. I told you what would happen if I ever saw you again. Way I see it, I don't need you. I just need the girl to lead me to the hard drive.'

'You're wrong. That drive is DNA locked.'

Caine's stare did not waver. 'You're lying.'

Bernatto's lips curled into a smug grin. 'Afraid not, Tom. Only I can access it. The data is scrambled using military-grade encryption, AES-256 standard. The drive contains a sample of my DNA on file. When the mechanism is activated, a biometric pad takes a blood sample from the user. If anyone who isn't a close enough DNA match to my file tries to access it, it erases all the data in a matter of seconds.'

'Bullshit. Defense contractors have been playing with DNA locks for years. No one's been able to make them work. There's always a margin of error.'

Bernatto pushed his glasses up his nose and grunted. 'Yes, the technology isn't perfect, but it's secure enough for my needs. Only I or an immediate family member can open that drive. And as I'm sure you know... I have no family.'

'Now *that* I believe,' Caine replied.

'Hey!' Both men turned their heads at the sound of the girl's voice. Trina stood in the room's entrance. 'We made food. Let's eat.'

Caine stood up.

The girl eyed the pistol in his hand. 'Could we maybe have no guns at the dinner table?' she snapped.

Caine glared at Bernatto then slipped the CZ into his waistband. 'Fine. But this man... He isn't who you think he is.'

Trina bit her lip. 'Neither are you. Come on. My grandfather needs to eat to get his strength up. We can talk over food.'

Bernatto followed her into the kitchen. He glared back at Caine but said nothing.

Caine clenched his fists one last time then followed them out of the room.

Keep it together. When this is over, when you have the intel you need... Bernatto will pay. For what he did to you. To Jack, and Galloway...

And most of all, for what he did to Rebecca.

28

The young man named Vinh hunched his shoulders as he lit a cigarette. The brief flare of the lighter illuminated his scowling face as he pushed his way through the crowd of bodies inside the club. The pulsing beat of electronic music drowned out the complaints of the dancing patrons as he shoved them out of his way.

Moving toward the bar, he blew a cloud of smoke into the air. The atmosphere in the dark room was already a thick haze of smoke. A miasma of sweat, body odor, and human excess swirled in the lights above the dancing crowd.

He leaned against the counter. The bartender, a petite local girl with long hair and a round face, set a Tiger beer on the counter next to him. He stared at the bottle for a moment, watching the beads of condensation drip down the blue foil label.

The girl leaned over the bar, staring at him with wide eyes. Even in the dim lights of the club, he could see she was wearing bright-blue contact lenses. Her pupils were two tiny dots, black pinpricks surrounded by a sea of sapphire blue.

'Hey, man,' she shouted over the music. 'You got my stuff or what?'

Vinh fished a wad of small bills from his pocket and slid the money across the counter. The girl fanned through the bills and removed a small white packet. Glancing around to make sure no one was watching, she slipped it down the plunging neckline of her glittering dress. Then she looked Vinh up and down, seeming to notice for the first time the mud on his clothes. *'Chuyện gì đã xảy ra với anh vậy?* What the hell happened to you?'

'You seen Trina?' he asked, ignoring her question.

She shook her head. 'Nah... Told you she'd dump your ass.'

Vinh grabbed the beer and lurched away from the bar. The girl called after him, but her words got lost in the music and crowd.

He looked up as he pushed his way across the dance floor. The Hero Club was a local hotspot, popular with the younger local crowd as well as expats looking to party. The sweeping lights and neon beams revealed girls dressed in skimpy black bikinis dancing in cages that hung over the dance floor. A sea of mirrored balls descended from the ceiling, refracting the beams of light into a rainbow haze.

Vinh chugged down his beer then dropped his cigarette in the empty bottle. He hurled it at the parked war-era Soviet truck that filled the northern corner of the club. The truck's rear bed served as a tiny stage, and a DJ hunched over his turntables, spinning the tunes that ignited the crowd.

Vinh shook his head and turned down a narrow corridor, making his way past a long line of girls waiting for the restroom. He pushed a twenty-something backpacker out of the way, giving the young man a fierce look. Then he swung open the men's room door and entered.

People were using the urinals, so instead he opened a door to a stall and unbuckled his pants. He sighed as he urinated. He swayed in time to the music, causing his stream to splash the toilet seat and stall floor.

As he hummed to himself, he heard the creak of the door opening. Then footsteps, shuffling across the tile floor. People were exiting the men's room in a hurry. He wondered if someone was going up on stage.

He heard more footsteps, this time coming toward him. The stall door next to him creaked, and he heard someone sit down. The bathroom was quiet. For a moment, the only sound was his pissing. Then a man's voice broke the silence.

'I heard you're the man to talk to around here. For certain... party favors?'

The voice echoed off the bathroom's tile walls. Vinh said nothing. He had learned long ago not to do business with people he didn't know. He finished urinating, letting the last few drops trickle into the toilet.

'Not much of a talker, eh? I respect that. I let my money do my talking for me.'

Vinh heard something hit the floor. A booted foot kicked a thick white envelope underneath the wall and into his stall. A rubber band held the envelope closed, but he could see the colorful edge of a thick wad of bills stuffed inside.

'I don't know what you're talking about.' He kicked the envelope back under the wall.

The mysterious speaker chuckled. Outside, the music was a dull bass thud, a distant background hum. 'You don't, huh? Yeah, I could tell you're a hard-ass. You know your problem, Vinh? You're not a carrot guy.'

The young man zipped up his fly. 'Hey, how you know my name, asshole?' he said.

'You're not my first stop tonight. I had a word with one of your boys. Another hard-ass. He didn't appreciate the value of a good carrot either. See for yourself.'

The man kicked the envelope under the wall again.

'I told you, not interested,' Vinh snapped.

'Oh, I disagree. I think you're about to become very interested. Go on. Look.'

Vinh reached down and picked up the envelope. He pulled off the rubber band and opened it. A crumbled plastic baggie lay within, wrapped in the stack of bills. He pulled it out, and a splatter of red struck the grimy tiles beneath his feet.

'*Cái quái g' thế*... What the fuck!' He felt something soft and fleshy in the baggie. He held the plastic bundle by one corner, lifting it up to the light.

Inside was a severed human ear.

Vinh screamed and dropped the grisly package. He spun around, but before he could open the stall door, it swung toward him and slammed him in the face. He stumbled backward and fell to the floor. His head struck the side of the toilet with a loud crack.

His vision blurred, and a tunnel of shadow seemed to close in around him. Before darkness engulfed him completely, he heard the stall door swing open again. A pair of hands dragged him back into the light.

He felt himself flying through the air. His head thudded into a mirror, and he heard the crash of shattering glass. He fell to the floor. All he could see was blinding white light. The faucet knobs squeaked, and the sound of running water filled the room.

The hands were grabbing him again, lifting him up. He swung his fist, but he was weak and barely conscious... He couldn't even tell if he hit anything.

Suddenly, cold darkness surrounded him again. Water stung the cuts on his face, and tiny bubbles exploded from his nose. When he gasped for air, a torrent of chlorine and tap water rushed into his mouth.

The hands pulled him out, and the blinding white light surrounded him again.

'See, me, I respect a good stick man,' the American voice said. 'But I gotta tell you, the carrot is a hell of a lot easier for both of us. And after the day I've had, you just get tired of all the bullshit. You know what I mean?'

Sploosh! He was back underwater. He blinked, and his vision focused a bit. His thoughts cleared. They were drowning him, shoving his head in the sink. He kicked and struggled, but he couldn't break the iron grip holding his head underwater. The dark tunnel closed around him once again, and he felt his chest burn.

Then, with a loud splash, they yanked him out. He coughed and sputtered as he gasped for air. A blurry figure shoved something in his mouth. He looked down... A carrot protruded from his mashed, bloody lips.

Two burly Vietnamese men in military uniforms held his arms in a brutally tight grip. He heard fingers snap. He turned and saw a tan, leathery face hovering before him. Gray buzz-cut hair and eyes like black opals. The man smiled.

'That's better. I can see I'm getting through. Now, my name is Boone Riley. And like I said, I've had one hell of a day. So here's how we're gonna do this. A helpful local citizen reported seeing a man and a woman drop you off, outside the city. By the river.'

Riley held up his phone. A blurry traffic-cam photo filled the screen. Vinh's eyes opened wide. It was her, Trina. And the American, the one she drove off with.

'Now, before you waste both our time lying, I already know you're dating her. I also know you kept your little side racket here behind her back. Hell, I know you think she's been two-timing you with that British geologist from the tour company she works for.'

Vinh struggled to form words, but the carrot was wedged tight between his teeth. Boone laughed and grabbed the orange vegetable. He yanked it from the terrified youth's mouth. A single tooth flew out with the carrot and clattered across the floor.

Vinh spat blood across the filthy white tiles. 'Who... who the fuck are you, man?'

'Me?' Boone thought for a moment. He took a bite of the carrot and chewed slowly. Then he drew a pistol from his waistband. He pressed the barrel of the gun into Vinh's temple. 'That all depends on what choice you make. I tried the carrot. Now you get the stick.'

'Trina Phan!' Vinh shouted. 'Her name is Trina Phan!'

'I already know that,' Boone said. He took another bite of carrot. 'Have to do better, my friend. Where is she going?'

'I don't know, I... Wait! She has a grandfather, south of here. In Ha Tinh!'

Boone titled his head. 'Grandfather. Interesting. What's his name?'

'I don't fucking know, man!'

Boone made a clicking sound with his tongue. 'And just when you were being so helpful.' The tall, muscular man lunged forward and drove his fist into Vinh's abdomen.

The youth made a retching sound and curled into a ball. Only the two men holding his arms kept him from sprawling on the floor.

'Last chance for the carrot,' Boone snapped. 'Give me a name. Now!'

'Nhan...' Vinh mumbled. Blood rolled from his mangled lips as he spoke. 'His name... is Nhan. Nhan Thien. He's just an old man...'

Boone nodded at one of the Vietnamese soldiers. They released Vinh's arms, and the young man collapsed to the floor. The soldier tapped on the screen of a rugged smartphone. He squinted at the display then looked at Boone. 'Got him.'

Boone knelt. 'See? Carrot's always easier. Why you gotta be such a hard-ass?'

He stuffed the half-eaten carrot in Vinh's mouth. 'Enjoy. You earned it.' Before Vinh could answer, Boone looped an arm around his neck. Vinh struggled as the burly man dragged him across the floor, but he barely had the strength to move, let alone break the iron grip.

The two soldiers looked at each other in silence as Boone yanked Vinh into the bathroom stall and kicked the door closed behind him. They heard a muted scream and frantic splashing behind the dented plastic door. Water sloshed across the floor.

Silence followed. A few seconds later, Boone opened the stall and took a deep breath. He washed his hands at the sink and dried them on a paper towel. Then he grinned at the soldiers.

'What are you two waiting for? You heard the kid. Let's go visit Grandpa.'

* * *

Caine's stomach rumbled as soon as he set foot in the tiny kitchen. He realized he had not eaten since his breakfast the day before, and the smell of grilled pork and seafood made his mouth water.

He tensed as he watched Bernatto scoop a mound of rice from a clay pot onto his plate. Trina used a pair of tongs to arrange some crab legs on her grandfather's plate.

She looked up at Caine and pursed her lips. 'Are you going to sit down and eat or not?'

Keeping an eye on Bernatto, Caine sat at the opposite end of the table. Trina placed some crab on his plate then lifted the lid off a bamboo steamer. Inside, several summer rolls lay stacked in a tight bundle. Each roll consisted of translucent rice paper, wrapped around bundles of fresh herbs, vegetables, and slices of pork sausage.

Using a pair of long chopsticks, she deposited two of the rolls onto his plate. Caine stuffed one in his mouth. The crisp vegetables complemented the fatty sausage well. He finished the roll then pried some crab from its shell with a fork. The meat was white and sweet. A simple coating of fresh black pepper and lime juice enhanced the natural flavor. Before he knew it, he had devoured his entire plate.

At the other end of the table, Nhan took a long sip of beer. He set down the bottle and sighed. The wrinkles in his face seemed to sink even deeper, and his eyes looked tired. He pointed at Bernatto.

'You... You lie to me.'

Caine washed down his food with some cold tea. 'He's not who he says he is. His name is—'

'I know his name,' Nhan snapped. 'Let me speak.' He returned his dark, tired gaze to Bernatto. 'You tell me hard drive worth money. Help me and Trina. But not dangerous.'

Bernatto took a sip of tea. 'Yes,' he said. The old Vietnamese man's dark eyes bored into his. Bernatto looked down. 'That was a lie.'

'Now, men come looking for this drive? Looking for me?'

'I didn't know. I thought they—'

The old man slammed his fist on the table. 'You put my granddaughter in danger. She is all I have left!'

'I...' Bernatto paused. 'I'm sorry, Nhan. You're right.'

Trina swallowed some crab meat then toyed with the shell on her plate. 'So what's on this drive? Why is it so important, anyway?'

Bernatto cleared his throat. 'It's better that you don't know.'

The girl leaned back in her chair. 'Better for who?'

'The more you know, the more danger you'll be in,' Caine said. 'Trina, you hid the drive somewhere, didn't you? Look, just tell us where it is, and we'll take it off your hands. The longer we stay here, the more danger you're both in.'

Nhan shook his head. 'No. We all in danger now. These men will come for us, yes? Even if you leave?'

Caine was silent. Bernatto stared at him then turned to Nhan. 'Yes. They will.'

The old man nodded and took another sip of beer. 'We all in danger. So we all go with you. Americans come, take you away with drive, yes?'

'Maybe,' Caine said. 'To be honest, I haven't planned that far ahead yet.'

'Then we go where you go.'

Trina laughed. 'What? I can't go to America! I start school in—'

'Too dangerous to stay now,' the old man replied. 'You will be safer with them.'

'Where is this drive?' Caine asked. 'Where did you hide it?'

'You can't get to it by yourself,' she said, taking another bite of food. She chewed angrily, glancing at him from the corner of her eye. 'It's in Hang Son Doong.'

Caine's mind raced... The name sounded familiar to him, but he couldn't quite place it.

'Hang Son Doong?' Bernatto said, glaring at the girl over the rims of his glasses. 'You hid it in a cave?'

'It's not just a cave,' she snapped, glancing between Caine and Bernatto. 'Hang Son Doong is the largest cavern system in the world. Only one tour company in the world is allowed there. You can count the number of qualified guides on one hand, and I'm one of them. It's a hell of a lot safer there than in my apartment.'

'So where in this cave did you hide it?' Caine asked.

She took a breath. 'An underground river system runs beneath the cavern. The last expedition there found a new tributary, branching off from the main tunnel. I put the drive in a waterproof case and weighed it down in a smaller cave, beneath the surface. There won't be any tours there now until after the rainy season... Trust me, no one is going to go looking there.'

29

Caine stood on the house's porch, staring out into the darkness. A warm night breeze whipped across the yard. The wind rustled the thin fabric of his shirt and mussed his hair. Beads of sweat dripped down his skin. He looked down at the burner phone in his shaking hands. A part of him wanted to hurl it into the trees or smash it on the ground. Blood pounded in his temples.

Finally, he took a deep breath and closed his eyes. He forced himself to slow his breathing.

Focus on the mission. The mission is all that matters...

For so long, his mission had simply been survival. Then, when events finally brought him face-to-face with Bernatto years after his betrayal, his mission changed. It became revenge.

But now? Now, he wasn't sure.

He took another breath. The anger and adrenaline rush faded from his body, leaving him numb and tired. He dialed a number.

After the standard clicks and beeps, her voice answered. 'Hello?'

'It's me.'

'No code phrase?' she asked, sounding cautious. Guarded.

He was silent for a moment. He didn't know what to say.

'Tom?' she replied. 'Are you okay?'

'Did you know?' he finally asked.

'Did I know what?'

'The asset. Did you know it was Bernatto?'

'What?' She sounded as shocked as he felt.

'Allan Bernatto is Larkspur,' Caine said, forcing himself to remain calm. 'He's here, in Vietnam. Did you know?'

'Of course not! I'm just as surprised as you are.'

'But Paulis knew, didn't he?'

'I have no idea. But Tom, that doesn't matter right now.'

'How can you say that? After what he did to... After you, and...'

'Say it, Tom. Say his name.'

Caine looked back at the house. He heard pots and pans clanking in the kitchen. The old man jabbered instructions to his granddaughter.

'He hurt us both, Rebecca. And he hurt people we cared about.'

'You think I don't know that? You think I don't want him dead?'

Caine was silent.

'Listen, this is bigger than either of us. Paulis just got out of another Senate hearing. You're not going to believe this, but they're considering granting Grissom a pardon. They want to use his private military company as some kind of counterterrorism program. Everything we've done, all we've been working on for the last year... Grissom, Blackwing, undoing the damage he caused. It's like they're pretending it never happened!'

Caine pondered her words. 'Bernatto says he has intel, a

hard drive he stole from Grissom's complex in Sudan. Something called ACHERON. Grissom's contingency plan, in case things went wrong.'

He heard Rebecca suck in her breath on the other end of the line. He knew the sound meant she was thinking, turning over the various angles in her mind.

'Paulis had an off-books meeting with the new DNI, Alex Maddison,' she said in a rushed, breathy voice. 'According to Maddison, ACHERON is Grissom's bargaining chip. If we can get our hands on that, he loses all his leverage!'

'Assuming Bernatto is telling the truth,' Caine replied. 'But there's a problem. He says he's the only one who can access it.'

'What, like a code or password?'

'More than that. Some kind of DNA lock on the drive.'

Rebecca fell silent. 'Could be a prototype,' she finally said. 'I've heard of DNA-based security measures, but the technology isn't reliable yet.'

'Do you want to take that risk?' Caine replied.

Static crackled over the line. 'Is he with you now?' she asked.

'We're with an old contact of his. A man named Nhan Thien. Someone he knew from the war.'

'Have you secured the ACHERON drive?'

Caine glanced at the house again. 'Negative. It's not here. Nhan gave it to his granddaughter for safekeeping. She hid it somewhere. We have to go retrieve it.'

'Then find it. Let me know when you have the drive.'

Caine heard footsteps creaking across the floor in the house. 'I will,' he muttered. 'And Rebecca... We agreed, no more secrets between us. So I need you to understand. Once I have the intel on that drive, once I don't need Bernatto anymore, I'm ending this. One way or another.'

'Understood,' Rebecca said, her voice cold and quiet. 'Be careful.' Then she hung up.

The screen door swung open behind him. Caine pocketed the phone and turned around. Trina stood on the porch. Despite the tropical heat, she hugged herself as if she were cold.

'Hey,' she said, peering out into the darkness beyond the house.

'Are you all right?' Caine asked. In the distance, waves crashed against the beach. Their gentle lapping provided a soft rhythm behind the chirping and clicking of insects in the trees.

'I didn't... I just didn't expect him to be so bad. I knew he was sick, but...' She turned to him. 'What about you? You have family?' He stared back at her but said nothing. The girl nodded. 'Yeah, didn't think so,' she added.

'People in my profession usually don't.'

She looked up at him, tucking strands of blonde hair behind her ear. 'What profession is that?'

Caine sighed. 'Trina, the less you know, the safer you and your grandfather are. All I can tell you is, it's vital I retrieve the information on that hard drive.'

His emerald stare bored into her. She took a deep breath then blinked. 'Okay, okay, I'll take you there. We'll leave tomorrow. I assume you can swim?'

He smiled. 'Don't worry about me.'

She gave him a concerned look. 'I'm serious. Cave diving is dangerous. It's dark. You get lost, run out of air... You can't tell which way is up. And the river will be harder to cross this time of year. *Lắng nghe tôi*, listen to me. This is the kind of thing that gets people killed. You can't just—'

Bzzzzzzt!

A burst of static erupted from the walkie attached to Caine's belt, cutting off her warning. She glanced at the walkie in surprise. Caine adjusted the channel and held the radio to his ear.

'Hey, Tom.' Boone's voice crackled through the speaker. 'Knock, knock...'

Something caught Caine's eye, and he looked across the yard, peering into the shadowy trees. He saw two tiny pinpoints of light in the distance, moving closer to the village... Headlights on the dark jungle road. He spotted another pair behind the first.

Then another.

'They've found us,' he snapped. 'Get inside.'

Trina followed the trail of headlights with her eyes. The dark vehicles sped closer to the house. 'What? Are you sure? How could they—'

Caine drew his pistol from his waistband and grabbed her arm. 'I don't know, but they're here. Move!'

He pulled her inside the house as the trail of lights rushed closer.

30

'Nhan,' Caine shouted as he and Trina raced back into the house. 'Do you have any weapons?'

The old man rose from the table and stood on shaky legs. 'Weapons? Just shotgun, why?'

'Grab it,' Caine snapped. 'We'll need everything we can get our hands on.'

Bernatto held out his hand. 'Give me your pistol. I can help.'

Caine gave him a withering look. 'I'm not stupid or desperate enough to trust you, Allan.'

The older man's lips curled into a grim smile. 'Put your personal feelings aside, Tom. You're outnumbered and outgunned.'

Caine grabbed Bernatto by his shirt collar and dragged him closer. 'I don't know what you've told these people or what the hell you're doing here. And frankly, I don't care. Mission or not, you know I'm looking to put a bullet in you. I see you even look at a weapon, I'll have a reason to. Understood?'

Allan nodded. 'Fine. So how do you plan to get us out of this mess?'

Before Caine could answer, a blinding light beamed through the front windows of the house. The intense brilliance cast long, dark shadows across the walls.

Caine cursed and threw Bernatto to the floor. 'Everyone, get down!' He dropped to the floor and crawled toward the sofa.

A hail of gunfire exploded through the windows. Trina screamed as a line of bullet holes perforated the wall behind them. Bernatto covered his head and huddled on the floor. The gunfire knocked the old pictures from the wall, shattering the glass in their frames.

Caine crouched next to the sofa. Another burst of automatic weapons fire screamed above his head. When the gunfire paused, he leapt up and darted across the room.

A bright white circle shined in the front yard: a searchlight mounted on a truck. Caine fired twice. He heard the tinkle of broken glass as he dove to the floor. The blinding light went dim, cloaking the house in darkness.

A hail of bullets tore through the air where he had been standing. Tufts of white foam exploded from the back of the couch. He heard Trina scream again, this time from the kitchen.

'Allan, you alive?' Caine hissed.

Bernatto grunted in acknowledgment.

'Stay low... Get to the back of the house,' Caine snapped. He rolled onto his back and sent three bullets thudding into the door. He knew the shots wouldn't stop anyone on the other side, but it might give them pause before they breached.

Then he crept along the wall, moving in a low crouch to the kitchen. Nhan and Trina were hiding behind the overturned table. The old man held a short-barreled shotgun in a trembling grip. 'Who are these men?' he shouted. 'Who you bring to my house?'

'Special forces,' Caine growled. 'T2, Vietnamese People's Army.'

'We are Vietnamese citizens!' Nhan shouted, shaking his fist.

'It doesn't matter,' Caine snapped. 'You can't trust them. They're working for a man, an American. Someone who wants us all dead.'

'Why?'

'Ask him!' Caine hooked a thumb over his shoulder. He pointed at Bernatto as the older man shuffled behind him.

'No time for that now,' Bernatto hissed. 'We have to get out through the back. Then make our way—'

The roar of gunfire drowned out his words as more bullets swept through the house. Caine tilted his head, listening. This time, the shots came from the side of the house. As the gunfire ceased, he heard a popping sound from the living room.

'Close your eyes!' he shouted.

A loud hiss came from the front of the house. Caine grabbed a towel from the floor and dunked it in one of the steamer pots sitting on the counter. He wrapped the wet rag around his face as tendrils of white mist billowed into the kitchen.

The tear gas stung his eyes, but he blinked and kept moving. Caine yanked the shotgun from Nhan's trembling hands and pumped the slide. The gun had a perforated barrel and a walnut stock. He recognized the weapon as a Stevens Model 520-30 trench gun. An old but reliable model left over from the war, it held five twenty-gauge shells in a tubular magazine under the barrel.

His nostrils burned as he navigated through the haze. He kept his breathing shallow to avoid drawing the gas deeper into his lungs. Moving toward the living room, he pressed his back against the wall. He peered around the corner. A pair of men in drab camouflage uniforms were picking through the rubble of the couch. They both wore gas masks and carried automatic rifles.

Caine raised the shotgun and fired. The single barrel roared, and one of the soldiers collapsed to the floor. The other spun around and fired. Bullets tore through the walls as Caine sprinted across the gap between the rooms. A chunk of drywall exploded next to him, leaving a gaping hole in the wall. Caine jammed the barrel of the shotgun through the hole and pulled the trigger. The gun kicked in his hands, and the soldier staggered backward.

Keeping his finger pressed against the trigger, Caine pumped the shotgun again. With a loud boom, the weapon fired. The old Stevens M520 lacked a trigger disengage system and would continuously discharge shells as long as the trigger was held down. The shotgun roared three more times as Caine slam-fired through the hole in the wall. The soldier's body jerked and spasmed then fell. His rifle clattered to the floor as his arms flailed behind him.

Caine raced into the living room, still moving in a low crouch. The burning in his eyes grew worse as the white vapor swirled around him, but he ignored the pain. He had trained to push through the effects of tear gas and other chemical irritants. He yanked off one soldier's gas mask and slid his radio from his belt. Then he grabbed the man's discarded rifle and jogged back into the kitchen.

'Nhan, here!' He tossed the old man the rubber mask. The man stared at it then doubled over in a fit of coughing.

'Grandpa, let me help you.' Trina took the mask and slipped it over his head.

'The longer we stay here, the worse our situation gets!'

Bernatto shouted, coughing and wheezing as the gas continued to fill the room. He crawled toward the rear of the house. 'We have to get out while we still—'

'No.' Caine grabbed Bernatto's shirt and dragged him back behind the table. The older man peered at him over the rims of his glasses. His eyes were bloodshot and watery. 'What do you mean?'

Caine held up the radio he had acquired in Hanoi. 'Boone Riley contacted me just before these men attacked. He warned me they were coming. Why would he do that?'

Bernatto narrowed his eyes. 'He's controlling the battle-field, manipulating the enemy's responses. Just like I taught him.'

Caine nodded. 'He knew we'd see the lights out front. He wants us to flee out the back.'

Caine turned to Nhan. 'Is there any other way out of this house?'

The old man stared at him through the mask's goggles. He blinked then smiled. 'Yes! Follow me. Trina, stay here. Get behind table.'

Nhan crawled across the floor and toward the pantry. He reached up, opened the door, and crept inside. Caine and Bernatto followed.

'I live through the war,' he said in a wheezing voice. 'Much trouble back then. And more trouble after. I build tunnel here, under house. Just in case.'

A dusty, faded carpet lined the floor of the pantry. The shelves were bare save for a few cans of vegetables and preserved meat glinting in the dim light. Nhan threw the carpet aside, revealing a trap door in the floor.

'Just like Cu Chi,' Bernatto muttered.

Nhan looked back at him. 'Yes. I was trained to live in these tunnels for weeks, months if needed. I was what you Americans called a tunnel rat.'

'No time for history lessons,' Caine snapped. 'Where does this lead?'

Nhan heaved the door open. A dank, musty breeze moaned through the dark hole underneath. It smelled like mud and animal excrement.

'Goes to my old fishing boat,' Nhan said. 'In the yard, next to house.'

'I'll need a flashlight.'

The old man fished around in his pockets and removed a scuffed metal cigarette lighter.

Caine took the lighter and shoved it in his pocket. 'That will have to do. Nhan, take these.' Caine handed him the shotgun and his CZ pistol. 'Reload the trench gun and give the pistol to Trina. Stay low. Find cover. You see anything moving outside, you shoot. One round only. Conserve ammo. You need to delay their breach as long as possible.'

'I understand,' the old man replied.

Caine adjusted the walkie's frequency then handed it to Bernatto. 'I'll circle around and take out any sentries. When the coast is clear, I'll contact you on this channel. Then you get everyone out the back.'

Bernatto grunted. 'Not much of a plan.'

'You got any better ideas?'

Bernatto shook his head.

Caine turned to Nhan. 'Listen to me... Under no circumstances do you give this man a gun. You can't trust him.'

'I know him better than you ever will,' Nhan said. 'Enough talk. Go!'

Caine glared at Bernatto one last time then lowered himself into the dark hole.

31

Caine slithered through the dank, narrow passageway. The tunnel was pitch black, and he didn't dare use the cigarette lighter for fear the light would give away his position on the opposite side. He kept moving, ignoring the feeling of the mud and rocks closing in around him. He could feel beams of wood set into the damp earth – reinforcements, put in place by Nhan. He hoped the old man knew what he was doing when he built the secret passageway.

The sound of dripping water rang out in the distance. Caine knew the infamous Cu Chi tunnels were larger than this, but not by much. He found it hard to believe soldiers could live in such conditions for weeks at a time.

Amazing what you can do when your life depends on it.

The passageway sloped up, growing even narrower. He grunted with exertion as he forced himself forward through a tight gap in the rocks, moving just a few inches at a time.

He was what he estimated to be about halfway through the tunnel when he froze. He felt something moving across his clothes in the darkness. Something long, smooth, and cool.

A hiss echoed off the rocks. The thing, whatever it was, continued moving up his leg. He felt pressure on his back... a wriggling, slithering sensation.

He closed his eyes. His heart beat like a drum, pounding in the darkness. He took a deep breath, knowing that whatever animal lurked in the shadows, his fear would only attract its attention. He forced himself to calm down, to slow his racing heart.

The thing slithered across his neck. He felt the rasp of cold, dry scales moving across his skin.

Snake. But what kind?

The thing moved over his head. He felt the snake's weight mussing his hair, and a smooth, sinewy body brushed the top of his ear. He heard it drop to the ground and rustle through the dirt in front of him. Then there was silence.

He waited. There were no more sounds. He blinked, struggling to make out a shadow or some sign of movement. But he was cut off from any starlight, and the tunnel was completely black... He couldn't see a thing.

Moving as slowly as he could, he reached into his pocket. His fingers wrapped around the tiny lighter Nhan had given him. He slipped it out of his pocket and held it before him. He hated taking the risk, but Vietnam was home to several species of venomous snakes and he had to know what he was dealing with.

Taking a long, slow breath, he flicked the lighter.

He squinted as the tiny orange flame lit the darkness. The shadows receded across the rocks, driven away by the faint, flickering glow.

Hissssssss...

The sound echoed through the tunnel, and the long, sinewy body reared up at the sight of the flame. The snake's body measured over ten feet long and as thick around as Caine's wrist. At first, he couldn't tell what species the reptile was in the dim light. Its scales were a dark olive gray. Their pattern shifted to a creamy white under the serpent's raised chin.

The snake hissed again. Droplets of venom glistened on its long, curved fangs. An oval flap of skin snapped in place behind its head, and the animal swayed back and forth in the tunnel.

Caine held his breath. The markings and hood were unmistakable. The animal before him was a king cobra, one of the deadliest snakes in Southeast Asia, possibly in the entire world.

Caine instinctively shifted backward, crawling as slowly as he could. The snake hissed again and darted forward, snapping at the air. Caine froze. His emerald-green eyes locked with the snake's golden orbs. He could see its diamond-shaped pupils tracking his every move.

Caine dipped his arm down to his waist. He moved at an agonizingly slow pace, but still, the animal grew more agitated. It hissed and darted forward then reared back. Caine continued the slow movement until he felt his fingers wrap around the hilt of his knife.

The serpent swayed in the lighter's faint glow and hissed again. The sound was low-pitched, almost a growl. It reverberated off the rocks surrounding him and echoed through the tunnel, sending a chill down his spine. Caine had never heard anything like it. He couldn't believe any snake could make such a loud noise.

As he raised the knife, Caine tried to recall what little he knew about the deadly serpents. They weren't usually aggressive, preferring to flee rather than fight. But this specimen seemed more than willing to make a stand. Perhaps it was protecting eggs in a nearby nest.

Cobra venom was a potent mix of neurotoxins and could

kill a man within thirty minutes. Death resulted from a combination of cardio paralysis and respiratory failure unless the proper antivenom was on hand. Caine didn't fancy his chances down here, trapped in a tunnel beneath a hostile force.

Like a lion extending a claw, Caine gently pressed the lever on the back of the knife, and the curved karambit blade extended from its sheath. He slowly lowered the lighter to the ground then he moved his arm into position.

A new sound echoed through the tunnel... Distant gunfire, muted by the rock and mud surrounding him. The snake's hood flared even larger in response. Again, it uttered its low, growling hiss. The serpent's head swayed back and forth as it tried to home in on the unfamiliar sound.

Now!

His left arm shot forward and grabbed the snake just below its fanged snout. The creature thrashed in his grip. Its tail lashed at his arm like a whip. Caine rolled over onto his back and slashed with the knife, hooking the blade under the reptile's tiny head. The fanged maw hissed one last time then fell to the ground.

Blood sprayed from the reptile's severed neck. Caine grimaced and tossed the decapitated snake down the tunnel. The body continued to undulate and move as synapses fired along its length.

He extinguished the lighter and continued crawling forward into the darkness. If some of the men were shooting up above, that meant others would breach the house soon. He was running out of time.

After a few more minutes of shimmying through the damp shadows, the tunnel sloped up. Caine winced as his head thudded into a piece of wood. He flicked the lighter again. In the dim orange glow, he saw another wooden hatch, mounted above a square hole in the tunnel's roof.

He pushed up on the hatch, and it gave way. After sliding the wood cover aside, he pulled himself up through the narrow opening. He extinguished the lighter and blinked, giving his eyes a few minutes to adapt to the darkness. Moonlight poured into the dark space through narrow slits. He reached out and touched the walls. His fingers brushed against curved wood slats crusted with rough barnacles and flaking paint.

I made it. I'm inside Nhan's boat.

He crawled along the side of the old vessel until he found the gaping hole in the side. Peering through the gap, he could make out the tiny house and the flat grasslands surrounding it. A dark grove of trees bordered the rear of the property. Beyond that, a sloped expanse of jungle led up into the mountains.

Caine crawled out the hole and sprinted to the shadowy trees. He kept his rifle slung over his shoulder and the knife in his hand. He knew if he fired now, he would alert the soldiers to his position.

Weaving through the trees, he moved as fast as he could without making too much noise. He was positive sentries were hiding in the foliage, but he doubted they expected anyone to flank them from behind.

His feet crunched across the grass and vines as he crept forward. A gentle breeze rustled the surrounding foliage. He tried to match the sounds, moving on the balls of his feet. He gripped his rifle tight in one hand, making sure the strap didn't rattle or clink.

He made his way to a thick, tall Hopea tree and ducked behind its trunk. A soft murmuring came from the leaves ahead: men whispering. He peered around the tree. A pair of men in camouflage uniforms crouched in the brush with their backs to him. They trained their rifles on the rear of Nhan's house.

Gritting his teeth, Caine debated how to proceed. He knew he was running out of time, but any shooting here would attract attention...

A second later, the men decided for him. Gunfire exploded from the house. He saw flashes of white light in the windows... Flashbang grenades!

Raising his rifle, Caine stalked forward. He closed the gap between himself and the men. Ten meters. Five meters. Three meters...

Caine opened fire and sent a quick burst into each of the men. The explosive gunfire echoed through the trees. The sound was deafening at close range, but Caine could only hope noise from the house would mask his location.

The soldiers crumpled forward and fell limp into the brush. Lowering his rifle, Caine knelt beside the bodies, stripped them of their spare magazines, then raised his walkie to his lips.

'Bernatto, now! Get out of the house! They're going to—'

Before he could finish his sentence, more gunfire roared beyond the trees. Caine saw muzzle flash blazing from the right side of the house. Bullets tore into the nearby foliage.

He dropped prone and crawled across the jungle floor, moving as fast as possible to the nearest copse. Another hail of bullets whizzed overhead. Caine rose to his feet and pressed his back against the rough bark. He heard the percussive thud of slugs tearing into the wood behind him. A splinter flew across his face, cutting his cheek. He licked his lips and tasted blood.

Spinning around, Caine returned fire. The two soldiers ducked behind the house, taking cover as Caine's burst lit up the night.

He emptied the magazine then ducked behind the tree

again. He heard men shouting as reinforcements moved along the side of the house.

If they don't get out now, they're not getting out at all.

He ejected the empty magazine then grabbed one of the spares and slammed it into the rifle. Caine pulled back the charging handle and opened fire again, driving the men back around the house.

'Allan,' he hissed into the walkie. 'We're running out of time! I can cover you, but not for much long—'

'*Thả súng trường!* Drop your rifle!'

Caine spun around as another soldier stalked out from the trees.

Should have checked for a third man. Sloppy.

'I said, drop your weapon!' The soldier jabbed his rifle barrel forward. 'Do it now!'

'*Được...* Okay,' Caine whispered. 'Take it easy...' He lowered the rifle to the ground and raised his hands.

32

'Hands on head!'

Caine raised his arms and laced his fingers behind his head. He kept the karambit knife folded in his palm, hoping it was too dark for the soldier to spot it at a distance.

For all the good it will do me...

The soldier stalked forward, keeping his rifle trained on Caine. He toggled a microphone clipped to his lapel and spoke in rapid Vietnamese. Caine wasn't sure what he was saying, but a moment later, he heard more gunfire from the front of the house. The familiar thump of an exploding flashbang grenade followed.

'Turn around,' the soldier shouted in English. 'Keep hands on head. Don't make any—'

Before he could finish his sentence, something fell from the trees and struck his arm. The man looked down, and his eyes opened wide. A thick, mottled snake writhed and coiled around his forearm.

The man lowered his rifle as he struggled to shake off the thrashing reptile.

Caine moved without thought, acting on instincts honed by years of bloody combat. He lunged forward, sweeping out his left arm and extending the karambit's blade with his right. Grabbing the soldier's rifle, he shoved the barrel aside. The man fired, and again, muzzle flash lit up the trees. In the brief burst of light, Caine saw a panicked look cross the soldier's face. The man's jaw dropped, and his eyes opened wide. He knew he had made a fatal mistake.

Before the man could adjust his aim and fire again, Caine slammed his fist into his opponent's abdomen, using the knife's handle as a force multiplier. He didn't bother trying to stab the soldier with the curved blade. The metal talon was designed for slashing. It was too short to inflict serious damage through multiple layers of clothing.

The soldier grunted in pain. With his right arm tangled in Caine's grip, he launched a quick left hook, but Caine was ready. He released his hold on the weapon and ducked under the blow. Spinning the man's torso around, Caine used the momentum of his punch against him. Then he hooked his right arm around the soldier's throat.

With a quick slicing motion, he dragged his blade across the man's neck. Hot blood sloshed across the back of his hand, and the soldier uttered a hoarse cry. He fell to his knees and collapsed in the brush. His body twitched for a moment then lay still.

Caine shook the knife then ran the blade over his clothes to wipe off the blood. He glanced down at the fallen soldier. The snake coiled around his arm was already dead, its head severed from its long, sinewy body.

The cobra. The one I killed in the tunnel...

He tensed as footsteps shuffled toward him in the darkness. Allan Bernatto stepped out into the moonlight.

Caine raised the knife in a defensive posture. 'Allan?' he whispered. 'What the hell are you doing here? I told you—'

'I couldn't do any good in there without a weapon,' Bernatto whispered, keeping his hands up where Caine could see them.

'So you followed me with a dead snake?'

The older man smirked. 'Snakes are cold-blooded. They can take up to twenty minutes to bleed out and die. That's one thing I learned here... If you're smart, the jungle itself can be a weapon.'

Suddenly, the rear door of the house burst open, and Nhan and Trina stumbled out. Caine watched as they hobbled across the yard. He ducked and retrieved his rifle. They were moving as fast as they could, but the old man could barely walk, let alone run. Trina slung his arm over her shoulder as Caine stepped out of the grove. He gestured with his hands.

'It's no good, Tom,' Bernatto hissed behind him.

Before Caine could respond, another pair of soldiers rounded the corner of the house. Caine stepped back into the shadows and pulled the trigger of his rifle. The gun spat a curtain of suppressing fire, sending bits of dirt and vegetation flying into the air. The men retreated, taking cover behind the house.

In the yard, Nhan stumbled and fell to the ground. 'Go,' he wheezed.

Trina tugged at his arm. 'Damn it, *ông nội!* Get up!'

Thump! Thump!

Caine recognized the sound. He opened fire again, sending a hail of bullets into the side of the house and shattering a window. But it was too late. Two metal canisters landed in the yard a few meters away from Trina and her grandfather, kicking up a spray of dirt. A cloud of hissing white smoke erupted from the impact zone. Within seconds, Caine lost sight of the two figures in the haze.

He felt a hand on his shoulder and whirled around. Bernatto stood behind him. Caine was shocked that the old man had moved so close without him noticing.

You let your guard down, the old familiar voice said. The voice that would never be silenced... the voice of the killer inside.

Caine took a step back and aimed the rifle at him. 'Touch me again, you're dead,' he snarled.

'Tom, we have to pull back. Look...'

Caine stared at Bernatto then shot a quick glance over his shoulder. He saw a squad of armed men storming through the tear gas cloud. Trina made a retching sound then fell to her hands and knees. Two men wearing gas masks grabbed her arms and dragged her back to the house. Caine raised the rifle and took aim.

'Don't,' Bernatto whispered. 'You can't win. Better to fall back and fight another day.'

'Abandon your friends to the wolves?' Caine snarled. 'Why am I not surprised?'

'Tom, I'm the asset. That means I'm the mission. If those men find us, the mission fails.'

'You worried about the mission? Or just saving your own skin?'

Bernatto peered at him over the arm of his glasses. 'In this case, they're the same.'

Caine watched the soldiers as they grabbed Nhan and yanked the old man to his feet. The white haze dissipated. He smelled the acrid chemical tang on the breeze as it drifted through the grove.

He stepped back into the darkness. Then he turned to Bernatto and lowered his rifle. 'Fine. But this isn't over.'

'Agreed.' The old man met his emerald stare head-on. 'We need Trina to get us to the hard drive. But we can't help her if we get captured or killed.'

Caine nodded. 'Follow me. Keep up. You fall behind, I leave your ass in the jungle.'

Bernatto said nothing, but he followed Caine into the dark foliage.

33

The thumping of the UH-1 helicopter's blades was deafening as it descended upon the jungle clearing. Known as an Iroquois, it was originally made by Bell Helicopters in the United States to serve as a medical evac and transportation vehicle for US and South Vietnamese forces. Despite the design's age, its versatility and easy engine maintenance led the People's Airforce of Vietnam to keep more than a dozen of the workhorse choppers for its own use, mostly reclaimed from the South after the war.

The chopper's skids touched down on the windswept grass, and two figures hopped out the rear door. They kept their heads down as the twin rotors continued spinning overhead, rippling the tall grass surrounding them like an ocean wave. One man gestured to a row of molding, vine-encrusted buildings at the far side of the clearing. The other nodded, and they both plodded toward the decaying structures.

The chopper's rotors slowed, and the engine roar turned to a high-pitched whine. One of the men looked up, revealing the face of Lt. Colonel Tranh Nguyen.

'Tell Grissom we have to wrap this up quickly,' the Vietnamese officer hissed. 'I can't keep this quiet much longer. The helicopter, the men... My superiors will—'

Boone Riley ran a hand over his buzzed hair, swiping away some loose grass and debris blown up by the helicopter. 'In case you didn't figure it out, Grissom is your superior now. I take my orders from him. You take your orders from me. At least until this is over.'

'And when will that be?' Nguyen shouted back.

'Keep your shirt on, Tranh.' Boone shot the man a manic grin. 'I see the light at the end of the tunnel. Don't you?'

The Vietnamese officer shook his head. 'No. I see an unsanctioned military operation on Vietnamese soil. One that's getting out of control!'

'That's why we're using this old Russian supply base. Grissom checked. It's not on any of your country's maps. Hell, I doubt your superiors even remember it's here.' Boone shot the man a withering glance. 'So buck up and grow a pair, Tranh.'

Boone grabbed a rusty metal handle and slid aside the door to one of the ancient hangars. A few of Tranh's handpicked soldiers sat at a card table inside. Others were cleaning their weapons at a workbench running along the wall.

A row of offices lined the rear of the building, their ceilings rotted and sagging. An explosion of green foliage obscured the hangar's roof. Vines and plants hung down from the jungle canopy, and a steady shower of water droplets cascaded through gaping holes in the roof. The runoff collected in muddy pools on the floor.

Boone whistled. 'Christ, this place is a dump.'

'What did you expect?' Tranh asked. 'It's over fifty years old. Besides, what the hell do Russians know about building in the jungle?'

As Tranh walked over, the men at the table stood at attention. They snapped up their arms in a salute, and the lieutenant colonel returned the gesture. '*Họ ở đâu?*' he asked. 'Where are they?'

One of the soldiers lowered his arm then led them to the offices. 'Over here. We got the girl and the old man.'

'What about Caine?' Boone snapped.

The soldier gave him a confused look. '*Xin lỗi, nhưng...* Pardon me, but I don't know who that is?'

'American, little younger than me. Ex-military, you know the type. Probably took out a few of your men.'

The soldier nodded. 'There was another man in the jungle, but none of us got a good look at him. None that survived, at least. Whoever he was, he escaped. We searched around the house but found no trace of him. Then we reported here.'

Boone wiped a film of sweat from his forehead and sighed. 'Yeah, I figured as much. Well, show me what you got.'

The soldier opened an office door. Inside, an elderly Vietnamese man sat in a chair. A length of rope bound his arms behind his back, and a filthy cloth gagged his mouth. The man did not react as the old door creaked open. He stared off into space as if he were looking through the walls of the moldy old structure.

Boone chuckled and shook his head. 'Jesus, guys, you're batting a thousand. Wrong old man. I said Bernatto. American, glasses?'

'We found no one matching that description,' the soldier answered. 'But we secured one other prisoner.' He shut the door and stepped over to the next office. The door creaked open.

A Vietnamese woman sat inside, tied to a chair like the old man. Unlike him, however, she struggled at her bonds and glared at Boone as he stepped into the room. She cursed and howled in anger, but the gag reduced her cries to a series of unintelligible grunts.

'Well, this is a little more interesting. Ms. Trina Phan, I take it?'

After Trina uttered another series of angry grunts, the soldier consulted his cell phone. 'That's her. She's a graduate student at the Vietnam National University, Hanoi, but police have linked her to a small organized-crime network operating out of the city. The man in the other room is her grandfather.'

Boone knelt in front of her. 'Funny, she doesn't look like a hardened criminal. Let me guess – you like bad boys, don't you? Mommy and Daddy died and left you all alone, and now you've got a chip on your shoulder the size of a Cadillac?'

The girl heaved in the chair and cursed again. Boone laughed.

'Hell, bet you've screwed your way through every punk with a gang tattoo in Hanoi.'

The girl strained forward in the chair again. The wood creaked, but the rope around her wrists held her in place.

Boone looked up. 'I like her. Send some men back to the house. Keep searching for Caine and Bernatto. They can't have gotten far in this jungle.'

Nguyen looked through the open door at the girl. She glared back at him, snarling through her gag. 'What about her?' he asked in a hesitant voice. 'What are you—'

'Don't worry about me,' Boone said, cutting him off. 'Me and Miss Trina here, we're gonna have a little chat.' He slammed the door shut.

Nguyen peered at Boone's shadow through the frosted glass. Then he turned around and began jabbering orders to his men.

* * *

Caine peered across the lake's smooth, glassy waters. In the amplified starlight of the night-vision goggles, the water was a vast black mirror, dotted with glowing green particles – swimming animals and detritus sinking into the depths. Zooming in closer, Caine could make out the rotting supports of a mangled pier that pierced the depths of the dark water at the edge of the abandoned base.

'What the hell is this place?' Caine whispered, tracking the movements of soldiers patrolling along the jungle-covered shore.

'Old supply base,' Bernatto hissed back. 'Most likely Russian or Eastern European.'

'Yeah? How the hell would you know that?'

Bernatto shifted slightly in the brush and glanced at Caine. 'Because my unit was assigned to take out places like this in the war. Russians used them to helicopter in weapons... mostly Dragunov sniper rifles. Then they'd use the lake and river system to distribute them to the Vietcong. Lost a lot of good men blowing up places like this.' Bernatto sighed. 'For all the good it did.'

'We're all expendable, Bernatto,' Caine whispered back. 'Isn't that what you told me?'

'Expendable and wasteful are two different things.'

Caine lowered his goggles and glared at the older man. Bernatto's clothes were damp and wrinkled. Sweat plastered his white hair to his scalp. The skin on his neck and arms sagged, giving his body a tired, withered appearance.

Still, Caine had to admit Bernatto was a tough old bastard. Few men his age could navigate this far into the jungle while hiding their tracks from patrols. And despite the smothering heat, his eyes still looked sharp and alert.

'So, are you going to tell me about your connection to

Nhan?' Caine asked. 'There's no way I'm buying that you're doing all this for some old war debt.'

'I told you the truth.' Bernatto took the night-vision system from Caine and peered through it at the encampment below. 'You served. You know what it means when you make a promise on the battlefield. Allies, enemies... sometimes the line gets blurred. There are some debts you can't repay... and some promises you just can't break.'

'I know,' Caine whispered. 'But for as long as I've known you, Allan, you've never given a damn about anyone but yourself. Whatever happened between you and the old man down there, I don't believe that's changed.'

Bernatto continued surveying the camp. 'Regardless, we need Trina.' He lowered the goggles. 'Unless you think you can navigate the largest cave system in the world, find where she hid the case, and get us back out on your own?'

'Who are you trying to convince? Me or yourself?'

Bernatto grunted. 'They're refueling the helicopter. That means Boone will take off soon, probably taking Trina and Nhan with him. So do you want to waste time arguing with me? Or figure out a way to get them out of there without getting us all killed?'

Caine reached into the tall grass and grabbed a canvas duffel bag by the handle. It was a go bag that Bernatto had stashed in an old shed on the edge of Nhan's property. Along with the night-vision goggles, Bernatto had packed some MREs, water, a stack of local currency, and a Browning Hi-Power pistol. Caine carried the gun and two spare magazines in a nylon belt around his waist.

With his naked eyes, he spotted a tiny light moving along the edge of the lake. He focused on the glowing pinpoint, letting his eyes drink in what little detail they could pick up through the inky black night.

The light was a cigarette. As the smoking man took another drag, Caine could make out a dim face, partially hidden in the shadows.

Boone...

'Boone Riley, Simon Takuba, Arinori Kusaka. You seem to have a penchant for working with psychopaths, Bernatto.'

'I worked with you as well. Until you lost your nerve.'

'You mean until I came to my senses.'

Bernatto grinned at him in the darkness. Caine looked away. 'Now who are *you* trying to convince?' Bernatto whispered. 'Me? Or yourself?'

Caine watched as a fuel truck wheeled into the clearing. A group of soldiers attached a hose to the side of the helicopter.

'Come on,' Caine whispered. 'We're going in closer. I have an idea...'

'If you're planning what I think you're planning, I'll need a weapon to back you up,' Bernatto replied.

'We'll see,' Caine muttered. He slid forward and crawled through the muddy grass, moving closer to the lake's edge.

34

The walls of the dilapidated hangar shook when Boone Riley slammed the office door. The men outside looked up but said nothing. Instead, they shot Lt. Col. Nguyen a questioning glance. The older man adjusted his uniform then stepped over to Boone.

'What did you find out?'

Boone grinned. 'Interrogation takes time, my friend. She's just beginning to realize how deep in the shit she is. Next time I go in, she'll sing a pretty tune. But I gotta tell you...' He eyed the other office door. 'I think the key is the old man in there.'

The Vietnamese officer gave the frosted glass panel an uneasy look. 'Him? He's just a broke fisherman. What could he possibly—'

'He's all she's got. You threaten him, she'll spill whatever she knows.'

Boone turned and started toward the table that ran along the side of the building. Nguyen grabbed his shoulder. 'Wait!'

Boone spun around and glanced down at the man's hand. 'Best take your hand back, Nguyen. While you still can.'

The officer let go. 'This must end!' he whispered. 'Quickly! The base is asking questions. That helicopter was meant to transport—'

'Plans change, don't they?' Boone replied with a chuckle. 'Hell, I was about to call Grissom and tell him we've hit a delay, but you and your men have been so gosh-darned helpful. I'd stress to him how important our relationship is and how we should do whatever we can to help you succeed in your ah... extracurricular endeavors. But if you'd prefer to sever our partnership now? Well, I'll put you on the line, and you can tell him yourself.'

Nguyen stepped back and shook his head. 'No... I... I mean—'

'Yeah,' Boone said in a lower voice. 'Thought so. Let me give you some advice, friend. Once you start dancing with the devil, you best wait for the song to end. 'Cause you step out early, and—'

Kablaam!

The hangar shook, and a massive fireball exploded through the building. The rotting walls gave way. Something large roared through, smashing them to bits.

An orange glow filled the room as a burning truck rumbled through the hangar. Flames licked at the vines and weeds covering the ceiling. Nguyen's men scattered, opening fire on the flaming vehicle as it tore through the building. One soldier failed to clear the rampaging truck's path. He screamed and raised his hands, but the gesture was futile... The fiery metal grille slammed into his chest, and he crumpled under the wheels.

Boone glanced up as the truck hurtled through the other side of the hangar. 'It's the fuel truck! Caine is here!'

The remaining soldiers raced after the burning vehicle. The

incinerated truck's chassis sped across the grass and rolled toward the lake. Boone picked himself up off the floor and drew a pistol from a shoulder holster. He stormed over to the office doors and threw a door open. Nhan glanced up, peering at him with black, sunken eyes. The wrinkles at the corners of his mouth deepened.

He was smiling.

Boone slammed the door and marched over to Trina's cell. He opened the door. The girl was still there, glaring back at him. She muttered a stream of Vietnamese profanity behind her gag.

Gunfire roared in the distance. Boone cursed and slammed the door shut.

'Okay, Tom,' he muttered to himself. 'Let's play.'

He marched through the charred hole left in the hangar's side and headed toward the lake.

* * *

As the office door slammed shut, Bernatto darted out of the shadows. Trina looked at him with wide eyes as he tugged the gag from her mouth. 'Are you crazy?' she whispered. 'What if he comes back into the room?'

'As plans go, I'd consider this one suboptimal,' Bernatto muttered. 'But I wasn't exactly in a position to argue.'

He drew a knife from a sheath at his waist and severed her bonds. He pointed at the vines and weeds covering the ceiling. 'Grab the rope... It's up there, just past the vines.'

Trina stood on the chair and pushed aside the foliage covering the hole Bernatto had cut in the waterlogged roof. It was just large enough for a person to crawl through. She grabbed the rope. 'I have it... What about my grandfather?'

Bernatto unslung a rifle from his shoulder. 'He's in the next room. Climb up and wait for my signal. I'm going for him next.'

'What signal?'

'Most likely more shooting.'

She grimaced then shinnied up the rope.

Bernatto gritted his teeth as he pulled back the charging handle on the rifle. His body ached, and his breathing was labored. The heat of the jungle was wearing him down. But his thin, wrinkled lips curled into a cynical smile. 'Never thought I'd be doing this again,' he muttered to nobody.

Then he kicked open the door. Two soldiers stood in the hangar, guarding the room that held Nhan. The rest had pursued the burning fuel truck into the surrounding jungle.

The men spun around as the door slammed into the wall. Bernatto opened fire. A quick burst silenced one man instantly. The other man raised his rifle and returned fire. Bullets thudded into the wood next to Bernatto's face, missing him by inches.

Bernatto winced and pulled the trigger again. A red splatter painted the frosted glass behind the soldier. The man groaned as he clutched the wound in his chest. He slumped to the ground and lay still. Bernatto advanced, sweeping the rifle left and right. Beads of sweat trickled down his forehead. Once he determined he was alone in the hangar, he wiped them away. Then he threw open the door to Nhan's cell.

The old Vietnamese man spat and coughed as Bernatto removed his gag. 'Are you all right?' Bernatto asked.

Nhan shook his head. 'I... I don't have much left. Cancer... taken its toll. This is better way to die.'

Bernatto shook his head. 'No, I'm getting you out of here.' He sliced through the ropes holding the elderly man to the chair. Nhan slumped forward and fell to the floor. Bernatto cradled him in his arms, lifting his head from the floor.

'Nhan. Nhan, get up.'

The old man closed his eyes. 'I'm tired. So tired. Need rest...'

'Nhan, Trina is waiting. We have to get to her.'

Nhan's eyes opened. 'Trina?'

Bernatto pressed the butt of his pistol into Nhan's limp hand. 'Yes... Trina. She's waiting outside. Can you shoot?'

Nhan flashed him a toothy grin. 'Shoot, yes. Walk, no.'

'I'll walk for both of us,' Bernatto muttered. With a grunt, he hoisted Nhan off the floor and slung the man's arm over his shoulder. He held his automatic rifle with one hand and supported the feeble man's waist with the other. 'I clocked three guards at the chopper landing zone... The Iroquois is twelve. You take the man at ten o'clock. I'll handle one and three.'

Nhan gave him a weak nod. 'I understand.'

An explosion rumbled through the faraway jungle. Bernatto took a deep breath. 'Here we go...'

They shuffled out of the hangar wall. Bernatto swung his rifle, firing two short bursts. One of the chopper guards jerked and spasmed then fell to the ground. The other stumbled back but stayed on his feet.

Nhan's pistol roared. The soldier standing closest to the hangar collapsed and fell face-down in the grass. Bernatto fired again, but his shots ricocheted off the fuselage of the helicopter. The wounded soldier returned fire. Clumps of dirt and grass flew up in their path.

Nhan adjusted his aim and fired again. The remaining soldier gurgled as a trickle of blood spilled from his mouth. He slumped against the helicopter, and he fell to the ground.

'You always were a bad shot,' the old man wheezed.

Bernatto whistled loudly. Trina slid down the curved hangar

and rushed over to them. 'What the hell is going on? Where's Tom?' she asked in a breathless voice.

'Help me!' Bernatto snapped.

Trina slung Nhan's free arm over her shoulder. The three of them hobbled toward the helicopter as quickly as they could.

'Caine is by the lake,' Bernatto said. 'He used the fuel truck as a distraction, drew away some men.'

Trina glanced around the dark clearing. A pale-orange glow rose over the roof of the hangar... In the distance, the jungle was burning. Distant cries echoed through the trees, and staccato bursts of gunfire chattered in the darkness.

'What about the crazy one?' she asked.

'You'll have to be more specific,' Bernatto hissed. He threw open the rear door and laid Nhan in the back of the helicopter.

'The guy with the buzz cut and those devil eyes.' She shivered. '*Chúa tôi*... My God, he scared me. When he looked at me, it felt like someone walking over my grave.'

'Boone has his issues,' Bernatto said, settling into the pilot's seat. 'So does Caine, for that matter.' He peered out the front cockpit window, and for a moment, his hands froze on the controls. He glanced down at his fingers. They were shaking.

He clenched them in a fist. 'What we do, the things we've seen... It leaves scars. Gets to us all in the end.'

He relaxed his hand and began flipping switches on the chopper's controls, powering up the engine. The rotors slowly whined to life.

Trina hopped in the back and cradled her grandfather's head in her lap.

'Hang on,' Bernatto called back as he worked the flight controls. The Bell helicopter lifted into the night sky, leaving the flaming jungle and rotting hangars behind.

35

Caine felt the cold lake water slosh against his legs as he backpedaled through the mire. He raised his rifle. Ahead of him, a dim blaze lit up the jungle as flames from the crashed fuel truck crawled up the surrounding trees. The vines criss-crossing overhead became sparkling tendrils of fire and quickly disintegrated into trails of glowing ash.

He sent another burst of gunfire into the trees as he moved along the edge of the lake. The weapon clicked empty, and he dove under the water's black surface. He kicked off the bottom, swimming along the shallow, undulating coast. A few minutes later, he surfaced and examined the rifle in his hands. So far, the water had not damaged the gun's ability to fire. He could only hope his good luck would continue. But either way, his shots were merely a distraction.

More gunfire crackled in the jungle. The men were firing wild, unable to zero in on his position. So long as the blaze from the wreckage lit up the jungle, he knew the men darting through the trees could not see him in the black water. He ejected the spent magazine and slammed a fresh one into the rifle. He pulled back the charging handle and opened fire again, sending two quick sprays into the shadowy trees.

A pair of thick black leeches hung from his left arm, but he ignored them and dove underwater again. He felt reeds and other plant life brushing against his body as he kicked forward and dove into the dark depths. The lake bed sloped up beneath him. He swam forward, heading back to the coast. With any luck, Bernatto and the others had made it to the helicopter and would pick him up shortly.

He surfaced again, gasping for breath. He kept his body low in the water, allowing only his head to break the surface. He scanned the coastline, making sure no men were advancing on his position. In the distance, he heard more shouting and the faint crackle of gunfire. The blaze burned brighter. A thick cloud of smoke billowed into the purple night sky.

Caine rose a few more inches from the water. He raised his rifle, preparing to fire.

Suddenly, he heard a splash. Vegetation snapped behind him. Before he could turn around, a muscular arm wrapped around his throat, and a fist pummeled his side. He gasped in pain as the blow slammed into his kidney. A wave of agony shot through his body. His hands spasmed, releasing their grip on the rifle.

As the weapon sank into the shadows, his attacker dragged him backward and pulled him from the lake. 'Nice try, Tom,' Boone hissed in his ear. 'Keep the fire between you and your targets, hide in the shadows. Perfect spot to pick off a few stragglers.'

Caine grabbed the arm around his throat and struggled to pry it loose. But the man's grip was like a steel vise. His nails clawed at Boone's flesh, but the older man continued dragging Caine out of the water and up onto the grass.

Caine felt Boone's hand drop to his waist and remove his pistol. He tossed the weapon into the water then threw Caine loose. He struck the ground and rolled a few feet away, gasping and sputtering for breath.

'What's the plan, Tom? Bernatto gonna fly out of here? You think he'll risk his ass to come back and get you?'

Caine rose to his feet. He slid the karambit knife from his pocket.

Boone grinned. 'Hell, you know how he thinks. We're all expendable, right? He'll just betray you again. Like you betrayed me.'

'Grissom betrayed us both,' Caine snarled as he circled around Boone. 'He sent us on an unsanctioned op. He hung us out to dry and—'

'Bullshit!' Boone drew a knife. The blade made a metallic hiss as it left the sheath at his waist. The long, serrated weapon glinted in the moonlight. Boone darted the knife back and forth in the air, like a snake preparing to strike. 'Grissom came back for me, sent men to get me out of that Chinese hellhole you left me in. You know what they did to me there?'

'I can guess.'

Boone laughed. 'Yeah, I'll bet you can. Same thing they did to you in Afghanistan, right? Bet those White Leopard assholes worked you over good once they got their hands on you.'

Caine narrowed his eyes. 'How did you know about that?'

Boone kept his eyes on Caine as he laughed. He tossed the knife from hand to hand, following Caine's circular pattern through the grass. 'How do I know? Who do you think led that convoy in the desert, Tom? Hey, there's one thing I always wanted to know.'

Caine kept his attention on the knife and Boone's shoulders, waiting for any sign of an impending attack. From afar, he heard the thumping of the helicopter as it took off.

They made it. They're in the air, which means...

'Why do you do it, Tom?' Boone asked.

The words sent a chill down Caine's spine, like a blade of ice had cut through his skin.

'What did you say?' he growled.

'Jack asked you that in the tunnel, underneath the collapsed well, right? But you never answered. See, me, I know exactly why I do it. Like I said before, on the radio. There are wolves, and there are sheep. And I'm no sheep.'

Boone advanced, darting with the knife. Caine continued circling, avoiding the bait.

'But you didn't say anything. Jack wasted his last breath on you, and you couldn't answer. So I have to ask... Is it because you don't know? Or because you can't face the truth?'

The sound of the chopper grew fainter. Caine glanced up at the horizon... He saw the dark shape of the Bell turning south, moving farther away from his position.

Bernatto, you son of a bitch!

'Just you and me now, Tom,' Boone said, noticing the fury in Caine's eyes. 'So, what's it gonna be, brother? You a wolf? Or a sheep?'

Boone lunged forward. Caine pivoted to the side, but he was too late... His opponent's blade cut across his arm, and a spatter of blood struck the grass. The wind picked up, whipping through Caine's hair.

Caine lowered his stance and adjusted his grip on the knife. Boone grinned and feinted forward. Caine shifted his weight, pretending to step back. But at the last second, he dodged sideways. Boone's feint turned into a downward slash, but Caine was already moving. As the attack sliced through thin air, Caine swung his left arm and knocked the blade clear of the strike zone.

Boone's body turned to the left, following the direction of his blade. Caine's knife slashed a vicious gash across the man's ribs. But before he could step back, Boone slammed his head forward, cracking the top of his skull into Caine's face.

A flash of white exploded across Caine's eyes. The cartilage in his nose snapped. He stumbled backward, raising his knife to block any oncoming attack.

Boone put some distance between them and continued circling. He gingerly prodded the bloody wound in his side. 'That's it, Tom. I don't want to fight the sheep. I want the real deal. I want the killer... the bastard who left me to die!'

'You want him?' Caine snarled, locking his emerald eyes with Boone's manic stare. 'You got him!'

Caine darted forward again. Boone moved to block, but before his arm could connect, Caine switched the knife to his left hand, locked Boone's blocking arm, and slashed at the man's neck with the curved blade.

Boone dropped his blade and threw his free arm up, blocking Caine's strike. Before Caine could disengage, Boone's knee shot up. Caine felt the blow slam into his solar plexus, and a gagging cough erupted from his lips. Before he could catch his breath, he felt himself stumbling backward... Boone charged forward and pushed him toward the lake.

Caine dropped the knife, and his fingers clawed at Boone's throat. He wrapped them around the man's thick neck and squeezed as hard as he could. But his enemy only grinned back at him, his black eyes wide and bloodshot.

Caine felt himself trip over a log or rock... It was impossible to tell in the darkness. All he knew was that he was falling. He heard a splash, and cold water stung his cheeks. The murky haze closed over him, distorting his view of Boone and his wild-eyed gaze.

As he slipped beneath the water, Caine felt Boone's hands wrap around his throat. The man's face was a warped mask of rage and bloodlust, a twisted shadow barely visible through the dark, swirling water. Caine coughed again, sending more bubbles streaming to the surface.

His vision faded to black as he and Boone continued to strangle each other.

36

The Bell helicopter swung right as Bernatto's feet slipped on the torque pedals. Trina screamed as the sudden motion threw her against the wall.

'Calm down, we're fine,' he shouted back as he veered away from the abandoned hangar buildings. 'I'm just out of practice, that's all.'

Trina watched the lake vanish behind them as they soared away from the camp. 'Wait,' she shouted. 'What about Tom?'

'Don't worry. Caine can take care of himself.'

'What?' She stormed up to the cockpit and braced herself against the empty co-pilot's chair. 'We can't just leave him behind. We have to go back!'

Nhan erupted in a fit of coughing behind her. She turned and gave him a concerned look.

'Trina, my dear, Caine is not the priority. You hid the intel. I can unlock it. And that should be enough to secure safe passage to America for you and your grandfather.'

'So you're just going to leave him to die?'

'Better him than me. Once he no longer needs me, he has

no reason to keep me alive. You saw it with your own eyes. He'll kill me in a heartbeat.'

'Why? What the hell did you do to him?'

Bernatto looked up at her for a moment then turned back to the instruments as the helicopter shuddered in an updraft.

'Neither of us were saints, Trina. I did... terrible things. Terrible but necessary. Caine will never forgive me. Either he dies here, or I do.'

Trina bit her lip and thought for a moment. She walked back to Nhan and cradled his head in her arm. He coughed again then closed his eyes and patted her arm. 'You good girl. Good... to... me.'

His breathing slowed as he fell asleep. The gun in his hand struck the floor with a loud thud. She slid a folded blanket under the old man's head. Then she picked up the pistol.

Bernatto pulled up on the stick, gaining altitude and climbing over the treetops. Then he froze. He heard a metallic click behind him. The sound of a racking pistol slide.

'Turn around,' Trina snapped. 'We're going back.'

'Trina, you can't trust Caine. You don't know him like I do. He'll—'

'Whoever he is, he saved my life. I'm not leaving him here to die. Turn around, now.'

Bernatto sighed. 'You won't shoot me, Trina. Not with Nhan in—'

Blam!

The roar of the gunshot was deafening in the tiny cockpit. The bullet ricocheted off the helicopter's controls. Sparks leapt from the control panel, and a warning light flickered to life. Bernatto gripped the control stick as the helicopter shuddered. 'Trina! You could have damaged the controls!'

Trina aimed the gun at Bernatto again. 'Đúng rồi... That's

right. So turn around now, or I might have to fire another warning shot!'

A low chuckle sounded from the rear of the helicopter. 'You better listen to her,' Nhan wheezed. 'Trina is stubborn girl. She take after me.'

Bernatto glared at her but said nothing. He swung the helicopter around. Trina lowered the weapon as they circled back toward the encampment.

* * *

Caine thrashed beneath the surface of the water. A dark, bloody haze hovered around the edge of his vision. He felt a burning sensation rising in his lungs, and more bubbles escaped his lips.

He needed air.

He clenched Boone's neck tighter and felt cords of muscle ripple beneath his fingers. Boone was a few years older than he was, but the man had kept in perfect physical condition. Caine could just make out Boone's savage grin through the murky depths. The man had suffered; it was obvious. Behind his black-eyed stare, Caine saw a familiar sight... Rage, hatred, betrayal. The same things he saw when his own face peered back at him in the mirror.

Boone was strong, but Caine knew that wasn't why he was losing. It was because Boone had nothing to live for... nothing but revenge. Once, Caine had possessed that same singular purpose. But now...

Rebecca... you finally have a chance to fix things with Rebecca. To put the past behind you.

In his mind, he heard a cackle. Instead of Boone, he saw a woman, ancient and withered. A dream, a hazy memory from his past. Anna, the godmother of Thailand's most powerful organized-crime family. The *Chao Mae*... An old woman with pitch-black eyes like Boone's, cradling a porcelain doll in her lap.

'You can be both an angel and a devil for only so long,' she croaked, her voice a throaty rasp from years of smoking. 'Sooner or later, you have to choose...'

Angel or devil, he thought. *Wolf or sheep...*

A brilliant white light exploded across the water. For a second, Caine was blind. Boone's face, the jungle, the water... Everything vanished in the blinding flash. For that one moment, Caine thought the lack of oxygen had done its job, and his brain cells were dying in a beautiful display of mental fireworks.

Then he heard a sound over the churning water and the roar of blood in his ears. Gunfire swept across the water's edge. He felt Boone's choking fingers loosen their grip. The man grabbed his shirt and yanked him from the water, dragging him back toward the jungle at the edge of the lake.

The mechanical growl of rotors thundered through the air. A searchlight beamed across the shore. It was a helicopter... Bernatto had returned!

The Bell lowered, hovering a meter above the lake. Its prop wash sent water droplets spraying through the air, and circular ripples erupted beneath the aircraft. Trina stood in the open side door, holding Bernatto's pistol in a quivering grip. Caine shook his head, fighting to clear his vision as Boone continued pulling him backward.

He's using me as a shield, he thought. *Keeping me between him and the chopper until he can finish me in the jungle.*

He coughed as he sucked in a lungful of oxygen.

Once he gets me into those trees, Trina doesn't have a shot.

He struggled to break free of Boone's grip. But Caine was

weak from lack of oxygen, and his limbs felt like jelly. His arm dropped to his side. He felt warm blood run across his palm.

Not my blood... I wounded him! He remembered dragging the knife across Boone's side. The haze lifted from his oxygen-starved brain.

Taking a deep breath, he clenched his hand into a fist and swung it like a hammer, pummeling the gash in Boone's torso. Boone grunted in pain, and Caine felt the iron grip around his throat loosen. He struck the weak spot again then dipped his shoulder down to the left.

Caine stepped back and drove his left foot into Boone's knee. The man slipped in the mud, and his hold broke. Caine lurched free and sprinted for the helicopter. He zagged right as Trina opened fire again, sending three shots into the brush. Boone cursed behind him and dove into the undergrowth.

Caine's feet splashed through the shallow water at the edge of the lake. He could see Bernatto in the pilot's chair, struggling to keep the aircraft level over the water. The curved landing skid swung ahead of him.

Caine leapt into the air and grabbed hold. His fingers wrapped around the metal perch, and he held on for dear life. The helicopter lurched up, gaining altitude. He heard the crackling of gunfire behind him. Sparks flew from the fuselage, and a series of holes tore through the metal tail.

Caine heaved himself up onto the skid. Trina grabbed his hand and pulled him into the helicopter. He rolled onto his back, gasping for breath. Another volley of gunfire struck the aircraft. Caine pulled Trina down as bullets tore through the sidewall. He turned his head and saw Boone shooting blindly into the night sky. The helicopter swooped over the lake and disappeared behind a jungle-covered hill.

'Are you okay?' Caine said, still cradling Trina in his arms.

She looked him in the eye and nodded. 'I... I think so.'

Caine wrapped his hand around hers. 'You're okay. Give me the gun.'

She released the pistol. Caine stood up and ejected the magazine, checking to make sure it still had a few shots left. Then he slammed it back into place and stormed into the cockpit.

'Bernatto, you son of a bitch!' he shouted.

A beeping sound filled the cabin, and Bernatto struggled to work the controls.

'You were going to leave me behind!'

'Now is not the time, Tom,' Bernatto shouted back. A red warning light flickered on the console.

'You're right, Allan. Now is not the time. I should have shot you on sight, back at the house. Then maybe we—'

'Enough!' Trina shouted. 'No more shooting! No more killing! I can't... Nhan is...'

Caine wasn't sure if Nhan's condition had worsened or if the girl was in shock. He opened his mouth to speak, but no words came. He didn't know what he could possibly say that would make any difference.

She broke down in tears. 'Just, no one has to die, okay?'

'I'm afraid that may not be an accurate statement,' Bernatto muttered.

Caine glanced down at him. 'What are you talking about?'

'Riley's shots pierced the fuel tank, and it wasn't full to begin with.'

The helicopter lurched again. Caine leaned over Bernatto's chair and eyed the fuel gauge. The thick white needles bounced within the circular gauge as the aircraft dropped again. Then it settled at the far left of the meter, dipping below the red warning line.

'The gauge reads empty. Do we have enough to—'

The engine whined and coughed then grew silent. The sound of rotors grew quiet... The engine stopped spinning.

'No,' Bernatto snapped. 'We don't. Everyone, brace for impact!'

37

Caine tumbled forward into the co-pilot's seat. His stomach lurched as Bernatto adjusted the falling aircraft's pitch. The nose of the aircraft tilted forward as Bernatto lowered the pitch with the cyclic control lever.

Caine braced himself against the control panel. He reached back and grabbed the flight harness then clicked it into place. 'Trina,' he shouted. 'Strap in, now!'

He didn't wait for her response, instead turning to Bernatto. 'Disengage the clutch! Let the rotors spin free, or—'

'I know how autorotation works, Tom.' Bernatto's arms trembled as he gripped the controls tighter. 'We need to descend at the proper angle to keep the rotors spinning. But it's been decades since I flew one of these. Landing without engine power isn't something I ever—'

Whack!

Before he could finish his sentence, the landing skids pierced the jungle canopy beneath them. Leaves and vines slapped against the belly of the aircraft.

'I can't find a clearing,' Bernatto shouted.

ANDREW WARREN

The fuel alarm continued wailing, and the impacts against the metal fuselage grew louder. Caine peered out the cockpit windows. Any minute now, they'd drop below the tree line, and when that happened...

He narrowed his eyes, scanning the tilted horizon. He pointed out the cockpit window. 'There, I see a clearing... If you can—'

Suddenly, the tail of the helicopter spun, throwing them to the left. Caine heard Trina scream, and the sound of grinding metal screeched in the back of the helicopter.

Bernatto grabbed the main stick with both hands, fighting to keep the aircraft level. 'It's no good,' he shouted. 'Tail rotor's jammed!'

The helicopter lurched again, dropping several meters. Caine heard the scream of rending metal and a loud snap. The chopper tipped to the right then began tumbling through the air.

'Brace for impact!' he shouted.

A sea of green rushed toward him. The aircraft shuddered as it struck the canopy of trees. Then, with a sudden, violent shock, the helicopter snapped backward. Caine felt his skull rattle as his head slammed into the back of his seat. The last sound he heard was the shattering of glass. The cockpit imploded, and a hail of glittering shards rushed toward him.

* * *

Caine blinked. The darkness clouding his vision lifted – but only a bit. He cracked his eyes open more... A pale shaft of light pierced the mangled metal shell hanging over his head. For a moment, he thought another helicopter must be hovering above them, beaming a searchlight down on their position.

Then the image snapped into focus, and the light seemed to fade. He realized it was only the moon, bathing them in its soft, silvery glow. He reached up to undo his harness. His hand missed the release and slapped against the edge of his seat. He grunted and tried again.

He heard a click, and his body fell sideways. He struck the ground with a loud thud. The surrounding wreckage shuddered. Looking up, he saw the control panel next to his head. Everything seemed to be pointing in the wrong direction... The dials and gauges were a dark blur.

He shook his head, clearing the remaining haze from his vision. He blinked and looked at the panel again. It was sideways. The helicopter was lying on its side on the jungle floor. Water dripped through the torn metal fuselage, and green leaves jutted through the broken glass of the cockpit.

Bernatto hung limp in his seat. He was unconscious, and a trickle of blood ran down his nose. Caine stared at him for a moment, listening to the dripping water and creaking metal surrounding them.

Allan Bernatto... His old handler and Grissom's successor at the CIA. The man who had framed him for treason and left him to die in the deserts of Afghanistan.

In the years after his betrayal, Caine had dreamt many times of killing Bernatto. The thought kept him going through days of torture and captivity. And later, through long, sleepless nights, checkered with nightmares of his past. Bernatto had lied to him, manipulated him, used him for his own ends. He had killed Caine's partner, Jack Tyler, and countless others.

Jack was a father, a good man. A better man than Caine...

For a time, Caine had put his hunger for revenge behind him. Instead, he focused on survival. He lived off the grid, leaving all traces of his old life behind. Then Rebecca came into his life again. Somehow, she found him.

And Bernatto... He hurt her, put her in a wheelchair. Then he killed Josh Galloway, a man Rebecca had turned to for comfort when Caine abandoned her in the shadows. Another good man dead.

Do it. The voice in his head was cold, calculating, like a serpent coiling around his skull. *How many times will you let him betray you? Take him off the board before it's too late.*

Caine closed his eyes and swallowed. The mission. He needed Bernatto alive.

Bullshit. There's always another excuse. Always another lie.

Caine opened his eyes. His hands reached out toward the unconscious man's neck. It would be so easy... No gun, no knife. Just the satisfaction of seeing one last look of fear on the man's face. One last hissing gasp of breath as he choked the life out of him.

'Help! Please, help me...' The voice was weak and tinged with pain.

Caine rolled around. He heard someone moving in the back of the helicopter. Trina.

'Are you all right?' he shouted back.

'No, it's my grandfather! Please help!'

Caine gave one last glance at the unconscious man strapped in his seat. Then he slowly stood up. A wave of dizziness hit him. Swaying on his feet, he reached out and steadied himself against the metal fuselage. He touched his head and felt blood.

Might have a concussion, he thought. *Take it easy...*

'Tom,' Trina shouted. 'Where are you?'

'Just stay where you are. I'm coming to you.'

He felt the crumpled aircraft shudder as he moved into the back. He squinted, struggling to see in the dim light. Suddenly, a green phosphorescence lit up the back of the helicopter. Trina's terrified face peered up at him, lit from below by a fluorescent glow stick. Blood speckled her face, and her lips looked bruised. But other than that, she appeared unharmed.

'I found this in a first aid kit,' she said, her words slurring together. 'I can't find a flashlight. I don't know where...' Her voice trailed off to a faint whisper.

Caine put a hand on her shoulder. 'You're all right. We just—'

'My grandfather, I think he's hurt bad!'

Using the glow stick, she led him farther back into the mangled fuselage. Nhan lay against the side of the helicopter. His breath was a damp wheeze, and he groaned in pain.

Caine took the glow stick from her shivering grasp and ran it over the old man's body. In the pale green light, he saw a black, sticky pool of liquid seeping beneath Nhan's body. He rolled the man on his side.

Nhan gasped in pain.

'Stop it, you're hurting him!' Trina shouted.

'Keep your voice down,' Caine hissed. 'I don't know how far from their camp we are. There could be patrols.'

He moved the light closer, examining the area behind the old man's body. The helicopter's side had a large gash torn through it. A thick shard of metal pierced the fuselage and ran along the side of the wreckage. The edge of the metal blade sliced a long, bloody cut across the old man's back and spine.

As he ran the light along the metal fragment, Caine realized a rotor had snapped off and bounced back into the aircraft. He glanced down at Nhan's trembling body. The man was sick and old, and now he had lost a significant amount of blood.

He saw the whites of Nhan's eyes roll up as the old man met his gaze. 'Not in here,' he muttered. '*Đưa tôi ra ngoài...*'

Trina choked back a sob. 'He wants us to take him outside,' she said. 'I don't know – should we move him?'

'We should do what he wants,' Caine murmured.

Trina sobbed again. She grabbed her grandfather's legs, and Caine slid his arms under the man's shoulders. Nhan hissed but nodded.

They carried him from the wreckage as slowly as they could and laid him gently on the ground. Caine heard footsteps behind them. He looked up, and his hand darted to his waistband. But it was only Bernatto, staggering toward them from the wreckage.

Caine glared at him for a moment then turned back to Nhan. 'Can you move your legs?'

Nhan uttered a high-pitched grunt. It took Caine a moment to realize he was laughing. 'If I can, I don't want to.'

Trina looked at the old man's withered body. The jungle was alive with the sounds of insects. A monkey howled in the distance. Trina opened her mouth to speak but burst into tears instead. She slumped over his body and sobbed into his chest. 'No... Please, I'm not ready. Not like this, not out here...'

The old man patted her back. 'No, no... Out here is good. Look at the moon. Listen to the crickets. Beautiful here. Good place to rest.'

He gently pushed her away and turned to Bernatto. 'You keep your promise. Keep her safe.'

'I... I'll try, Nhan, but—'

The old man shook his head. 'No excuse. You keep her safe, or I come back to haunt you.' He turned to Caine. 'You... you don't trust him, do you?'

Caine shook his head. 'Not for a second.'

The old man nodded. His face looked pale and gaunt in the

moonlight. 'Good. You smart. You watch out for my Trina. Help keep her safe.'

Caine clenched his jaw then nodded. 'I will.'

Nhan closed his eyes and smiled. 'Better, out here. Soon, I will see beautiful Mai. And then Linh, Trina's mother. Better... better like this. Tired of waiting. It is good. It is...'

His voice faded away, and a final wheeze escaped his throat.

Trina lowered her head and wailed. The sound echoed through the trees, and for a moment, the jungle sounds ceased, as if the animals also mourned Nhan's passing. Then, a few seconds later, the crickets resumed their chirping. The night birds continued their cries. All was as it had been.

Caine returned to the wreckage and searched through the mangled metal. He found his duffel bag and pulled it out then dropped Trina's first aid kit in. He fished Bernatto's pistol out from under the seat.

'We should go,' Caine said. 'Put as much distance between us and them as we can before sunrise.'

'First, we bury him,' Bernatto murmured.

'There's no time. We have to—'

'I said we bury him,' Bernatto snapped in a raised voice. 'It will go faster if you help.' The man glowered at Caine over the rims of his glasses. The blood from the gash in his head continued to drip down his nose.

Caine sighed. 'Fine. We bury him.' He tossed a mangled shard of metal to Bernatto, then grabbed one himself. The two men worked in silence as they carved dirt from the jungle floor. The only sounds were the jungle animals' cries and Trina's muted tears.

38

The trek to the mouth of Hang Son Doong cave was a blur. Caine remembered little of their journey save the ever-present heat and the constant chirping of insects. They traveled through the night and reached the dark, gaping mouth of the cavern by dawn. As the sun rose over the jungle, Caine paused and took a deep breath. The ground beneath their feet had become rocky and steep. A tapestry of clouds stretched across the pale-blue morning sky, trails of pink, gold, and magenta hanging behind the jagged rock outcropping ahead of them. Beyond that, the darkness of the cave lay waiting.

The cave entrance was massive, looming over them like the mouth of some ancient predatory beast. Standing in the cave's shadow, Caine felt small and insignificant. The wind picked up, and a cool morning breeze blew through his clothes and hair and made a faint moaning sound as it moved through the dark interior of the cavern.

Trina stepped next to him and paused, looking up at the rocks. 'Impressive, isn't it?' she asked quietly.

Caine nodded. 'It's bigger than I thought. How deep does it go?'

She grinned. 'Honestly? No one can say for sure. You could fly a 747 through the original cavern. And expeditions keep finding more chambers and passageways. Last year, the divers who rescued those children from the collapsed cave in Thailand? They dove over eighty meters into a new underwater tunnel here. It links this entire system to a whole other cavern. That's like finding a second peak at the top of Mount Everest.'

'And that's where you hid the drive?'

She nodded. 'Yes. That's where we're going. After we rest at the camp.'

Caine brushed his windswept hair from his forehead. 'There's no time to wait. The men chasing us could be—'

'Tom, I get it.' She looked back at Bernatto as he clambered up the trail after them. His skin was already flushed red, and he struggled to keep pace. Sweat soaked his clothes, and he panted for breath. 'But we're hurt. We're tired. We're hungry. It's dangerous in there... more dangerous than you can imagine. You know what I said before, about Mount Everest?'

Caine nodded.

She gave him a concerned look. 'More people have summited Everest than have stood inside this cave. If you make a mistake diving in here, there's nowhere to go. You can't surface. You run out of air, and you die in the shadows. Most likely, no one will even find your body.' She rested a hand on his shoulder. 'We have to get to camp and rest. Eat some food, drink some water.'

Caine glared at her. The sun shifted behind the rocks, and golden beams of light moved across the foliage. He gave her a reluctant nod. 'Fine. We rest for a couple hours. Then we have to move.'

She smiled. 'Good man. Now, follow me. Prepare to see a genuine wonder of the natural world.'

She continued up the trail. Caine waited for Bernatto to catch up. Then he followed her, vanishing into the looming shadow of the overhanging rocks.

* * *

Caine woke up in a cold sweat. He shot up into a sitting position, gasping for breath. It took him a second to remember where he was. The fabric walls of the tent seemed to close in around him. He and his companions were several hundred meters into the cave, and the rock blocked all but a thin shaft of sunlight from entering the mouth of the cave. He could have sworn he had heard the fluttering of wings. But it was so loud... as if hundreds of bats had swooped through his tent.

He reached up and wiped his hair from his face.

Just a nightmare. Memories from the past. Just like always...

He slid out of the sleeping bag and checked his watch. Two hours had passed. Despite the rest, his nerves still jangled with adrenaline, and his body ached. But they couldn't afford to wait any longer. Boone would have patrols in the jungle looking for them, and it was only a matter of time before someone picked up their trail.

Caine grabbed a bottle of water Trina had provided from a cooler and took a few shallow sips. Then he peeled open a protein bar and took a bite. As the dry, chewy paste touched his tongue, he realized how hungry he was. He devoured the rest of the bar then exited the tent.

Trina was standing outside with Bernatto, examining a map on a foldable table. Despite the man's earlier condition, he now looked calm and well-rested. He peered up at Caine over the rims of his glasses. 'Welcome back to the land of the living, Tom.'

A piercing screech echoed through the cave. Caine tensed and looked up into the darkness, but Trina rested a hand on his shoulder. 'It's all right. It's just an eagle owl.'

Caine narrowed his eyes. 'That was a bird?'

Trina laughed. 'Well, it's quite a bird. They have a wingspan of over six feet. Sometimes they nest in the trees down here.'

The thought of trees in a cave seemed odd to Caine, but he ignored her comment and examined the map on the table. 'So, what are we looking at here?'

Trina spun the map around to face him. 'This is a map of the cave system. We're here, in the mouth.' She traced a fine line with a pen, leading through a large interior cavern. 'We have to cross the underground river here...' She gestured on the map with her pen. 'There are guide ropes set up, but this is the rainy season, so the water level will be higher than normal. That's why the tours are shut down now.'

Caine glanced over his shoulder at the two tiny tents. 'Then who set these up? What is the camp still doing here?'

Trina bit her lip. 'Look... you saw my grandfather's house. You heard him cough...' She paused, taking a deep breath. 'He's been sick for years. The hospitals here... they couldn't do anything for him. He needed medicine. Expensive medicine.'

Bernatto gazed up at her. 'So you led tours here yourself? Off season?'

She nodded. 'Only seasoned cave divers. People I know can handle it. I don't let them post pictures. They're just doing it for the experience. And if we find a new system, there's a lot of money in that. Enough to take care of... I mean, there would have been.'

A sob wracked her body, and she coughed. 'Forget it. Doesn't matter now.'

'All right,' Caine said in a soft voice. 'What next?'

'After we cross the river, we reach the first doline.'

'Doline?' Caine raised an eyebrow.

She pointed up at the cavern roof with her pen. 'These caves are mostly limestone. It's relatively brittle. A doline is where the underground river carved away too much rock, eons ago. The cave roof couldn't support its own weight and collapsed, forming a sinkhole that lets in light and air. Huge rainforests grow there, underground. They even have their own rain clouds and weather systems.'

She tapped on the map and drew a line with her pen. 'And here is where the underwater tunnel leads to Hang Thung. It's deep... The standard gas mix the divers were breathing would only allow them to descend eighty meters, but they estimated that it must go down at least another 200 meters beyond that.'

Caine whistled. 'That's a serious dive. You'd need a special nitrogen mix at that depth.'

She nodded, giving him a surprised look. 'Have you worked with nitrox?'

Caine smiled. 'Here and there.'

Trina cocked her head. '*Hấp dẫn*... Interesting. You're a more serious diver than I thought. But we won't be going that deep. A client and I found an offshoot from the main tunnel, here.'

Using her pen, she drew a line that diverged from the serpentine tunnel. 'It's not on any of the maps yet. Compared to the size of this cavern, it's relatively small. That's where I hid the case. I figured it was the last place anyone would think to look for it.'

'An underwater cavern nobody knows about?' Bernatto muttered. 'Safe but hardly convenient for retrieval.'

'You have equipment?' Caine asked.

She nodded toward her tent. 'Tanks and dive skins for two. I don't have full wetsuits... too bulky. The skins will help hold in some warmth, but it will still be very cold down there.' She looked Caine up and down. 'Luckily, my client was about your size.'

Caine studied the map for a few seconds then looked up. 'We'd better get going then.'

Trina tucked her hands in her pockets and gave him an uncertain look.

'What is it?' Caine asked.

She stared into his eyes. 'Every brain cell in my head is screaming this is a terrible idea. We're underequipped, and nobody knows we're here. With the rainy season starting up, we have no idea what the currents will be like down there. No one does. This is uncharted territory. And I still don't know your skill level.'

'I can vouch for Tom's experience,' Bernatto interjected. 'He's a trained combat diver. Earned his master diver insignia badge and served over four years with—'

'None of that matters down there,' Caine snapped. He returned Trina's stare. 'And you're right – it is dangerous. But we came here to get that drive back. And if we fail, then Nhan died for nothing.'

'What the hell is on that drive?' Trina asked in a defiant voice.

'Information,' Bernatto replied. 'Information that can stop a very dangerous man from getting what he wants.'

'What man?' she snapped.

'His old boss,' Caine replied. 'The one holding Boone Riley's leash.'

Trina sighed. 'Fine.' Again, she nodded toward the tent. 'But down there, you follow my lead. If I say we turn back, we turn back. And since you're so eager to get going, you can carry the gear.'

She went back to her tent. Caine stood where he was, watching as she ducked beneath the canvas flap. He turned and glared at Bernatto.

The older man raised a single eyebrow. 'You heard the lady, Tom.'

Caine shook his head and marched after her. High above them, the massive eagle owl circled through the air, its screeching cry echoing through the shadowy cavern.

39

The inky-black water was so cold Caine was amazed his limbs could still move. It wasn't freezing; he knew that was impossible. But as he and his companion began their descent into the dark depths, he felt like he was falling into a deep pool of icy needles, each one stabbing at his flesh.

After a few minutes of swimming through the narrow underwater tunnel, his muscles loosened up. The Lycra dive skin trapped a thin layer of water next to his skin, which soon grew warm from his body heat. The skin was nowhere near as pleasant as a wetsuit, but it was better than nothing.

Ahead of him, Trina kicked her fins and maneuvered under a hanging rock. The light strapped to her head cast a stark white circle over its craggy surface as she swam around it. Caine had a similar light attached to a strap around his head and a smaller flashlight tethered to his wrist. A waterproof Maglite was strapped to his ankle as an emergency backup.

'When you get in trouble underwater, your instinct is to swim up. But most of our dive will have no vertical exit point,'

Trina had explained on the shore of the submerged tunnel. 'So to maintain safety, we use the rule of threes. Three sources of light. And we divide our air supply into thirds.' Caine remembered the metallic clang his tank had made when she rapped her knuckles on its side. 'Each of these cylinders holds about an hour of breathable air, give or take. So that's twenty minutes down, twenty minutes back, and twenty minutes reserve. We hit minute twenty-one, we turn back, case or no case. *Hiểu không?* Got it?'

Caine had assured her he understood. But now, after about ten minutes of swimming through a dark, twisting tunnel of rock, he wasn't so sure. The topography of the passageway seemed strange and alien. At some points, it was so narrow he could hear his scuba tank scraping on the walls. Then, with no warning, the passage would open wider, and he would find himself surrounded by darkness, with only the tiny pinpoint of Trina's headlamp to guide him.

His breathing sent a constant stream of bubbles into the water, and the hiss of his regulator was a comforting presence in the silent blackness. He glanced at the glowing pips on his steel dive watch. Eleven minutes down, nine to go. Despite his promise, he had no intention of turning back without the case in his possession. He had no desire to risk Trina's life. He would plunge deeper into the blackness on his own if need be.

Then he saw her light move to the right. The tunnel narrowed again, and he could tell that Trina was feeling her way along the western wall. As Caine swam closer, he saw a dark, narrow crevice bisecting the rocky wall.

Trina spun around in the murky water and faced him. Her dark-brown eyes peered out at him from behind her mask. She pointed at him then held up her two index fingers. Then she straightened the fingers of her right hand and slashed toward the crevice in a karate chop motion.

Caine recognized her hand signals instantly. They were familiar to all trained divers. *Stay together. Go this way.*

He watched as she slid sideways into the dark opening. Their lights were almost blinding in the tight confines of the passage, and Caine squinted at the brilliant strata of rock just beyond his mask. He heard the metallic scrape of his tank as he slid after her. As they moved through the crevice, the darkness behind them grew even blacker, as if a cold shadow was chasing after them.

Caine felt his pulse quicken as his tank scraped again. Despite his experience, he had never dived in such claustrophobic conditions before. He knew if something went wrong, if they got stuck, or if some rocks shifted... no one would come to their aid. They would drown, cold and alone, in the shadows.

After a few meters, the crevice expanded into a wider tunnel, though it was still a tight fit, and several times Caine felt his tank scrape against the rocks as he swam behind Trina. Ahead of him, she kicked with her fins, stirring up a cloud of sediment in the water. She was a skilled swimmer, and as she sped ahead, Caine lost sight of her. The black water beyond the tunnel seemed to engulf her, devouring the tiny glow of her light.

Caine increased his speed, eager to catch up. As he propelled himself down the tunnel, he squinted. He saw movement up ahead, but it wasn't Trina. Something large and pale streaked toward him through the water. He checked his tank's air gauge. Was he hallucinating? What looked like a giant skull swam closer, its bloodred eyes blazing in the shadows.

When he threw up a hand to ward off whatever it was, he felt something cold and rough brush against his skin. He looked closer: dozens of tiny fish clustered around him. Their sleek, narrow bodies were pale white, with crimson membranes running along their cheeks. Their eyes, if they possessed any, were so tiny as to be invisible.

The small, shimmering bodies beat against his hands and mask. Caine chuckled to himself. Each fish was less than a foot long, but together, they gave the appearance of a large white mass. In the narrow confines of the tunnel, the shape had appeared like that of a skull, and their gill membranes glowed bloodred in the beam of his light.

He swam through the annoying but harmless cave fish, moving into the deeper water beyond. With no warning, the narrow tunnel disappeared, making him feel like he was drifting in an infinite black void. For a moment, he could see nothing beyond the faint light cast by his lamp. It was as though he had stepped off the planet and fallen into outer space.

Then his eyes adjusted to the darkness. He could make out the faint outline of stalactites above their heads, plunging down into the cavernous chamber. Another light bobbed ahead of him. Trina was floating in the water, maintaining her position as she waited for him to catch up.

As he swam over to her, she swept her light over the rocks above. Although the chamber was smaller than the massive caverns above, it still seemed immense. It would be incredibly easy to get lost in the dark, black expanse, and he now understood her concern. Looking up, he saw only jagged rocks and more water. If anything happened to them down here, a treacherous crevice and a long, confined swim stood between them and fresh air.

Trina reached out, took his hand, and pointed down. He nodded, and they swam together, descending deeper into the underwater cave. The water here was surprisingly clear, and he could make out tiny shapes flitting through the beams of their lights: more of the translucent fish he had seen in the crevice.

As Caine and Trina continued their descent, the floor of the cavern came into view. They swam through a forest of stalagmites and fallen boulders. The walls of the cave were a smooth, undulating curtain of flowing limestone... sediment carried by falling water, hardened over the millennia.

Trina grabbed hold of a rock formation near the cavern floor, lowered herself underneath, and swam into a small, hollow pocket. The tiny cave was less than three meters across, and the two of them could barely fit inside. A tiny bundle wrapped in a clear plastic tarp lay nestled within the rocks. Bungee cords anchored to the rugged terrain held it in place.

Trina released a strap and handed it to Caine. Then she removed another, grabbing it as it floated toward the roof of the cave. The package, no longer held down by the elastic cords, drifted from its resting place. She grabbed it and slid a small waterproof plastic case from the tarp.

She gave Caine the 'OK' symbol, and they turned to the mouth of the tiny cave. Using the rocks, they pulled themselves back out into the main chamber. Caine checked his watch... They were just about at the twenty-minute mark. Time to head back.

He made knifelike motions, pointing up the cavern entrance. Trina nodded. She turned and grabbed the floating tarp, bundling it up and shoving it into a pouch on her belt.

Caine watched her as she worked. A flicker of motion caught his eye, and he turned his head. He saw a sliver of light piercing the darkness. At first, he thought it was more fish, darting above them. Then the light grew brighter, closer.

Caine grabbed the case and ripped it from Trina's hands. Behind her mask, her eyes shot open with surprise as he shoved her behind him. As a trail of bubbles streaked through the water toward them, he threw up the case like a shield. Something struck the plastic shell with a muted thump.

He tilted the case down. A harpoon pierced the thick plastic lid. He reached down and drew his knife from his belt as three divers in black wetsuits descended upon them.

40

Caine dropped the case and swam up to meet their attackers. Kicking hard, he closed the distance before either man could fire another bolt. He reached out, grabbed the closest enemy's speargun, and shoved it aside. Then he slashed with his knife, but the water slowed his movements. His opponent grabbed his wrist, blocking the attack. As they struggled, the two of them tumbled through the water, creating a cloud of bubbles as they panted into their regulators.

Caine glanced down at Trina. He could just barely see her in the dim light. She swam fast, darting through the water toward the case. She grabbed it with her free hand. One of the enemy divers grabbed her fin, but she spun around and kicked at his face. The blow struck his head, slamming it against the rocks.

Caine's opponent drove a knee into his abdomen, sending another blast of bubbles cascading through the dark water. He shifted his body, blocking another knee attack as they floated above Trina and the other divers. She dove low, threading through the rock formations below. One of the black-clad men reloaded his speargun and fired. The metal shaft tore through the water, narrowly missing Trina's leg. She swam around a stalagmite on the cave floor, taking cover behind a rock spire.

Caine gave his opponent's arm a violent twist, forcing him to drop the speargun. It sank in a lazy spiral, landing on the rocks below. But before Caine could press his attack, his opponent hit him with another knee strike. Caine doubled over in pain, fighting to catch his breath. Without warning, his attacker reached out and tore off his dive mask.

He blinked, blinded from the chilling water flooding his eyes. Peering through the haze, he saw his opponent slide a long, serrated dive knife from a sheath at his ankle. Caine reached for the man's arm, but he was too late... The shimmering blade swung out, slashing through his regulator hose.

A cloud of bubbles surrounded the two men as oxygen vented into the water from the severed tube. Caine kicked hard, trying to put some distance between himself and the blade. But his attacker still held his knife arm in a tight grip.

Can't breathe... running out of air. Have to end this now!

Caine threw his head forward, slamming it into the man's mask. He ignored the flash of pain as the bridge of his nose struck the hard glass. His opponent's head snapped back. Caine reached down and grabbed the man's belt, shifting his weight in the water. He kicked his legs, powering them both up toward the roof of the cavern.

His attacker kicked and struggled to break free, but Caine spun him around in the water, holding him face up above him. A brief, muted scream exploded through the depths as they ascended toward the jagged rocks.

Caine grunted with exertion. He felt the body in his grasp thrash and writhe as he impaled it on the tip of the sharp stalactite hanging above. His swaying light cast a crimson beam through the water. Blood gushed from the massive puncture wound.

A fire burned in Caine's lungs. He unbuckled the scuba tank from the thrashing body above him. As he slipped the tank off, the corpse went still. A final burst of bubbles slipped through the man's lips.

Caine's vision was hazy, and a drumbeat of blood and desperation thundered in his temples. Every instinct in his body screamed at him to swim up, but he fought the urge... He knew the shadows above held no salvation. No way to surface and suck air into his oxygen-starved body.

Instead, he forced himself to remove the tank from the corpse. He slipped the regulator into his mouth and blew out to clear the hose. Then he breathed in.

The haze lifted, and his heartbeat slowly returned to normal. He spun the tank over his back and clipped the straps in place. Then he slipped his mask back over his eyes, blowing through his nose to clear the water out.

He spun around, getting his bearings in the dark water. Another spear streaked through the water, missing his arm by inches. The spear struck the corpse behind him, hitting the limp flesh with a dull thud. Caine saw a shadowy figure kicking toward him. He dove deep, propelling himself to the floor of the cave as quickly as he could.

Thwack! Another spear streaked past his head, rebounding off the rocks before him. He swam under a narrow ledge, hoping to hide in the shadows. Then he muttered a silent curse as his light reflected off the rock walls like a blinding spotlight. He twisted the flashlight, turning it off and letting it dangle from his wrist.

Darkness engulfed him. The water was cold, black, and silent. He reached down, using the rocks to pull himself along the cavern floor. Up ahead, he saw a dim pinpoint of light bobbing among the rocks.

Trina...

He swam toward her position. As he hugged the bottom of the cave, his hands bumped against something long and metallic. He grabbed it but could not see the object in the darkness. He continued paddling toward the light. Spinning around in the water, he glanced over his shoulder but could see nothing in the blackness. The other diver had also turned off his light... He could be less than a meter away, and Caine would never spot him.

He turned and paddled closer to Trina, swimming at a steady speed, no longer bothering to hide among the rocks. As he moved close to the light, he could see more details in the water. A quick glance at the object he was carrying confirmed what he had suspected... it was a loaded speargun. The other diver had dropped it during their struggle.

Trina floated in the hazy water ahead of him, crouching behind one of the fallen boulders that littered the submerged chamber. Caine turned on his light and swam closer. Glancing over his shoulder, he could see the other diver now. The man was only a few meters behind him. Caine sucked in his breath as his enemy raised his speargun and swam toward him.

41

Caine circled around the rock, and his opponent followed. But as they rounded the massive boulder, Trina sped out between them, swinging the plastic case through the water. The blow clipped the enemy diver on his chin, sending him careening backward. His speargun fired, but the projectile shot off at an angle and vanished into the shadows.

Caine planted his feet on the rocky ground and pushed off, spinning around to face his pursuer. At the same instant, Trina kicked up toward the roof of the cave, crossing his line of sight. The enemy diver looked up, following her light through the water.

Took your eye off the target, Caine thought. *That's a mistake...*

He aimed the long, narrow weapon and pulled the trigger.

Whoosh! The spear darted forward, streaking through the water like a predatory barracuda. It struck the diver in the head, shattering his mask and piercing his left eye. His neck snapped back, his body went limp, and he hung motionless in the water for a moment. Then his corpse floated up toward the jagged rocks.

Caine grabbed Trina's arm and peered through her mask. She furrowed her brow and stared back at him through the glass. Despite days of running, fighting, and cheating death, she still seemed clear and focused. She was tough and resourceful, but Caine knew fear and panic would set in eventually. Down here, one wrong decision could mean life or death. The men who had attacked them were no doubt local soldiers, co-opted by Boone and Grissom. And he knew more could be waiting above...

She closed her hand in a fist and thumped her chest. Then she pointed at the crevice in the cavern's rocks. Caine knew the diving signals by heart.

Running low on air... Time to leave...

He checked the gauge on the side of her tank. Although she still had her reserve, the increased activity had depleted some of the supply for the return trip. Caine had Trina check the tank he'd taken from one of their attackers... he was low too. She was right. It was time to leave. Whatever was waiting for them up above, they would have to deal with it later.

They kicked toward the dark, narrow gap in the cavern wall. Caine let Trina enter first then glanced back at the cavern behind him. Beyond the radius of his feeble light, the water was a flat, black pane, impossible to penetrate. He followed Trina into the tunnel.

They made it a mere few meters down the tight passageway when Caine felt something tug on one of his fins. He spun around, hearing a dull metal clang as his tank scraped against the rocks. A diver clad in a sleek black wetsuit hung in the water behind them.

The diver Trina knocked out. He must have recovered...

Trina spun around in the tunnel. A burst of bubbles

exploded from her regulator as she gasped. He stabbed forward with his fingers, indicating that she should keep going. Then he kicked his attacker's face.

The water dulled the force of the blow, and the man grappled with his legs. Caine pulled back, tucking his feet in close. He spun in the water, struggling to maneuver in the tight space. Above them, the crevice grew even narrower, the rocks sloping together in a tight V-shaped formation.

Caine darted to the side as his opponent slashed through the water with a knife. The attack missed his regulator hose by inches. Caine grabbed the man's knife arm, pushed the blade away, and jabbed forward, stabbing the fingers of his free hand into his attacker's throat.

A cloud of bubbles filled the tunnel as the man gasped for air. Caine could barely see his enemy as they struggled in the swirling haze, but he saw the man push off the rocks with his legs, driving Caine backward. A metallic clang echoed through the passage as his tank slammed into the rocks. Another stream of bubbles exploded over his shoulder.

Caine muttered a silent curse. The impact had damaged a valve on his tank, causing him to vent oxygen into the water. Soon, he would run out of air.

He darted left as the diver slashed again with his knife. The shimmering blade scraped against the rocks, barely missing his shoulder. Caine pushed off the rocks, launching himself forward and driving his shoulder into his attacker's chest. His motion propelled the two of them up, and Caine felt his skull slam into the edge of the narrow rock crevice above them.

As they struggled in the water, Caine noticed the man was wearing a buoyancy-control-device vest over his wetsuit. The weights and air bladders in the vest controlled his buoyancy, allowing him to spend less energy maintaining his depth in the water.

The man drove an elbow into Caine's shoulder, knocking him away, then lashed out with the knife again. Caine winced as the blade tore across his arm and a cloud of blood stained the surrounding water.

Caine grabbed the man's knife arm again, halting another strike. He grabbed the control knob of the diver's BCD and turned it up all the way. The vest hissed as it inflated with air. The diver's eyes opened wide with surprise and terror. He shot up like a rocket, ascending toward the roof of the passage. His head and shoulders wedged into the crevice above, leaving his legs kicking below.

The panicked man dropped his knife and struggled to free himself from the narrow gap in the rocks. But the vest continued inflating, wedging him even more tightly. His tank scraped against the opening, unable to fit through.

Caine grabbed the sinking knife. He swam up and slashed the blade through the trapped man's air hose. As another burst of bubbles filled the passage, Caine spun around and navigated the dark tunnel, leaving the trapped man behind. He could hear the diver's bubbling screams and feel the gentle motion of his thrashing through the water.

Then the thrashing stopped, and silence fell.

A few seconds later, he emerged from the crevice. He could feel the air he was breathing grow thin and stale. His damaged tank was almost empty. Trina, noticing the trail of bubbles leaving his tank, swam over to him. She removed her regulator from her mouth and handed it to him.

He ejected his mouthpiece and took a deep breath from Trina's air supply. Then he handed her regulator back and released his damaged tank, letting it sink into the depths. She grabbed his hand, and they swam together through the darkness. They took turns breathing, sharing her remaining air as they ascended to the dim, distant light above.

42

Despite the brutal heat outside, the air inside the massive
cavern was perpetually cool. Caine felt a shiver run through his
wet, soaking body as he and Trina walked back to their campsite. After hours of swimming and climbing, his muscles felt
like warm jelly. His head throbbed from lack of sleep and food,
but his nerves were razor-sharp, still tingling with adrenaline
from the tunnel battle.

As they approached the camp, he grabbed Trina's arm and
pulled her behind a rock formation. Pistol in hand, he peered at
the colorful tents in the distance.

'What are you doing?' Trina whispered.

'Those divers knew where they were going,' Caine muttered.
'Bernatto must have given them our position.'

'What the hell is it between you two?' she asked, peering
into his intense green stare. 'What did he do to you?'

Caine glared back at her. 'He betrayed me,' he finally said.
'He hurt people I cared about.'

'People? Or person?'

Caine gave her a strange look. 'What do you mean?'

She tilted her head and peered into his eyes. 'After my parents died, I ran with a bad crowd. We call them "black families" here, gangs. I've seen plenty of guys out for revenge. And no matter what they say, no matter who got hurt, it usually comes down to one person. Sometimes, it's grief. But usually, it's ego or guilt. At the end of the day, revenge is a selfish thing. And it's always personal.'

Caine said nothing, returning his gaze to the camp in time to see a man duck out of a tent. He wore camouflage fatigues and carried an assault rifle. His features looked Vietnamese.

'There, see?' Caine nodded toward the distant man as he began patrolling around the tents.

Trina ducked out from behind the rocks. 'I see him. Do you think he—'

Caine yanked her back. 'Quiet! There could be more of them.'

'So what do we do?'

He eyed the man. 'Any gunfire in here will echo for miles. If there are others like him in the caves, they'll hear and come running.'

Trina gave him a mischievous grin. 'Sounds like you need a distraction.'

'No, we should—'

Before he could finish his sentence, Trina pulled back her hair, stepped out from behind the rocks, and walked briskly toward the armed man.

Caine cursed to himself, then ducked back into the shadows.

* * *

'*Xin lỗi*, excuse me,' Trina said, walking up to the armed soldier.

The man aimed his rifle at her. 'Hey! *Đặt hai tay của bạn lên đầu của bạn*! Put your hands on your head! Now!'

Trina did as he asked. 'Jeez, sorry! I'm just lost. Okay? Can you tell me how to get to the second doline?'

The soldier advanced toward her, ignoring her question. 'Turn around!' he shouted.

Trina narrowed her eyes. 'Pervert!'

The guard paused. He seemed confused by her nonchalant attitude. 'You! You were with the American. Where is he? You tell me now!'

She blinked, turning to face him. 'What American? I booked a tour of the cave, but I got separated from my group.'

She stretched her arms over her head and yawned. The glistening material of her wet dive suit clung to her like a second skin. 'All this climbing and swimming... It's exhausting. I should have stuck to the foodie tour in Hanoi.'

The guard lowered his rifle a bit. His lecherous gaze traveled across her body. 'Bullshit,' he muttered. 'Tell me where he is. It will be better for you that way. Trust me.'

'Trust you?' She raised an eyebrow, noting his angry stare. 'Oh, well, in that case, he's right behind you.'

The man lunged toward her, reaching out to grab her arm. 'No more games! Tell me now or—'

Thunk! A dull thud ended the man's shouting. His rifle fell from his hands and clattered on the rocks. He toppled over, landing at Trina's feet. A dive knife protruded from the back of his neck.

Caine stood a few meters behind him.

'Nice shot,' Trina said.

'That was stupid.' He grabbed the man's fallen rifle and inspected the magazine. 'You could have been killed.'

'That's what I've been telling myself every second since I met you,' she snapped.

The body on the ground made a faint gurgling sound. Caine kicked the man over and aimed the rifle at his head. A trickle of blood ran from his lips, and a wet, rattling cough erupted from his throat.

'Who are you?' Caine demanded. 'Are there others?'

'He... He will come for you...' the man gasped.

'Who will?'

'The man with... the devil's eyes...'

His head tilted to the side, and he made no further sound. The corpse peered up at Caine with the cold, lifeless stare of death.

'Devil's eyes,' Trina breathed. 'Sounds like your friend, Boone.'

Caine's head snapped up. 'How do you know that?'

She shivered. 'He came to me when I was tied up, after they took us from the house. I thought he... thought he would...'

Caine's jaw clenched. 'Did he hurt you?'

She shook her head. 'No. He showed me his scars. His body was... It was brutal. And the entire time, he was smiling, laughing. He's insane, isn't he?'

Caine thought for a moment. 'I don't know. He used to be like me. Now, we're different.'

She shook her head. 'I can't imagine that. You're nothing like him. Nothing at all.'

Caine lowered his gaze to the dead man on the cavern floor and said nothing.

A series of muffled grunts came from the tent. Caine spun around. He motioned for Trina to stay still then advanced on the tent. He flipped open the canvas flap. Bernatto lay on the ground inside, bound and gagged.

Caine dragged him out and ripped the tape off his mouth. 'Did you tell them where to find us?' he demanded. 'Did you sell us out?'

'What the hell are you talking about, Caine?'

'Divers came straight to us! Biggest cave in the world, and they knew exactly which tunnel we were in!'

'Trina... She marked it on the map,' Bernatto snapped. 'Once they subdued me, it was a simple matter to figure out where you went. They probably suspected already, since they brought diving equipment.'

'But how did they get in here without you seeing?' Caine demanded.

'There are other ways into the cave,' Trina said in an uncertain voice. 'But...'

A distant noise echoed through the dark cavern. Caine looked up, trying to pinpoint the location of the sound. At first, he thought it was the massive wings of the eagle owl, beating overhead once again. But as the sound grew louder, he realized it was no bird. He quickly released Bernatto's bonds.

'Take cover!' he shouted. 'Move, now!'

Grabbing Trina, he sprinted across the cave, taking cover behind the jagged rocks at the edge of the cave. Bernatto moved in the opposite direction, pausing to retrieve his pistol from the dead guard.

In the distance, a helicopter swooped around the foliage-covered plateau that lay beneath the first doline.

'How the hell did they get in here?' Caine snapped.

'Both the dolines are big enough for that thing to fit through. But it's incredibly dangerous!' Her dark eyes gave him a concerned look, and she brushed her lock of blonde hair from her face. '*Khùng quá*! They really want to kill you!'

'Maybe,' Caine shouted back, watching as Bernatto sprinted

toward the rocks on the opposite side of the cavern. 'But it looks like I'm not at the top of their list!'

The roar of gunfire resounded through the cave, and bright-orange muzzle flash exploded from the front of the helicopter, strafing the ground behind Bernatto and sending a barrage of high-caliber slugs into the rocks. Puffs of dust kicked up behind his feet as he limped toward cover.

'He's not going to make it,' Caine hissed. 'Stay down!' He pulled back the charging handle of his rifle then darted between a gap in the rocks. His weapon spat a burst of slugs through the air, and sparks leapt from the tiny aircraft's fuse-lage. He ducked behind another rock as the helicopter spun around and flew toward his position.

As the tiny helicopter flew over the rocks, Caine got a closer look at the aircraft's size and shape. Its body was narrow and sleek, and a triple-blade rotor spun in a blur above the cockpit. The craft resembled a Polish PZL SW-4 helicopter. Caine wasn't aware of any major arms deals between Poland and Vietnam. But the tiny multipurpose aircraft was built at a jointly owned factory in China, so anything was possible.

The chopper swung back over the rocks, making a second pass at Caine's hiding place. The light machine gun blazed to life, the roar of the gunfire like thunder in the domed rock chamber. Caine ducked low to the ground and covered his ears as the chopper flew overhead. Dust and stone shards rained into his hair as slugs tore through the rocks.

As the thumping of the rotors faded, Caine leaned out from his hiding place and opened fire again. He emptied the maga-zine into the rear of the aircraft, causing smoke to billow from the tiny tail rotor. But the helicopter continued buzzing over-head and swooped toward Bernatto's position.

The staccato beat of bullets pummeling rock echoed

through the cavern. Then the aircraft swung around again, heading back toward Caine. He peered around the chipped remains of his cover. The chopper had come to a stop and hovered twenty meters from his position. It pivoted, turning its right flank toward him. Caine heard the swift report of Bernatto's pistol in the distance, but his shots had little effect on the aircraft.

A side door in the aircraft slid open, and a man leaned out of the rear compartment. He raised a thick metal tube and balanced it on his shoulder. Caine tensed, preparing to sprint.

M72 LAW, he thought. *Light anti-tank weapon.* The weapon was practically an antique. A relic of the Vietnam War but a particularly deadly one.

As he raced from behind the rocks, he heard a loud whoosh and saw a trail of orange smoke streak from the rear of the helicopter. The cavern shook and rumbled as the explosive projectile struck the rocks. A pillar of fire erupted from the cavern floor, and Caine felt the heat of the explosion scorch his back. Shards of rock flew like shrapnel, slicing across his shoulder and arms. He fell to the floor of the cave, gasping for breath. Before he could get his bearings, the scream of the machine gun tore through the chamber. A line of bullets traced across the cavern floor, heading straight for him. Caine rolled backward then dove behind another rock outcropping. The bullets followed his path, pounding against his cover like a thousand sledgehammers. He hunkered down as far as he could, wincing as rock fragments exploded around him.

The barrage ceased, and the helicopter swooped overhead. It bore down on Bernatto, opening fire again with its machine gun. Caine glanced down at the rifle in his hands. His weapon was useless unless he could get back to the camp and reload.

He looked toward the table, trying to spot the spare magazines in the debris, and was surprised to see Trina sprinting across the rocks. She was making a beeline for the torn, frayed tents. Their canvas flaps billowed in the prop wash of the helicopter as it circled overhead.

'Trina, get out of there!' Caine shouted. 'Take cover, now!'

Trina ducked behind the overturned table. Caine eyed the chopper as it hovered before her. The helicopter spun around, and the man in the rear compartment aimed another rocket at her. Caine ran faster, knowing the plastic table would provide no cover against the explosive projectile.

As the aircraft bore down on her, Caine raced toward Trina's position. But before he could reach her, she stood up, holding a weapon in both hands. She aimed the sleek black barrel at the man in the chopper's rear. A loud twang echoed through the cave. Her target clutched his chest, a slim spear piercing his heart. He toppled from the aircraft, striking the rocks below with a strangled cry.

The aircraft veered off, heading toward the rocks beneath the doline. Caine skidded behind the table and grabbed Trina.

'What the hell were you thinking?' he shouted, shaking her by the shoulders. 'They could have killed you!'

'Someone had to do something!' she shouted back.

He ignored her, glancing up at the golden shafts of sunlight descending through the mists above. The dark shadow of the helicopter circled around and flew toward the dedicated campsite.

'We have to move,' he said, keeping his eyes on the aircraft. 'On my mark...'

He scooped up an extra magazine from the debris, and as he slammed it into his rifle, a crumpled scrap of paper caught his eye... It looked like an old black-and-white photo, and he was certain it had not been among their papers earlier.

'They're coming closer,' Trina shouted, her wide eyes following the flight path of the helicopter.

Caine grabbed the photo and shoved it in his pocket. Then he took Trina's hand. 'Now!' he shouted, pulling her toward the opposite side of the cavern. They slid behind the rocks next to Bernatto.

'What's your ammo situation?' Caine asked.

'I'm on my last spare,' Bernatto hissed. 'Eight left, plus one in the chamber.'

The thunder of the rotors beat the air as the chopper swooped above. Bullets screamed past his ear, and more chips of rock exploded from their cover.

Caine and Bernatto circled around the rock, opening fire on the helicopter's unguarded flank. Their bullets sparked against the long, narrow tail of the aircraft but did little damage. The aircraft turned in the air then swooped away again, leaving a cloud of black smoke drifting in its wake.

Bernatto crouched behind the rock. 'I'm out.'

'We don't have enough firepower to take that thing down anyway,' Caine replied, peering into the mist. The beating rotors grew distant as the aircraft made another pass around the green cliffs.

'There's still a chance,' Bernatto said, pointing at the corpse lying in the center of the cavern. 'There.'

'I got a good look at his weapon before he fired it,' Caine snapped. 'M72 LAW. It's a single-use weapon.' He gave Bernatto an annoyed glance. 'You should remember. It's from your war.'

'I *do* remember. I also remember the postwar reports from a CIA liaison. The Vietnamese Army modified the design to use incendiary rounds. And to fire multiple times.'

Caine eyed the body. The corpse had a large, heavy pack strapped to its shoulders. 'So if he has more ammo...'

'Exactly,' Bernatto replied. 'If one of us can get to his rocket launcher, we can take that helicopter down.'

Trina looked back and forth between the two of them.

Caine sighed. 'Guess that would be me.'

Bernatto grinned. 'My assessment as well. Give me the rifle. I'll cover you.'

Caine shook his head. 'Not on your life.' He tried to hand the weapon to Trina. She held up her hands and backed away.

'Are you kidding me? I don't know how to shoot one of those things!'

Caine glared at Bernatto then handed him the rifle. 'Fine. If this doesn't work, we're all dead anyway.'

The sound of the rotors grew louder.

'We're running out of time,' Bernatto snapped. 'Go!'

Caine sprinted out from behind the rocks. As the helicopter veered in his direction, Bernatto leaned out and opened fire, sending a spray of bullets into the aircraft's glass canopy.

The helicopter spun around in the air, moving toward the armed threat.

Bernatto turned to Trina. 'Stay here. I'm going to draw their fire.'

Her face was pale, her dark eyes wide with fear. But she bit her lip and nodded. 'Be careful.'

The older man smiled at her. '*Đừng lo lắng*... Don't worry, I will.'

He limped to another set of rocks, firing short, controlled bursts as he ran. The helicopter swooped closer, its gun screaming a trail of death through the misty air. Bullets nipped at Bernatto's heels as he ducked behind another rock.

As the helicopter opened fire, Caine slid across the cavern floor, coming to a stop next to the dead soldier's body. He hugged the ground, using the corpse for cover as he opened the pack and rummaged inside. Sure enough, four more rockets lay inside, nestled within a protective foam insert. He grabbed two, set one down, and slid the other into the barrel of the launcher.

The helicopter veered toward him, machine gun blazing. Caine rolled across the ground, narrowly evading the trail of bullets streaking closer. He fell into a shallow gully and curled into a tight ball as the rain of death shattered the surrounding rocks. Then the helicopter ceased firing and swooped overhead, flying back toward the doline.

Caine popped up from the gully, rested the rocket launcher on his shoulder, and zeroed in on the fleeing aircraft, lining it up between the front and rear sights mounted to the barrel.

Got you, you son of... His lips curled into a savage grin as he squeezed the trigger.

A loud whoosh echoed through the cavern, and a plume of smoke and fire over a hundred feet long erupted from the rear of the launcher. The explosive projectile streaked toward the distant helicopter.

The chopper spun in the air, swooping in the opposite direction, but the last-minute evasive maneuver was too late. The incendiary round slammed into the side of the fuselage, engulfing the aircraft in a fiery explosion.

The helicopter swung sideways then dropped from the air. The mangled, burning hulk struck the green cliffs beneath the doline and tumbled down the rock face.

Then it began rolling straight toward Caine. He turned and raced back toward the campsite. 'Everyone move! Now!'

Bernatto and Trina joined him, sprinting away from the tumbling wreckage.

Seconds later, the helicopter's reserve fuel tank exploded, blasting their backs with a wave of searing heat. The wreckage tore through the campsite, scattering remnants of the tents and papers as it rolled toward them.

Caine reached the steep, rocky climb that led back to the cave's entrance. Their guide ropes were still in place. He grabbed one, took a step up the rock face, and held out his hand. 'Allan, let's go.'

Bernatto grabbed it, and Caine pulled him up. Trina took the other rope and also began climbing. The burning wreck tumbled closer, and Caine felt another blast of infernal air scorch his face. Together, they scrambled up to a narrow rock ledge, just before the burning copter hit. With a metallic scream, the wreckage slammed into the base of the rocks, only a few meters beneath them. A wall of fire erupted from below, bathing them in scorching heat.

Then the blaze subsided, and they rested on the ledge for a moment, panting for breath. Caine turned to Trina. 'Please tell me you have the drive?'

She gestured to her pack. 'Safe and sound.'

He nodded then looked up. His muscles ached, and he was short of breath. But he knew they had no time to spare.

'When the helicopter doesn't report back, they'll send more men,' Bernatto said.

Caine nodded. 'Then we'd better get moving.'

Together, they continued the long climb up from the depths of the cavern. After several minutes of climbing, Caine heard the loud screech of the eagle owl again. The massive bird circled the cavern, its black wings silhouetted against the flames below.

43

CIA OLD HEADQUARTERS BUILDING, LANGLEY, VIRGINIA

Director Paulis hung up the phone and leaned back in his chair. He turned and glanced out the panoramic window behind him at a swath of the Virginia countryside, the trees in the distance a mottled collage of red and orange hues. He heard one of his two secretaries shout from the hallway and spun around to face the door.

'Sir, please, you can't go in there right now. The director is on—'

The doors to his office swung open, and Alex Maddison marched into the room. The secretary stood behind him, hands on her hips and a scowl on her face. 'Sir, I'm sorry! He—'

Paulis raised his hand and sighed. 'It's all right, Ms. Pryce. I finished my call. Could you please give us a bit of privacy?'

The woman glared at Maddison. The handsome man responded with a grin and a nod. She swung the doors closed.

Maddison sat down opposite Paulis and glanced at the modern paintings hanging from the walls. 'Nice, Michael. Bit colorful for my taste, but it suits you.'

Paulis steepled his fingers and looked Maddison in the eye.

'Thank you, Alex. But perhaps I should have someone send them back to the museum. Not sure how much longer I'll be sitting in this chair.'

The DNI chuckled. 'I take it you heard from the big man himself?'

Paulis shook his head. 'No, the president asked his chief of staff to convey his wishes in this matter.'

Maddison nodded. 'Well, he is a busy man. Still, no need to get dramatic. No one's asking you to resign. But it's time to pull the plug on this while we still can.'

Paulis grunted. 'You mean abandon my man in the field? Let Grissom and his hired thugs murder him and multiple innocent bystanders so the president can get an edge in his trade negotiation?'

Maddison leaned forward in his chair. 'Look, Michael, I gave you a shot, but the clock ran out. I know it's not pretty, but this is the way the game is played. Sometimes, you have to make the hard calls.'

Paulis nodded. 'I know. I'm making one now.'

Maddison sighed. 'Stop wasting time. Call Freeling and tell her to wrap this up. Now.'

Paulis leaned back in his chair. He said nothing.

The DNI slid his phone from his jacket. 'Fine. I'll do this myself. I know you redirected Rebecca to the station house in Prague. I already alerted the director there that something like this might happen.'

Paulis heard a muted voice pick up on the other end of the line. Maddison looked at him then spoke into the cell phone.

'Do it,' the DNI snapped. 'And please confine Director Freeling until further notice.'

He pocketed the phone. 'I'm sorry about this, Michael. I

really am. But I need someone in that chair who I can trust to make the right decisions.'

Paulis stood up. 'There's a difference between following orders and making decisions. And like I said, I already made the hard call. Made it as soon as you walked through that door.'

The younger man looked up at him in surprise. 'Oh? And what was that?'

'If this is the price of my chair, you can have it back.'

Paulis buttoned his jacket, turned his back on the DNI, and left the room.

44

HANOI, SOCIALIST REPUBLIC OF VIETNAM

It was a three-hour hike from the gaping cavern mouth to the closest trail. There, Caine and his companions flagged down a rickety flatbed truck delivering livestock to Phong Nha, a village where tours to the cave departed from. The three of them collapsed in the back of the truck, a small herd of goats braying and milling around them. Bernatto's skin was badly sunburned, and he gulped air as he leaned against the side of the vehicle. One of the animals defecated in the straw covering the flatbed next to him. Bernatto wrinkled his nose in disgust.

Caine grinned. He watched Trina as she dug through her pack and pulled out the thick black hard drive. A strip of LED lights ran across the top of the drive, but they were all dark.

'This is what my grandfather died for?' She held the drive up to the light, examining the thick, ugly lump of metal with tired eyes. She turned and looked at Caine. 'Was it worth it?'

Caine took the drive from her hands. 'It never is,' he muttered. He held it out to Bernatto. 'Open it. Now.'

The older man shook his head. 'Won't work here,' he wheezed. 'Needs an external power source. Besides, once I do unlock it, it won't stay that way forever. You have to authenticate every fifteen minutes.' He closed his eyes and rested his head against the side of the truck as it rumbled through the dense jungle. 'Face it, Tom. You still need me.'

Caine glared at him then handed the drive back to Trina, who slipped it into her pack. He watched as a pair of brown goat kids nudged her legs then curled up and fell asleep beside her. Flies buzzed in the air around them, but Trina was so tired she didn't seem to notice.

'They might have the right idea,' Caine said. 'We could all use some sleep.'

She closed her eyes, but he could tell she was still awake. 'I don't think I can,' she mumbled. 'Too many nightmares.'

Caine sighed and closed his eyes. 'Yeah, I know what you mean.'

'Will I really be safe in America?' she asked in a quiet, exhausted voice. But Caine couldn't miss the hopeful tone of her question.

He thought for a moment. 'I don't know,' he replied finally. 'The people who are chasing us have money, power. I don't think anywhere will be safe as long as they're out there. But I do think we can protect you better there.'

She sighed. 'When my parents died, it felt like my whole world was torn away from me. Everything I've done since then, running with the gangs, grifting tourists, even going to school... I was just trying to find a place to belong. Nhan gave me that. He gave me a home. My grandfather was the only family I had left.' She shifted her position, and her voice grew faint. 'Now, I'm alone again. There is nothing left for me here, no reason to stay.'

'I'm sorry about your grandfather, Trina,' Caine said. 'I know it doesn't seem like much, but if we get this drive to the right people, then the man responsible for all this... It will hurt him. Take away some of his power.'

'Then that's what we will do,' she said. Her voice faded, and her breathing grew louder as the rattling of the truck finally lulled her to sleep. Caine watched over her in silence for a few minutes, struggling to stay awake. He was wary of dropping his guard with Bernatto so close. But soon, Caine also slipped into oblivion's embrace.

After a couple of hours on the road, they reached Phong Nha. The driver let them out then motored off down the road, vanishing in a cloud of dust.

The town was fairly large for the region. Two rows of colorful buildings flanked a dust-swept highway. Miles of dense jungle surrounded the area, and jagged green hills rose from the distant mist. In the stifling late-afternoon heat, Caine felt a trickle of sweat run down his forehead. Next to him, Bernatto panted for breath as he took a step forward. He reeled on his feet, and Caine grabbed his shoulder to steady him.

'Easy. We've been going nonstop.'

Trina, accustomed to the heat, seemed to be doing the best of all of them. She knelt and rested her arms on her knees for a moment. Then she stood and pointed at a shack with faded green paint a few hundred meters away.

'They sell water and food there. Wait here. I'll get us some.'

Caine watched as she walked away. She carried the pack slung over her shoulder, the hard drive tucked in among her supplies. He didn't like letting the drive out of his sight, but he saw no logical reason why it would be safer with him, out in the open. He glanced at Bernatto. The old man sat down in the grass at the edge of the road, wiping sweat from his forehead as he glared up at Caine.

'I'd like to see you do better when you get to my age, Tom.'

Caine shook his head and smirked. He looked around the village and spotted a battered, mud-streaked Ford SUV, parked in front of a block of houses. A heavyset Vietnamese woman with tattoos and long, dark hair leaned over the open hood and tilted a metal oilcan into a funnel.

'Allan, give me your wallet.'

Bernatto gave Caine a suspicious look. Caine held out his hand and said nothing.

Sighing, the older man reached into his back pocket and slipped out a worn, creased billfold. Caine opened it, removed a wad of bills, then tossed the empty wallet in the grass. He fanned out the money, counting it in his head. 'And your watch.'

Bernatto narrowed his eyes. 'Why?'

Caine glanced down at him. 'You want to walk to Da Nang?'

Bernatto unbuckled the metal clasp of his Rolex, slipped it off his sweat-soaked wrist, and handed it to Caine. 'Fine. But it's worth a hell of a lot more than that rust bucket over there.'

Caine held the shimmering dial up to the light. He disliked ostentatious watches, but during his time as a smuggler in Thailand, he had learned to appraise their value. Bernatto's Rolex, a Cosmograph Daytona model, was indeed worth more than most people's cars.

'I'll be sure to get you a receipt,' Caine snapped.

He walked across the moist grass and approached the woman by the Ford. 'Excuse me?' he called out. 'Do you speak English?'

The woman nodded. 'A little, yes. You here for tour of caves? Too late, season over!'

Caine held out the stack of money and dangled the watch from his fingers. 'No. But I'd like to buy your truck.'

She rested her hands on her hips and gave him a suspicious look. 'What? Truck old, not worth so much!'

Caine handed her the wad of cash. 'Our car died on a trail a few kilometers from here. Please, you'd really be helping me out.'

The woman snatched the bills from his hand and counted them. 'Okay, okay.' She glanced at the watch and shook her head. 'This plenty, no need watch. Too hard to sell.'

Caine glanced back at Bernatto and grinned. He dropped the heavy piece of jewelry in her hand. 'Take it... I insist.'

The woman reached into her back pocket and handed him the keys. 'This your lucky day... I just changed oil. Here you go.'

Caine slammed the hood closed as the woman ambled back to her shack. He climbed into the passenger seat and turned the key as Bernatto stood up and walked over.

The engine whined and chugged. Then it died. Caine sighed and turned the key again. Once more, the engine sputtered and coughed.

'Well done,' Bernatto grumbled, standing by the open window. 'You traded the last of our cash for a clunker with a bad engine.'

Caine looked up to respond, but the words froze in his throat. A cloud of dust rose in the distance, spiraling down the mountain trail that led to the village.

Convoy. Multiple vehicles, heading this way.

'Get in the truck,' he snapped. 'Now.'

'Sure you don't want me to push?' the older man snapped.

Caine turned the key again. This time, the engine rumbled to life. 'Get in, or I leave you here.'

Bernatto noticed the look on Caine's face then spun around. He followed the trail of dust as it streaked closer to the village. The hood of a military vehicle emerged from the haze down the center street. Then another. They swerved across the road as they roared past the brightly painted buildings.

'Boone found us,' the older man muttered. He opened the rear door and slid onto the seat. 'How could he—'

'He knew we were at the cave,' Caine growled. 'This is the closest village. We should have assumed he would send men here as well.'

The wheels spun in the dirt, and the truck lurched across the street. Bernatto braced himself as the sudden motion jostled the rear of the truck. On the opposite side of the street, Trina exited the store, carrying a few bottles of water and a plastic grocery bag. She looked up, surprised by the noise of the truck roaring her way.

The military vehicles turned onto the main road and rushed closer to the village. In the distance, Caine spotted a soldier leaning out the side window of the nearest truck.

The man aimed a rifle at Trina.

'Get down!' Caine shouted out the window. 'Take cover!'

The scream of automatic rifle fire tore through the village. Panicked shouts filled the air as locals took cover in the small dwellings on either side of the trail. Trina dropped the water bottles and stumbled backward as a row of bullets tore across the trail, sending puffs of dirt into the air.

She shrieked and crawled back into the store as Caine spun the truck's wheel. The vehicle skidded to a stop, blocking the middle of the road from the approaching convoy. Caine leaned across the seat and opened the passenger door.

'Trina, get in! Now!'

The woman sprinted from her cover as another volley of gunfire tore into the shack's walls. Dust and wood splinters exploded into the air, and the store's windows shattered. Trina dove into the passenger seat, and Caine stepped on the gas. The truck lurched forward, tearing away from the village. But behind them, the cloud of dust moved closer.

The convoy was gaining on them.

'Sat phone,' Caine snapped, glancing at their pursuers in the rearview mirror.

Trina slid her pack off her shoulder and rummaged around.

Caine returned his eyes to the road and swerved around a bend. 'Trina, I need the phone, now!'

'Hey, don't blame me!' the woman snapped. 'Why the hell am I carrying everything, anyway?'

Caine gritted his teeth as the truck skidded over the muddy trail. 'Good point,' he muttered.

She handed him the chunky black phone. 'Here.'

Caine grabbed it with one hand as gunfire ricocheted off the trees behind them. He dialed a number from memory then held the phone to his ear, turning the wheel with his free hand.

'Tom,' Rebecca's voice crackled over the line. 'What the hell is going on there? It looks like a military convoy is converging on your position, and—'

'Rebecca, there's no time! I have ACHERON and Bernatto. We need an extraction. Now!'

'I thought you were heading for Da Nang?' she replied. 'I can't just—'

The chatter of gunfire cut her off, and the rear window of the truck exploded into glass shards.

Trina screamed and ducked in her seat. Caine jerked the wheel, and the vehicle lurched off the trail into the jungle. Leaves slapped the windshield, and branches whipped against the sides of the truck.

'Rebecca, Da Nang is not going to work. We need something closer!'

'Tom, Paulis just texted me,' Rebecca snapped back. 'The DNI ordered him to scrap the operation. Paulis resigned in protest! They're going to come for me next, and you want me to authorize an illegal incursion into Vietnamese airspace?'

Caine was silent for a moment. He spun the wheel as the truck burst through the leaves, skidding back onto the trail. More bullets whizzed past, tearing through the surrounding foliage.

'It's either that, or we don't make it,' he finally answered.

Rebecca exhaled.

'All right. Let me see what I can do.' She hung up, and the line went dead.

Trina looked up at Caine with wide, terrified eyes. 'Are they coming for us?'

'Doesn't sound promising,' Bernatto muttered from the back seat.

Caine looked Trina in the eye but said nothing. Then he glanced back up at the mirror as their pursuers closed the gap on the rugged, mud-slicked trail.

45

PRAGUE, CZECH REPUBLIC

'Where the hell are they?' Rebecca snapped. 'We need visual!'

The flickering bank of monitors bathed her face in a harsh electric glow. A shiver ran through Rebecca's body despite the overcoat she had thrown on over her suit. But she ignored the cold and continued focusing on the monitors. 'Come on, we're wasting time!' she snapped.

'I'm sorry, ma'am,' Anastazie replied. 'The nearest satellite is still moving into position. We should have video feed... now!'

Rebecca winced at the word 'ma'am,' but she didn't bother to correct the young woman. Instead, she watched the image on one of the screens. She narrowed her eyes as she examined what looked like an endless expanse of mountainous jungle. 'Center on their last known coordinates and zoom in.'

Lukas unbuttoned his red cardigan sweater and wiped a few drops of sweat from his brow. He pecked at his keyboard with one hand, adjusting the image. A pair of crosshairs pinpointed a region on the map. The image zoomed in closer, focusing on a tiny village near a winding mountain road. A convoy of vehicles cut through a dense swath of jungle on either side.

'I have them, Director.' He pointed at a small white dot on a winding mountain trail. The road cut through the dense swath of jungle and wound its way deeper into the mountains. 'The road they're on does lead to Da Nang. But it looks like they're not alone.'

'Get their coordinates and send them to my phone.'

'Yes, ma'am.'

'I need a secure line to Naval Coms. Patch me through to the bridge of the *USS Carl Vinson*.' She rested her hand on Anastazie's shoulder. 'And I really need you to stop calling me ma'am.'

'Yes, ma'am, I—'

'Belay that order!' a curt, imperious voice shouted across the room.

Rebecca spun around as Joseph Wimmer emerged from the elevator at the far end of the ops center. He was flanked by a pair of beefy security guards in ill-fitting suits.

She glared at the station house director with a defiant stare. 'Joseph, I know this isn't standard procedure, but I have a man in the field who needs—'

Wimmer clasped his hands behind his back. 'Director Freeling, I am aware of the situation. Unfortunately, the DNI has ordered us to terminate this operation. You are to be removed from the operations room and held until such time as Director Paulis can debrief you.'

'What?' Rebecca snapped. 'Are you insane? We're in the middle of—'

The tall, gaunt man leaned forward. 'Director Freeling, please,' he hissed. 'Don't make this harder than it has to be.'

Rebecca felt her cell phone vibrate in her bag. She exhaled, then nodded. 'Fine. Lead the way.'

Wimmer turned to the two technicians. 'Shut this down.' He

gestured with his hands, stabbing a long, narrow finger at the bank of monitors. 'All of it.'

Anastazie gave him a wide-eyed stare then tapped a command into the keyboard. The screens went dark.

Wimmer grinned. 'Excellent. Director Freeling...' He extended a hand toward the elevator.

Rebecca marched into the tiny silver car, the two security guards following behind her.

'I'll wrap things up down here,' he told the lead guard. 'Take her to the holding office on the second floor.'

'Understood,' the muscular man grunted.

The door began to slide shut. Suddenly, Wimmer's hand slid through the crack and stopped it. The door chimed and slid open once again. 'Oh, one last thing, Ms. Freeling. I'll need your cell phone, please.'

Rebecca froze.

He held out his hand. 'Now.'

Rebecca sighed and dug a hand into the Hermès purse hanging from her shoulder. 'You mean I can't even play *Candy Crush* while I wait for you idiots to straighten this out?'

Wimmer frowned as Rebecca continued to rummage through the contents of her purse.

'I'm just following orders,' he snapped. 'I'm sure once you speak to Director Paulis, we can put this all behind us and—'

He paused as Rebecca slid a small black slab of plastic from the purse. 'Ms. Freeling, that's not—'

Rebecca swung her purse by the strap, slamming the heavy bag into his chin. Using the impact as a momentary distraction, she jabbed with her cane. The lanky older man grunted as she drove the tip into his abdomen. He stumbled away from the elevator doors as Rebecca jammed the tiny black square into the shoulder of the closest security guard. Ten thousand volts of electricity crackled through him, forcing his body to jerk and spasm like a marionette.

As he slumped to the floor, the other guard grabbed her by the shoulders and slammed her against the elevator wall. The tiny car shook, and Rebecca winced as a throbbing pain rippled through her spine. Her face flushed red, and her nostrils flared. Blowing a strand of hair from her face, she held her cane horizontally with both hands and jammed the rod into her attacker's windpipe.

A strangled grunt emerged from the man. He stepped back, trying to relieve the pressure on his throat.

Despite the pain in her back, Rebecca grinned. *Got you...*

Without his bulk pinned against her, she was free to move. She drove a knee up into his groin. The guard shifted his leg to counter the blow, but before he could strike back, Rebecca stabbed the taser into his chest.

As he collapsed to the floor, she knelt and reached into the twitching guard's jacket. Grabbing the man's pistol from a shoulder rig, she aimed the gun through the open doors at Wimmer.

'Ms. Freeling, please, be reasonable!' the older man whined.

She pressed the door close button with her free hand. 'Get back, Joseph. I don't want to hurt you.'

He did as she asked, glaring at her as the elevator doors slid shut.

With a low hum, the car ascended from the basement, traveling up to the ground floor. Rebecca slumped against the wall, panting for breath. The men on the floor twitched and groaned. She had no idea how long the jolts from the taser would keep them stunned...

'Stay down, both of you,' she snarled. 'Or I'll use this again.'

The elevator chimed, and the doors slid open. Rebecca

stepped over one of the men and emerged into a sterile white corridor. She walked into the corridor and proceeded to a pair of double doors at the end of the hall. Through the glass panels in the door, she could see rows of office workers in the distance. Employees, hired to maintain the station house's cover as a small marketing firm.

Before she could reach the exit, a pair of hulking figures approached the door from the opposite side. The double doors crashed open, and two men in dark suits marched toward her.

She spun around, heading back the way she came. The elevator doors dinged open, and one of the security guards she'd attacked stumbled into the corridor. He rubbed his neck and glared at her. 'Director Freeling, stand down! Come with us, or—'

Rebecca darted down a side corridor, her cane frantically tapping on the tile floor.

Dammit! she thought. *So slow! If only I could run!*

She heard footsteps racing on the tile behind her. She considered firing a warning shot in their direction, but she knew that would cause panic and likely expose the station house to unwanted scrutiny. Instead, she limped over to a red fire alarm mounted on the wall. As she reached it, the two security officers ran around the corner.

'Director Freeling,' one of them shouted. 'You were ordered to—'

Rebecca grabbed the alarm's handle and yanked down. A siren wailed through the corridor, drowning out the guard's shouting.

The men started toward her, but the doors on both sides of the corridor swung open, and a flood of panicked employees filled the corridor. The throng of bodies pushed and shoved past the security guards, heading for the emergency exits.

Rebecca grinned and continued limping down the hall, moving to the edge of the crowd. She could still feel a faint buzzing vibration in her purse... She pulled her phone from her bag and glanced at the screen. The armed men shouted behind her, ordering the office workers to get out of their way. She knew she was running out of time.

She ducked into a now-empty office and slammed the door behind her. Locking the door, she accepted the call and held the phone up to her ear.

'Rebecca!' a warm, gruff voice said. 'Couldn't believe it when the comms officer told me Director Freeling was calling me from Prague. When did they promote—'

'Admiral Adamcik! I'm sorry, but I'm short on time, and this is an emergency!'

The door shook, men pounding on it from the other side. Rebecca grunted in pain, using her body weight to shove a desk across the room.

'Rebecca, what the hell is going on over there? Are you all right?'

'I'm fine, Admiral,' she replied, panting for breath as the desk slammed up against the door. The pounding grew louder. She heard Director Wimmer's muted voice berating the men in the hall. Ignoring the chaos outside, she tapped frantically on the phone's screen. 'I wish we had more time to catch up, but I'm afraid there's been a change of plans. The people I was sending to the *Carl Vinson* are cut off. They're not going to make it.'

The admiral grunted. 'Just got a text from you. I take it these are coordinates?'

The door shook again and opened a crack. A dark-sleeved arm slid in, and a meaty fist grabbed the edge of the doorframe. Rebecca threw her weight against the desk, forcing the door closed. The man on the other side yelped and withdrew his arm.

'Yes, sir,' she answered, panting for breath. 'And a sat phone where they can be reached. They can't get to Da Nang. They're being pursued by hostile forces and are carrying vital intelligence that could expose corrupt elements within the United States government.'

'Rebecca, that's quite an accusation. Are you sure about this?'

'As sure as I possibly can be.'

'You realize you're asking me to violate Vietnamese airspace, here? Not to mention international law?'

The pounding grew louder.

'I do, sir.' She paused, struggling to find words. 'Admiral, you know I wouldn't ask unless I was out of options.'

The admiral coughed. 'Well, hell. Your father bent the rules for me on more than a few occasions. Guess it's time I returned the favor.'

Rebecca sighed with relief. 'Thank you, sir. I assure you, I'll take full responsibility for—'

'Never mind that.' She heard him bark orders to another officer on the ship's bridge. 'I just ordered a chopper to take off,' he said to her. 'Once they get to these coordinates, how will they find your man?'

Rebecca frowned as she examined the pictures the technicians had sent her. 'Trust me, Admiral. You can't miss them. Just hurry... Please.'

46

SOCIALIST REPUBLIC OF VIETNAM

The battered SUV shook and rattled as it tore down the narrow jungle trail. Caine gripped the wheel in his hands, struggling to maintain control as he stamped on the accelerator. The truck leapt forward, its engine groaning in protest as the foliage hanging over the trail slapped against the vehicle's windows. Up ahead, a small tree lay in their path, blocking the dusty road. Caine gritted his teeth as he downshifted into a lower gear.

'Hold on!' he shouted.

The truck leapt into the air as its wheels bounced over the tree. Trina braced her arm against the dashboard as they crashed back down onto the road with a metallic crunch. The vehicle skidded in the dirt then straightened out and resumed speeding forward.

Caine glanced in the rearview mirror. The cloud of dust receded behind them. With any luck, they could lose their pursuers somewhere in the sprawling jungle until Rebecca figured out an extraction plan.

A crack of thunder split the sky. A jet engine roared overhead, and the roof of the vehicle shook.

'*Thật to!*' Trina shouted. 'What the hell was that?'

Bernatto leaned forward from the rear seat. He peered out the side window, watching the distant jungle speeding by. 'Sukhoi Su-17 fighter-bomber.'

'You don't know that,' Caine shouted back. 'It could be a surveillance aircraft, or—'

'Trust me,' Bernatto snapped. 'I know what they sound like. Watch.' He pointed out the window.

A series of distant explosions ripped through the jungle. The vegetation trembled, and heat waves rippled up from the ground. A wall of smoke and flame erupted from the foliage, several kilometers away.

'Napalm bombs,' Bernatto said in a strangely calm voice. 'They're trying to cut off our escape route.'

Caine's eyes darted back to the rearview mirror. The vehicles behind them were gaining. To his right, the dirt trail beckoned, leading off the main road and away from the billowing clouds of smoke.

Caine spun the wheel, guiding the SUV down the narrow track.

'What are you doing?' Trina said, giving him a concerned look.

Caine kept his eyes on the trail. The truck jostled as its wheels tore over clumps of dirt and vines. 'We have no choice. If we stop now, Boone and his men have us outnumbered ten to one. Our only hope is to navigate around the fire before it gets too bad.'

'Each of those bombs can incinerate 2500 square yards of jungle,' Bernatto said. 'You can't outrun it. You're about to drive into hell itself.'

Caine looked up at him in the mirror. 'If you have a better idea, I'm listening.'

Bernatto narrowed his eyes and thought. Finally, he nodded. 'I'm afraid I don't.'

Caine pressed down on the accelerator again, speeding faster down the narrow dirt road. 'Then hell it is.'

* * *

'What the hell are you doing?' Boone Riley snapped. 'Why have we stopped?'

The soldier behind the wheel gave him a surprised look. The man gestured out the windshield. 'Jungle on fire. We can't go in.'

Boone drew his pistol. 'Caine went in there. So we go after him. Understand?'

Someone rapped on the glass behind him. Boone lowered the panel, letting the hot, humid air seep into the vehicle. Nguyen stood outside, staring at him through the open window.

'Mr. Riley, I have done all you ask. Men, weapons, air support... Now the jungle burns, and my superiors have ordered me to report back to Hanoi. You must call Mr. Grissom, tell him to intercede on my behalf, or—'

'Intercede? Now there's a two-dollar word.' Boone glared at the man through the window. 'Let me give you another one. Reciprocity, Nguyen. Grissom gets what he wants. Then you get what you want. That's how this works, understand?'

The lieutenant colonel shook his head. 'No more, Mr. Riley. It's over! If I do not report back and explain myself, I will be court-martialed and relieved of duty. The fire will take care of these men you seek.'

Boone looked back and forth between the two men. The driver twitched in his seat, his eyes flicking down to Boone's pistol. The other vehicles sat idling in the dirt road, their rumbling engines kicking up clouds of dust.

Boone looked back at Nguyen and gave a wolfish smile. 'Maybe you're right. I got a bit of the hound in me. Too focused on the hunt to see straight. Come here. Let's call Mr. Grissom together. I'm sure we can straighten this mess out.'

The Vietnamese officer nodded. 'Yes, very good.' He leaned in the window as Boone reached for the sat phone hanging from his belt.

Boone's free hand darted to the window's controls. He pressed a button, raising the panel. Quickly dropping the sat phone, Boone grabbed the colonel's hair and held him in place as the window closed, trapping the colonel's neck in the opening. The man grunted as the glass pane dug into his throat.

Boone kept his pistol trained on the driver as he slid a knife from his boot. With a single, lightning-fast thrust, he drove the blade into Nguyen's mouth and up into his skull.

The man gasped then went limp. The driver's hand crept to the pistol at his waist.

'You're looking at this all wrong, son,' Boone drawled. His voice was cold as ice, and his eyes did not blink. The soldier withdrew his hand. 'Nguyen was your commanding officer, right?'

The soldier nodded.

Boone chuckled. 'I just promoted you. Now get out of the car. You can show your gratitude by ordering the rest of these men back to Hanoi.'

'But, I—'

'Maybe I should promote someone else?'

The soldier shook his head.

Boone gestured to the door with the barrel of the gun. 'Slowly, now. Leave your sidearm here.'

The man unbuckled his seat belt, slid his pistol from its holster, and set it down. Then he opened the door and exited the vehicle. Boone climbed into the driver's seat and shut the door, keeping his pistol aimed at the man. He toggled the passenger window, lowering the glass panel. Nguyen's body fell limp to the ground.

Boone grinned. 'Congratulations, Sergeant.'

He stepped on the gas, and the vehicle charged down the trail, leaving the other men and Nguyen's corpse behind in the sweltering heat. The sky grew dark and hazy with smoke as the jungle continued to burn.

47

A hellish orange glow bathed the interior of the SUV. Sweat dripped down Caine's face as the heat in the cabin intensified. Trina's clothes clung to her skin, stuck by a film of sweat and dirt. Bernatto panted for breath in the back seat.

The branches and vines lining the sides of the trail erupted into flame, and smoke swirled ahead of them. As Bernatto had predicted, the fire had outpaced them. The smoking blaze engulfed the surrounding jungle. Suddenly, a loud cracking sound echoed above the flames. A clump of burning trees and vegetation fell across the trail, blocking their way.

'Look out!' Trina shouted, pointing at the fiery obstacle.

'I see it,' Caine snapped. He spun the wheel to the right, and the vehicle lurched down an even narrower path.

'Where does this trail go?' he shouted.

Trina shook her head. 'I don't even know if this is really a trail!'

Bernatto pointed at the windshield. 'Look!'

Up ahead, the vegetation cleared, and a vine-covered observation tower rose above the jungle. The inferno tore through the surrounding area, devouring the trees and vegetation like a hungry beast. As they sped closer to the clearing at the end of the trail, a loud pop exploded through the cabin. The truck dipped lower to the ground.

'Is someone shooting at us?' Trina asked, craning her head to look out the back window.

'No,' Caine replied. 'One of our tires blew out... Probably caught on fire.'

The vehicle exploded through a curtain of burning leaves then skidded into the clearing. The front end dug into the ground, throwing a plume of dirt into the air.

'We can't go any further like this,' Caine said. 'Everyone out. Run for the tower!'

The trio exited the burning truck and sprinted toward the tall wood structure. The air was thick with ash and smoke. Bernatto doubled over in a fit of coughing.

'Move!' Caine shouted. 'Get up into the tower!'

The old man nodded, recovering his breath. Trina leapt onto the ladder. The structure shook and rattled as she climbed up one rung at a time, Bernatto right behind her.

More loud pops exploded beneath them, and Trina screamed. The crackling of the flames was deafening, and smoke stung Caine's eyes as he ascended the ladder behind them.

'Keep going,' he shouted. 'It's just the other tires!'

He glanced down into the smoky haze. The inferno was engulfing the truck. He could barely see the charred black metal frame beneath the hungry tongues of fire. Another pop sounded, and the vehicle sank lower to the ground. The heat had melted the rubber tires, causing them to swell and explode.

Sweat poured down Caine's face and dripped from his hair.

Hearing Bernatto gasp for breath, he looked up and saw the old man pause, hanging from the ladder with limp fingers.

The heat within the inferno was pushing them to their limits. If they didn't escape soon, he knew it would only be a matter of minutes before they succumbed to smoke and exhaustion.

'Allan, keep climbing! We're almost there!' Caine shouted.

Bernatto glared down at him then gave a weak nod. They continued climbing.

The tower creaked and swayed as the group moved higher up the ladder. Caine wasn't sure if it was their combined weight or the extreme heat. Once the fire consumed the tower, he doubted it would remain standing for long. He could only hope that Rebecca's helicopter was in the air and would spot them in the blaze.

The ladder trembled again. The wind picked up, and Caine was certain they were swaying back and forth. But as they moved higher and put some distance between themselves and the raging inferno, the temperature cooled slightly. He sucked in a lungful of air and pulled himself up faster.

The ladder led up into a tiny office perched sixty feet above the jungle floor. The windows surrounding the tiny room were cracked and yellow with dust and age. A chipped, faded green door led out to a rotting wood balcony that ran along the edge of the tiny shack. Beneath them, the sea of fire stretched as far as the eye could see. A thick gray cloud billowed up into the sky.

'Well,' Caine muttered, coughing as fresh air filled his lungs. 'If a chopper is on the way, they can't miss us.'

'What the hell is this place?' Trina said, pulling her sweat-soaked hair from her face. She glanced around at the cobwebs and mold covering the walls. 'It looks about a hundred years old.'

Bernatto limped over to a metal file cabinet tilted on its side. He pulled open the drawer and combed through its contents. 'These documents are illegible. Could be from the war. Or perhaps built by a rubber plantation.'

Caine moved toward the nearest window. He picked up a rusted, sagging metal chair and used it to smash the glass. Then he ran it around the edges of the window frame, clearing away the sharp fragments that clung to it. The open window let in more fresh air and helped clear out the smoke rising from below.

He craned his neck out the open window and examined the sky. At first, he saw nothing. Then, in the distance, a tiny silver dot streaked closer, moving over the sliver of water and the rolling green hills on the horizon.

A low thumping sound rose above the snarling inferno.

'Helicopter inbound,' Caine shouted. 'Get ready, we're getting out of here!'

Click...

Caine knew the sound as intimately as a lover's sigh. It was the sound of a pistol hammer being cocked. A Browning Hi-Power pistol.

Allan Bernatto's pistol.

'Knew I shouldn't have given you a gun,' Caine said in a low voice without turning around.

'You were right,' Bernatto said. 'Step away from the window. Slowly, please. Hands in the air.'

Caine did as Bernatto asked. 'You're just like that snake in the jungle, Allan,' he said, his emerald eyes locked with Bernatto's beady stare. 'You really can't help yourself, can you?'

'Allan, stop!' Trina said. 'What the hell are you—'

'Stay back,' Bernatto snapped. Trina froze in her tracks. 'Believe me, Trina, I have no wish to hurt you. I promised Nhan I'd see you to safety, and I intend to keep that promise. But we have the drive, and we have me. That's enough for the United States to grant us safe passage. We don't need Caine.'

Caine nodded. 'You're probably right, Allan. It's like you always say: we're all expendable in the end.'

'That's true, Tom. You may not believe me, but I *am* sorry. I wish this could end another way. But we both know sooner or later, when circumstances change, you'd come looking for me again. Looking for your revenge.'

Caine's emerald eyes blazed. 'I told you before, nothing would stop me from killing you. For Jack. For Galloway and Rebecca. Take your pick.'

The thumping of the helicopter grew louder. Bernatto gestured with the gun. 'And I always believed you. Now step away from the window. Put your hands on your head and get on your knees.'

Caine stepped away from the window but ignored the man's other commands. 'But you were wrong, Allan. Not everyone is expendable. Not even to you.'

Bernatto glared at him in silence. He tightened his grip, the gun shaking slightly in his hand.

'Before you go, I have something of yours,' Caine said.

The older man narrowed his eyes. 'What are you talking about?'

Caine lowered his hands and glanced toward his pocket.

Bernatto nodded. 'Slowly.'

Caine removed the crumpled scrap of paper. He tossed it on the floor in front of them. Bernatto kept the gun trained on him.

'What's that?' Trina asked, her voice quivering slightly. The tower swayed as the fire crackled below.

'It's nothing,' Bernatto snapped. 'Leave it.'

'Let her see,' Caine said. 'She's as much a part of this as we are. More so, in fact.'

Trina glanced at Bernatto then bent down. Her hand shot out and snatched the crumpled photo.

'Trina, don't listen to him,' Bernatto wheezed. 'He's just trying to—'

She unfolded the picture, revealing a faded, creased black-and-white photo from Nhan's home. A photo of Mai, her mother. The woman was beaming at the camera, wearing her beautifully embroidered *ao dai* dress.

'Where... where did you get that?' Bernatto growled, his eyes darting from the photo back to Caine.

'You know where,' Caine replied. 'You took it from the mantel in Nhan's house. When Boone's men tied you up in the cave, they searched your pockets. They left it on the table.'

'This belonged to my grandfather,' Trina muttered, staring at the photo. 'Why... why would you take this?'

Bernatto said nothing.

'Why?' Trina said, raising her voice. 'Why do you have this?'

'He has it because Nhan's not your grandfather,' Caine answered, his voice as hard as cold steel. 'Isn't that right, Allan?'

The gun trembled in Bernatto's hands. He clutched it tighter, his mouth a thin slash of rage. But he did not pull the trigger.

'What?' More tears streamed down Trina's face. 'What the hell is he talking about? Is that true?'

'Mai... She...' Bernatto lowered the gun. 'She was so beautiful. And after the war ended... Nothing was the same. Nhan was taken for questioning by the Vietnamese government. I worked behind the scenes, used my connections to protect him, get him released. But it took time. Mai... We became close. And one night...'

His voice trailed off. The pistol stopped quivering in his hand, and his eyes had a faraway, distant look. Caine knew that look well. Bernatto wasn't staring at him or the tower or even the raging fire outside. He was looking into the past, lost in a tide of memories. Dragged under dark waters by phantoms of forgotten pain and lingering regrets.

'I guess you just can't help betraying the people close to you, Allan,' Caine said. 'It's in your nature.'

Bernatto lowered the gun and turned to Trina. 'I... Trina, I wanted...'

She stared at him, shocked. 'Is it true?' she asked, her voice shrill. 'Are you... You're my grandfather?'

'I wanted to tell you, so many times. But Nhan... It would have destroyed him. And I thought it was safer this way.'

'Safer?' Trina's eyes grew wide. She balled her hands into fists. 'Everyone I care about has been lying to me my entire life!' She pounded Bernatto's chest. 'Nhan wasn't... All this time, I thought he was family!'

'He *was* family!' Bernatto snapped. 'He loved you. He cared for you. He gave you and your mother what I couldn't. And you gave him a purpose... Something to live for.'

As they argued, Caine turned his head. In the distance, he heard a sound loud enough to pierce the crackling flames and billowing smoke. He peered out the window, narrowing his eyes. A bright silver speck hugged the horizon, streaking toward them at incredible speed.

'Everyone get down!' he shouted. He dove forward, grabbing Trina and rolling behind the toppled file cabinet. The ACHERON hard drive clattered from her pack and bounced under a rotting wood shelf.

Bernatto spun around, but before he could move, a deafening roar filled the air... The sound of rapid-fire autocannons screamed above them, and the wood walls of the tower cracked and splintered. High-velocity slugs tore through the air, shattering the windows. Bernatto's body jerked and spun around like a marionette. Then he collapsed to the floor. Jet engines thundered overhead, shaking the tower walls.

'Fighter jet,' Caine shouted over the noise. 'Stay down!' Rotted papers and dead leaves swirled around the tiny chamber as the jet streaked above them.

'Is it gone?' Trina screamed.

Caine leapt to his feet and peered out the window. He shook his head. 'Negative. It's coming around for another pass!'

Caine's eyes swept across the moldy, rotting office, searching for anything that could help their situation. But he saw nothing... His firearms were useless against the fast-moving jet.

Caine grabbed another file cabinet from the opposite side of the room and dragged it over to their position, stacking it on top of the first. He knew such a barrier would probably not stop the depleted-uranium slugs launched by the aircraft's autocannons, but it was the best he could do.

As he dropped the heavy cabinet into place, he spotted a squat red can leaning against the wall. The cabinet had previously blocked it from view.

Generator fuel. Kerosene...

The roar of the fighter jet's engines grew louder. It was circling back.

Caine ducked beneath the file cabinets. Trina pressed up against him, her body shivering, her face pale. Her dilated pupils looked like two black saucers in the dim light.

She's in shock. Terrified...

Caine draped an arm around her shoulder. 'Trina, you're all right. We're going to be okay.'

She peered into his eyes. 'You really believe that?'

He looked down at her and forced himself to smile. 'Yeah.'

She bit her lip. '*Nhảm nhí!* For a spy, you're a terrible liar.'

Before he could respond, the scream of weapons fire again filled the tower. The fighter's twin Gryazev-Shipunov GSh-23 autocannons filled the air with a barrage of metal slugs, and the file cabinets shook and rattled like tin drums. The tower creaked and swayed as the roar of the jet's engines passed overhead. When the sound died down, he heard a soft beeping noise...

'Trina, your pack... Give it to me!'

She slid her arms out of the straps and handed the bag to Caine. He pulled out the sat phone. The compact unit buzzed with an incoming call.

'Go ahead,' he said, answering the phone.

'This is United States Navy Helicopter 11-248, from the *USS Carl Vinson*. Director Freeling at Langley patched us through to this channel. Looks like we're late to the party down there!'

'Better late than never,' Caine replied. 'Be advised, hostile aircraft in the area. Sukhoi Su-30, Russian made, armed with—'

'Yep, we saw it. Bugged out the second we got within shooting range.'

Caine breathed a sigh of relief. 'Whoever's calling the shots, I doubt they're authorized to engage with a US aircraft.'

'Well, I wouldn't put too much faith in that,' the pilot answered. 'We're violating Vietnamese airspace, under orders from Langley. We're about two minutes from your position. Stand by and... Oh, crap!'

'What is it?' Caine asked.

'Missile launch detected! Inbound, sixty seconds to impact!'

Caine dropped the sat phone and leapt to his feet.

'Where are you going?' Trina shouted.

'That jet carries KH-29 air-to-surface missiles,' Caine snapped. He grabbed the battered fuel can and poured the contents out the window, soaking the sides of the tower. As the flammable liquid struck the inferno below, the fire leapt higher, climbing up the side of the rickety structure. A thick black cloud of smoke billowed into the air, blocking their view through the shattered window.

'So your plan is to burn us down before it hits?' Trina snapped.

'Those missiles are laser guided! Smoke can throw off their targeting mechanism!'

'Missile in range,' the voice crackled over the phone. 'It's locked on to your position!'

Caine finished dumping the fuel over the side. He dropped the can, coughing and gagging as the smoke cloud drifted into the tiny cabin.

'Impact in ten seconds,' the pilot's voice said. 'Seven... six... five...'

Caine grabbed Trina and dove behind the file cabinets.

'Wait! The missile, it's losing altitude!' the pilot shouted. 'It's dropping fast!'

Kaboom!

The streaking projectile struck the ground less than a hundred meters from the tower. The explosion hurtled trees and dirt into the air. Debris pelted Caine and Trina through the windows, and the walls shook more loudly than before. Caine heard snapping wood and the groan of bending metal.

'Hang on!' he shouted.

'What happened? Did the missile hit?'

'The smoke threw it off course, but the impact damaged the tower! We're—'

Caine stumbled as the floor shifted beneath his feet. Trina screamed, and Caine felt a sickening feeling rise in the pit of his stomach. They were moving. The tower groaned then slowly, inexorably toppled sideways. Through the filthy, cracked window, Caine saw the burning jungle rush up to meet them as the tower collapsed.

49

With a shriek of rending metal, the tower slammed into a cluster of trees and hung suspended at a steep angle. One of the file cabinets crashed against the floor and slid across the tiny office. The remaining glass windows shattered beneath its weight, and the metal case tumbled out. The blaze on the jungle floor incinerated its contents.

Caine struggled to stop his own sliding motion, digging his feet into the angled floor. But the dust and ash made it impossible to get a firm grip, and he, too, slid toward the shattered windows. Trina screamed, and he grabbed her hand as they skidded through the gaping hole in the tower's side.

A blast of hot, dry air assaulted Caine's skin as he fell out of the tower. His flailing arm grabbed the edge of the windowsill, and he grimaced in pain as shards of broken glass tore into his hand. A wrenching pain tore through his shoulder. He looked down and saw Trina hanging from his other arm, her feet kicking in the air above the infernal blaze.

As the tower lurched and fell another meter, Caine winced

as the frantic girl tugged on his arm. He held on to the sill with a white-knuckled grip.

'Trina, stop kicking. Just relax!'

She stared up at him in disbelief. 'Relax? Are you crazy?' she shrieked as the weight of the tower shifted again. The trees supporting its weight buckled and snapped. The inferno crawled up their trunks, moving into the branches that supported the tower's weight.

'The more we move around, the faster this thing will collapse,' Caine hissed. He grunted in exertion as he pulled her body up. She grabbed the edge of the window frame and scrambled back into the lopsided room then helped Caine crawl in after her. He stumbled over to Bernatto's body.

'Allan!' He touched the man's neck... and felt a faint pulse. Bernatto moaned, and a trickle of blood fell from his lips.

Caine spun around. 'Trina, where's the drive?'

She rummaged in the bag slung over her shoulder. 'I don't... I don't see it. It must have fallen out!'

Bernatto clawed at Caine's sleeve. He glanced down and saw blood staining his torn shirt. Bernatto's arm was covered in it. The thumping of the helicopter grew louder. The aircraft was hovering above them.

'Tom... Get Trina... out of here,' Bernatto said in a harsh wheeze. Deep, ragged red holes pierced his body in at least six places, and a dark puddle spread underneath him. The flames outside the tower shimmered in the blood's wet crimson surface.

'Trina, help him!' Caine ordered. He stood and looked around the smoke-filled office. The sat phone on the floor crackled to life.

'We're in position over the tower. Lowering rescue collar now!'

Caine cursed as he peered through the smoke. The helicopter hovered over them. The blaze from the jungle floor crawled up the tower walls, fueled by the rotors' rushing air. Fangs of red and orange flame crackled through the shattered windows along the tower's side.

He didn't see the hard drive...

Caine peered out the door, now a horizontal slash in the tower walls. Through the swirling smoke, he could see a bright-yellow harness descending from a steel cable.

'Trina, let's go! You're getting out of here.'

'What?' she shouted. 'What about—'

'Go!' Bernatto lifted a weak arm and pointed at the angled door. 'You don't need me, Tom. Get her out of here now!'

Caine grabbed Trina's arm and helped her climb some toppled file cabinets. Avoiding the flames and broken glass, he and Trina teetered across the angled room and leaned out the doorway. Trina squinted as the prop wash from the chopper's rotors struck her face. A blistering wind assaulted their skin as the heat from the fire engulfed them.

Caine reached out and grabbed the harness. 'Lift your arms,' he shouted. He buckled the thick padded strap around her torso. 'Your body weight will lock it in place. Just go limp!'

'Tom, wait, I don't—'

He shook his head. 'There's no time!'

'What about you?' She gave him a concerned look. Caine glanced back at Bernatto then looked her in the eye. He gave her a reassuring smile. 'I'll be right behind you!'

'But I don't think I can—' Before she could finish her sentence, Caine pushed her backward. She screamed as she swung away from the tower. The steel cable connected to the harness went taut as the helicopter's winch lifted her into the air.

Caine turned and made his way back into the tower. He knelt on the floor next to Bernatto. 'Allan, I can't find the drive. Is there a copy, another server where—'

Bernatto shook his head. 'You have... everything. Trina... Get Trina out of—'

'She's safe, Allan! But the drive, what about—'

'Everything... Everything you need...'

Caine shook the old man then slapped his face. 'Allan, I've wanted you dead for as long as I can remember. I've dreamed about wrapping my fingers around your throat, choking the life out of you. But right now, I need you, dammit! There has to be a backup somewhere—'

Gunfire screamed through the air. Caine spun around as the pilot's panicked voice crackled over the sat phone.

'Shots fired, shots fired! Hostile on tower! Repeat—'

Another burst of gunfire cut him off. The helicopter veered away from the tower, yanking Trina up into the azure sky.

Boone Riley balanced in the doorway, holding an assault rifle. The right side of his face was charred and blackened, and savage third-degree burns covered his right arm. He aimed the rifle at Caine. 'Well, isn't this a touching scene?'

'Boone,' Caine snarled. 'Looks like I made the same mistake again.'

The burned man grinned. 'Don't worry, partner. We all make mistakes. But this will be your last.'

Boone lowered himself into the angled room, keeping his eyes on Caine. 'Now, before we settle things up, I have a little business to take care of. The drive. Give it to me.'

Caine shrugged. 'Don't have it.'

Caine winced as Boone fired a quick burst into the air. The cabin swayed, and the fire continued to eat at the trees and foliage below. 'No time for games, Tom. Give me the drive, and I'll give you a quick death. Least I can do for an old friend.'

Caine rose to his feet. Boone trailed his movement with the barrel of the rifle. Caine leaned against the file cabinet and coughed. A low chuckle escaped his lips.

'What's so funny, partner?' Boone snapped. He stepped closer, making his way through the smoke-filled air.

Caine glared at him and smiled. 'Just the way things work out. You. Me. Bernatto... All these years, all the betrayals. And now we're all going to burn together.'

Boone glanced down at the old man. Bernatto's eyes twitched beneath his closed lids. His breathing was a low, rasping wheeze. 'Speak for yourself, pal. I think poor old Allan's just about checked out. And me? Well, you left me to burn once before. Didn't work out so well for either of us.'

'Yeah...' Caine leaned harder on the file cabinet and coughed. He shot a glance at the broken windows. Through the smoke and flames, he could see a crisscrossed web of vines. The delicate foliage was all that supported the weight of the tower.

He shifted his weight, angling forward on his right foot. 'Well, like I said, I won't make the same mistake again.'

'Meaning what, exactly?'

Caine smiled. 'Meaning this time, we finish it.'

Caine lurched forward, tearing the file cabinet away from the wall. He dove to the floor as Boone opened fire. The bullets tore above his head, penetrating the weakened wall of the cabin. But before Boone could adjust his aim, the falling cabinet crashed through the broken windows and plummeted down. The heavy slab of metal ripped a clump of burning vines, and the tower lurched closer to the blaze.

Boone grunted as he lost his balance and fell to the floor. He yelped, letting go of the rifle as flames crawled up his arm. The rifle clattered across the shifting floor and fell out the window.

Boone coughed in the swirling smoke. He stumbled to his feet and spun around, but he was too late. Caine swung a broken wooden beam and struck him in the face. Boone grunted and staggered backward, bracing himself against the angled walls.

Caine swung again, but Boone recovered his balance and blocked with his forearm. He kicked Caine in the gut, and the two men shuffled apart. They stood facing each other as the hungry flames crawled up the walls surrounding them.

Caine's emerald eyes sparkled in the flickering light. He hefted his makeshift club and adjusted his stance. 'Now,' he snarled. 'About that unfinished business...'

Boone flashed a manic grin. His coal-black eyes looked like dark, bottomless pits in the flickering light. He screamed with rage, uttering an inhuman wail like nothing Caine had ever heard. Then Boone charged forward, his footsteps thundering across the shaking tower's floor.

50

Caine saw the glint of a blade flash in Boone's right hand as the man lumbered toward him. The bigger man stabbed forward, but Caine pivoted sideways, letting the blade slip past him. He swung his fiery club down, sending burning embers into the air as the charred wood slammed into Boone's arm.

Boone stomped his foot, driving his boot into Caine's shin. He slashed again with the knife, and Caine felt the serrated blade tear across his arm. Limping backward, he swung the club in front of him, forcing Boone to retreat out of attack range.

The two men circled each other, stepping over the broken windows and burning patches in the floor. Caine swung again, but Boone ducked. He slammed his shoulder into Caine's chest, knocking him backward. The wall behind him buckled as they crashed into it. The tower shifted again, and the straining wood creaked under their weight.

Caine slammed a knee into Boone's solar plexus. The man grunted and backed off, raising his knife in an overhand grip.

He stabbed down, but Caine drove the blow aside with the wood beam. He jabbed the end of the club into Boone's face.

Boone grunted in pain and covered a bruised eye with one hand as he stumbled back. Caine took a step forward then bent over in a fit of coughing. A thin, red haze clung to the edge of his vision. The smoke and heat overpowered him... and the blood loss from his wounds was taking a heavy toll.

Can't keep going much longer.

'Getting tired, huh?' Boone taunted him. 'Shit, Caine, I'm just a grunt! You think you can knock Grissom down from his castle? Gonna have to try harder than that!'

Caine stumbled sideways, barely dodging another jab of Boone's blade.

The taller man made a clicking sound with his tongue. 'All this pain. All this death... If you had just died that day, none of this would be happening. Rebecca would never have ended up in that chair. Galloway would be alive.'

'Rebecca is alive, asshole. The only person dying today is you!' Caine spat back.

He swung his club again, but Boone was already moving, darting around the broken windows and stabbing down with the knife. Caine staggered back, raising the wood beam over his head. He felt the impact of the knife tremble through his arms, saw the steel blade pierce the splintered wood. Its glittering tip hung inches above his right eye.

Boone pushed down, driving the blade closer. Caine twisted the wood in a circle, breaking his opponent's grip on the knife handle. He tossed the club aside, letting it clatter to the ground.

Boone swung his fist, but Caine threw his left arm and shoulder up, blocking the punch. He exploded to his feet and moved in close. He looped an arm around Boone's neck, pulled the man's head down, and slammed his knee into his opponent's face.

Boone roared in fury. He broke Caine's hold and lumbered backward, cradling his bloody nose in his hands. Reaching down, he grabbed the handle of a drawer in the toppled file cabinet. He yanked the drawer free and swung it through the air, clipping Caine's chin.

Caine's head snapped back. Blood dribbled from his mouth. Blinding white spots hovered before his eyes. He couldn't see, couldn't breathe.

Need to get some distance... clear my head...

But before he could regain his balance, Boone struck with the drawer again. The slab of metal pounded into Caine's side, and he felt old wounds tear open. He took another step back and looked up... Through the smoke and haze, he saw a shaft of sunlight beaming in from the shattered windows above.

Boone charged toward him again, swinging the drawer like a battering ram. Caine leapt up, grabbing the edge of the windowsill above him. He swung his legs forward, striking Boone in the chest with both feet.

The kick sent the bigger man reeling backward. Boone tripped and stumbled over to the file cabinet then struck the wall with a loud thud. The tower shook again, but the tangle of vines and trees held.

The wood beneath Caine's fingers snapped and crumbled under his weight. He fell to the floor and slammed onto his back. He felt the air explode from his lungs. He coughed again, gasping for breath in the smoky haze.

Boone staggered to his feet. 'It's over, Tom. You got nothing left.' He stepped forward and raised the heavy metal drawer. 'And me? I'm just getting started.'

Caine narrowed his eyes. He saw a glint of metal glowing in

the firelight. The board, impaled by Boone's knife, lay less than a meter away. So close but just out of reach.

Boone grinned as he hefted the drawer over his head with both hands. Caine knew the next blow would crush his skull, leaving him barely conscious as he burned alive in the tower.

'This time,' Boone gasped. 'This time, I leave you to burn!'

Suddenly, Boone stumbled backward. Caine narrowed his eyes... and saw a shadowy figure standing behind him.

Bernatto!

The older man wrapped his arms around Boone in a bear hug. Bernatto fell backward, and Boone toppled over with him. The two men crashed through what was left of the windows. A cloud of glowing ash exploded into the air as the inferno consumed the falling wood and glass.

Caine crawled over to the hole in the floor and peered down. Bernatto hung above the blaze, his right leg entangled in the clump of vines. Boone clung to his torn shirt as the hellish blaze rose beneath them. He glared up at Caine, his obsidian eyes dark with rage.

'No!' he screamed. 'It's your turn to die! Your turn to burn!'

Bernatto tilted his head, looked up at Caine. His face was pale and covered with soot. But his gaze was clear, his jaw firm.

'We're expendable, Tom,' he shouted. 'But not her...'

Caine rolled over. His fingers wrapped around the wood beam. He grasped the knife's pommel and pried the blade from the splintered wood. Then he crawled back to the gaping hole in the tower.

Looking down, he watched as Boone climbed up the web of vines next to Bernatto. The man's charred fingers reached for the edge of the windowsill. Bernatto grabbed his leather belt with a shaking hand, holding him back. He locked eyes with Caine and nodded. 'Do it.'

'Goodbye, Allan,' Caine said. He drove the knife down, slashing through the vines with the razor-sharp blade.

For a brief second, Bernatto's face seemed frozen in time, a pale, gaunt mask, staring up at Caine like the emotionless features of a porcelain doll. Then the old man plunged into the inferno, dragging Boone with him. The raging flames engulfed their bodies, and they vanished from sight. Within seconds, the hellish blaze consumed them both.

Caine thought he heard one last scream. It sounded like Boone, but it was impossible to be sure. He rolled over onto his back. The tower dropped another meter, and a burst of fire exploded through the shattered windows.

Choking and gasping for breath, Caine staggered to his hands and knees. He narrowed his eyes. Through the swirling, superheated air, he could see a small metal object wedged under one of the rotting desks.

The hard drive, he realized. Bernatto's words echoed in his mind. *We're all expendable, Tom. But not her...*

The distant thumping of the helicopter returned. The aircraft hovered a few meters away from the burning tower. The structure shook again as more trees and vines disintegrated in the blaze.

Almost out of time...

Caine leapt to his feet and rushed over to the drive. He reached out to grab it but drew back his hand in pain... The drive's metal body was red-hot, heated by the surrounding flames.

Wincing as the skin on his hand became red and blistered, Caine tore off a shirt sleeve. He wound it around the hard drive and tied the bundle to his belt. The thumping of the rotors grew louder. The helicopter hovered just above the doorway. He saw the rescue collar lower again, but the wood walls around him groaned and buckled.

The tower rotated sideways again as another vine snapped. Caine's view of the helicopter spun through the windows. The door was nearly vertical now. The chopper's curved landing skid hung just beyond the crumbling balcony.

Caine took a step back. Then he sprinted forward, ignoring the pain in his lungs and the burning flames nipping at his skin. He raced toward the door and pushed off with his legs, throwing all his strength into one last jump.

As he sailed through the air, a cloud of fire burst out the door behind him. He saw Trina standing in the open side door of the helicopter. She gasped as she watched the tower collapse behind him. Caine felt his fingers touch the cold metal of the skid. One hand slipped off...

But the other held tight.

The helicopter lifted off, carrying him higher into the air. As his body spun below the chopper, he caught a glimpse of the fiery blaze beneath him. The last of the vines gave way, and the tower fell into the raging inferno. The wooden beams and rotting walls disintegrated into a cloud of ash and smoke as the jungle continued to burn.

He felt someone grab his arm. Looking up, he saw Trina and a naval officer reaching for him. He took her hand, and they helped him climb up into the helicopter's rear cabin.

'Sir, are you all—' the officer began, but Caine shook his head.

'No time,' he croaked. His voice was a harsh rasp, little more than a whisper. 'Need a satellite uplink to the *Carl Vinson*.'

'We'll be there in five minutes, sir,' the officer replied, holding up a canteen. 'You need water and—'

Caine swatted the canteen away. 'We have to get the contents of this drive to Langley, now! Do it!'

The officer nodded. 'Yes, sir!'

The officer handed Caine a power cable for the drive then attached some other cables to a portable transmitter. Caine tugged the hard drive from his belt.

He unwrapped it and examined it in the dim light. 'You can open this,' he said to Trina as he connected the power lead.

She looked at him in surprise. 'Me? But I don't—'

'Bernatto told me the DNA lock has a 20... 23 percent variance. That's not a coincidence.'

'I... I'm his granddaughter,' she breathed.

Caine nodded. 'Finish it, Trina. You're the only one who can.'

She took the drive from his hands. 'Okay. What do I do?'

Caine took her hand and pressed her thumb down on the pad.

Nothing happened.

'No,' he wheezed. 'It should work... It has to work.'

She tried again. 'Tom, it's not doing anything!'

The officer handed him a cable. 'Satellite uplink ready, sir! We'll be landing in four minutes.'

Caine examined the hard drive's metal casing. It was dented, charred, and still warm to the touch. The strip of lights on its surface was dark.

Caine spotted a fire extinguisher bolted to the wall. Grabbing a cargo strap for support, he pulled himself to his feet. Then he yanked the canister from the wall.

'Stand back!' he shouted.

Trina and the officer stepped away as he blasted the metal drive with the freezing CO_2 mist.

He picked up the device. The lights were still dark.

'Damn you, Bernatto!' he rasped. He slammed the drive against the wall. 'You're not going to screw me over again!'

Trina put a hand on his shoulder. 'Tom, please—'

He shrugged her hand away and slammed the drive again. The metal drive clanged against the helicopter's fuselage. The officer gave him a concerned frown. 'Sir, we can have our technicians take a look when we—'

Caine slammed the drive again. Suddenly, the strip of LEDs flickered then lit up red. 'Trina,' he shouted, spinning around. 'Now!'

She pressed her thumb on the pad, wincing as a tiny needle pricked her skin. 'Ow!' she cried, yanking her hand away.

The lights flickered once more then cycled through red and green. A second later, they flashed blue.

'It worked,' Caine said. He plugged the uplink cable into the drive and handed it to the officer. 'Transmit all the data on this drive to your ship. Have them relay the signal to Langley!'

The officer took the drive. 'Yes, sir!'

Caine slumped to the floor. His eyes fluttered, and he hung his head forward. A series of powerful coughs wracked his lungs, making his body shake.

Trina sat next to him. 'You did it,' she sighed.

He gave her a tired grin. His bright-green eyes were half open, and his sweat-soaked hair hung in his face. '*We* did it. Together.'

She held up the canteen. Caine took a long sip. Then he tilted his head back and closed his eyes.

Trina rested her head on his shoulder. 'So I guess I'm going to America now.' She looked out over the jungle as the helicopter streaked toward the crystal-blue waters. 'This... this is all over.'

Caine sighed. 'No, it's not over. Not yet.' He looked down at her. Her eyes were closed, and her breathing was heavy. He realized she had passed out.

'Not for me,' he whispered.

51

CIA OLD HEADQUARTERS BUILDING, LANGLEY,
VIRGINIA

It was strange to be back...

Once again, Caine felt out of place, out of his element. Only this time, he was not working in the field. The air was cool and dry, and he was surrounded by white columns and potted plants, not the lush tropical trees and opulent hotels of Singapore.

A few minutes ago, he had walked across a vast lobby of marble and granite. The echo of his footsteps bounced off the towering ceilings overhead as he walked over the decorative seal set in the checkerboard floor. The design was a black circle, sixteen feet in diameter. In the center of the black granite disk, a white badge crested with the head of an eagle surrounded a sixteen-pointed compass star.

The eagle symbolized the United States. The shield stood for defense, and the star was a compass rose... A representation of intelligence data from all over the world, converging at a central point. Surrounding the emblem, the words 'Central Intelligence Agency – United States of America' wreathed the black circle.

Now, he stood facing the north wall. Six rows of black stars lined the wall, flanked by two flags. On the left side, the Stars and Stripes hung from a pole mounted on the wall; on the right was the navy-blue CIA flag, bearing the eagle-crested seal.

Beneath the stars, a slim steel case jutted from the wall, topped with an inch-thick sheet of glass. Inside the case sat a book, bound in black Moroccan goatskin. Known as the book of honor, its pages contained the names of CIA employees who had died in the line of duty. Each name sat next to a gold star in the book. Not every star had a name... Some were still classified, even in death. But every entry matched one of the black stars carved into the wall. Although Caine had not been in the building for some time, he knew that before today, 133 stars marked the white marble expanse.

Today, they numbered 134.

Silently, he read the inscription carved over the rows of stars. *In honor of those members of the Central Intelligence Agency who gave their lives in the service of their country.*

A tapping sound across the lobby caused him to look over his shoulder. Rebecca walked toward him, her copper-red hair gleaming like crimson fire in the sunbeams falling through the skylights. As always, she was impeccably dressed. Her sleek gray suit fit her slim, athletic body perfectly, and dark sunglasses covered her eyes.

When she saw Caine, she pushed her glasses up and smiled. He grinned back. The tapping grew louder as she walked over and joined him at the wall. For a moment, he frowned at the sight of her leaning on her cane.

Still, he had to admit, it beat her wheelchair. Things were getting better. For both of them...

'It feels like an eternity since we talked about this,' she said, her eyes slowly moving across the rows of black stars. 'I have to admit... I wasn't sure it would really happen.'

Caine felt her clothes brush against his skin as she leaned closer. The smell of her hair, her skin. He closed his eyes, and for a moment, he felt the darkness finally lift. The curse of death and bloodshed that had haunted him for so long was finally gone. The voice of the killer inside was silenced, and he was transported back in time. Back before Bernatto, Blackwing, and betrayal...

There was always betrayal, the voice in the back of his mind hissed. The voice of the killer inside, the one he could never quite silence. *Always...*

Rebecca looked up at him, and he was surprised to see the look of concern on her face. He realized that she had looked briefly in his eyes. She saw what he saw, every day, staring back at him in the mirror. The haunted look, the darkness he kept inside.

'Are you okay?' she asked in a quiet voice.

He nodded. 'I'm fine. Just having a hard time believing I'm here myself. Josh was a good man. I wish I could have gotten to know him better.'

She stepped away from him. The air suddenly felt colder, as if an emptiness had opened between them.

'Tom, thank you for being here. It means a lot to me.'

Caine smiled. 'I feel like there's a "but" coming.'

She grinned back and shook her head. 'No, it's just... Things are...'

'Complicated?'

Rebecca laughed. 'Yeah, I guess so. You remember by the lake, in Hanoi? When I tried to abort the mission?'

'Well, I didn't exactly make it easy for you.'

'No, you didn't,' she answered, returning her gaze to the wall.

'Rebecca, I...' Caine paused, struggling to think of the right words. 'It's going to take me some time. I've been on my own for so long, I've seen and done things, I... Trust is going to take time.'

She reached up and touched the side of his face. Her eyes met his. 'No, Tom, that's not what I mean. I was thinking about it later, and I realized something. Something that was hard for me to admit.'

'What was that?'

'I wasn't thinking about the mission or protecting the asset. That's not why I wanted to abort.'

'Then why?'

She smiled. 'I was worried about you.'

Caine took her hand in his. 'Rebecca, I...'

A loud cough sounded behind them. Caine dropped her hand, and they both turned around. Director Paulis stood behind them. 'I hope I'm not interrupting anything,' he grunted.

Rebecca flushed but quickly regained her composure. 'Not at all. We just came to pay our respects.'

Paulis removed his glasses. He looked up at the wall and sighed. 'I was hoping I'd serve my tenure here without adding any more stars to this damn rock. But here we are.'

'Is his name in the book?' Caine asked, glancing at the glass case.

Director Paulis shook his head. 'Negative. I'm afraid his work in Sudan was classified. And it will have to remain so.'

'Of course,' Rebecca said. She turned away from the wall to face Paulis.

Caine did the same. 'So what happens now?' he asked.

Paulis replaced his glasses and offered them a warm smile. 'That's what I came to tell you. Our techs are still pouring through ACHERON, but we've already turned over a mountain of intel to the DNI, as well as FBI counterintelligence. China came back to the table, and it looks like the trade talks were reasonably successful. But more importantly, half the Senate Intelligence Committee is about to be indicted on charges of bribery and violations of the Foreign Agents Registration Act.'

'What about the other half?' Caine grunted.

Paulis chuckled. 'Well, to quote Khalil Gibran, "tomorrow is today's dream."' The director looked Caine in the eye. 'And, I'm pleased to say, it seems I was right about you.'

'Right about what?'

Paulis held out his hand. 'Code Green. All the way.'

Caine paused then shook Paulis's hand. 'Thank you, Director. But I had a lot of help.'

'Yes, like Ms. Trina Phan.'

'What will happen to her?' Caine asked.

'Of course, she's free to return to Vietnam if she wishes. But I understand Director Freeling has made her a rather lucrative offer.'

Caine glanced at the fiery-haired woman, a surprised expression on his face. 'Really? She didn't mention it.'

Rebecca shrugged. 'Believe it or not, geology plays a large part in our intelligence efforts. Rare earth elements are a critical component of everything from jet engines to night-vision goggles and computer chips. And we're not the only country looking to increase our supply. The CIA works with a number of consulting firms to identify and monitor valuable deposits around the world.' She gave Caine a warm smile. 'I just made a few introductions. Ms. Phan is an intelligent, resourceful woman. I'm sure she'll have her choice of offers.'

Caine chuckled, remembering their dive in the caves and their flight through the jungle. 'I'm not sure I can picture her giving PowerPoint presentations behind a desk, but I appreciate it. She deserves a break.' He turned back to Paulis. 'And what about Grissom? Blackwing?'

Paulis frowned. 'We're in a holding pattern there. The president wants a more detailed assessment of ACHERON before he makes his decision. But for now, Axion has been denied its military contract. And amnesty for Grissom is off the table.'

'For now,' Caine repeated.

'Meanwhile, Mr. Caine, I believe you've earned some leave. When you get back, I look forward to us working to rebuild our mutual trust.'

Caine nodded. 'I look forward to that as well.'

'I'll leave you to it, then.' The heavyset man turned and walked away, vanishing among the lobby's scurrying workers and white marble columns.

'This isn't over,' Caine muttered. 'Not as long as Grissom and his network are still out there.'

Rebecca tucked a strand of fiery hair behind her ear. She stared at the final star in the last row on the memorial wall. She bit her lip then turned to Caine. 'I haven't had time to go through the entire ACHERON file, but there was one piece of intel that stood out to me.'

Caine glanced around, making sure no one in the building was paying attention to them. 'Go on,' he whispered.

Rebecca leaned in close and embraced him. 'Another Blackwing company,' she whispered. 'Not defense or communications tech. A construction firm, specializing in historical recreations. We connected them to a project in Geneva. Someone there is using them to rebuild an old castle.'

'Boone Riley said something about a castle,' he whispered

into her ear. '*You think you can knock Grissom down from his castle?* Those were his exact words.'

Rebecca placed her hands on his chest, pushing him away, breaking their embrace. 'When you get back, we can talk... about us. The future.' She smiled. 'Like he said, tomorrow is today's dream.'

Caine tilted his head, looking down at her. 'Who said I'm going anywhere?'

She grinned. 'Just a feeling. I'll see you soon, Tom.'

Then she turned and walked away. Her cane tapped on the marble, the sound growing distant and faint as she disappeared into the crowd.

52

GENEVA, SWITZERLAND

Walter Grissom peered over the edge of the balcony and sighed. In the dim foyer below, shipping crates lined the walls of the room, disappearing into the shadows like the steps of an ancient pyramid. Each one was packed with memories of a forgotten past and dreams of a future that would not be.

Grissom held his arms behind his back and tapped his foot. 'Well, you win some, you lose some,' he muttered to himself. 'Stings like hell, but that's why the Good Lord created whisky.'

He looked down at the massive animal carcass dominating the center of the foyer, a striped ox he had bagged in North Africa. Its gray, spiral horns seemed to point up at him, and its dark, artificial eyes took on a sinister gleam in the overhead lights.

'You lost that day, my friend,' Grissom continued, staring into the animal's glassy eyes. 'Today, looks like it's my turn. But unlike you, I can still pick myself up and brush off the dirt. For now, at least.'

He sighed and paced away from the balcony. 'Well, how we

lookin', Karl? If we have to leave, let's get on with it. Last thing I want to do is twiddle my thumbs in an empty house.'

Karl stood at attention in front of his desk. He wore a thick roll-neck sweater and gray flannel trousers, and his metal arm gleamed in the light. The burly man gave Grissom a brisk nod. 'Yes, sir. Security thinks it's wise for you to lie low for a few months. Indonesia, perhaps? Bali is lovely this time of year.'

Grissom shook his head. 'Hell no. Local cuisine doesn't agree with me. Let's stick to Europe. Reach out to our friends in Ukraine. See if we can work something out. Lots of folks owe me favors in that neck of the woods.'

Karl nodded. 'Sir, I'll see what I can do. But either way, it would be best to get you in the air sooner rather than later. I have men to see to your things. We will store them until you've made your final travel arrangements.'

Grissom thought for a moment. 'Make sure they pack up old Jimmy, downstairs.'

Karl gave him a confused look. 'Jimmy, sir?'

Grissom chuckled as he settled down in the leather chair behind his desk. He removed a thick brown cigar and clipped the end with a pair of metal shears. 'The ox,' he replied. He lit the cigar and puffed a cloud of smoke in the air. The leather chair creaked as he leaned back. 'Named him after a senator who was a particular thorn in my side. They're both dead now. Nice to keep a record of your wins, know what I mean?'

Karl gave him a thin smile. 'I'll see to it.' He turned and walked toward the door.

'Oh, Karl?' Grissom called after him. 'Round up Benicio for me. I want to talk to him about a few security concerns. Loose ends, you know how it is.'

Karl paused. 'Of course, sir.' He exited the room, leaving the door open.

Grissom took another puff of his cigar, savoring the taste of the thick, fragrant smoke. He glanced around the room. His eyes traveled across the wildlife stuffed and mounted to the walls, the glass cases filled with artifacts and fossilized bones. Mementos of the slow, inevitable decay of the natural world.

He set the cigar down on the edge of an ashtray, taking care not to spill any ash on his desk.

A roar of anger exploded from his throat. He swept an arm across his desk, knocking the books, papers, and trophies to the ground. The cigar flared bright red as it tumbled through the air. Then it landed in a pile of debris. A thin stream of smoke rose to the ceiling.

'Mr. Grissom?'

Grissom turned and saw a figure standing in the doorway. He wore black tactical pants and a Kevlar vest over a gray shirt. The brim of a blue cap tilted over his face, covering his features in shadow.

'What the hell do you want?' Grissom snapped. He turned and examined himself in the mirror running along the wall. His skin was flushed red, and beads of sweat dotted his face. His wispy white hair was messy and out of place.

He held up his hand and took a deep breath. 'Benicio, sorry. My temper gets the better of me sometimes. Have a seat. We need to have a chat about—'

'Benicio won't be reporting for duty, I'm afraid.'

The man stepped forward into the light. A pair of emerald-green eyes blazed beneath the brim of his cap. Grissom's jaw dropped, but he made no sound. He stared into Caine's eyes, unable to break away from the power of their cold gaze.

'Caine...' he whispered.

Caine raised a pistol in his hand. The silenced Beretta Px4

Storm fired. The gunshot sounded like a loud cough and echoed through the vast, empty foyer below.

Grissom grunted and stumbled backward. Caine fired again. His target slumped into a leather chair, blood trickling from two holes in his chest. He sucked in a deep breath, and a wet, rattling wheeze emitted from his lungs.

'Son of a bitch!' Grissom gasped. 'Paulis grew a spine, eh? Sent you to finish me off.'

Caine stared back at him. 'Paulis doesn't know I'm here. I came on my own.'

'I see. So that's it, then? Two bullets to the chest. No last words? No goodbyes?'

'I said goodbye a long time ago,' Caine replied.

Grissom laughed. The sound was like a diesel engine stalling. Blood continued to spill from the wounds in his chest, and his face turned pale and ashen.

'And Bernatto?' he asked.

'Dead.' Caine took another step forward. 'Along with Boone Riley.'

The old man's pale-blue eyes squinted. He looked at Caine, but his stare seemed distant and unfocused. 'Shucks, they were dead a long time ago. Grim Reaper just took a while to catch up with them. It's the same for me. And it'll be the same for you.'

Caine aimed his pistol at Grissom's head. 'Maybe. We'll see.'

'You think killing me will fix everything, don't you?' The old man's soft, pale-blue eyes stared back at him over the pistol's barrel. 'But it's not that easy, Tom. Some mistakes are harder to fix than others. Sometimes you're too far down the trail to turn around. And even if you do, by the time you get back, every-thing's changed. Things won't look the way they once did. The world has moved on without you.'

Caine gave a slight shrug. 'The world isn't your problem anymore.'

Grissom laughed again. 'I always thought I'd at least have the luxury of passing at home. I'm a Tennessee boy, you know. Born there. Planned to die there.' His eyes darted around the room. The animal heads mounted on the wall loomed over him, their glassy eyes staring down in silent judgement. 'Guess this will have to do.'

Grissom rolled his chair back a few inches. Caine narrowed his eyes and took another step toward the desk and adjusted his aim. 'Guess so.'

Before he could fire, he felt a sudden tingling on the back of his neck...

He drew you in... You fell for it!

The killer's voice screamed in the back of his head, drowning out all conscious thought. Once again, he turned over control of his body to his instincts, the same instincts that had kept him alive for all these years.

He spun around as he heard the soft whir of a motor on the far wall. The mouths of the animal heads lowered on hydraulic hinges. He saw a glint of metal in the dim light... Slim metal barrels emerged from the beasts' gaping maws.

Caine dove to the floor and grabbed one of the thick leather-bound books lying in the pile of debris. A soft whooshing filled the air as the high-powered dart guns sprang to life. He rolled across the floor, darts thudding in his wake. The gun barrels were moving, tracking him through the room.

Motion sensors.

He felt the rush of air as the tiny projectiles whizzed past his face. Caine raised the book, blocking his face. The darts struck the heavy volume, their razor-sharp tips penetrating the leather cover. The firing stopped. Caine glanced down at the book. A dozen darts impaled its cover. Droplets of liquid ran down the cracked leather binding.

Suddenly, something knocked the wind from his lungs. He felt as if a freight train had struck him at full speed. He caught a glimpse of blond hair and snarling lips curled over perfect white teeth. Then Karl tackled him to the floor.

Caine gasped for breath again as the weight of the man slammed into his chest. He threw up his arms to cover his face as Karl punched with his good hand. Caine's instinctive block deflected the blow. But as the haze cleared from his vision, he saw Karl's other arm swing up, poised to strike. The limb ended in an artificial prosthesis of some kind. The metal claw at the end looked heavy enough to crush Caine's skull.

Caine drove his knee up and slammed it into the blond man's inner thigh. Karl grunted and shifted his weight, allowing Caine to roll to the side. The metal arm struck the floor with a thunderous crack. The wooden beam next to Caine's head split down the middle. Torn papers flew through the air like confetti.

The muscles in Caine's shoulder burned as he heaved the larger man off of him. Caine rolled across the floor and darted under the nearest trophy case. Snarling like a wild animal, Karl leapt to his feet. He swung his metal arm like a battering ram and shattered the glass case, sending sparkling shards raining down into Caine's hair. He kept rolling and sprang up on the other side.

Karl advanced through the wreckage of the smashed case. Caine retreated, keeping his arms up in a defensive posture. Karl swung again, but Caine leaned away from the attack. The weight of the man's swinging claw left him off balance. Caine darted in close, landing a pair of jabs into Karl's solar plexus.

Karl shoved Caine backward with his good arm. The blow

sent Caine flying. He slammed into a wooden pillar, and another wave of pain exploded through his back and shoulders.

Torn a muscle. Have to end this now!

Before he could recover, Karl swung his metal arm again. Caine dropped to his knees as the metal club slammed into the beam. It snapped in two, sending a cloud of splinters and plaster dust into the air.

Karl reached down with his good hand and grabbed Caine by the neck. Grunting with exertion, he hoisted him up into the air. 'You...' the blond man snarled. 'You are nothing. You are an insect compared to him.'

Struggling to free his throat from the iron grip, Caine grabbed the man's wrist. He lashed out with a kick, but again, the blow seemed to have no effect. The muscles in Karl's arm flexed, and he hurled Caine through the air.

Caine's arms and legs pinwheeled as he slammed into another display case. Shards of glass tore through his clothes as he crashed through the case and fell to the floor. His vision grew hazy and dark once more, and blood trickled down his chest. He heard the clomping of Karl's boots marching toward him. His hands darted through the debris as he struggled to find a weapon, anything that could give him an advantage over his larger, unstoppable opponent.

Once again, he felt Karl yank him to his feet. He blinked as the image of his attacker's face came into focus. Karl's lips twisted in a cruel grin, and his eyes glowered with bloodlust. Dust streaked his blond hair and covered his face, giving him a ghostly appearance.

'This is not a place for weak, broken men like you,' Karl hissed. 'This is the wild, the jungle. Here, you are not a predator...' Karl raised his arm to strike. 'You are prey...'

Now! The sound exploded in Caine's mind like a gunshot, spurring him to action.

He stabbed forward, driving a piece of debris into Karl's chest.

The man gasped as he looked down at the wound. A broken arrow shaft protruded from his chest. His arm went limp, and Caine fell to the floor, holding the other half of the arrow in a trembling grip. Landing on his feet, he gritted his teeth and wrapped his arms around Karl in a bear hug. He charged forward, pushing the hulking man backward.

Karl swung his metal claw down and slammed it into Caine's right shoulder. A starburst of agony exploded across Caine's eyes, but he kept moving. Karl gasped in pain as Caine slammed him backward into the balcony. Then he heaved the man up and over the edge.

He heard a brief, strangled scream, followed by a wet thud.

Then silence.

Caine peered over the edge of the balcony. Karl lay motionless, impaled on the horns of the stuffed buffalo in the foyer below. A trail of blood flowed down his metal arm and pooled on the dark wood floor. His blue eyes peered up at the ceiling, as lifeless as the mounted heads in Grissom's office.

'Welcome to the jungle,' Caine muttered.

He picked up his gun from the floor, wincing as the bones in his shoulder shifted. Limping back to Grissom's desk, he transferred the weapon to his left hand. The old man lay slumped in his chair, barely able to move. He coughed then gave Caine a weak smile. 'We trained you well. This was my last chance, my big play.' He bent over, coughing again, and sucked in a deep breath. 'Looks like it's not in the cards,' he wheezed.

The gun trembled in Caine's hand as another wave of pain

and nausea tore through his battered body. 'What was it all about? ACHERON, blackmailing the senators, sabotaging the trade talks... What the hell did you want?'

Grissom straightened up in his chair. 'Isn't it obvious? I wanted to come home.'

'Bullshit,' Caine snarled.

Grissom peered up at Caine with half-closed eyes. 'I know how it is,' he grunted. 'You spend enough time in the shadows, you get used to it. You don't trust the light of day anymore, can't believe what you see with your own eyes, what's right in front of you. But sometimes, the answer really is that simple.'

'Right now, I know exactly what I see,' Caine replied. 'The end to all this.'

'You're lucky you have her, you know,' Grissom wheezed. 'Rebecca. Without her, I honestly think you'd still be lost out there. Still afraid to come out into the light.'

'You're right.' Caine raised the gun and aimed it at Grissom's head. 'And you'll never hurt her again.'

'Waste of a bullet, son,' Grissom said. He laughed then coughed some more. 'Mother Nature already took her shot.'

Caine narrowed his eyes. 'What are you talking about?'

Grissom coughed again. 'Tumor. It's in my head, size of an apple. Inoperable. I told you that's what this was all about. Sometimes, all you have left is a legacy to leave behind. And a peaceful place to die.'

The old man's eyes flared with rage, glaring at him with such infernal intensity that Caine almost took a step back. Grissom's withered lips curled into a snarl, and his fingers tensed on the desk. 'Now,' he said in a low, guttural voice, 'let's get on with it. We both know how this ends.'

Blam!

Caine fired. A crimson hole opened in Grissom's skull, and the man collapsed over the desk.

Caine tossed the gun to the floor. Then he turned and limped to the door. He stopped, taking one last look at the shattered cases, broken trophies, and mounted carcasses lining the walls.

Reaching into his pocket, he removed a tiny gray cylinder. He pulled the pin on the AN-M14 TH3 incendiary hand grenade and tossed the canister into the room. With a brief white flash, the thermite in the grenade ignited, burning at over 4000 degrees. Orange flames leapt up from the floor, devouring the scattered papers and debris.

Caine watched as the fire crept up the walls. The animal heads burst into flames, and within seconds, the air reeked of charred flesh and formaldehyde. As the inferno cast a hellish orange glow over his face, Caine thought back to Director Paulis and his quote from Khalil Gibran.

Tomorrow is today's dream. Caine had googled the words on his flight to Geneva. He was surprised to find there was more to the quote. The preceding line read *Yesterday is but today's memory...*

Grissom's legacy. Bernatto, Jack, my past... and Rebecca's.

He turned and limped out the door, vanishing into the shadows of the corridor. Behind him, the fire raged on. The roaring blaze burned away all traces of the past, all memories of pain. The flames left nothing but smoke and crumbling gray ash in their wake.

* * *

MORE FROM ANDREW WARREN

Another book from Andrew Warren, *Hell & Ice*, is available to order now here:

https://mybook.to/HellandIceBackAd

ACKNOWLEDGEMENTS

This book could not have been written without the very gracious help of the following.

As usual, thanks must go to Sam Carver for his insights into Southeast Asian history and geopolitics. And of course for serving as Mr. Caine's armorer and sharing his encyclopedic knowledge of weapons and military hardware.

Thank you to Amanda Mortimer for recounting her experiences living in Singapore; the vivid details she shared helped me bring this fascinating part of the world to life.

Thank you to Howard Limbert for taking the time to discuss his knowledge of Hang Son Doong cave. As the leader of the expedition that first explored this magnificent cavern, his insights were critical to one of my favorite portions of this book. If you are interested in learning more about this natural wonder, please contact Oxalis Adventure.

Thank you to Kronos Ananth and Bodo Phundl (AKA the Typo Assassin) for their help proofreading this manuscript.

To paraphrase the great Stephen King, what I got right is thanks to them; what I got wrong is thanks to me.

I'd also like to thank my editor Vic Britton and the entire Boldwood Books team. They've helped take the Thomas Caine series to the next level, and I couldn't be more thrilled.

A very special thank you to my beautiful and brilliant wife, Mimi. I'm grateful to have you beside me for this, and all our other journeys...

Finally, thanks to you, the reader, for taking the time to read this book. Without you, none of this is possible! I hope you will join me on Thomas Caine's next adventure.

ABOUT THE AUTHOR

Andrew Warren is the international bestselling author of the Thomas Caine thriller series. Andrew was born in New Jersey and has over a decade of experience in the television and motion picture industry, where he has worked as a writer, story producer, and post production supervisor. He currently lives in Southern California with his wife and trusty dachshund sidekick.

Sign up to Andrew Warren's mailing list for news, competitions and updates on future books.

Visit Andrew's website: www.andrewwarrenbooks.com

Follow Andrew on social media here:

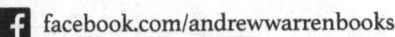

facebook.com/andrewwarrenbooks

instagram.com/andrewwarrenbooks

bookbub.com/authors/andrew-warren

bsky.app/profile/aawarren.bsky.social

ALSO BY ANDREW WARREN

Boldwood

Boldwood Books is an award-winning fiction publishing company seeking out the best stories from around the world.

Find out more at www.boldwoodbooks.com

Join our reader community for brilliant books, competitions and offers!

Follow us
@BoldwoodBooks
@TheBoldBookClub

Sign up to our weekly deals newsletter

https://bit.ly/BoldwoodBNewsletter